A Plague on Both Your Houses

By the Same Author

Whitechapel
Suffragette Autumn Women's Spring

A Plague on Both Your Houses

Ian Porter

Matador
9 Priory Business Park,
Wistow Road, Kibworth Beauchamp,
Leicestershire. LE8 0RX
Tel: 0116 279 2299
Email: books@troubador.co.uk
Web: www.troubador.co.uk/matador
Twitter: @matadorbooks

ISBN 978 1789010 183

British Library Cataloguing in Publication Data.
A catalogue record for this book is available from the British Library.

Printed and bound by CPI Group (UK) Ltd, Croydon, CR0 4YY
Typeset in 11pt Bembo Std by Troubador Publishing Ltd, Leicester, UK

Matador is an imprint of Troubador Publishing Ltd

To the memory of all the women and men of Britain and Germany, sacrificed on their respective Home Fronts in the Great War.

Prologue:

In April 1917 the United States declare war on Germany.

There had been German air-raids on Britain by Zepplin earlier in the war but now the first bombing by Gotha planes takes place.

By October US troops have arrived in France and are involved in their first action.

The following February British women aged over 30, with some added provisos, gain the vote. Lower working class men also gain the vote.

In March Russia signs a peace-treaty with Germany, allowing millions of German troops to be transferred from the Eastern to the Western Front. Within two months they have broken through at Arras, then Ypres and are now advancing on Rheims. The Germans are winning the war, militarily at least.

But their Home Front is struggling badly. The Allied blockade of imported foodstuffs, poor government organisation of their remaining food resources and a potato blight has left the German people hungry.

The Allied Home Front is also struggling, with shortages and huge queues for food, but the introduction of rationing, with its fairer system of distribution, proves a great boon for morale.

And it's much needed because the US troops have

brought with them something from America which is far more deadly than their own fire power. It threatens the Home Fronts of both sides and may be about to bring the war to its conclusion…

Chapter 1

"The home front is always underrated by generals in the field. And yet that is where the Great War was won and lost. The Russian, Bulgarian, Austrian and German home fronts fell to pieces before their armies collapsed."

British Prime Minister David Lloyd-George,

War Memoirs

East End of London, May 1918

The Votes for Women campaign had been so all encompassing, taking over entire lives, Suffragette Ruby Nash had often wondered how her situation would change once the vote had been won. Would she use the skills that she had learned during the campaign? Public speaking; the ability to plot, manage, organise, motivate, subvert, deceive, and when all else failed strike out or hitch up her skirts and make a run for it.

Her previous life as a cashier on an ocean liner, followed by a brief spell working in a biscuit factory, seemed a world away. And, frankly, a waste of her newly acquired talents.

But now the vote had indeed been won, there had been no great earth shattering change in her life. That had happened four years earlier with the outbreak of war. She now simply continued with what she had been doing these past four years, working for Sylvia Pankhurst in London's poverty stricken East End.

Sylvia and her East London Federation of Suffragette colleagues had continued to fight for the vote for women throughout the war, but such action had taken a backseat to the more pressing matters of helping the starving, widowed, gassed, blinded and injured whom the government had cast aside like so much useless flotsam and jetsam.

Ruby had multiple jobs which included managing the Mother's Arms, a cleverly renamed ex-pub which had been converted into a nursery and Montessori playschool. It enabled local women to take on decently paid work in nearby factories while their infants were well looked after in clean, cheap, professionally run surroundings.

She also kept an eye on Sylvia's Cost Price restaurant and oversaw her toy factory, and assisted her employer in badgering officialdom about everything from the paltry level of child allowances to high rents and their resulting evictions, to the need to nationalise food supply. Luckily all of these jobs were sited only a few hundred yards from each other, a stone's throw from where Ruby lived with her husband, in Bow. But her duties involved long days, seven days a week. Exhaustion had set in.

She had just left the restaurant hoping that a bit of fresh air, or at least as fresh as the Bow slaughterhouse, soap-works and tannery infused miasma ever got, would freshen her up. It hadn't. A decision was made to abandon going to check up on the toy factory and head for home.

Ruby was walking slowly along Roman Road, eyes

down, feeling sorry for herself, when she heard an explosion. Since the huge munitions factory explosion the previous year, just down the road in Silvertown, which had laid waste the surrounding area, and could have killed thousands had it gone up during working hours, any explosion had Ruby fearing the worst. She processed the information the noise had given her. It was the harrumph of a distant explosion. But was it a big one miles away or somewhat smaller but closer? Then came another blast sound. Nearer this time. Then another, closer still. It was no munitions factory being blown to smithereens. Bombs were landing. The sounds had initially raised her head to the horizon; now she looked higher, up to the sky. There they were. Little bi-winged affairs. German Gotha IV planes with three men aboard, close enough for each of their heads to be seen from the ground. It was an air-raid, and the bombers were about to fly over her nursery, full of children. She started running towards the nursery, eyes fixed skywards. Not watching where she was going, she soon collided with someone running in the opposite direction and was knocked to the ground. As she started to pick herself up, she made a speedy return trip to the cobbles courtesy of another collision. A wave of people, like an escaping relief-filled crowd at the end of a shift flowing through factory gates, were heading in the opposite direction to her.

The first person with whom she had collided, a teenage lad, had stayed on his feet and had not given her a backward glance. The second, a young woman, had fallen to join her on the street. She got back on her feet in double quick time, neither cursing Ruby for bringing her down nor the graze that was now on her knee. She simply shouted some advice to her assailant before continuing her panic stricken journey.

"Leg it! Tube!"

It was short speak for 'run to the nearest underground station'.

As Ruby slowly got on one knee to get up again, she saw two trousered tree trunk legs arrive next to her, offering protection from the on rushing crowd. She peered up and a huge belt appeared in her eye-line. She knew who was standing over her before he spoke.

"First time I ever saw you down here in Bow, you were on the ground. Things don't change much do they?"

"And the first time I ever saw you dear husband, you were lost. Didn't know where you were. So less of your lip, help me up and get me to that bloody nursery so we can get those children safe!"

Duly put in his place, Alexander Nash, who everyone, including his wife, knew as Nashey, stuck out a huge mitt of a hand and pulled Ruby to her feet. Without a further word they started running. Nash led the way, slicing through the crowd with the wave of an arm to anyone in his way, with his wife in his slipstream.

The brief conversation had alluded to Ruby and her husband meeting for the first time, six years earlier, in the bowels of the Titanic just as it was about to sink beneath the waves. They had saved each other's lives that terrible night. It was quite a bond between them. They had gone their separate ways afterwards, but months later their paths had crossed again when Ruby had visited Bow for the first time. She was there on Suffragette duties and had been knocked to the ground during a typically lively,

4

violent exchange of views with men who believed that women should know their place. And that was rather closer to the kitchen than the ballot box. Nash had been among the pro Suffragette men at the altercation, who had sent the bullies on their way, care of giving them a good hiding. And he had plucked Ruby off the pavement in much the same way as he had just done again. Though the exact manner of that meeting was happenstance, it was no coincidence that Ruby had travelled to Bow. Despite a seventeen year age gap, there had been chemistry between her and Nash from the first moment they met. She knew he lived in Bow and had been hoping to meet up with him again while she was there. And the two had remained close ever since.

Nash dived down an alley to get away from the crowds heading past them down the main street. Ruby always marvelled at how her husband seemingly knew every alley, and where it led, in the area. It was a useful legacy from the years he spent as Sylvia Pankhurst's bodyguard, assisting her to evade capture by the police. Several twists and turns later she was not surprised when they popped out within yards of the nursery in half the time it would have taken on the main thoroughfare. Doctor Alice Johnson and Nurses Hebbes, Burgess and Clarke were carrying babies out of the building and heading towards them. Ruby immediately took over, shouting instructions.

"Turn round! Get in the park!"

Nurse Hebbes queried the order.

"Tube?!"

"Too late for that. They must have done the docks. Now they're trying to hit Bryant & May's. You'd be running towards the target. Get in the park. They won't waste dropping bombs there. Move!"

Nurses and doctor nodded in unison. The Bryant & May match factory, of Victorian phossy jaw infamy, was the largest in the country, and like all big factories had now been converted to war work. It was only a few hundred yards away and surely a plum target. The four women, each awkwardly cradling three babies wedged together in their arms, ran across a little bridge over a canal that ran alongside the nursery, and into the vast open space of Victoria Park.

Ruby and Nash ran into the nursery. Nash took the stairs two at a time, shouting over his shoulder.

"I'll have a look upstairs!"

The ground floor was mayhem. The nurses and doctor had managed to take all the youngest babes in arms but the nursery still had many screaming infants within its walls. One year olds lay grizzling on their afternoon nap sleeping stretchers. Toddlers were barely able to get their breath such was the depth of their panic stricken sobbing and snot-filled drooling. Some stood at the bars of their dainty little cots like demented prisoners; others tottered about on the floor, tripping and falling over a scattering of dolls, bricks and tiles, setting off yet more frenzied crying.

Ruby found a large crate-like box full of playthings; dumped the cargo and refilled it with all the remaining children she could see, laying them down, trying the best she could to avoid having them smother each other. She then quickly grabbed as many soft toys as she could find and placed them on top of the infants. Being smothered by teddy bears caused the more claustrophobically inclined little ones to increase their decibels, but Ruby could not worry about that now.

The crate was too big, and now too heavy, to lift, so she dragged it with some back straining effort, unceremoniously towards the open front door. Just before she reached the entrance another bomb landed nearby on the canal next to the small factory opposite. The factory took the brunt of the blast. Water, large sods of soil and shards of wood and metal thudded into the nursery's old Victorian pub walls and windows, smashing the latter to smithereens.

Ruby had been lucky to have been bending down low to drag the crate and therefore escaped much of the flying glass that penetrated the building. Nonetheless she felt pain and reached up with her hand to find her hair was a sticky bloody mess. But she barely registered the damage as she gazed down at the little bundles below her in the box. There were small pieces of glass and other detritus resting on top of the teddies and children, but thankfully she could see no smears of blood or any evidence that any injuries had occurred.

Had the nursery staff headed towards the underground station as they had wanted, they would have been nowhere near the bomb. But Ruby had sent them into its path. She shifted her gaze with dread to where the bomb had landed. The factory was on fire but through the smoke she could see the nursery staff and their charges had safely reached the centre of the park, and were heading round to the far side of the impressive Burdett-Coutts Memorial Fountain, which might afford some protection should another bomb land nearby.

Ruby took a huge gulp of air. But the momentary relief of tension didn't last long.

Nashey! Where the bloody hell is he?!

The sudden realisation that her husband disappeared upstairs just before the bomb exploded, and had not since returned, resulted in a wave of adrenalin pumping through her.

The burning factory, and the toxic blackened rectangular shards of indeterminate material that were floating down through the air with the incongruous spinning grace of a ballerina, meant it would be hazardous to drag the box outside. She took one more check of the box of infants. Still no sign of blood. What to do? Events had proved that the children were probably safer inside than out. She dragged the crate round behind the old pub's bar, which was still in place as a nursery reception desk, and wedged it into a corner. She looked around the nursery for inspiration. The floor was covered in a confection of milk, infant health leaflets and feeding charts. There were bright coloured pictures on white walls full of marks made by sticky little fingers. A wonderful doll's house, donated by a wealthy supporter. A rocking horse that had seen better days. A pram. Boxes of Virol, Glaxo baby food, eggs and barley. Then she saw the staff's coats hanging up on hooks. She grabbed them and draped them carefully on top of the seething mass of mini humanity and their soft ursine minders, careful not to replace one danger with another. That would have to do until she returned.

Within seconds she was leaping up the bare wooden stairs just as her husband had done a few minutes earlier. She reached the top of the steps and hurtled through the open doorway. A single room took up the whole of the first floor. Seven children aged three to five years were sitting, cowering on the floor, shaking with fear, arms around knees brought up to their chins. Some had hair and faces covered in dust; some had scratches on them. Ruby gave them a rudimentary inspection for injuries but they all appeared unharmed, physically at least. The smell of urine was clear. Most, if not all, had wet themselves. There were no adults to be seen.

Where was Miss Matters and her assistant Hildegarde? And where was Nashey? The roof!

She started to take another flight of steps, two at a time at full pelt, not noticing the red marks on them. A few feet from her destination, she could see through the open doorway to the roof. For the briefest moment she glimpsed her husband, lying on the ground covered in blood, and then everything went black.

******

Nash had arrived on the first floor to find three screaming children sat on the floor. Knowing how many children were usually in the nursery, he wondered if there should not be more of them. His wife had once told him the nursery used the old pub's roof as a place to get some fresh air in to the lungs of the tots. Better check it.

The audience of three continued to show their displeasure. Nash looked back at them, hesitating for a moment. He wasn't used to dealing with tiny tots. What should he do for the best?

"Stay there!" was all he managed, unaware of the

harshness with which he had blurted out the words. The children's decibels increased if that were possible, and the sentence, such as it was, had been redundant. They were not going anywhere.

He raced up to the roof. A woman Nash recognised as Muriel Matters was just about to bring another two children down the steps. Her assistant Hildegarde was trying to catch a child that was running round the roof like a whirling dervish. This was being made more difficult by an additional tot clinging to her skirt. Both children were attempting to scream but could barely get their breath to do so.

No one other than Nash called the highly respected Montessori education pioneer by any name other than 'Miss Matters'.

"Mure, chuck me them two and go back and help Hild get the others down!" barked Nash. Mure did as she was told. Nash quickly placed the children with the others and returned to the roof. The two women now had a child each. Nash took hold of Muriel's. The boy who had been running around the roof, was now thrashing his arms and legs about, making it difficult for the stooping petite young Hildegarde while she attempted to hand him over. Nash reached forward with his spare hand and grabbed the child roughly from behind via his shirt collar. The relieved young woman straightened and there was just a hint of a smile of thanks starting to cross her face when the bomb landed on the canal. She was no more than a couple of feet away from her colleague, Nash and the two children, but it was enough. A piece of shrapnel hit her square in the neck. The rest of them didn't receive a scratch from the metal but were splattered with blood.

Blood poured out of the woman's severed jugular vein as she fell to the floor. She gurgled and spluttered her death throes. Nash immediately knew she was beyond help, so turned his back to shield the children from the horror and rushed them down the steps to join the others. He returned equally quickly to find the dying woman being cradled by her boss. Nash new it was hopeless but threw himself to the ground in any case and tried covering the wound with his hand. Blood poured over his fingers. The heart continued to pump blood over both him and Muriel for a while and then it ceased. She was gone. Nash leaned back and lay on the ground, his red hands holding the top of his head in despair. At that moment Ruby appeared in the doorway.

******

It was strange. Ruby felt her head was both floating on air and also a ton weight. If she made any movement the weight toppled forward and her head started to spin. It reminded her of how she felt when she had been force-fed for the first time in Holloway prison. There was a racket going on outside. It was what must have awoken her. Where was she anyway? She daren't move her head sideways. A Victorian pub's tin ceiling gazed down, informing her that she was lying on the ground floor of the nursery. She listened intently to make sense of the din. What sounded like a firework went off. That would be the all-clear maroon. This was almost immediately confirmed by an all-clear bugle, no doubt being blown by a boy scout atop a bicycle. There was the clattering of what sounded like heavy buckets on the cobbles, a squeak of something metallic being turned, and then metal being scrapped along the ground. And above these noises came the sound of shouting from young women and a lone male voice. She recognised the latter. What the hell was her husband doing outside?

Nash was shouting up at someone crouched awkwardly half out of a first floor window in the factory.

"Stay there I'm telling you!"

But his subject was not being as compliant as the tots. A panicking young man was threatening to jump.

A dozen members of the Bow Women's Fire Brigade, less than resplendent in the most unflattering garb of neck-to-ankle blue overall uniforms with loose fitting black waist belts, were buzzing around. One of them was attending an unconscious female factory worker, lying on the cobbles face down. The firewoman crouched down to flip the teenage girl over, then grabbed hold of her and completed a fire officer's lift, carrying the youngster off matter-of-factly over her shoulder like a sack of coal, towards an arriving ambulance.

Another firewoman had just busied herself using two special wrenches to unlock a water supply cover. A couple of her colleagues had then dragged the heavy metal cover a few feet so others could manhandle their hose contraption onto the water supply outlet. Other women were ferrying huge empty fire buckets in each hand.

Nash had taken all this in, and was impressed. But it did not stop him from trying to take charge.

"Don't worry about the factory! Drop them buckets and get your catching thing over here sharp!"

The women ignored this bystander to begin with, but his shout did cause one of them to look his way for a moment. She then followed his gaze.

"Ethel, jumper!" shouted the fire officer.

The senior firewoman quickly reacted to her colleague's cry.

"Everyone stop action! Get the Browder!"

Every woman stopped what she was doing and rushed to their fire engine. Moments later they were assembling a Browder Life Safety Net. Within seconds the dozen women were running with it to get below the young man perched precariously above them. The Browder was built to optimise the chances of catching someone falling from a far greater height. It had a big enough circumference for twenty fire officers to get around. The dozen in situ were finding it an unwieldy beast.

Nash attempted to take charge again, pointing at some of the women at one edge of the safety net.

"You four move over the other side, I'll take the strain here!"

Chief fire officer Ethel Robson was used to having to deal with men who thought they knew best.

"Sir, will you kindly step aside and leave this to the professionals," she retorted.

"Let him help! He's got experience of this sort of thing!" It was a wobbly Ruby, holding uncertainly on to the door arch of the nursery.

She was somewhat guilty of exaggeration. Shortly after they had met, Nash had thrown Ruby off the deck of the Titanic, into the last lifeboat which had already started to be lowered. If anyone had experience of catching people

13

falling through the air, it was the poor officer in the lifeboat on whom Ruby had landed.

The man above was now so precariously balanced on the window ledge that if he did not soon jump he would surely fall. The chief made an executive decision.

"All right that man, get hold!"

Nash did as he was told and the young man above took this as his cue. He thudded into the net with quite a bump but the net held.

"Blimey, just like a Charlie Chase comedy!" commented a relieved Nash.

"No laughing matter actually sir," retorted fire officer Robson, before turning on her heel to shout further orders to her team to get back to the factory fire and its casualties.

"Yeah all right! Christ, that's the thanks I get!" said Nash, with a twinkle in his eye to show it was only mock affront.

At which point the oldest of the other fire officers, a woman in her forties, entered the fray.

"I thought it was more like Harold Lloyd myself. And you look like a Keystone Cop if you ask me."

This was said with rather too saucy a purse of the lips as far as Ruby was concerned. She left the safety of her door arch support and approached.

"Well, no one did ask you did they? I'll give you Harold Lloyd!" she said knowingly, before she made the mistake of nodding her head to the side to add emphasis as she told the firewoman to "hop it" back to her fire duties.

Everything started to spin.

The next time Ruby opened her eyes she was back staring at the nursery ceiling again.

"That's three times I've picked you up off the floor today. You going to stay down this time?" scolded Nash.

The reproach in Nash's voice was his way of showing concern for his wife's health.

"Thank you for your concern darling. Perhaps if a member of the fire brigade hadn't been inviting you to the pictures, when she should have been getting on with putting out a fire, I might not have ended up on the floor a third time, eh?"

"People have different ways of dealing with this here war. One minute she was helping save a life, the next she was having a bit of fun. There's no harm in that is there darling?"

When Mr & Mrs Nash started calling each other 'darling', it was a sign that their conversation was not without tension. A conversation then ensued which involved several more 'darling' broadsides before Ruby's foggy mind suddenly wondered what had happened on the roof. Nash explained.

"The stairs to the roof had just been hit. They must have been like Swiss cheese. Your weight on 'em finished 'em off. You fell through to the stairs below. You've got a gash on your leg and some scratches, and you must have copped a bash on the nut in to the bargain. Dr Alice has already given you a quick once over and drugged you up. She'll be back to see you proper soon enough. She's got her hands full right now mind."

He had said the last sentence with such gravity in his voice that Ruby knew something else had happened. She waited to hear the worst. Nash went on to explain that Hildegarde was dead. The planes had flown off. The body was still up there. An ambulance was on its way. People would have to use a ladder up to the roof for the time being. Muriel was on her way to tell Hildegarde's parents. The nursing staff had returned, as had some of the parents of the children, and things were under control.

Ruby felt terrible for the dead young woman and her loved ones. Then a huge sense of relief that it hadn't been her husband flooded through her, immediately followed by an accompanying sense of guilt.

Chapter 2

"The disease simply had its way. It came like a thief in the night and stole treasure."

George Newman, Ministry of Health Report
on the Pandemic of Influenza

Dr Alice Johnson's career had been determined by something as mundane as an ear infection. She had been twelve years old when her mother had dragged her daughter from their home in a leafy upper working class part of Stepney Green to see the new 'doctoress' who had started work at the local children's hospital in nearby Shadwell.

Alice had not relished the prospect of being seen by a young woman doctor down in darkest Shadwell, where the poorest of the poor lived. What would a woman in such a place know about medical matters? And from what Alice had heard of the death rate of children admitted to the hospital, the answer to that question was not much.

She was even less enthusiastic when, after some painful poking about in her ear, the woman had diagnosed something called mastoiditis and insisted she have an operation, injections and, worst of all, a stay in the hospital as an in-patient for some time while all this was going on.

Couldn't she just have some more ear drops like the Leman Street dispensary had given her last week? The no-nonsense doctor had asked her without any semblance of sarcasm if the drops had worked. Alice had to admit that they had not. She hated it when adults asked her questions they already knew the answer to. And more to the point, they knew the answer was not the one she wished to convey.

By the time her thirteenth birthday had rolled around, the now healthy again young girl had decided she would become a medical practitioner, just like her doctor, heroine and torchbearer, Miss Elizabeth Garrett.

The success of Miss Garrett had so horrified the British medical establishment that they had made it more difficult for further women to take her path, but a dozen years later Alice passed her final MD's examination in more medical woman-friendly Switzerland. And she had been a doctor running her own practice in the East End, specialising in women and children for over three decades since.

And now, with so many male doctors in France for the past four years, she felt that the war had, if nothing else, allowed women doctors to get a firmer toehold on the medical ladder. In her case this had manifested itself in her being appointed to a role whereby she was representing East End MDs in liaising with the local sanitary authorities, local medical officer of health, the chief medical officer of the London County Council, local education authorities and the Board of Education, regarding all matters medical.

And very little social work went on in the East End without Sylvia Pankhurst and her assistants becoming involved in it. Thus Alice found herself in the unenviable position of being the middle woman, stuck in the no man's land between the warring factions of the authorities and Miss Pankhurst's impressive organisation. And the latter were not interested in excuses, explanations, logistics or anything else other than getting things done. They repeatedly asked the one word question so beloved of the enquiring minds of four year olds. 'Why?' And the problem was that, like the parents and teachers of young tots, Alice could rarely articulate an acceptable answer.

It was particularly difficult when she had to deal with her friend and Miss Pankhurst acolyte, Ruby Nash. And today was going to be such an occasion because she had received a note from Ruby stating that she would like to see her local doctor. The summons was short and to the point.

'Alice, the flu is taking hold round here. I've heard the trenches have it bad. Sylvia tells me Madrid in Spain has it worst of all. There are people dead there. Are people going to die round here? What can we do? I will be at the nursery to receive you on your visit this morning'.

Ruby had clearly recovered from her fall. That was for sure. The problem was that as regards most of the comments in the note, Alice did not know what her friend was talking about. As usual, the Nash's and Miss Pankhurst's grapevines were way ahead of her own official sources of information.

******

The Cost Price restaurant provided good nutritious meals. There were significant shortages in most food staples, which had led to huge queues at shops and galloping price inflation. Sylvia's organisation, which was now a sizable war charity with multi donation and subscription income streams, was able to buy in bulk and therefore cheaply, and also use its contacts to get hold of not just food, but coal with which to cook. This was a commodity often unavailable through local shops or the coalman. Thus it was much cheaper, healthier and more palatable for people to eat at the restaurant rather than in their own home.

The first news to greet the newly restored to health Ruby on arrival back at the restaurant was that Sylvia had taken to her bed. The number of recent influenza victims in the area had Ruby immediately make an assumption.

"Flu?" she asked, concern verbally etched into the solitary word.

No it wasn't the flu. One of the kitchen workers informed her that Miss Pankhurst's fragile digestive system had not been able to cope with the restaurant cook's latest culinary attempt at 'food reformist vegetarianism', as she called it. Mrs Richmond had apparently taken it upon herself to add cooking to Sylvia's vast portfolio of reform work.

Sylvia had done more hunger strikes than most during the Suffragette years. And during the particularly stressful final two years of the struggle leading up to the outbreak of war, she had taken to adding thirst strikes to her prison repertoire, because the body deteriorated quicker so she was released from prison on health grounds that much more speedily. And now, four years later, her digestive system had still not recovered. At least, not enough to tackle dishes involving the cook's new penchant for pulses.

Ruby quickly popped round to see Sylvia. This great champion, who had single-handedly forced the Prime Minister's hand in 1914, bringing him to the negotiation table for the first time, and whom, Ruby believed, but for war breaking out, would have won the vote for women immediately thereafter, had been laid low by dried beans. She lay on her bed, feeling extremely sorry for herself, clutching a hot water bottle to her stomach to ease the pain.

The two women discussed the restaurant; the need for the government to extend countrywide the present Home Counties rationing system on all important foodstuffs; and they also spoke of the flu. Sylvia had received further news from Spain that the illness there had reached epidemic proportions. Ever insightful, she had questioned whether Spain could be the only country suffering in such a way. She suspected it was highly likely that because it was not in the war, Spain was the one country that was allowing its newspapers to tell the truth about the disease. Meeting and chinwag over, Ruby returned to the restaurant with orders to get the cook under some sort of control.

The raison d'etre of the restaurant was to provide four hundred good filling two-course meals per day for tuppence per adult, a penny for children. And each evening a pint of hot soup and a chunk of bread for another penny. But not everyone could afford even these prices. Aware of the stigma attached to charity, Ruby had come up with an ingenious method to help those who could not afford to pay for their meals. Tickets for the meal were purchased at the door and free tickets given to those without means. No one sitting at the tables was aware of whether the people beside them had bought their ticket or not.

Ruby thought meat pudding, greens and potatoes, followed by a nice slice of spotted dick, or something along those lines, should be the dinner order of the day, every day. Serving dried bean concoctions was not in the script.

As Ruby got within yards of the restaurant in Old Ford Road, she was met by would-be customers turning away in disgust and demanding their food ticket back from the girl on the door. Ruby caught the eye of some, who simply shook their heads at her and muttered things under their breath, some of which, unfortunately, Ruby heard. It was not the most constructive of criticism but certainly got to the point. Moments later Ruby had detected the root cause of the problem. A restaurant helper was stirring a huge cauldron, doing a reasonable impersonation of ye olde medieval crone knocking up a batch of eye of newt. Ruby looked over the woman's shoulder and she too was less than impressed by what she saw.

"Mrs Richmond!" she exclaimed across the kitchen. "You cannot serve unpeeled potatoes in the soup!"

There followed a heated discussion, rather unprofessionally held in front of all and sundry in the restaurant, as to the benefits of roughage as provided by potato skins. It finished with Ruby losing her temper.

"Mrs Richmond, we are a charity who rely on benefactors! People bring us crockery, utensils, chickens, eggs, homemade pickles, jams. One man brings us a dozen loaves a day. Many send us money. If word gets out we are serving this muck we will lose their goodwill! People have had to learn to like your unseasoned butter beans, spinach, brown breadcrumbs and grape nuts, but potato dirt is too much! You have already poisoned poor Miss Pankhurst with your pulses and now you're going to starve the people of Bow into defeat quicker than our own stupid government are by not introducing full rationing!"

There was silence in the restaurant. Everyone was either staring at Ruby or had suddenly found the scuffs on their shoes most fascinating. Mrs Nash had gone way too far. And she herself immediately knew it. This war was fraying her nerves, and the shock of her recent fall had clearly left a mental scar.

She couldn't think of what to say. It had been her experience throughout life that whenever men had reached a point in an argument where they could no longer think of anything more to add, they would simply state they were 'going up the pub!' and would then storm off slamming the door behind them. She did something similar.

"Oh, do what you like! I'm off to the toy factory!"

******

The Nashes usually ate at the Cost Price restaurant but as relations were rather strained with that establishment at the moment, the man of the house had been packed off to line up to get some meat from the butcher's. Unfortunately for Nash, word had spread like wildfire that a supply of rabbits and some beef brisket had come in. The line stretched for hundreds of yards. He blasphemed to himself before taking up his place at the rear. He was not usually one for making small talk to anyone, let alone strangers, but he could see he was going to be on his feet for half an hour or so before passing through the butcher's doors, so he started up a conversation with the young woman in front of him. It would pass the time. He vaguely recognised her. She was a local munitions factory worker who had a little one at the Mother's Arms. Nash had no idea whether her tot had been one of those he had taken off the roof. He thought it best not to bring up the subject.

"How long do you reckon?"

The woman crooked her neck to look back. She recognised him and smiled.

"Queueing?" she said.

It was the start of a rather staccato conversation.

"Eh?" asked Nash. He wasn't sure he had heard correctly. The only cueing he knew of was in a snooker hall.

"You asking how long we'll be in the queue Mr Nash?"

"In the what?"

"Queue. Line up. Queue's what they call a line up now. You want to know how long we'll be?"

"Yeah."

"Couple of hours I shouldn't wonder."

"Christ! Bleeding butcher likes gassing to everyone I suppose?"

"No, it just takes longer nowadays, by the time you hand over your meat card, then your bacon card if you're of a mind to get bacon an' all, and then they have to stamp it. All takes time don't it?"

"I fought this new rationing lark was supposed to get rid of line ups."

"It has mostly. It's only because they've just had some

rabbits in. You don't have to queue for sugar or marge or coal no more like you used to. And you get your fair share. That's the most important thing, I say."

Nash grunted his grudging agreement.

"Saves all them lot in Mayfair getting it all I suppose. Like they have been," he said.

It was her turn to grunt in agreement. She was about to change the subject but was not given the opportunity.

"Oi! Chinkey!"

An errand boy cycling past was likening the young woman to someone of Chinese extraction because her skin had been turned yellow by working with TNT in the munitions factory. Such women had acquired the generally used nickname of 'canaries'. The target of the abuse did not react to the lad's more unpleasant epithet but Nash did.

"Come 'ere!! You little cowson!"

The errand boy may not have been the brightest crayon in the box, but he knew enough not to follow that sort of order. He took his right hand off the handlebars, turned his wrist and without so much as a backward glance at his protagonist gave him the two fingered salute.

Nash immediately looked into the gutter for anything resembling a projectile. There was a piece of rotting fruit lying there. He grabbed it and threw it at the boy. But Nash's heavily muscled arms meant he lacked the speed of lever required. His effort fell well short of the fast disappearing young scamp, splattering on the pavement next to those standing further up the queue. A member of the Volunteer Force inspected his newly decorated shoes with less than enthusiasm.

The Volunteer Force was made up of men who were

unable to serve, mostly due to health reasons or being over military age. Others were in a reserved occupation. They were mostly old men often ridiculed in public. They wore GR armlets which had given rise to them being given the poetically licensed nickname, Gorgeous Wrecks. This particular sixty year old had been assigned to patrol the queue to ensure no disorder occurred. When a shop ran out of a popular foodstuff before those who had been lining up for hours had received their fair share, it could lead to some unpleasantness in the best of places. In the East End it could end in a riot.

The man looked down the queue and spotted the fruit-throwing troublemaker. He then slowly sidled up to Nash with the passive aggressive body language only a seasoned jobsworth could perfect.

"What's your game?" he enquired.

"Not cricket, that's for sure eh gov?" said Nash smiling. He had almost called the man Gorgeous but had just stopped himself in time.

"Never mind all that," replied the man waving away Nash's bonhomie with a backhanded flick of the wrist a table tennis player would have been proud of, "look at the state of my shoes!"

Nash appreciated the old boys in the VF. They were just trying to be useful after all. And he had seen them doing good work moving patients during air raids and helping returning soldiers at mainline railway stations who were too tired, bewildered or simply ignorant of London to understand how to get themselves home. And he was himself rather too close in age to some of the Volunteers than he cared to admit. So he was far more conciliatory than he would normally be, and accepted the good talking to, he no doubt deserved. This included Nash being told that if there was any more trouble from him, a special constable would be called. Nash had nodded in all the right places but his contrition did little to improve the old man's mood. The conversation ended with Nash being told in no uncertain terms that had the Volunteer been ten years younger he'd have given him a good hiding. And with this he strutted, stiff-backed up the queue.

"That was good of you to let him have his moment Mr Nash," said the young munitions worker.

Nash winked at her.

"And thanks for going after that little perisher. I'm Anne by the way. Anne Geoghegan."

She now changed the subject to the one she had in mind as soon as she recognised Nash. She started by asking a question to which she already knew the answer.

"Anyhow, I did hear of Mrs Nash having a bad fall. How is she?"

"She's all right. Tough as old boots she is. She's up and about. She's already upset 'em all down at the restaurant, so there can't be too much wrong with her can there?"

"Running round doing all them jobs for Miss Pankhurst and with husband at home to look after. Keeps her on the go I'll wager. She looks fit and strong mind."

"Well she don't have to do a twelve hour shift in a factory and then look after five kids like some, does she? But yeah she's fit and strong all right."

It was time for the question Anne had been angling towards.

"Don't suppose she could play football Saturday

afternoon? My shells team are playing forgings but our factory welfare officer won't let me and some of me mates play on account of us being yellow. They like us canaries to keep out the way when we're not in the factory. Don't look good see. So we're a bit short."

Nash sighed deeply, gave the wryest of smiles and shook his head. He did not even bother to make his thoughts known on a country that didn't mind its workforce poisoning itself, just so long as the fewest number of people knew about it. After all, it was only the same as the cannon fodder in the trenches.

Anne took the shake of the head to be a refusal. She upped her sales pitch.

"She don't have to be no good mind. And one of the girls is bound to have the same size feet so can lend her some boots. And we've got team shirts, socks, caps and shorts. You'd be letting her do a good turn. The match is in aid of the Disabled Soldiers Fund mostly. And for poor children. And for Stepney railway station buffet."

The last sentence was so absurd that it tickled Nash's funny bone. He appreciated his mood being lifted away from the war for a moment.

"Blimey, why didn't you say before girl?!" he said with eyes wide open with enthusiasm. "I've had many a good plate of whelks in Stepney station. You don't have to get my permission mind. Just ask her yourself. "

Chapter 3

"Why is Mr Utz bad now? They've been buying tripe off him for years and he wasn't bad then. Has the badness got something to do with the brawn or has it got something to do with Utz himself, with the very name Utz maybe?"

Melanie McGrath, Silvertown
– An East End Family Memoir

Conscience. Conscientious. Strange words; strange notions. That was, as far as Nash was concerned. There had been a time in his life when, as a young man living by nefarious means in the East End of London's Whitechapel slums thirty years earlier, neither word would have related to him.

And even now, he found it difficult to understand what all this conscientious objection lark was all about. Conchies were rum coves. Why would a man refuse to fight just because of some religious belief he held?

Yet, conscience now drove him to protect the conscientious. He spent most of his waking day hiding men, who refused to fight for their country, from the authorities.

Weeks earlier, Nash saw irony, and now he was ashamed to remember the tiniest flicker of jet black humour, in a desperate British government raising the maximum age for conscription to the army to fifty one years of age. He was just too old a fly to fall into that spider's net. Pity. He would have loved to have gone to an Objectors' Tribunal to tell them of the beatings he had handed out to many a man over the years, many of whom would have been in uniform, because they had dared to be, or at least been unlucky enough to find themselves, in opposition to him. And then, just when the inquisition's faces would have failed to hide their consternation at this seemingly ideal bit of cannon fodder in front of them refusing to fight, he would have told them why he was there and where they could stick their war. No conscientious objection. Just objection. It was not his fight. It was as simple as that.

He was brought up in a part of Whitechapel which had a large German population. Nash had lived close to the German Lutheran Church in Alie Street. Some of the German lads living in the area were members of the street gang that he led in his teenage years. He fought with them at his side. He felt he had much more in common with them and other German working people than the British establishment who had taken the country in to war against them.

As far as he was concerned, if that lying cowson of a Prime Minister Asquith and his blithering idiot of a Foreign Affairs wallah Grey, and Asquith's replacement, that self-seeking weasel Lloyd-George, wanted to fight the Germans, let *them* do it. These and their other merry men in Cabinet, were the very opponents he had been fighting against for the past six years since his recruitment into Sylvia Pankhurst's women's suffrage campaign. He failed to see why, just because he had been born on the same bit of turf as them, he should fight their battles for them.

And when he and his colleagues had finally won their battle for Votes for Women two months ago, he too, as a man of the urban poor, had won the right to vote for the first time. He had not been able to vote at the last general election, and neither had a good chunk of the British army, many of whom had been near-starved into voluntarily taking the king's shilling at the start of the war. But he was luckier than many of them. He had no children to support or aged parents to keep out of the workhouse. He had a wife, but she didn't need support from anyone. He had not voted for the Liberal government that took the country into war; had a very low opinion of the present coalition mob that obstinately continued the disaster; and would not have fought for either lot even if he *had* voted for them.

As for his new conscientious objector friends, they were sometimes religious men, sometimes not. Some simply pacifists who could not take another man's life, or even assist in helping others take lives. And other people, such as his Bow neighbour Sylvia Pankhurst, were always going on about the evils of capitalism, and why this terrible war was just a capitalist power, money and land grabbing exercise, using the workers as their poor, unknowing tools in the greatest confidence trick in history. He didn't know anything about all that conchie or commie talk. He just knew that fighting the men of Germany simply because our politicians could not come to terms with their lot, was wrong.

Nash also had an old fashioned Victorian sense of fair play. It was what had drawn him into the Suffragette struggle. He had initially had no particular interest in Votes for Women, but once he saw how the government were treating the opposite sex in their struggle, he dug his heels in and helped the women in any way he could. And now he didn't like the way conscience objectors were being treated. After being court marshalled they were given the most severe sentence possible in law, which earlier in the war had been one hundred and twelve days hard labour, but was being increased more and more as the conflict proceeded. The sentence began with a month in solitary on bread and water, performing arduous and boring tasks such as breaking stone, hand-sewing mailbags or picking oakum. After release they could be immediately arrested again as a deserter, court marshalled and returned to prison.

The picking of oakum was far too close to home for Nash. It was a duplication of the duties he and his family had performed in the Poplar workhouse, when they had been forced behind its walls when he was a young lad. And being rearrested after release from gaol was far too similar to the dreaded Cat & Mouse Act, which five years earlier the government had rushed through Parliament as a very successful tactic to undermine the Suffragettes. It had almost killed his friend Sylvia Pankhurst, though he had to admit that was as much about her being so bloody-minded, as anything else. But it took one to know one. Nash was now bloody-mindedly helping conscientious objectors whenever and wherever he could.

But as such a notoriously tough, violent man, Nash was the last person the authorities would suspect as having conscience objector sympathies. Yes, he had been Sylvia Pankhurst's bodyguard for two years during her East End Suffragette campaign, and yes she was one of the most vocal anti-war, pacifist voices in the country, but in defending her, Nash had handed out many a good hiding to anyone who had opposed him. He was certainly no pacifist.

And a twist of fate had sealed Nash in the authorities' minds as being someone they need not be concerned about. At the beginning of the war, there had been an outbreak of anti-German rioting and many people with foreign sounding names in the cosmopolitan East End, whether they were German or not, had been attacked or their properties ransacked. And after the sinking of the Lusitania, when a new outbreak of anti-German rioting had taken place in the East End, Nash had become embroiled in it. His likeable local corner shop owners, the Plotskys, on seeing rioters coming down the street, had quickly painted 'We are Russians' on their shopfront. Nash saw what was happening and knew a mob would not be placated by a mere sign. He stood in front of the shop to see what he could do to help. Behind him, a mischievous young man was putting his old school geography classes to good use in painting a P at the front of Russians to give the word a very different meaning. With the mob only yards away, Nash spotted the miscreant.

"Oi!" he shouted as he made a grab for the man, who quickly made a run for it, hitting out at Nash with his paint brush-filled right hand. Nash captured the brush and a splodge of paint for his trouble, but the troublemaker escaped his clutches. Nash turned to find the mob was upon him. He tried shouting at them but there was little he could do against such a large crowd and the shop was duly ransacked.

He had been seen with the paint brush in his hand, shouting at the front of the mob. There was some poor arithmetic involving the addition of two and two, which had Nash implicated in the attack. Two policemen, who had no interest in detaining anyone involved, later questioned him about his part in the melee. Nash had a policy never to tell the police anything about anything, so they got very short shrift. This confirmed his guilt as far as the authorities were concerned, but he heard nothing more about it.

It was shortly after this that the No Conscription Fellowship contacted him. Through their links with Sylvia Pankhurst they knew full well the truth of the story, and of Nash's dislike of the war. They asked him if he would like to work for them. His previous life on the wrong side of the law had left him with skills that could be usefully deployed in helping conscientious objectors avoid capture by the authorities. He was also known to be the antithesis of a pacifist and thanks to the paint brush incident was now believed to be a German hating patriot as far as the authorities were concerned, which was an ideal cover.

He was duly recruited and worked under the less than original name of Smith to his objectors, though he asked them to call him Smithy. He had successfully worked undetected by the authorities for the past three years. Only Sylvia, his wife and a few trusted friends from either his villainous or Suffragette days knew of his work. He avoided talking about the war but when forced to offer something to a related conversation in a pub or wherever, he would simply state that he would never forgive the Germans for sinking the Lusitania. Everyone knew of the horrors he had faced on the Titanic and in the ocean afterwards, and they also knew not to bring up the subject, so this usually killed the conversation stone dead, which was just how

Nash wanted it. And his hatred of the Germans for sinking the Lusitania was true. The difference between him and most of his fellow Englishmen was that when he said 'the Germans' he meant purely the German government. Not ordinary German people.

It was an unusual stance on the war. But not unique. Ruby shared his beliefs. When she had first confirmed this to her husband, he had asked her if she was just being a supportive wife. If so, he would prefer it if she followed her own instincts even if they were opposed to his own. She had taken offense at this and told him so in no uncertain terms. He was informed that, as he very well knew, she was certainly no pacifist during her Suffragette time, and years of conversations with Sylvia had her seeing the war for what it was; economic imperialism gone mad. And having worked with so many nationalities while working on board ocean liners, she was convinced that if left to their own devices away from being corrupted by bigots, people were pretty much the same everywhere. And that included Germans. Admittedly, had she never met Nashey or Sylvia she thought she probably would be working in a munitions factory as a willing bit of Home Front cannon fodder, but fate had decreed something different for her.

But she had never become involved in her husband's work. Which was on his insistence. If and when he was held to account by the government for what he was doing, it was important to him that Ruby not be implicated. When she had argued with him about this, he had told her that she needed to keep herself in reserve for the next women's battle. Who knew what this government might get up to next against women? Perhaps conscription would be brought in for them too? Perhaps the vote would be taken away once the war was over? And when would women under 30 get the vote? She needed to be there to fight the good fight as and when.

She had agreed to keep her distance from his work, but it was difficult for her not to worry about the danger in which her husband was putting himself.

His most pressing problem at the moment was to find a hiding place for an objector named Wal Gilbert who had been to France as a non-combative soldier. The job Wal had been assigned by the army was digging up dead bodies for their identification discs, so the men could be confirmed dead rather than merely 'missing in action' and word sent home to their loved ones. The man he had been working with, a combative soldier in one of the 'Pals' battalions had by chance dug up his own brother and cried like a baby. It was at that point Wal had decided that if he ever made it back to Blighty, he would go Absent Without Leave. And this he had done, making contact with the No Conscription Fellowship, who had eventually passed him into Nash's care.

Nash was having difficulty finding safe houses. He was a victim of his own success. He had successfully hidden so many men that he was being inundated with requests to hide even more. A further problem was that while some of his objectors were middle class men with private incomes, some were far less fortunate and had to be found work so that they could pay their way. But it could not be just any work. It needed to be the sort of casual, back street employment where no questions were asked about from where the latest recruit had appeared. These were usually poorly paid, physically demanding jobs that others wouldn't do, but beggars could not be choosers. Nash had got employment for his objectors at a Bethnal Green coal yard loading wagons; at a Spitalfields brewery heaving barrels off brewers' drays; at an Aldgate slaughterhouse lugging carcasses and sorting cow bones for glue.

And now he was going to deliver his latest man to a new safe house in nearby Mile End. The tenant of the house was Kosher Bill, a likeable gentle giant ex-boxer who had helped Nash protect Sylvia when the police were continually trying to re-arrest her under the Cat & Mouse Act in the Suffragette years. Bill was a man of limited intellectual capacity. Nash suspected that he had taken one fight too many and was a little punch drunk, though others who had known Bill longer insisted he had always been that way. As a Jew, Bill knew what it was like to be on the wrong end of a phobia, and he was also sometimes taunted for his simplicity by children in the street, so it was not so surprising that he would be accepting of someone who also faced challenges. Bill could also get Wal employment in his family's cigarette-making business. And Bill's very simple nature meant that he was the last person the authorities would suspect of being involved in any sort of subversive matters. But there was the rub. Could Nash trust him not to speak out of turn? Bill was no great conversationalist. Anyone standing at the bar of his local pub engaging him in a chat would be lucky to get much more than 'yus', 'dunno' and other vague one word answers. After a lot of thought Nash had decided that he could not think of anyone better. And besides, it appeared the war was drawing to an end in any case.

Wal had told Nash something that the government and newspapers were keeping from the populace. During his time in France he had joined demonstrations and strikes by troops at Etaples over mistreatment, and when he was on his way back home he had seen more protests in Boulogne. He had also heard of scores of Chinese and Egyptian soldiers in the British Expeditionary Forces having been shot and wounded after they had tried to break out of their camp. And there were rumours of even more serious and widespread protests with men being sentenced to death and shot for mutiny or sedition.

The Germans would be in Paris soon enough. Wal believed the only thing holding them back was widespread flu, of all things. The slowing of their Spring Offensive meant they must have the flu at least as bad as our boys, which was pretty bad. But it wouldn't last of course.

Nash decided that even if Bill was to speak out of turn and get them all arrested, they might not have to spend too long putting up with the terrible punishment usually reserved for conchies and anyone who aided and abetted them.

Chapter 4

"In the mind of all the English soldiers there is absolutely no hate for the Germans, but a kind of brotherly though slightly contemptuous kindness – as to men who are going through a bad time as well as ourselves."

British army officer and poet,
Ivor Gurney, letter from the trenches

Berlin, May 1918:

There were rooks; fine glossy specimens. They made quite a din in their amiable rook way. Their musical accompaniment was the metallic screech of a rusting bar, swinging in the breeze somewhere nearby.

If this had been enough to initially rouse Dorothea Lipp from sleep, there were plenty of other noises-off to ensure turning over in bed and returning to the land of dreams was out of the question. Her bedroom's window faced out on to a main road, where stallholders were setting up. They were seemingly engaged in some voice exercises in readiness for the day's advertising that lay ahead. Their ribald humour, volleyed backwards and forwards at each other like tennis players at the net, filled the air while failing miserably to drown out the noisy clatter of stall erection.

Not that Dorothea minded the cacophony. The atmospheric, down to earth, cosmopolitan nature of the area, along with a good central location at a reasonable price, had been what had attracted her to move there five years earlier.

She was soon leaving her front door to set off for the first day at a new job. A rook caw welcomed her as she stepped onto the pavement of the main road.

Invalidenstrasse had been built by people who refused compromise with the local churchyard's leafiness to the north or the River Spree and its attendant canals to the south. The road was a wide, straight, treeless main thoroughfare of faded, shabby chic Victorian grandeur.

Dorothea lived in one of the smallest houses along the street, less than a kilometre from where, a dozen years earlier, she had trained at the old Charite medical school and hospital. She remembered the concern of her family and friends when she had informed them she intended to live alone in such a down at heel area while training to be a nurse. She had reassured them that she would spend her entire time within the walls of the hospital or in her lodgings in a respectable house in Mitte, the much more affluent area nearby. She had kept to her word and waited for ragged evidence of the area's poverty to walk through the hospital doors.

But it was one thing to have seen the walking wounded of the poor, it was another to actually see the cause of their afflictions. She had seen plenty of extreme poverty in her years at the hospital but from what she had heard of late, the war torn slums of Berlin appeared to be on a whole different level of horror.

Heading for the local railway station, Dorothea took a short cut through the poorest part of her neighbourhood. It only saved her a couple of minutes, and the additional exercise would have done her good, but she wanted to remain aware of what this war was doing to people.

Her nose wrinkled as she passed courts, yards and alleys piled with stinking, rotting refuse which had mounted up quicker than the rooks, dogs and assorted vermin could recycle it. On her return, she would take the longer way round, sticking to the main roads. Not because she couldn't face another taster of urban blight, but it would be dark then, and mean streets like these were no place for a lady at such time. On walking in through the entrance of the railway station she took a deep breath, followed by, she had to admit, a sigh of relief.

The extreme coal shortage, not to mention the paucity of locomotives, meant that trains were few and far between, and the timetable was a work of fiction. But within minutes, with some pleasant surprise, though not a little discomfort, she was standing on a packed train she had wedged herself on to, heading towards the East End.

The train passed alongside a canal. Towpath lamps were strung out in blinking white lines like a frost covered spider's web illuminated by a sunrise. They provided a false sense of occasion before the train's wheels rattled over points as rails funnelled to give a more accurate hint as to what was to come. The incongruously fine signage and insignia of a railway station terminus peeked out from beneath a liberal incrustation of soot.

Berlin's Borse railway station enjoyed neither the cosmopolitan excitement nor the efficient blandness natural to such a place. The arms of its clock had lost their battle with gravity, twice daily accurately reporting to the world it was six thirty. Most of the artificial illumination had failed to spark into life, leaving the improving light to reveal the shape of waiting room, café and other facilities.

There were no voices, just the dreary procession of sleepwalking commuters, to give the bleak scene limited animation. The platform end, where a line of passengers allowed the ticket collector to live up to his job title, was decorated, as if by design, by tiny ragged creatures, elfin but clearly adult, since some of the female variety nursed at their breast perfect miniatures of themselves. Little groups of them sat independently apart, faces suitably haggard, hands in laps, watching the world pass them by.

They were there as Dorothea and her fellow early morning passengers arrived, and would no doubt still be there, squatting silent and motionless in unchanged positions, when the last trains departed.

Dorothea thought how much had changed since she had last used the station a decade ago, just before her new husband-to-be had insisted she give up nursing on marrying. A wife's place was in the home. With great regret, she had demurred. All that training wasted. All those skills lost. But that was the way. Had she refused, his offer may have been retracted. And after all, as an upper working class woman, she was well aware how lucky she had been to have the good looks to attract a middle class suitor.

But when, five years earlier, her husband had died suddenly of cancer, she had resisted the urge to return to her old calling. For one thing, nursing was a tough life for any woman, let alone one on the wrong side of thirty. And whom had settled into a comfortable middle class ladies' life which, in recent years had included little more physically demanding than bending down to show an errant gardener where he had been going wrong. And secondly, she'd had other things on her mind.

The life assurance money from her husband's death and the nice house she then owned, had left Dorothea in a position where, if she moved to a more manageable abode where servants were no longer necessary, she need not work again. This she had achieved, before becoming an unpaid volunteer, working for the Bund Deutscher Frauen Vereine, a union of numerous feminist organisations, fighting for a variety of women's rights.

The job had taken her over to England, the year before the war began, to meet, as well as look and learn from, British Suffragists. They had over twenty different law abiding groups campaigning for the vote for women, plus three militant organisations fighting for the same thing but by different methods.

She had done the rounds, visiting numerous groups, sitting in on meetings, going on marches, and her faltering but improving English had managed many an interesting conversation. She had found England fascinating. It was far more modern than Germany in its thinking towards women. Apparently a woman had swept to a landslide victory, with by far the most votes of anyone in the whole of London, in an election for a School Board, as long ago as 1870. And every Suffragist procession Dorothea had joined had been met by huge, friendly cheering crowds, many of them full of men. Her conversations had also informed her that a large majority of British MPs believed women should have the vote. And but for their Prime Minister Mr Asquith, and the machinations of politicians like Mr Lloyd-George, who would have welcomed women into the electorate with open arms if it had benefited his own career, British women would have had the vote years ago.

Before the visit, she had felt other feminist goals in Germany were more important than gaining the vote. Access to higher education, an end to state-regulated prostitution, free access to contraception and abortion, and divorce law reform. The last one, after she had been stuck in a loveless marriage for years, was particularly close to her own heart. But English women had impressed upon her that it was the gaining of the vote that was crucial, because once one got the cross in the box on election-day, all those other goals could rapidly be achieved.

Three years ago, with the war in full cry, she had journeyed to The Hague to attend an international women's peace meeting. She and her friend Anita had represented their feminist organisation, and several other German women were also among the one hundred and twenty present. But due to the British government restricting their movement, only three British women had managed to attend. One of them, Mrs Pethick-Lawrence, had been a co-leader and the chief fund-raiser of the notorious Suffragettes. This woman had gone to prison early on in the Votes for Women struggle, which had such an effect on her that she had suffered a mental breakdown. Yet she went back to prison to serve another six terms. This had all been told to Dorothea in a matter-of-fact manner by the Suffragette as if it had been a perfectly natural and obvious thing to do. Long conversations between the two women had Dorothea fall under Mrs Pethick-Lawrence's spell. She thought her the most amazing woman she had ever met, and when she asked her who she herself held as a heroine, she had replied in the same matter-of-fact manner.

"Why, most certainly it would be Miss Sylvia Pankhurst."

When the obvious question was asked, Dorothea was told all about Sylvia and amongst other things, her exploits in the East End of London. And two of her acolytes there, a Mr & Mrs Nash, were mentioned too.

******

Klaus Winterhager was a bitter man. He believed his stupid government had ridden roughshod over him and his fellow farmers, and everyone else in food production, without any proper planning or vision. Having to run his farm without farmers and horses was bad enough, but running it without its stock in trade was ridiculous. The army had stolen all his skilled two and four-legged workers, and then the government had slaughtered a total of nine million pigs countrywide, including all of his, in the great schweinenmord of three years earlier. It had been an attempt to divert grain consumption from animals to humans, and had been a temporary boon to meat eaters. But now meat was scarce and without pigs, or nitrates and phosphates for that matter because the munitions factories had first refusal on those, there was no fertiliser. He had been reduced to being little more than a cow, chicken, turnip and grain farmer.

Klaus would shake his head with contempt every time he thought of such things. He also had a very low opinion of Austria. It was their useless railway system that failed to move grain efficiently from Hungary to Germany.

So now he was expected to do the government's job for them. And how was he supposed to achieve even this? By acting as nursemaid to injured soldiers, prisoners of war and women; his new unskilled workforce. And as if that were not bad enough, the closing down of his much loved sport, shooting, meant he now also had to fend off armies of game birds from eating his crops.

The last straw had been when he visited the city with a consignment of eggs for the black market. He had felt a tinge of guilt as he loaded his truck with the contraband, only to arrive at his destination by passing city backyards and parks full of goats, rabbits, vegetables and pigs. Apparently such animal husbandry existed because city people believed their misery was due to inflation caused by exploitative farmers making huge profits from the war!

If he was believed to be an exploiter, then so be it. He would become one. It had been at this time that he had thrown in his lot with the black market. Rather than provide them with just a few excess eggs, they became his main buyer, at a better price than anyone else could give him.

His main contact was a man by the name of Fritz Patemann who worked directly with a network of spivs. But the old farmer would also do business with any of the semi-professional cadgers who ventured into the countryside on foraging jaunts, on behalf of relatives, friends and neighbours. They all paid him a lot more than the legitimate market did for his produce, so he kept his official output as low as possible, but just high enough to stop any snoopers from a government ministry asking questions he could not answer.

Klaus was due to receive a visit from Patemann, but wanted to make his rounds beforehand. He set off to see how his British POWs were getting along. He spoke a bit of English and had to admit that he rather enjoyed a bit of banter with the enemy. Before the war he had encouraged a robust sense of humour between his workers. He remembered one occasion when a university agriculture student had asked him if he could come along and measure how the men worked. The young man had turned up with a stopwatch.

"You don't need a watch lad," Klaus had boomed for all his men to hear. "You need a calendar to measure this lots' speed of work!"

Cue much good natured swearing at their employer from his workforce.

But now the injured ex-soldiers he had working for him were a mix of the physically and mentally delicate, so he tended to be respectful and rather formal with them. And though ribald with men, he had never liked the sort of coarse talk that was often the norm between men and women working together. And flirting was out of the question for the happily married old farmer, so he had always been rather guarded with his new army of women farmhands. But he missed his robust manly badinage. So the arrival of POWs had allowed him to revert somewhat to his old self. They had been a forlorn lot when they arrived, but soon picked up on the twinkle in his eye when he insulted them, and started to enjoy giving as good as they got.

Klaus now arrived in his first field to find a small group of men standing on a large mound of hay in a cart, making hard work of emptying it on to the ground. A one-legged German soldier hobbled nearby, carrying a shotgun, supposedly to ensure the enemy did not suddenly run amok with their pitchforks.

"Fussballindianer!" shouted Klaus.

Soon after they had first arrived on the farm, the Englishmen had been both perplexed and amused by being told that German trench soldiers called their enemy counterparts 'Football Indians'. Perhaps the football was a reference to the Christmas ceasefire matches that had been played at the start of the war. But what did Indians have to do with anything?

"Dreckfresser!" came the Englishmen's reply, mostly in cockney accents.

It was quite a mouthful for a Londoner to get his tongue around. But calling their German host a 'mud glutton', a term taught to them via a game of translation charades by their non-English-speaking guards, appeared to keep the old farmer in a good mood, so why not?

But the injured German soldiers had got one over on their captives. The POWs had been led to believe they were using a term of abuse used against farmers, but in fact it was another expression used to deride Allied soldiers in the trenches. The Englishmen were themselves the mud gluttons.

The rest of the conversation took place in English, but the quality of debate did not rise.

"Poor bloody infantry! How are my coat-hangers today?" Klaus inquired.

Klaus had been most amused when, during their first conversation together, the men had told him that British Tommies called themselves PBI – poor bloody infantry. And that they were 'something to hang things on', referring to the amount of kit they had to carry to the Front.

A few more epithets were volleyed back and forth while Klaus handed out cigarettes. He told the men that German doctors believed that cigarettes were good at staving off the flu. Factories had cancelled their no-smoking rule and workers were now actively encouraged to smoke in the workplace. The Englishmen were dubious, stating that 'fags' must surely be bad for the flu, given that both attack the chest. They implied the old farmer was trying to kill them as a crafty enemy ruse. But they all took the cigarettes and lit up in any case, much to his amusement.

Klaus was quite outspoken with his thoughts on the German government's war effort when it came to all matters relating to food supply in general and farming in particular. None of the German soldiers on the farm knew a word of English, so it would not go any further. And it did him good to vent his spleen to some fellow working men, even if they were the enemy.

At one point the farmer asked Albert Walker, a man he already knew from a previous conversation was a conscientious objector, whether there were any Englishmen who were, like Klaus, not conscientious but simply objectors.

Albert told of him of a chap he knew back in London. A fellow called Smithy. The man had been his protector for a while. Despite being in his fifties, Smithy had been the scariest, most intimidating man he had ever met. He had told Albert stories of some of the things he had got up to in his younger days in the East End. It was frightening stuff. He was most certainly not the sort of man you would expect to be a conchie sympathiser. So Albert had asked him once why he was helping men like him, and he simply said the war was not his fight. He had nothing against the German people. And that once the war was over, both country's businessmen will have made a few bob on the deal, and then everything would just go back to as it was.

Klaus nodded, momentarily deep in thought. He then, having previously added 'fags' to his glossary of English words, now inquired as to what 'bob' meant.

And after providing the translation, Albert went on to say that on being arrested he had been beaten up and threatened with being sent to the Front, where he would be expected to fight, and if he didn't he would be shot for cowardice. Or he could tell them about the man who had protected him, and then they would arrange for Albert to be either a despatch rider for a non-combat unit or a stretcher bearer at the Front. He was ashamed to admit that he had been so worn down by being a conchie that he had agreed to their terms and told them what little he knew of the man called Smithy.

Chapter 5

"We will fight for what we choose to fight for; we will never fight simply because we are ordered to fight."

No Conscription Fellowship,
1917 Manifesto

Nash may have been too old to be conscripted into the army but he had always looked after himself, and still retained the fine physique that had made him the toughest man on the cobbles back in late Victorian Whitechapel. He still looked, and could be when the occasion required, a nasty bit of work. His tough looks belied his years so hardly a day went by without him being stopped by a policeman and asked for his discharge or exemption papers.

He had just been stopped and asked the question by a police officer.

"Don't have any. I'm a Cuthbert," said Nash.

Nash always enjoyed these little contretemps. He particularly liked the irony of telling a policeman that he was a conscientious objector. Or Cuthbert to use a nickname in common parlance which was his preferred term of choice for those men whom he helped.

He then wasted the policeman's time, being as evasive,

uncooperative and confrontational as he could, before the inevitable mention of arrest crossed the policeman's lips.

"You ain't going to arrest me boy," warned Nash with menace, as he moved his hand inside his coat.

The policeman made for his truncheon, only for Nash to whip out ID that showed him to be just too old for conscription.

The policeman attempted to tell Nash the error of his ways while receiving nothing but the grimmest of smiles in return. The one-way conversation ended with the almost obligatory "next time I'll nick you for wasting police time" when both he and Nash knew that was not going to happen.

And with the closest thing Nash ever had to a spring in his step, he made his way to a meeting with his latest Conscription Fellowship contact.

******

John Jameson had told the tribunal that he was conscientiously objecting on religious grounds, to which the chairman took exception.

"You are exploiting God to save your skin, a deliberate and rank blasphemer, a coward and a cad, nothing but a disgusting mass of quivering fat!"

Another tribunal member, who was the owner of a wood mill business which had reserved occupation status for some of its workers, tried a more considered approach.

"Will you do non-combatant work? A considerable number of Society of Friends are doing ambulance work."

The Quaker was shaking his head.

"I cannot be governed by their convictions My conviction is such that I cannot take any sort of non-combatant work."

Tribunal members had become increasingly bewildered and angered by such a stance. They could perhaps just accept, however much they disliked it, an objector who was prepared to do something for his country as long as it did not involve bearing arms, but a conchie who would do nothing at all to support the war effort in any way was beyond belief.

This Quaker was too much for the chairman.

"It seems to me that there are two things you possess – cowardice and insolence. It is the duty of Christians to fight the Devil, and if the Kaiser is not worse than the Devil I am a Dutchman!"

On entering the room, Jameson had recognised some of the men in front of him. They were local businessmen and councillors. He addressed them directly.

"Is it asking too much of grocers, haberdashers and retired colonels to rise above the general body of mankind to such a height to behave with reasonable forbearance?"

Fearful his now purple chairman was about to have a seizure, the tribunal clerk took up the cudgels.

"The conscientious objector is a fungus growth. A human toadstool which should be uprooted without further delay. You are the most awful pack that ever walked on this earth. To think that you would not defend our women and children from the ravages of the Germans. Is that Christianity?"

Jameson failed to understand why these men had to

be quite so rude. And even a Quaker could be brought to sarcasm by such behaviour.

"Perhaps you would prefer if I objected on political grounds? I am also a socialist."

"Since you are a socialist you cannot have a conscience!" declared the clerk with the superior air of a man who had reached a QED moment. "You sir are only fit to be on the point of a German bayonet!"

The Quaker was duly dispatched to France where his absolutist stance had him soon receiving Field Punishment no. 1, trussed to a gun carriage wheel, arms spread-eagled in the crucifixion position for two hours. He was then sent to the fish market on Boulogne Docks, which had been turned into a punishment barracks. Here he joined several other such men in a twelve feet square cell, where they were each fed water and just a few small dry biscuits all day. They were eventually taken out together to stand in line outside the adjutant's field office. Jameson was the first to be ordered inside. He was accompanied by a soldier carrying the charge sheet. As they marched side by side the soldier appeared to haphazardly allow Jameson to catch a glimpse of what was written on the paper. Printed at the top in large red letters and doubly underlined was 'Death'. As Jameson came to attention in front of him, the adjutant read out his name and serial number, the charge, then the sentence.

"Sentenced to death by being shot." There was then a pause before he continued. "Confirmed by Sir Douglas Haig". A second pause was longer, then, "And committed to ten years penal servitude."

Two weeks later he stepped ashore at Southampton

Docks where jeering bystanders had gathered to throw eggs and tomatoes at him and his fellow objectors.

He was thrown into a penal settlement in Ponders End, on the northern outskirts of London, where he had been due to spend the rest of the war doing deliberately valueless tasks. His latest job had him and fourteen other objectors get taken to a farm where they took three weeks to dig a field for oats which a single horse and plough could have completed in a day. They were just coming to the end of the job when there was an air-raid by a single plane. All raids were a shock, but this one being out in the countryside was a greater one than usual. A bomb landed in the reservoir next to the farm throwing up a spectacular plume of water.

Jameson supposed this lone bomber had probably been spooked by anti-aircraft fire, got confused by all the waterways in East London and flown up the River Lea in the wrong direction, away from the Thames. He suspected the plane's pilot probably spotted the Ponders End reservoirs and assumed they were part of the docks.

The little bi-plane came around again, very low, and dropped a bomb on the main farm building, blowing it to smithereens. Disabled soldiers, land army girls, prisoners of war and conscientious objectors, all of whom had been working on the farm in one capacity or another, ran around like headless chickens. Jameson was no different. Minutes of pandemonium later, he found himself in a forest, alone.

A week later he was about to meet a man called Smith who, he had been assured, would arrange a safe house for him.

Chapter 6

"The new hands they are taking on are only to receive 8s. a week…they cannot live on that – some have children to keep. The profits all around are large, and the Government … is shovelling out the money to help contractors buy machinery."

East End of London Munitions Worker
letter to Sylvia Pankhurst

Ruby had been amazed at how the introduction of rationing had improved everyone's morale. The ravages of war were worse than ever. Huge numbers of East End women had died of malnutrition and other related illnesses within months of becoming widowed, due to the government's failure to care for them. It was not just men in the trenches who were fodder. Old age pensioners were also starving. High rents resulted in mass evictions. There were strikes everywhere. The flu was laying people low. Yet working people were taking it all on the chin because they could finally get hold of a bit of sugar, meat and coal, and do so without lining up for hours. And the wealthy had the same rations so it was believed that they too were having to do their bit for a change.

Nobody showed this spirit better than the munitions girls' football teams. As well as losing husbands, fathers, sons and brothers at the Front, they had lost grandparents at home, and many had lost work colleagues to poisoning or explosions. And that was just the deaths. Many loved ones and acquaintances were still alive but mere living husks of their old selves, who would never work or laugh again.

Yet as soon as these women escaped their stultifying factories and terrible lives for a couple of hours on a Saturday afternoon, they came together in joking, giggling, mickey-taking female comradeship.

Many of the shells team were on 'danger work', handling explosives. It paid slightly better so those with children, parents, grandparents and avaricious landlords to support, committed themselves to such employment. This work could end with a woman's remains scattered over the factory floor.

The problem was that most of the shells footballers had been weakened by their duties. TNT was just one of the poisons with which they were working. Others didn't leave any visual trace on the body so women working with these were allowed to play for their team. But though they worked on their footballing skills while they had practice 'kickabouts' against the local lads outside the factory gates at lunch time, they would probably be too weak to be competitive against the healthier forgings team.

Thus Ruby, irrespective of whether or not she had any footballing skill, was a well-received injection of running power and physical strength. And despite her being an outsider who was a decade older than most of her teammates, she was welcomed into the team with open arms. That's not to say she didn't have to endure some good natured ribbing as her initiation. She was quickly nicknamed Gorgeous. She was, despite being older, clearly the best looking woman in the team, and it was known that she was married to a much older man, who was almost old enough to be a Gorgeous Wreck. And she had to field many a barb about that too. But she had to be careful with her comebacks about men, because she knew many of the women no longer had them in their lives.

Given that she was a ringer, she had to be careful; if she got talking to any of the opposition after the game, she was to tell them that she had only just started in the factory, in the TNT section, and the 'yellow girls' as they liked to call themselves wanted one of their lot to be in the team, so she had been drafted in at short notice.

Ruby had played a little football during her time working on ocean liners. When a ship was in port, she and the rest of the a la carte restaurant crew had a bit of rare free time so, when there were no officers around, Italy would play the Rest of Europe. Or to be more precise, her friend Claudio and his fellow waiters and cooks would take on a mixed sex team of mostly Swedish, Irish and English in a cargo bay. Her last team and its opposition had all died on one night. And if there was another explosion like the one at Silvertown last year, history could repeat itself. But she kept that thought locked in a dark recess while she enjoyed the company of her new friends.

Ruby had been expecting to play somewhere like the middle of Victoria Park, with the teams carrying their own goalposts to slot them into holes out in the middle of the park, with a few people going round with buckets to collect for their charities. So she was amazed when her team's horse-drawn charabanc deposited them outside Leyton football ground, which had a little stand and other terracing, all of which was packed full of people who had paid an entrance fee.

Leyton FC had been disbanded soon after the outbreak of war, when most of its unmarried players had volunteered for the army en bloc. And now, not just professional football but all spectator and participation sport had closed down, leaving the great British sports enthusiast desperate to enjoy some action.

And with women's football springing up everywhere, and raising money for war charities into the bargain, it was fast becoming a much loved national treasure. There was now a nationwide Munitionettes Cup competition, and thousands were watching the star team, Dick Kerr's Ladies, of Preston.

Consequently, even for an inter-factory match the Leyton ground was full to capacity to see the women play. And the players even had changing rooms, nets in the goals, and a fully qualified, uniformed male referee and linesmen.

Ruby's team ran on to the pitch, resplendent in their green & white hooped mop caps, matching vertical striped shirts with neck tie-ups, long black shorts and socks, plus heavy brown leather boots. They were met by huge deep throated cheers from the mostly male crowd. It reminded Ruby of her Suffragette years when she had to make speeches to a sea of cloth caps. Women then, as in this war, were too busy working, shopping, cleaning the house or caring for children to be in the audience.

Ruby was playing left back. Soon after kick off it was

obvious she was the worst player on the pitch. But her team mates were really skilful. So she decided that when the ball came to her she would simply attempt to hoof the ball as hard as she could away from her goal. It was the safest option. But fortunately the ball didn't come near her very often in the first half as her shells team dominated and pushed forward. They led 4-0 at half time. Everyone in the team was very happy and Ruby was praised for her no nonsense defending. A little old lady came on with a bucket of water and the remnants of a grey flannel that had seen better days, to slosh each woman in the face like a harassed mum unceremoniously wiping crumbs from a baby's mouth.

The second half was a much more even affair, as the shells team started to visibly tire. And their thirty six year old, less than skilful left back was in the fray rather more than she would have liked. But with about five minutes to go they led by seven goals to three. But then hitherto merely tired legs turned to jelly. And Ruby's recent fall, allied to the fact that she had never played a proper football match before, had left her almost as vulnerable to exhaustion as her teammates. The physical weakness of the shells team came home to roost as they mounted a Rorke's Drift defence against wave after wave of forgings attacks. But they were less successful than the British army had been in South Africa. They conceded four goals in little more than five minutes as they were overrun by an opposition not feeling the effects of having been poisoned.

There had not been many stoppages during the match so surely there would not be much injury time. Ruby spotted the referee's whistle was in his mouth. He was going to blow it to end the game and they would have escaped with a most creditable draw.

But forgings were coming forward with the ball again. Their star player, a big young woman with a donkey's kick on her, thumped the ball towards goal. It was heading straight at Ruby at head height. The only time she had previously headed the ball in the game she had used the top of her head like a battering ram against the ball rather than use her forehead in the prescribed manner, and had consequently seen stars for a few seconds afterwards. She had not learned her lesson and found her teeth juddering with the impact of mud covered heavy leather on skull. The impact knocked her hat off and through the pain she saw the ball spiral in the opposite direction to the one she had intended, straight back towards her own goal. It was too far from Betty, their goalkeeper to save it. In that split second Ruby saw she was about to score an own goal to lose the match. A moment later the ball flew an inch over the crossbar. No goal. And the referee's whistle blew for the end of the game. It was a draw. Her team gathered round her shrieking with delight and patting 'good old Gorgeous' on the back.

Chapter 7

"I knew that it was my business to protest however futile protest might be. I felt that for the honour of human nature those who were not swept off their feet should show that they stood firm."

Bertrand Russell, Conscientious Objector

Ruby had been asked by her husband if she would like him to come along to watch her at the football match, but she had put him off, concerned that she might make a fool of herself. This in itself did not worry her, but she had initially thought that there would only be a small crowd standing on the side-line to watch, and was afraid that some wag may shout abuse at her, which might result in the man being thumped by her husband.

But unbeknownst to her, Nash had found out the match was a rather bigger one than Ruby had realised, but kept this to himself lest his wife got stage fright. He had made his way along to the match, paid his contribution to charity, and had easily blended unnoticed into the sizeable crowd.

When the final whistle blew he had felt so proud of his wife, but on seeing the shells team gather round her, he resisted the temptation to run on to the pitch to tell her so. This was a moment for Ruby and her teammates to enjoy exclusively together. He had made his way home and waited for her to walk through the door. She was duly met with a "bleeding good header you did to save the game girl. I saw it. I'm proud of you Rubes," followed by a kiss.

But that had not stopped him from being highly amused the next morning, when his wife could barely get out of bed. She lit a bedside candle and groaned her way across the room to the kettle like a steam locomotive puffing to its water tower. She saw the smirk on her husband's face so retaliated by telling him her nickname with the girls, and why she had been given it.

Hours later she was still stiff as a board when she and Sylvia met Nash outside the British Museum underground station. He had spent the morning out in the countryside of Woodford, liaising with others in his cause and helping them put the finishing touches to a farm shed that had been converted into living quarters for objectors. The two women had led a League for the Right of Soldiers' and Sailors' Wives & Relations march to the War Office and 10 Downing Street. It was protesting against a new law that had been passed which made it illegal for a woman with venereal disease to have sexual intercourse with a member of the armed forces, even if that man was her husband and it was he who had given the woman the disease in the first place.

With deference to Ruby's stiff gait, they made their way slowly to Holborn Hall where Ruby and Sylvia were to attend a National Conscription Fellowship meeting where the ex-MP George Lansbury was to make an anti-war speech. Given Nash's work hiding objectors was tied up closely with the NCF, he needed to keep a low profile. He could not afford to be seen at such a meeting. He was there purely to protect his wife and friend if the inevitable unpleasantness outside the meeting became something a little more dangerous.

Nash left the women well before they reached the hall, and crossed the road to the Princess Louise pub. He bought himself a pint, grimaced first at the high cost and then at the watered down, low sugar nature of the beer.

"Nine-pence for a pint of piss," he muttered under his breath, as he took his beer on to the pavement to watch the proceedings across the road at the hall.

As expected there was an angry crowd of pro-war men outside. Fortunately the mob were too busy swearing at, and generally trying to intimidate, everyone entering, to recognise the infamous pacifist Sylvia Pankhurst. The two women were managing to slip through the crowd and into the hall suffering only minimal jostling.

But Nash had spotted a man standing at the edge of the swathe, who did not quite fit the surroundings. Nash's success over the years, first as someone who relieved gentleman of their valuables down dark alleyways, and then as Sylvia's bodyguard in his Suffragette years, was not based purely on his ability to beat up anyone who got in his way. He had a sixth sense for spotting plain clothes policeman, and any other men who were not quite whom they appeared to be. His antenna led him to keep his focus on this man. And as Sylvia passed by the fellow, Nash saw him react like a cat spotting a bird. The man went quickly to his pocket, fetched out notebook and pencil and started scribbling feverishly, continually glancing back and forth between his notes and Sylvia. He had obviously recognised her, and unsurprisingly followed her and Ruby into the hall. Nash did not think he had the stamp of a newspaper man. Whoever he was, Nash decided he better not be seen with Sylvia and Ruby when they came out of the meeting.

He quickly downed his pint and immediately wished he hadn't. He repeated his previous review of the quality of the beer, popped the empty glass back in the pub, and then went to head home. The women would realise he must have left for good reason.

But as he returned back through the pub's double doors onto the pavement, a large force of police and a number of soldiers arrived together on foot outside the hall. The men outside turned from jeering to cheering as they parted like the Red Sea to leave an avenue for the government forces to run through into the hall.

Nash could not worry about the weasel with the notebook now. He needed to protect his women. He ran across the road at full tilt. His momentum, along with some lusty thrusts of his elbows, had him crash through the avenue of cheering men just as they were starting to close back into a mass. Several oaths were shouted after him as he followed the police through the entrance area into the main hall. The last two policemen took hold of the large hall doors and started to close them but Nash was already through on their coat tails. One of them shouted "oi, what do you think you're doing?" after him, but immediately thereafter was too busy ensuring the doors got closed, to worry about a solitary gate-crasher.

Nash looked up to the speaker's platform to see George

Lansbury was already in position. But two military officers and six soldiers jumped up to join him and ordered the ex-MP not to attempt to start speaking. He was then told to procure order on their behalf.

Police officers were now going around demanding to see the identification papers of every man in the place. Men were attempting to leave but the doors were held firmly closed. Nash realised that the police had not shut the doors to keep the public out, but to keep them in.

There was uproar as police shouted to soldiers to come and round up a suspected conscription absentee whom they had caught. Four male peace campaigners were led away. A woman was arrested for attempting to help them. A young man, who had got up on the platform to wave his exemption papers, was then flung head-first several feet down to the hall floor.

Two policeman grabbed Nash from behind. Before he had time to react, a police officer in front of Nash shouted to his colleagues.

"Leave him, he's too old!"

It was the first time Nash had ever been correctly diagnosed as too old for conscription. A couple of years back, when the conscription age limit had been only forty-one, he had been delighted to be served a white feather by a nice young lady. And now apparently he didn't even pass for fifty. He had never been so insulted.

Duly released he fought the compulsion to show the policemen that he was not too old to dump the two of them on their backsides. He had other fish to fry. He looked around and eventually spotted Ruby and Sylvia. They were crouched on the floor assisting the young man who had been thrown off the platform. The lad was dazed and had a bloody nose but Nash thought he was no worse off than he would be after a lively Saturday night out in Bow.

Nash was relieved Ruby and Sylvia were out of trouble for once but you wouldn't have guessed it from his tone.

"Not arrested yet ladies? You two must be getting old!" he said, with a knowing smirk on his face.

Ruby wasn't going to let him get away with that.

"No policemen beaten to a pulp yet dear husband? You *are* old!"

Sylvia looked askance at them. It was neither the time nor the place for their silly banter. She had always found it extraordinary that they made fun of each other in the most inopportune circumstances. She put it down to the fact that having met just as the Titanic slid beneath the waves, no situation could seem too terrible after that. Duly chastised by Sylvia's withering look, the loving couple exchanged a 'that's us told' glance and got on with the serious job of extricating themselves from their predicament.

The two women helped the teenager up, but the three of them immediately gave a good impersonation of dominoes, when a man with a police officer clinging to him in a most unloving embrace, piled into them, causing them to fall to the floor in instalments.

Nash swept the lad up and threw him effortlessly over his right shoulder.

"Pick that tip up from your little firewomen friends did you?" asked Ruby, as she picked herself up stiffly from the floor.

Nash gave his wife a wink, before picking his way

through the mayhem to the hall's door, with the two women following in his wake.

At this point it was Ruby's turn to take charge, speaking oh so sweetly to the young policemen on the door, explaining that such roughness was no place for the sensibilities of ladies, so would the constables be kind enough to allow them to escape such tortures.

Ruby and Sylvia were each wearing a simple white blouse, ankle length plain skirt, old lace-up boots; and it had clearly been some time since their once fashionable, now battered velvet-trimmed chip hats had passed over the counter of Derry & Toms. They were hardly genteel middle class ladies about town. And Ruby's attempt to hide her working class Hampshire accent wasn't fooling anyone. Even wet behind the ears young police officers.

But one of them noticed the stiff way in which Ruby was moving and assumed she had just been injured in the melee. So after some umming & ahhing the young men allowed the women and their injured friend to slip out, and for the second time in five minutes, Nash was also allowed to go on his way on grounds of age.

It was only when they got outside and Nash found himself looking across at the pub, that he remembered the man with the notebook. He had forgotten to look for him in the melee.

Chapter 8

"No person shall by word of mouth or in writing spread
reports likely to cause disaffection or alarm among any of
His Majesty's forces or among the civilian population."

Defence of the Realm Act, 1914

The greater level of security being imposed by the
government posed new problems for Nash. He had always
taken the utmost care when meeting and transporting
his objectors, often choosing to travel when an incident
of sizeable proportions was due to take local police off
the streets. Best of all was an anti-war peace rally in the
East End. During the past year these rallies had become
increasingly well attended, but since the losses during the
German Spring Offensive people had once again closed
ranks behind the war effort. Thus such a rally was now
always good to spark a riot.

But the Holborn Hall incident had showed how the
police and army were becoming increasingly successful in
working together to chase down those who attempted to
evade fighting in the war. And Nash suspected that the
man who had been spying on Sylvia, had probably seen
him with her, and reported back to whatever government

agency for which he was working. It was possible they would find out in due course who he was, and then he might find himself under surveillance. He would need to be on his guard.

Ever careful to keep one step ahead of the government, Nash had a novel way of initially meeting his objectors. He had the No Conscription Fellowship drop off his new charges at the Woolwich Free Ferry.

The captains of the ferries had seen at first hand the appalling hardships of the people in the area caused by the explosion in the local Silvertown munitions factory the previous year.

The government had hushed up the largest explosion in history so, to the outside world gleaning their news from the press, there had merely been an explosion down at the docks. People throughout London had been left to ponder what that huge noise and bright light emanating from the East End had been. And just why had their windows rattled or smashed at the same time the very earth seemed to tremble?

But many East Enders were all too aware that much of Silvertown had been razed to the ground and thousands of already poverty stricken people had been left homeless. Local authorities set up temporary accommodation for many in local schools, churches and halls. Other people went to live with nearby relatives, returning mere slums to the overcrowded garrets and hovels they had been in a bygone era. And with coal in such short supply, and so expensive even when available, the inhabitants of churches, halls and slums alike lived in cold, damp misery.

The ferry captains responded by allowing as many

people as they could to ride in their cavernous engine rooms all day. Such places were as warm as toast. And someone could sit there all day, not only warm, but free from the prying eyes of police and military. So Nash had objectors dropped at the ferry, and they were told to ride it until they were approached.

Nash would make his way to the location by horse & cart. The latter was used to hide the objector. On the journey back to a safe house, the man would lie on the back of it, out of sight, under a pile of coal sacks.

Taking such transport on the ferry from Silvertown to Woolwich, and then immediately returning on the same boat without having alighted, might draw attention. Woolwich was where London's largest munitions factory was located. Travelling to Woolwich and back for no reason would seem odd to anyone who noticed. The whole population had been warned to look out for any sort of strange behaviour. It was believed they might spot a German spy. So Nash would leave his transportation outside Silvertown's Railway Hotel, which had survived the great blast.

On his initial reconnaissance of the area weeks earlier, Nash had spotted a one-legged young man with a cut down clothes prop as a crutch, probably a recently maimed soldier, scraping the barest of livings by calling passing cabs for drunks as they stumbled out of the hotel's saloon bar. Most would toss their unofficial concierge a penny, or if they were very drunk, their lack of coordination might result in them accidentally scattering a few coins over the cobbles for him to pick up with some difficulty.

Nash had asked the man to hold his horse until he

returned. And there would be more work where that came from; at a shilling each time. Good money for an hour's work, especially for a man who, assuming he was local to the area, was probably an ex-docker who would never be able to work in his chosen profession again.

Nash could have left his horse & cart closer to the ferry entrance but he had always liked crowds. A man could disappear into them. Being opposite Silvertown station and the only drinking den in the area to have escaped the catastrophe untouched, the pavement and street around the hotel was always thronged with local factory workers and the army of builders now constructing four hundred new homes to replace the thousand which had been lost. Workers from both the manure and animal rendering works were also on the pavement, always drinking outside as a courtesy to the noses of the pub landlord and his barmaids. The place was always very busy, so Nash's ex-soldier employee would probably not have seen which way he had gone, and assumed he always disappeared into the pub.

Nash would then pick his way past what was left of the great metal blots on the riverside landscape; the Tate & Lyle, Keller's, Trebor and assorted jam-making and biscuit factories; and through the devastation and construction to the Woolwich foot tunnel that ran adjacent to the ferry. He would then walk through the tunnel under the river to Woolwich, before riding the ferry back while he looked around the engine room to spot his man and to check all seemed in order.

Nash told the No Conscription Fellowship to dress the objector in the rags of the poor so he would not look out of place, but nonetheless he was usually easy to spot. He would probably have eaten many a meal of meat, vegetables and fruit throughout his life, so did not have the pallid, sallow complexion and wrinkled grey skin of the bread and scrape-fed, fag-end smoking East End poor. And just to make sure a mistake was not made in identification, he was to always wear a green muffler.

The objector had been given instructions on which one of the two ferries to ride. The engine room was packed with a huddled sea of misery that had it resemble a Victorian common lodging house. It was quite a performance for Nash to pick his way through the great unwashed, appearing to look for a place to sit while actually looking at each man's face in turn.

Once the flu had become commonplace, Nash had begun to put a handkerchief over his nose and mouth whenever he entered these packed confines. But he had noticed that while it was not always possible to tell the difference between the wretchedly poor and the wretchedly ill, there was usually little more than the odd clearing of the throat and following spit for him to worry about. Few of these poor devils appeared to suffer too badly from the flu, which given the overcrowded world in which they lived, seemed odd.

After the usual up toeing through the crowds, with the attendant oaths cursed his way when one of his huge boots made accidental contact with a foot or shin, he spotted his man, complete with green muffler. But as he made his way towards him, he caught the eye for the briefest moment of a second man with the same well-fed look about him. The man immediately looked away. A tad too quickly. And he was too well dressed in a decent looking suit to be a bona fide member of the engine room fraternity.

Nash's only prison term had come about from him single-handedly tackling half a dozen policemen who had made the mistake of attacking Ruby and a sister-in-arms during a Suffragette riot. He had never been caught by the police during his long spell as a Victorian hard man thanks to his intuition for smelling trouble.

And he now smelled a rodent that was all too prevalent in the slums, but this one did not have the customary tail and whiskers. Instead of making his way to his contact, he turned around, and when close to the door deliberately tripped over the foot of a poor wretch, grabbing at the door and swinging round quickly as if desperately regaining his balance. Again he caught the same man looking at him for the briefest moment before he looked away. The man would not be seeing Nash again. But Nash would be seeing him.

If this man was a rat, he had obviously followed the objector on to the ferry with a view to seeing who his contact was. Had the man already been given a description of him? He would be easy enough to spot. He was pretty distinctive after all. There were not many men in the East End, or anywhere else for that matter, who were in their fifties, over six feet tall with the physique of a brute half his age.

The government man would not have been stupid enough to come after him on his own. And he would want to arrest the objector too. There would be others, probably lurking just out of sight from the ferry. The agent would have to make a signal to them to rush on to the ferry to make their arrests, or perhaps they would hang back on the quayside to grab their prey as they came off the boat. Either way, this man could not be allowed anywhere within sight of the quayside.

If the unseen men were indeed in position, they were not the only ones lurking with intent. Nash stood just out of sight of the engine room exit and took a piece of lethal weaponry out of his pocket.

On leaving the engine room he had quickly reconnoitred his surroundings. The ferry was far from busy with traffic. Few men with their horses and carts were within sight.

The half a million horses seconded by the army during the war had left a shortage of four legged friends everywhere else. The law of supply and demand had pushed prices up for even the sorriest dobbin, the result of which was that many small businesses in the East End were now run out of a hand cart. And this limited the area over which the business could take its transactions. As for motor vehicles, these were a rare beast indeed this far into East London. Consequently the Woolwich Ferry may have been free, but the irony was this was a gift horse that many had to look in the mouth.

This left Nash with mixed feelings. There were few faces around to see what he was up to, but the lack of horses and carts meant there was little cover under which illicit deeds could be committed. Nash felt rather exposed on the deck of the large vessel so was well aware this was neither the time nor place to try and get any information out of the man spying on him.

And he had no particular desire to hurt the man any more than was necessary. After all, there was a chance the fellow was not from the government. He could just be some poor bugger who was so bored sitting in the engine room all day that he liked to look at everyone who came in. And maybe he had treated himself to a new whistle and flute in the not too dim and distant, and it had not yet had time to grow threadbare.

But Nash did not have to wait long to have his suspicions confirmed when the man alighted from the engine room within seconds. And with his back to Nash he stopped and peered up the ship. Nash took a quick look around to ensure no one was watching and before the man had a chance to change the direction of his search, calmly walked forward and without ceremony hit him behind both knees with his dockers' marlin spike. The force of the blow had the man airborne head back for a moment before crumpling on to the floor, face up. Nash bent down on one knee and punched the man once, to ensure his consciousness left him for a while. He then dragged his quarry away to the side of the boat, grabbed a long discarded moth-eaten old horse blanket that was lying nearby and covered him with it the best he could. The man wasn't fully out of sight, his legs and feet protruding, but it was the best Nash could do in the circumstances, and it should be sufficient in the short term, which was all he needed.

"Well my old mate, you were under cover, and now you are again," sneered Nash.

He then popped his head back through the engine door. There was not time for any subtle manoeuvrings so with the grimmest of expressions on his face Nash managed to combine both a shout and whisper in a deep voiced growl full of urgency.

"Richard!"

It was Nash's attempt at a bit of cloak & dagger stuff. With a nod to his favourite novel, The 39 Steps, his password for the objectors he met on the ferry, was Richard, after Richard Hannay.

It was not the most common name in these parts. East Enders' propensity for giving people nicknames meant that any parent would think twice about giving their offspring such a name. The only Richard most in the East End had ever heard of was Richard the Third, and this was too easily morphed into the Turd. Unsurprisingly, John Jameson was the only man to look up.

Nash waved aggressively at his charge to get up and head towards him. Nash was not a man to disobey at the best of times, and the immediately intimidated Quaker was on his feet and out the engine room in double quick time.

As Jameson stepped outside, Nash grabbed his arm, introduced himself as Smith, and pulled him to the side of the boat where the unconscious man lay under the blanket. He knew the Quaker would be horrified by the violence meted out to this man, especially if it were explained it was done on his behalf, so Nash casually shrugged as he told the conscientious objector not to worry, the man on the ground was just a drunk sleeping it off.

Nash quickly explained that he had reason to believe there was a group of men on the quayside at his usual disembarkation spot, Silvertown, waiting to arrest them. So the plan was to stay on the ship when it docked, then ride it back to Woolwich, where they would alight and make their way through the foot tunnel back to Silvertown.

Jameson asked why they didn't simply make their way

to the safe house from Woolwich, thus avoiding any risk of arrest at Silvertown.

"And what happens to me horse?" sneered Nash aggressively. "Can't just leave the poor little sod can I? He ain't even mine. He's worth a few bob an' all, what with horses being in such short supply now. Besides, Woolwich is the back of beyond. It'd take bleeding hours to get where we're going from there without horse. And I ain't got all day to molly coddle the likes of you!"

Jameson decided he would keep his thoughts to himself in future.

Half an hour later the two men were at the top of the stairs at the Silvertown exit of the foot tunnel. The less than fit Quaker had his hands on his knees gasping for oxygen, though as he breathed in the putrid smell of the local outfall sewer, he wondered whether this was indeed a sensible policy. His nose wrinkled while he wondered why they'd had to run the length of the tunnel and then take the steps two at a time when a perfectly respectable lift was available.

Nash saw his distress, caught his eye and winked conspiratorially.

"Keeps your stamina up boy. You never know in this game when you might need to run longer than some other bastard. Not quicker mind, but longer. Get my meaning?"

Nash didn't wait for an answer. He removed his coat and shirt, leaving just the thinnest white vest clinging to his muscled torso; then whipped off his belt. The clothing was given to his startled new valet, before a marlin spike was removed from the coat and stuffed down the side of Nash's trousers. Some words of explanation were necessary.

"I'm going to get me horse and cart but I got to walk

past the characters who are out to get us see, so it's best if I look the part."

With this, Nash bent down and grabbed some oozing filth from the gutter with his right hand, before slamming the disgusting mix into his body and rubbing it around his chest and then up his left arm. Then one final piece of something repellent was slapped round both cheeks.

He told his charge to stay out of sight inside the tunnel entrance. He would be back for him shortly. But if he wasn't back within twenty minutes, he wouldn't be coming back, in which case Jameson should leg it back through the tunnel, and make his way back to the No Conscription Fellowship the best way he could.

A group of builders, dirty from a day's hard graft, were coming along towards the tunnel entrance. Nash guessed they had just finished a shift at the George V Dock, which was under construction just to the north. One or two broke off and headed down the tunnel stairs. The rest headed west, either for the nearby railway station or the pub. Nash eased out of the tunnel entrance into the throng and made his way along the street with them. As they passed the ferry quay Nash scanned the alley to the side and sure enough, outside the front entrance of a soap-works, were two men hanging about looking bored while each kept a surreptitious eye in the direction of the ferry. They looked similar to the man Nash had left under the horse blanket. He had expected a larger number, but then he supposed wryly that needs must in war. One of them threw an uninterested glance at the group of dirty workmen passing along the street in front of him, before returning his gaze towards the ferry.

Minutes later Nash was paying the ex-soldier his

shilling. He then jumped up on his cart and took the reins from his employee. The man touched his cap in deference and went to go on his way, but Nash shouted after him.

"Oi! Can you catch?"

"Caught a package at Passchendale a twelve month since," said the man bitterly. "That was the end of me cricket. Then I caught the sodding flu. That nearly saw me off an' all. Yeah reckon I can catch all right."

Nash simply nodded and flicked a threepenny bit with his thumb, sending it accurately in a gentle arc towards the man's right side, so it was easy for him to catch it in the hand unencumbered by the crutch.

"That's thruppence more. Know the alley down the side of the ferry where the soap works is?" he asked. The man nodded. "Two fellers hanging about down there. Tell 'em their mate on the ferry's out cold under horse blanket. Got it?"

The young man nodded, showing no sign of surprise or enquiry, or any other emotion for that matter. Nash continued.

"Take your time getting down there mind. I need time to get well off."

The order was received with a sneer. Nash guessed the man was thinking to himself that everything he now did took plenty of time.

With a flick of his wrist Nash had the reins tell his horse it was time to go. He would pass the two government men, but they would not be taking any notice of someone travelling in his direction, towards the ferry. Though if they did, Nash had the reins in one hand, his marlin spike in the other.

He didn't really care if his message was delivered or not, though it would appeal to his sense of humour if it was. He imagined the look on the two men's faces. But if the bitter young perisher just stayed outside the hotel or scarpered off home, the threepenny bit was no more than the tip he deserved. The lad deserved a lot more.

Chapter 9

"Ah! You may laugh my boy, but it's no joke being funny with the influenza."

Mr Punch wrapped up in blankets
in front of the fire, eating gruel,
Punch Magazine, 1918

The Nashes thought the world of Charlie Chaplin. As well as enjoying his films, they had heard how military hospitals were now projecting his comedies on to the ceilings of wards so badly injured men who were unable to move, could watch them from their beds. Thus the war, and perhaps even their pain, ceased to exist for a few brief, precious moments in time. Charlie was a great hero with the boys in the trenches, and was clearly important to the war effort for his ability to make his fellow countrymen laugh, and for making personal appearances at huge war bond fund-raising events in America. But the British press hounded him as a shirker. They and their government string-pullers had to make an example out of any fit and healthy Englishman of fighting age, not in a reserved occupation, who was not in the trenches. And the more they did this, the more the Nashes loved the little genius.

Nash preferred his early, more unsophisticated stuff, where many an altercation ended with Charlie giving some wretch, often a policeman a swift kick up the backside, followed by a chase which saw the little hero make a successful getaway. Ruby preferred Charlie's more cleverly crafted recent work, and would tease her husband by asking him if he preferred the earlier films because they reminded him of his own early adult life. From what she had heard from both her husband and other sources, he had spent much of his time being chased by the police through the mean streets of Whitechapel. With so much practice she wondered why her husband was not quicker on his feet or had not been able to master Charlie's skidding stiff legged change of direction?

But such saucy comments were often in retaliation. Ruby was from Southampton originally, but had settled in South London on returning to Britain after the Titanic disaster. During the summer of 1912 she had lived no more than a couple of miles from the great clown, and worked in a Bermondsey biscuit factory, a stone's throw from where Charlie and his brother were living at the time in Kennington. She knew several people who claimed to have lived in the same street as the Chaplin boys, used the same pubs, saw Charlie perform in the local theatres and knew him well. Nash was his usual sceptical, argumentative self. He told his wife that if everyone who said they lived next to Charlie actually did, Kennington must have been a bloody crowded place. And given he seems to have drunk in every boozer in the Elephant & Castle area, Nash was surprised Charlie was ever in a fit state to tread the boards. No wonder he was so good at playing an inebriate. Maybe he wasn't acting?

But it was all good natured ribbing. They never got to calling each other 'darling'. And they had both equally loved last year's Easy Street and The Rink, though Ruby had noted that her husband had laughed loudest when Charlie encased a policeman's head in a gas lamp in the former film, and had caused people on roller skates to fly through the air to land painfully on their backsides in the latter.

The couple had just been to the early evening screening of Charlie's new film, A Dog's Life. Throughout the war they had got into the habit of going to the 'pictures' at this time of day to enjoy a bit of heating as well as the films. Every such visit was a shovelful of rare, precious coal not used at home. And although the longer days and milder temperatures of summer meant this was no longer necessary, they liked to keep their cinema dates as a regular day and time. Their lives during the war had become so frenetic, with quality time together snatched as and when they could, they liked to maintain any semblance of routine that was feasible.

They were part of a large crowd exiting down the steps between the cinema entrance and the street, giggling away to each other, blissfully oblivious of the war for a while, when they were brought back to reality with a bump. A thin, wizened man was shuffling along the pavement like a foot-wrapped geisha girl, head down, trying to negotiate his way through the throng. Neither the man, nor Nash, whose neck was turned looking down to his wife laughing, were looking where they were going. As Nash stepped off the final step onto the pavement the two men bumped into each other and, though the mildest of collisions, the man collapsed to the floor as if poleaxed.

"Steady on old feller," said Nash good-naturedly as he bent to help up the man.

He reached down, expecting the fellow to grab his arm and pull himself up. But the man just lay there, hapless, like a new born baby. He stared back at Nash and tried to speak but nothing but a gurgle was emitted. Nash dropped down on to his haunches and realised the inaccuracy of his initial assumption that the man was old. It was difficult to tell his age. Perhaps younger than Ruby. Perhaps not. The cheap suit he was wearing was many sizes too big for him, suggesting rapid weight loss, and his sallow, wrinkled skin reminded Nash of the poor wretches on the ferry. A couple of days' of unshaved greying chin whiskers completed the abject picture. His eyes then rolled up. He had passed out.

Nash felt his thin hand. Its skin had the feel of cold leather. Nash was wondering whether the flu could have done this to him, when Ruby took charge.

"Pick him up Nashey, we'll take him round to Dr Alice. She told one of my nurses she was going to make time to pop round to the nursery just before it closed to see if any of the children were showing signs of the flu. If we hurry we should just catch her."

Nash did as he was told, hoisting the man over his shoulder.

They were soon walking through the bomb ravaged entrance of the Mother's Arms. One of the nurses had been locking up, talking to Dr Alice as she did so. A quarter of an hour and a doctor's consultation later, the man was conscious and sitting, propped up against the bar of the ex-pub. The man couldn't speak and was not the best educated but through his scribbling of simple notes, they had ascertained he had been home from the trenches for three months, having been shot through the lungs and lost his speech.

Nash had just arrived back from the Cost Price restaurant with some potato soup for the patient. Ruby noticed the flaking potato skin floating unappetisingly in the liquid. She tried to think of a suitable simile for a moment, but could not think of anything disparaging enough so returned to the matter at hand.

She continued with the slow process of a note writing conversation while Dr Alice administered soup to the man. It transpired that he had been refused a full pension so had to go to work in a factory to make ends meet. After two months doing this he had collapsed and become paralysed in his hitherto stronger right arm. The authorities then offered him a job as a bookkeeper, and to punish him when he refused, his pension was reduced further. He had gone to see Miss Pankhurst for help. Sylvia had written to the authorities and tried to get his pension raised to that of a married man but she was told that because he had married since his discharge, his wife could not be expected to be kept by the government.

Ruby made all the right supportive noises, telling the man not to worry and so on. But as she did so she could not help less charitable thoughts entering her head.

He had married *since* his return from the trenches. A woman had married this pathetic husk of a man. Her sweetheart. But she had fallen in love with a man who no longer existed. Do you still marry the man anyway? Out of pity as much as love? Out of loyalty, not just to him but king and country? After all, the press were appealing to women to marry war-broken men.

She considered her own sweetheart standing a few feet away. The man who had saved her on the Titanic; had come to her rescue again on many an occasion during the Suffragette years; who was always there to look after her when she overworked and suffered a resultant slump, as was so often the case in this war; the tough East Ender who knew no fear and would always protect her; the saucy devil with a wry smile never far away when she was around; the clever Dick who put her in her place when she needed to be; the sarky so-and-so who would engage her in sharp tongued banter; the joker with such a sense of humour; the incorrigible lovable rogue; and let's face it, the good looking, huge hunk of a feller. If all these attributes were taken away by mustard gas or a German shell, and replaced by the man whose notes she was reading, could she stay with him?

She did not like herself sometimes.

A misty-eyed Ruby showed the notes of the conversation first to her husband, then the doctor. Nash flew into a rage. His wife had not seen him this angry since the first air raid of the war had brought Zeppelins to the East End. The deaths and injuries had been bad enough, but it was the sightseers who had arrived the next day on open-top buses to see the devastation that had sent Nash in to paroxysms. Many a sightseer had been on the end of Nash's fists and boots that day. In contrast Dr Alice simply nodded matter-of-factly. Ruby was not sure which reaction was scariest. And then, after a moment, she knew.

There was nothing more the doctor could do for her patient, so she started to tidy things into her bag. She was about to leave, but she was not going to escape that easily.

"Thank you doctor. We'll look after the poor little devil now," said Ruby, before completely changing tack. "By the way, you never did come to see me about the flu. I was upstairs sorting out the repair of the roof when you next came to the nursery after I sent you my note. But when I came down you'd gone. And I somehow managed to miss you the next time you visited as well. Lucky you told one of my nurses you'd be round today and I've managed to catch you."

"Oh, of course I must apologise Ruby," said Alice. "I have been such a busy bee of late your note completely slipped my mind and I forgot all about seeing you. I have to dash in and dash out of the nursery these days I'm afraid. Needs must and all that. I would have caught up with you sooner or later no doubt."

Alice was one of the two most intelligent women Ruby knew. She was perhaps not as intellectually clever as Sylvia; few were. But she had one of those minds that never missed a thing. And she certainly never forgot to answer questions that were asked of her, especially on medical matters. Ruby knew full well that the good doctor had been avoiding her lately because she clearly did not want to answer questions about the flu. But Ruby played along. Both women could be equally good actresses.

"Oh, I know Alice. These days you don't know whether you're coming or going I'll wager. Still, lucky we've bumped into each other now. Gives us a chance to talk about the flu."

Alice knew she had been backed into a corner. And Nashey was looking on, which didn't help. They were lovely people but she felt rather intimidated by Ruby and her husband. And she knew that if she refused to answer, Sylvia Pankhurst would be banging at her door within the hour. That would be even worse. So, having gained assurances from both Ruby and Nashey that whatever she told them was for their and Sylvia's ears only, she told them a little, though not all of what she had been told about the flu. She also told them her own thoughts as a doctor on the matter.

Chapter 10

"Soon the women who stood in the pallid queues before shops spoke more about their children's hunger than about the death of their husband."

German woman 1918

Before the war Fritz Patemann had been an entrepreneur. Though not a very good one. When he had left school with no qualifications or professional interests, he had drifted into the first job that had landed in his lap. He had become a bank clerk. And had hated it. He had quite liked the actual work, adding figures together and making them balance, but had despaired of the politics, back-biting, stuffiness and snobbery of it all. And he had despised the other young men in the bank. Many of them liked to play the working class hero, throwing their weight about. Fritz remembered them with contempt. They were bank clerks from a middle class area of Berlin. Not chain-makers from the toughest city slum in the Ruhr. They needed to come to terms with it!

He had stuck it out for almost four years, at the end of which he knew what he wanted to do. Become an entrepreneur. The only problem was that he lacked that essential quality that successful entrepreneurs tend to have. An understanding of what people want and, perhaps more importantly, before they know it themselves. Thus various business ventures failed.

When the war began he did the obvious thing for an entrepreneur with no real ability. He became a black marketeer. Nothing was available. People wanted everything. You couldn't go wrong. But it was too easy. And Fritz believed himself to be fundamentally an honest man. He needed to do something honest that showed entrepreneurial flair and ability.

And then a headline in a newspaper changed his life.

******

Fritz had begun by telling his farmer contact Klaus that he was arranging for five thousand eggs to be sent by train to Munich next month. And Klaus could supply as many of them as he wished. The deal was set up; payment and transportation logistics arranged.

The farmer was appreciative and advised his young business associate that he had heard on the grapevine that much of the potato harvest had been ruined by blight. As a result he was stockpiling turnips, confident that their price would rise. He thought this information might be useful to a young man with an eye for the main chance. Anything that went well with turnips, such as bones for a soup or anything that made a turnip marmalade, might be worth getting his hands on.

Fritz thanked him for the information but he made

it clear that he was not overly interested. He had another iron in the fire. And perhaps a friendly farmer could help him with this.

Moments later Klaus was having the best laugh he'd had all war. Fritz had just told him that an elephant had died in Dresden Zoo and that he had just bought the carcass. Cue Klaus' outburst of merriment. Once the laughter started to subside, Fritz informed him that he intended to butcher the elephant and sell the meat off to restaurants. More laughter. But only for a moment until the farmer realised this idea had legs. Big fat ones, plus a trunk and various other fine cuts.

Now he had a captive audience, Fritz went on to explain that he needed someone he trusted with some level of butchery experience. He needed someone who knew what they were talking about to liaise with a Dresden slaughterhouse to set up a deal, no questions asked, at a good rate. Someone like a farmer who dealt in the black market. Meanwhile he himself would hawk the idea of elephant steaks around the best restaurants in Dresden.

Chapter 11

"England looked strange to us returned soldiers. We could not understand the war-madness that ran wild everywhere... The civilians talked a different language. I found serious conversation with my parents all but impossible."

Robert Graves, Goodbye to All That

The fight for the vote for women had lost impetus in Germany during the war, but when eight and a half million British women had been added to their country's electoral register in February, the ears of German women had pricked up. And with the success of the Spring Offensive apparently about to bring the war to an end in Germany's favour, its women had been quick to mobilise. They could surely gain the vote during the Fatherland's warm glow of victory.

And though belief that the war was about to end had receded, optimism that women would gain the vote remained. Dorothea was starting work for the German Association for Women's Suffrage. She had shown her face at their headquarters to be introduced to a few people but soon enough was getting cracking down at the Borse marketplace. She was going to run a market stall, with the profits going directly into the coffers of her suffrage organisation.

Her fellow suffrage members had not exactly been lining up for the job. On busy days, it brought one into close contact with far too many people. The previous incumbent had unsurprisingly succumbed to the flu, which was laying low large numbers of people. And it was 'potato day' today, provided by the city authorities on a first-come-first-served basis. There was sure to be a rush.

But Dorothea had volunteered for the job. Although very intelligent, she actually preferred duties that did not involve much in the way of responsibility. When working as a nurse, she had always turned down opportunities to gain promotion. She always had plenty to say about women's rights, the war and all the subjects of the day, and was considered something of a sage with friends and suffrage colleagues alike, but the reality was that she preferred theory over practice. Where work was concerned, she liked an intellectually easy life. Rather than becoming a politician on women's rights, merely working on a market stall for the movement, was just fine with her.

And she hoped that her years in nursing, during which time she had caught the flu particularly badly on one occasion, may have left her with a certain level of immunity to the virus. That said, she was not taking any chances. As she got near the market, she donned a face mask before making her way through the busy narrow cobbled streets surrounding the large town square marketplace, past lines of empty hooks outside butchers' shops. Butchers stood forlorn in their doorways, their only stock on sale being 'ersatz' sausages.

Ersatz, meaning substitute, had a new pejorative meaning. There were eleven thousand ersatz food and drink products available throughout the country. Coffee made from tree bark was particularly despised as dishwater, though the empty butchers' shops were testament to the popularity or otherwise of meatless ersatz sausages, the ingredients of which few were brave enough to even hazard a guess at. But tomorrow was horse-meat day, when these same shops would be full of queues and dark red carcasses.

The potatoes had just been delivered, and another member was already busy awkwardly woman-handling the huge heavily laden hessian sacks, so they could be reached by the stall workers in an ergonomically efficient manner. Another colleague was standing in front of the produce, walking up and down pretending to busy herself getting the ration card punches ready, which took all of a few seconds, when in reality she was simply standing on guard to protect the stock from pilferage.

Potato stalls were scattered across the full width of the top of the square, and although still early, there were long queues for all of them stretching down the length of the marketplace like the tendrils of a giant jellyfish.

The women and children at the front of the lines stood on one foot, then another. They swayed and muttered.

Dorothea looked around the square. There must have been two thousand people in the marketplace. She whispered to her colleague.

"How long do you think the people in the front have been here?"

The woman nodded in the direction of the teenager at the front of their queue.

"I overheard that girl tell someone she got here at seven o'clock last night. But those at the back have slept in their beds and it will only take us and the other stalls three hours to reach them." She paused for effect before adding a wry aside. "If we don't all run out of stock by then of course."

******

During the success of the Spring Offensive, German soldiers had raided Allied supply depots and hearing of the shortages at home, had reversed the usual system of care-packages being sent by the Home Front to those in the trenches. Peter Fueschel, a veteran of the war, had received a Jammerbrief; a letter from his family complaining about their lot, so he had been only too happy to send such a package of tinned food, clothing and tobacco back home.

After each year in the trenches, German soldiers usually received two weeks home leave. But such was the decimation of the army by the flu that Peter's able-bodied presence had been required at the Front and his latest leave deferred. But now, with the Spring Offensive over, he had finally arrived home in Berlin on his fortnight's leave. He understood from the many Jammerbriefs he had received that morale on the Home Front was at its lowest ebb due to the shortages and flu. Nevertheless he was still expecting a little of the 'all hail the conquering hero' treatment. But he had barely taken off his boots and braces and taken the first swig of his father's weak beer, before he was being assailed by moaning. His father was quick to tell him that the beer was 'strechen'.

If ersatz had become the second most hated word in the German language, after 'Englisch', strechen, meaning stretched, had become a close third. Beer, as well as milk, was watered down. Bread was stretched with potato flour. And if one was really desperate almost any foodstuff could be stretched with turnip.

Peter had to listen to a long litany of gripes and ingratitude which showed little comprehension of his life at the Front. So despite feeling exhausted, it was with some relief that he was sent off to line up at the market for some potatoes. Being in uniform he could go straight to the head of the queue and he would be served immediately.

He duly arrived at a potato stall and looked at the queue. The people in it were eerily silent. The hungry stood four abreast and shuffled forward when they could with the orderliness of soldiers. It all added to the general air of depression in the square. He stood close to the head of the queue but hesitated about going right to the front. He looked down the line of people's anaemic faces, anxious and drawn, with puckered brows, lustreless eyes and dry cracked skins. Below some of them was the irony of swollen, bloated stomachs protruding from baggy trousers or skirts. One boy had bandy legs. Peter wondered if that at been caused by 'the English disease', rickets. How ironic.

It did not seem right to jump the queue. While contemplating whether to or not, he looked at the woman in charge of the stall. It was one of those moments when the person under scrutiny appears to have a sixth sense they are being watched and looks up and straight back at their voyeur. Their eyes met, but rather than the usual embarrassed look away, both parties held each other's gaze.

From what he could see of her face above the face mask, Peter thought her a good looking woman, but that would have been all the more reason to quickly avert his stare. There was something in the woman's eyes that held him. She was lost. That was it. She was lost too.

But then something as ridiculous as a sack of potatoes ended the moment.

One of the large hessian sacks, haphazardly propped up against Dorothea's stall, fell over and its contents spilled out. As the cascading produce started to tumble and roll along the cobbles, those in the queue closest to the incident surged forward to grab a free sample. But no sooner had they done so, and they were tossing them away in disgust. Others ran forward to grab the cast offs only to similarly reject them. A cry went up for people not to bother because the potatoes clearly had blight. Some accepted this while others, wanting to see for themselves, rushed forward to see the greenish blight-riddled pulp that had once been potatoes. Groans of despair issued forth. People looked around the marketplace with the thousand yard stare of the defeated. Did they give up and go home with empty bags to their starving children, or head for the back of another queue on the off chance other stalls had better produce?

Inspiration was to hand. One woman wondered whether she had just spent ten hours waiting for blighted potatoes. She pulled over the next sack to see if that too was afflicted. It wasn't. And with the die, not to mention the potatoes, cast, she sank to her knees and started helping herself to the produce. And she did not stop when her little bag was full. She put the bag down to free both arms to pull up the two bottom corners of her apron. She then barked under her breath to the child by her side to load more potatoes into what was now a cloth bowl. As the little girl did this, another woman rushed towards them with a grim look on her face. But rather them stop them she copied their larceny. The three pilferers almost immediately became four, then it was five; within a few seconds it was scores surging forward to scrabble on the ground helping themselves. All the stall's sacks were quickly pushed over and emptied as a free-for-all ensued. Some left their place in an adjacent queue to join the melee.

Dorothea looked around the square for a policeman to help her. She was not surprised when there was not one to be seen. Why would there be? The police had more important things to do than guard potatoes.

She looked at her assistants, who stared back at her in bewilderment. Her own look of disbelief went into the crowd, then to its periphery. Her eyes fell upon the soldier whom she had caught looking at her a short while earlier. But this time there was to be no return of her gaze.

Someone from the melee collided with the soldier, which had his army training kick in, and within seconds he was embroiled in an attempt to control the dangerous crush. He pulled people to their feet. Pushed others back. But it was hopeless. He tried shouting.

"German people! Fellow Germans!"

It was merely an attempt to gain people's attention. There was little point in shouting anything more complicated or meaningful to a mob. Most were ignoring him in any case, though not all. A little old woman glanced his way.

"I must have potatoes!" she shouted theatrically. "I

haven't had meat or fat for three weeks. My stomach has turned against marmalade. I can't live on it any longer."

And with that she dived to the floor to look for her food of choice.

"Curses on the military!" shouted another tiny woman over her shoulder as, bathed in sweat and bow-legged with the strain, she made off with a booty in her apron so large that it was doubtful she would get the whole load home without the contraband being reacquainted with the cobbles.

It was the last sight he saw before he blacked out.

The next thing he knew, he was being tended by the woman who had earlier caught his eye. She was on her haunches leaning over him.

"I see you are back with us soldier," she said matter-of-factly. "Someone hit you over the head with an ersatz sign. Rather ironic don't you think, as it was no substitute for the real thing, such as a cosh. That would have put your lights out quicker than an English air-raid. You'll be on your feet soon enough actually."

The soldier mistakenly took this to mean that he could be on his feet immediately. He attempted to get up but started to feel blackness threaten to close in on him again, so slumped back on to the cobbles of the square.

"Dried vegetables, dry bread, marmalade and a hero's death," said the woman. "A cheery little song we all sing here on the Home Front these days, soldier. And if you keep trying to get up, perhaps you will enjoy this fate sooner rather than later."

Peter looked at his nurse perplexed. What strange things to say to a man. She is not so lost perhaps. A good looking woman for sure, but an unusual one.

"Yes nurse," he said dryly.

"You are sarcastic I think soldier," she replied "But you are right of course. I am a nurse. Or at least I was. I will care for you now."

He had actually been right the first time about Dorothea's gaze. She *was* lost. Not being the confident woman she appeared to the rest of the world, it was only by retreating back into her clipped, rather arrogant nurse personae, the result of years of training by her intimidating no-nonsense matron, which enabled her to deal with this situation. She dropped to her knees and cradled the man in her lap. The light blow to his head would not normally have poleaxed a fit, tough soldier whom she suspected was a few years younger than her, perhaps thirty, though he looked older. She suspected it was only a temporary ageing. She could see it in his eyes. He had influenza.

Chapter 12

"I have so often advocated the communal kitchen as a solution of many of our present-day difficulties that it is heartening to find that the Ministry of Food is taking the matter up...The need of some communal system of catering and cooking is the deeply-felt want of the moment."

Women's Sphere, British Pictorial Newspaper 1918

The two most important skills for the driver of a motor car were to have the ability to swerve round horses safely and be a good mechanic. The new-fangled inventions were always breaking down. Klara Weber was almost unique in being a woman who possessed both skills. All those occasions she had balanced scenery precariously along the seats of an open motor charabanc and then driven it from one theatre to another, had come in useful. The ex-Berlin Opera Company chorus girl was now that very rare breed, a chauffeuse.

And she had just proven her credentials by jacking up her new employer's motor for a wheel change. The swap duly done, she now donned her military style tunic, dark brocade coat and peak cap complete with her pride and joy, her badge of driving proficiency. She then bent down and deftly rubbed road grit off her navy-blue serge skirt before clapping her hands, as much in enthusiasm for her job as to remove any dirt. Then on went her worn, wrinkled brown leather driving gauntlets, and she was ready.

Her employer, Frau Ute Burchardt, had remained on board during the stop, drafting her latest proposal. She considered motors were all very well but they were no replacement for the railway carriage when it came to writing while one was on the move. So this delay was not without its compensations.

"Well, this is a splurge!" shouted Klara as she leapt into the driver's seat, full of the joys of a job well done and keen to take on whatever the road next had in store for her.

"May I entreat you not to be so noisy and explosive Klara," came the rebuke from the back seat. "You must not lack dignity."

"I am such a goose. I think I must have a great deal of the child in me yet. Your advice will make me more than ever cautious," answered Klara with honest self-deprecation.

"Great heavens, no my dear, you have a grand character for brightness," reassured Frau Burchardt. "And what women need is a great deal more stirring up. It is simply that we must forever be on our guard to appear serious in front of those who would otherwise believe us frivolous."

"Right ho," said the chauffeuse. "Do call me Aldo by the way. It's a nickname I picked up because of my short hair. I did a spot of male impersonation on the boards you know."

"Very well my dear, Aldo it is. But promise me you will never do such work again. We are not here to impersonate. We are here to be ourselves." And with this, a gloved hand reached forwards out of the car window into her driver's eye-line, to beckon them forward. "From this time the road is open."

Aldo smiled and nodded enthusiastically in appreciation of her employer's somewhat theatrical gesture, as she wrestled with the heavy, unwieldy gear lever to set the car in motion.

This was the first journey they had undertaken together, and in the hour they had spent making their way from the suburbs to the city centre, Aldo had noticed what a charming woman her new employer appeared to be. She could seemingly admonish, praise, compliment and educate in one sentence. And she was so wonderfully informal. She had insisted that she be addressed as Frau Ute. Apparently she did this with many people. It was her way of retaining the respect a lady of her social standing expected, and a woman of her age deserved, while also retaining a level of conviviality.

Within ten minutes they were pulling up at their destination; the office of the Deputy Commanding General. This government department ran many aspects of the German Home Front. An old civil servant stood in attendance at the entrance and dutifully help up a hand in welcome and opened the front door for the affluent looking woman who had just alighted from the back of the motor car. The man's impassive expression belied the surprise he felt that the woman had not waited for her driver to help her out of the vehicle. His thoughts became rather more readable when said driver, another woman, appeared to have the audacity to wish to follow her employer into the building. But as the car owner passed him by, she had clearly seen his change of expression.

"Let her in my good man," she said casually over her shoulder without so much as a backward glance, as she carried on into the once grand, now faded reception area of the great building. "She's with me. We don't stand on ceremony nowadays. And please be kind enough to have someone guard the motor."

The man wanted to give her a 'who the hell do you think you are' look but kept his scorn and derision hidden beneath a veneer of respectful deference. His flat feet, not without difficulty, shuffled him ahead of the two women before he motioned that they should follow him.

"The dear old buffer," exclaimed Aldo warmly with only a whiff of unintended condescension.

Her employer let it pass.

******

Once the cost of the carcass, the farmer and the slaughterhouse had been taken into account, it was clear that Fritz did not have the working capital for such a venture. The deposit he had paid to secure the deal with the zoo had taken most of his available cash. He needed a loan. A big one. He could probably get the money through a black market contact but they would be sure to want to know what the money was for, and he was unwilling to tell such people his business. Firstly, once the underworld realised the value of the carcass, it might disappear from the zoo overnight. There was also the possibility that the enterprise could prove a flop. The difficulties of getting an elephant carcass from zoo to restaurant plates were many. Supposing restaurants wouldn't touch the meat? Or the meat went off? Merely transporting such a huge thing from the zoo to the slaughterhouse had its problems. The farmer or the slaughterhouse might pull a fast one on him. And then he would be in serious debt to serious men. And if he failed to make good the repayment, he could find his throat coming in to painful and deadly contact with a knife down a back alley.

And almost equally importantly, he wanted to do this as a legitimate enterprise. With no sordid backstreet loans. With no underworld involvement at all.

But when he considered his options, whom did he know, who was a legitimate, trustworthy, discreet person who was wealthy enough to fund such a venture, yet had perhaps an anti-establishment devilment within them that would entertain such an extraordinary operation? There was only one such person. The woman who bought black market petrol from him at vastly inflated prices for her motor car.

******

Aldo answered the knock on the door. The shortage of servants during the war meant that Frau Burchardt was now reduced to having just three. A cook who doubled as housekeeper; a maid who doubled, tripled and quadrupled as pretty much every other female servant; and a chauffeuse who not only dressed in trousers but did all the work that had hitherto been done by the butler and footmen. And this included answering the front door.

Fritz was not the sort of man who would have been expected to use the front entrance. Before the war, a liveried footman, rather too full of his own importance, would have cast a very wary eye down both his own nose and the length of Fritz's unkempt form. But these were different times. And young ex-stage performer Aldo, had not been trained in the finer points of servant snobbery.

"Good morning," she said before bending down to whisper. "You're the black market chap aren't you? Shouldn't you be coming round the back to see cook. No offence and all that."

Fritz bid her a good morning too, and assured her that no offence had been taken. He agreed that he would normally use the back entrance but then explained in hushed tones that he wished to see Frau Ute on a rather delicate business matter.

"Jolly good," said the chauffeuse conspiratorially, and quietly bid him to enter with some enthusiasm.

Chapter 13

"Were it not for the artistically painted signs you would never dream it was a National Kitchen...It is dainty and pleasing to the eye and the goods delivered are in appetising form. The business done is enormous."

Scarborough Evening Post, 1918

Dorothea was relieved to have a day off from the market stall. It being horse-meat day, everyone would swarm to the butchers' shops. This break in proceedings was allowing her to visit a woman whom she had been advised was well connected and was using her position within the upper middle classes to further the causes of women. Frau Burchardt had been pressuring the Ministry throughout the war to give women more responsible roles within the war effort. But she had been beating her head against a brick wall for much of the time, so had agreed by letter to have Dorothea come to visit at her home with a view to the two of them discussing how the Women's Suffrage movement may be able to offer assistance in some way.

As she made her way up the street towards Frau Burchardt's impressive home in the best part of town, Dorothea noticed a rather shady, rain-coated, high-lapelled man being ushered out of the front door and down the newly hearthstone rubbed steps by a young woman wearing, of all things, trousers. Dorothea was surprised at the young woman's smile. She did not appear to be sending the character away with a flea in his ear as one would have expected. The man negotiated the half a dozen steps onto the pavement with a spring in his step and headed her way. As he was about to pass her, he nodded and touched his wide brimmed felt hat in what could have been a mark of gentlemanly respect towards her, though she suspected it was more to shield his face than anything else.

The young woman was shutting the door when she spotted Dorothea at the foot of the steps looking up at her.

"Oh, you must be Frau Lipp!" she shouted enthusiastically. "Do come in won't you?"

Dorothea did as she was beckoned, and within moments the young woman had introduced herself as Aldo the chauffeuse, and gushingly told her how much she and Frau Burchardt had been looking forward to meeting her. Dorothea was then shown in to a sitting room and plied with a glass of lemonade. The lady of the house immediately glided in from another doorway, having just changed from the tweeds in which she had received her black marketeer, into the suitably light and flimsy affair that tea with a lady demanded. She welcomed her guest and offered her a seat. The two women sat down on formal hardback chairs facing each other a few feet apart. Dorothea assumed that the servant would now be dismissed from their presence, but to her surprise the young woman helped herself to another such chair and pulled it up next to her employer.

Such apparent temerity was readily explained.

"We don't stand on ceremony here Frau Lipp," said the lady of the house. "Aldo may only be a servant but she is also a woman, and therefore is germane to all my dealings concerning the woman's role. And she is a woman of many talents. She is a chauffeuse, or should I say chauffeur, as the role should not be made feminine I think you would agree. She is also a mechanic, footman, carpenter and maid. Just as all women are servants of the Fatherland at this terrible time. But are we not all asked to be mere maids? Maids of munitions, maids in hospitals, maids selling ersatz from market stalls. Our greatest talents, our great brains are not being used. Oh, and do call me Frau Ute by the way."

Dorothea's surprise was replaced by delight. She thought hospital nurses clearly did use their brains, but otherwise agreed with every word this woman had spoken. And she thought it was rather charming that the lady had replaced her surname with her Christian name. Dorothea believed she could work with this Frau Ute. The two women, with the occasional interjection from Aldo, then enjoyed an involved, animated conversation about German women's underused role during the war, and what could be done about it.

And the great attraction of this new relationship, from Dorothea's point of view, was that she herself could stick to being very much a backroom worker. This new acquaintance was the sort of woman who would actually take up the cudgels. For her part, Frau Burchardt was delighted that a clearly intelligent, middle class woman such as Frau Lipp had such a wonderfully common touch to the point where she was willing to work in a marketplace and serve ordinary people for the good of the cause.

The meeting ended with Frau Burchardt saying she would love to come and visit Dorothea in the marketplace sometime. She mentioned that she had a business meeting coming up next Thursday at her bank, which was quite close to the market area, so could pop along then if it were not inconvenient. She was told warmly that would be most fine indeed. It was lard day, so she would see the stall being busy.

"Perfect!" said Frau Burchardt, before adding conspiratorially, "my meeting is on a somewhat delicate matter you understand, and I would rather not advertise the fact that I am visiting my bank, so I will arrange for Aldo to drop me there a little early, and then she can drive the motor back to the square and help you on the stall for a while before returning in due course for me. How would that be?"

It was confirmed that it would be very nice. And Aldo too was her usual enthusiastic self about the chore.

Chapter 14

"Men burned and maimed to the condition of animals."

Harold Gillies, Queen Mary's Hospital

plastic surgeon, 1917

Nash was concerned that the net was drawing in on him. The man he had beaten up on the ferry had clearly followed the objector onto the ship and waited to see who he met. And now this man would have passed on a description of his assailant. Nash laid down the law to his contacts at the No Conscription Fellowship. They had to improve their security. The authorities being able to follow an objector needed to have been a one-off success. And Nash appreciated that he too had to be more careful in future. His Woolwich Ferry venue was no longer viable so he came up with not only an alternative venue, but a different method of meeting his objectors.

Queen Mary's Hospital Sidcup was dealing with the huge number of horrifying facial injuries incurred by men at the Front. Most were so badly injured that during their stay they never left the confines of the hospital, but there were still plenty who managed to get out for a walk in the grounds, and some even managed a little stroll in the nearby park or along Sidcup High Street. Consequently a man could roam around the area with bandages covering his entire face and nobody would bat an eyelid. And while Sidcup was a south of the river suburb, it was only seven or eight miles from the Blackwall Tunnel so was within range for Nash's horse.

His latest 'Richard' had been bandaged up, dropped at the hospital by the NCF and was waiting to be contacted. Ruby travelled with her husband by horse & cart as far as Sidcup railway station where, repeating his Silvertown modus operandi, he left the vehicle with some wreck of an injured soldier who was clearly too woebegone to make off with it. They then disappeared into a booth of the lady's toilet in the station, where Ruby bandaged her husband's head. She then got on a train heading for New Cross, and was to make her way home from there on the tube.

Nash was to walk up the hill from the station to the hospital, where his objector would be wearing a particular style of boots with a splash of red paint on the right one, so he could be recognised. The man had been told to roam around close to the hospital until he was contacted. Not having a set place to meet and both parties not being recognisable added a new level of security. Once Nash spotted his man, he would spend some time reconnoitring to ensure the coast was clear, before making contact. The two men would then pop into the gentlemen's toilet at the station to unravel their headgear before picking up the horse & cart and making their getaway.

Ruby's train stopped en route at St Johns, the place where she had lived when first settling in South London six years earlier. But since becoming a Suffragette and moving to the East End she had been so tied up, first of all with the Votes for Women campaign and then the war, that she had never found the time to go back to look up her old friends and acquaintances. She had not planned to get off the train at St Johns, but when it pulled in there, on a whim she jumped out.

She made her way along the road in which she had lived. On turning the corner she had been initially surprised not to see any little groups of gossiping pinafore-clad women on the pavement; nobody cleaning a front step or chastising a naughty child. But she soon appreciated that many would be working at a factory at this time of day; or some might be doing a shift on the railways or at one of the many other jobs women were now tackling that before the war had been the exclusive domain of men. Ruby smiled as she remembered ticking off her husband over the attention he had been given by that firewoman.

She knocked on the door of the woman who used to live next door to her. Lizzy was a real old character, who would know all the news and gossip. There was no answer. She was about to try the next door along when a young woman on a bicycle hove into view. It was Ruby's old mate Edna from when she worked at the Peek Frean's factory in Bermondsey. She was wearing a police woman's uniform.

"Gawd help us!" exclaimed Edna down the street. "Look what the cat's dragged in! Ruby Martin as I live and breathe!"

She jammed on the brakes, skidded to a halt, threw the bike into the gutter and moments later the two women were hugging. Ten minutes of excited catching up and leg-pulling followed. This included Ruby dropping the bombshell that she had married an older man whom she had met while working on an ocean liner, and she was now Mrs Nash if you please. Then accompanied by the sauciest, least subtle Marie Lloyd-like wink she could manage, Edna asked what it was like to be married to an old fellow. Ruby responded by asking how the most dishonest woman in Peek Freans, who somehow managed to regularly squirrel knickers full of bourbons and custard creams past the security guards, had managed to get herself into the police force.

"Takes one to know one see," said Edna. "If you've been on the other side of the law you know what to look for when you're a copper don't you."

"Well, you're the first copper this old Suffragette has ever hugged!" exclaimed Ruby, crying with laughter.

"Funny you should say that," said Edna enthusiastically, "I'll have you know you inspired me you did. After you went off to the East End I joined the cause! I didn't join your lot 'cause I didn't like the violence, but I joined the Lewisham branch of the Women's Freedom League. We might not have done the sort of stuff you lot did, burning things down and the like, but we still got up to some right old shenanigans I'll tell you. Managed to get myself pinched. Wouldn't pay the fine of course. Off to Holloway clink I went. Surprised I didn't bump into you there!"

"You didn't put all that on your police application form I'll wager!" giggled Ruby.

"Don't make me laugh! And now I'm the best copperette you'll ever see in all your life! Nick you as soon as look at you!"

"Remind me not to introduce you to my husband!" said Ruby knowingly.

The joy of so unexpectedly meeting an old friend, and such a character at that, had Ruby forgetting momentarily the horror she herself had endured in Holloway and the fact that loose talk could get her and Nashey into trouble. She had just hinted to a policewoman that her husband worked on the wrong side of the law.

"Oh, bit of a lad is he?" asked Edna. "Don't worry, old friends is old friends. And besides my job is to nick young lads up to no good, not old East End fellers doing what comes natural!"

They continued their merry banter for a while longer before Ruby crooked her head towards the front door outside of which they were standing.

"Where's old Lizzie Dripping then?" she asked.

Edna's face, and the conversation, plummeted.

"Passed away. Remember Joe, her husband? Got called up soon as they brought in conscription for married men. Quick as you like poor Joe cops it. Soon as he's dead the separation allowance is stopped. Army's on the ball when it wants to be. Not so clever with paying out the widow's pension mind. So she had no money coming in. Didn't have no one to look after the little uns. Couldn't get no home work. She were starved for weeks till the allowance came through. Gave every crumb she had to the little uns of course. Don't know what killed her in the end, tell you the truth. Flu probably. She had it right enough. She just faded away."

It was time for a cup of tea. Edna wheeled her bike with one arm, and put the other round her old friend as they walked up the road to her little terraced house. The conversation turned as melancholy as it had been joyful. Many of the women Ruby had known had died for a variety of reasons. Some were dead within a year of their husband being killed at the Front for similar reasons to Lizzy. Neighbours had rallied round the best they could, but they all had their own problems and responsibilities.

And Ruby realised that unlike in Bow, the women of St Johns didn't have Sylvia Pankhurst and her charities looking out for them.

Another young woman Ruby had known, had been working in Greenwich at the time of the Silvertown explosion. Ruby had heard that shrapnel from the blast flew across the river and into the Greenwich gasometer, causing the whole thing to blow up in a huge fireball. But there had been no coverage of such a thing in the press. Edna confirmed this to be true, and little Blondie, Ruby never had known her real name, had been killed in the inferno.

Ruby told Edna about her various jobs in Bow. For her part Edna relayed how interesting her work as a policewoman was, a lot of it helping fellow women in one way or another. But she had only just returned to duty after a bout of flu so was on more mundane work at the moment overseeing queues and the like, while she recovered her strength. Ruby questioned her friend further about her duties as a police officer, before going on to report that neither she nor her husband had caught the flu. She appreciated that they had been lucky, telling Edna that many of the girls in her football team and those she had played against, had been down with it.

"Football! You! At your age! Since when?!" exclaimed an incredulous Edna.

This led them back into the world of leg-pulling and giggling. The war was forgotten again for a while.

Chapter 15

"German spies continue to abound in France. They are met with all sorts of disguises. Simple looking peasants working in the fields, sham priests, Germans dressed as Sisters of Charity or as hospital nurses."

Illustrated London News

The trip to Sidcup went as planned. Nash was confident there were no government men around, and he duly picked up his objector without fuss.

The one injury Nash retained from his villainous days was a certain stiffness of the neck, courtesy of escaping from a burly policeman's headlock. It didn't give him any pain but his range of neck movement was impaired. So given that he didn't usually have a lot in common with his objectors, and was not one for idle small talk with men at the best of times, little attempt was made to crane his neck to speak once his charges were under the coal sacks on his cart. Journeys to the East End were quiet affairs.

But this man had recently come from the trenches and had some shocking news to relay so, when there was nobody on the street within listening distance, Nash found himself leaning back and swivelling a little to converse.

The man told Nash that he had seen huge numbers of soldiers in field hospitals with a new strain of flu. It was a far more deadly virus than the previous one, and that had been bad enough. A large number of soldiers had died. It was decimating the British army. Fortunately it was fairly clear that the Hun must have it in their ranks too, as trench warfare had been severely curtailed by both sides for a while, and now the Germans were even in retreat.

On arrival at their East End destination, Nash gave his new charge a walking tour of the area.

Many of Nash's safe houses were in Shoreditch and Spitalfields, the latter of which had been where a young prostitute friend of his had been killed by the Whitechapel Murderer thirty years earlier. The piecemeal, uncoordinated, unplanned slum clearance in the area that had followed the killings, had actually made the already appalling overcrowding worse for a while, as places such as the police no-go area known as the Flower & Dean Street rookery, were not adequately replaced. Only the destruction of the infamous slum known as the Jago, in Shoreditch's Old Nickel area, had been an unqualified success. Here now stood the impressive Arnold Circus development of decent tenement housing for the regularly employed poor. The novelist Arthur Morrison, who had written about the Old Nickel publicising its horrors, had succeeded where the area's most infamous son had not. The pen had been mightier than the knife.

The area as a whole remained a rabbit warren of slum alleys and courts, which Nash knew like the back of his hand. And while there were no longer any specific no-go areas for the authorities, there were still plenty of places that were probably best left unchecked, particularly at night, by anyone working alone in any sort of official capacity. This Victorian throw-back of a place was ideal for Nash's purposes. He could hide objectors here, away from prying eyes, with much more certainty than anywhere else. Men could be absorbed; disappear. But Nash had to accept that his objectors could stand out like a sore thumb. And most of his charges were middle class Quakers who had lived, at least until they had been abused, beaten and threatened during the war, very sheltered lives. Living in this area, they could be forgiven for believing they had simply swopped one living hell for another. Consequently Nash was careful where he placed his men. Shoreditch was his preferred spot. He now had a few objectors living at different addresses in the Arnold Circus development, and had others living together in a derelict Victorian furniture warehouse.

While a walking tour was useful in showing new arrivals where all the local infrastructure they were likely to need was located, the main purpose was to impress upon them how close the East End was to the City of London. One end of Petticoat Lane emptied out on to Bishopsgate, a main thoroughfare of the City. Battered cloth caps and horse dung gave way to shiny top hats and motor car fumes, like a muddy river cascading into a shimmering ocean. Liverpool Street railway station was only yards away, as for that matter was Bishopsgate police station, full of those who might ask a man for his identification papers.

Consequently these Quakers were under orders never to venture out on to the three main roads; Bishopsgate, Great Eastern Street and Commercial Street. These bay-windowed and beguiling streets held the slums within their grasp like a fisherman's net. The objectors were to stay inside the net. All the time these fish were beneath the surface they would survive.

The manager of their property, usually an old associate of Nash from his villainous days, was the only local person who knew their true identities. Their cover story when passing the time of day with anyone was that they were struggling artists attracted in to the area by low prices, the interesting racy character of the East End and the way this melting pot part of London accepted people who were a little different. They had not been recruited into the army for one reason or another. That reason could be kept vague so people could make up their own mind about what it may be. The manners, politeness and quietly spoken gentility of the men Nash was helping; the fact that they were thought to be artists and the tell-tale mention of them being different, led many locals to believe they were homosexuals. An assumption was made; the army didn't want 'cuddle pups'.

Nash would go into local pubs and make conversation with landlords and their bar flies about the local artist colony at the nearby warehouse, just to gauge what people's thoughts were about the men. Were there any suspicions?

Most people had not even noticed their arrival. The No Conscription Fellowship's good quality costume design had meant the men had blended in to their new surroundings nicely. Most people were far too busy with their own frantic lives to concern themselves with a few extra people adding to the overcrowding in the area. And when Nash had found drinkers willing to offer an opinion about the artists, it was clear there was no great love of these newcomers, and plenty of crude remarks were made about them, but nobody proffered any suspicions that they could be conchies.

One old bar-fly in the Ten Bells, several sheets to the wind, had once put forward the theory that they could be German spies, but Nash had quashed that easily enough. He had derided the man as being a daft old sod, because surely the whole idea of being a spy was to blend in to the surroundings to pass yourself off as a normal Englishman. And besides, what was there worth spying on in darkest Spitalfields? Passing yourself off as a rum cove artist, well away from the docks or any other place of spy interest, was hardly the best of tactics. Nash had gone on to jokingly accuse the accuser, suggesting he was more likely to be a German spy, as you couldn't get much more typical an Englishman than an East End drunk! This had set off plenty of good natured ribbing of the man by all and sundry, with the pub landlord's wife bringing out from behind the bar a battered old policeman's helmet. This she enthusiastically plonked on the man's head, suggesting as she did so, that he looked remarkably like the Kaiser in it. Cue much raucous merriment at the old man's expense.

Nash left his latest objector in Shoreditch with some confidence he would be safe there, and set off for home content with his long day's work. He was tired though not as tired as his horse. Nash let his old nag take a good swig from the horse trough in Brick Lane. Nash stepped down and gave his four legged friend an appreciative tap on the neck.

"I'll tell one of the girls to get you some feed, soon as we're home boy."

The horse brought his head up from the trough and looked at Nash with what the guilt ridden owner considered contempt. The guilty man felt the need to defend himself.

"Think yourself lucky. Know what they've brought in now to get us to eat? Bleeding tinned fish if you please. Muck! And horsemeat an' all. Plenty of that about I can assure you. And did you see all them motors south of the river. It'll be like that here soon enough. So don't give me that look."

Nash had reached the Whitechapel High Road when he realised that the latest victim of this war appeared to be his sanity. He was now explaining himself to a horse. He shook his head wearily.

"Christ, let's get home for Gawd's sake."

He was unsure whether he was talking to himself or the horse. Either way, it did not improve his mood.

******

Nash did not own his horse. He rented it from George Lansbury. The ex-MP's family business was a wood yard which had started to replace its horses with motor vehicles. Lansbury's daughters, Daisy and Minnie, both of whom were friends of Ruby's from their Suffragette years together, looked after the horses now that their stable lad had gone off to war. They were reluctant to sell off their equine friends, as they were concerned the poor things might end up in the horsemeat trade, so when Nash had mentioned that he would find a horse & cart useful but didn't have anywhere to keep it, they were quick to rent one to him. The women offered him free usage, and would continue to stable and look after the horse gratis, on the understanding that he paid for its feed. Lansbury had not been entirely happy with the arrangement, but if there was anyone more than Nash whom it was advisable to keep in the good books of, it was his feisty young daughters. He ceded and the deal had been done.

Nash dropped the horse & cart off with Daisy at the wood yard and trudged the short distance home.

The Nashes lived in part of a house in Selwyn Road, only a few minutes' walk from the nursery. And it was even closer to the restaurant and toy factory. It was, what had once been, a fine white plastered terraced cottage complete with bow windowed frontage, built a century earlier when the Industrial Revolution had arrived in Bow. It would have originally housed a skilled worker, his family, their servant and perhaps an aged parent or two. The couple now shared it with a recently widowed young woman, Maud Kemp, and her eighteen month old daughter, Rose. Ruby and Nash had the downstairs, the family the upstairs, and they shared the kitchen, scullery and outside toilet.

The Nashes had never met Maud's husband, Herbert. When he had joined up voluntarily the previous year, he had been accepted into the army even though he was below the minimum height requirement. The army was so desperate for men that they set up 'bantam' battalions. The slight man, stunted from the genes of descendants who had lived too long in poverty, had been one of the 20th Service Battalion (Shoreditch) Middlesex Regiment. On his departure, the government had been slow to pay his wife her separation allowance, so rather than live on 'air pie', she had moved to Selwyn Road because it was close to Sylvia's highly regarded nursery and within walking distance of munitions factories where she knew she would be able to find decently paid work.

Maud's parents were dead. She had sisters living nearby, but not all families were as close and supportive as the government's war propaganda would have everyone believe. Maud was on her own. It was Ruby who comforted her when the dreaded telegram arrived to inform her that her husband had been killed in action. The two women had always got on well, but now there was an intimate bond between them.

These sorts of events left Ruby with pangs of guilt over her and Nashey's stance on the war. Should they be assisting in the war effort, even though they didn't believe in it, just out of basic human decency? But when Maud's widow's pension failed to materialise, which meant that she had to continue to put herself at risk working with TNT in the munitions factory, the guilt was replaced by anger and contempt for a government that treated its people this way.

Not that working in such danger afforded her very much in the way of creature comforts. The Rents Restrictions Act, brought in by the government earlier in the war in reaction to rent strikes and protests against profiteering landlords, had capped rents at pre-war levels. But even before the war, the law of supply and demand assured that rents in the overcrowded East End were too high in relation to local wage levels. And with no additional funds arriving in their coffers at a time of galloping inflation, landlords had no desire to spend any money on their properties. Dwellings were thus returning to the slum condition of a bygone era.

The Nash & Kemp home had certainly seen better days. Lighting was of the wax variety; the outside plaster was flaking off and any part of the outside walls that could not easily be reached was caked in grime and soot; doors were warped and window seals failed to do their job so the place was rather too well aired in winter; and there was rising damp throughout. And the only reason there were no bugs in the walls, was that Nash, who had lived through the horrors of Victorian slums, spent much of his spare time scraping and wallpapering both his and Maud's section of the house.

The Nash half of this near-slum could only be afforded because Sylvia insisted Ruby draw a decent living wage from her charity's coffers and the man of the house had a part time job in George Lansbury's wood yard. The job was partly for the sake of appearances, so nobody would ever wonder what Nash got up to all hours of the day and night. Lansbury's son, Willie, under whom Nash worked, knew the score. If anyone asked, Nash was a full time employee. But in reality he spent half of his waking hours on his work protecting objectors.

These wages enabled the Nashes to pay their rent and keep a little aside for a rainy day. And if they didn't want to pay their landlord his prices, there were plenty of reasonably well paid munitions workers flooding into the area who would.

Nash found Ruby had only just got in herself, having spent the afternoon with a friend in South London. Once Nash had reassured his wife that his latest objector venture had passed off without incident, they ate a none-too romantic candlelit supper which was testament to them having already blown their rations cards for the week. The larder was bare, save for a few grain products. But Nash would not eat bread now that the government had changed it from white to brown, so the couple devoured maize semolina and, thanks to rationing and the warmer weather meaning coal was now much easier to come by, the kettle kept them supplied with copious amounts of tea.

The couple spent the evening swapping shocking stories they had heard from a woman police officer and a man recently returned from the trenches.

Chapter 16

"There will be work of all kinds that will want doing, and women will have to do it...But...there must be an absolute determination not to go back after the war to the old position of subordination. The new spirit of women inculcated during the last decade must strike through all their labours and illuminate all their actions."

Votes for Women newspaper 1914

The chatting and cosy snuggling up together of the previous evening had been replaced by a little early morning tension in the Nash household.

Nash never was at his best first thing in the morning, so Ruby's usual routine was to leave him in bed with a cup of tea, for which she might receive a grunt of gratitude if she was lucky. She would then pop out to the nursery to open up ready for the arrival of the nurses. By the time she returned to her husband, he would have risen, had a 'sloosh' from a bucket of water out the back; dressed and ceased to be a miserable old devil.

But this morning they were awoken by an unexpected knock on the door. In the line of work Nash was in, this was no mundane event. It could be men in uniform carrying a rifle or two, coming to pay him a visit. Nash jumped up from their creaking, drooping old bedstead and grabbed weaponry, trousers and boots in that order, while his wife shouted the obvious question. Nash was half way through donning his trousers, doing the one-legged hop that men do when attempting to complete the normally slow but sure exercise quicker than physics allows, when a man's voice boomed back an answer through the door.

"Taxi!"

"Hang about, we'll be out in a minute!" shouted Ruby, stepping into her clothes with far more speed not to mention grace than her husband.

Their bedroom being on the ground floor, they didn't need to be awoken by the local knocker-up's pea-shooter, but Ruby had paid Granny Brown her usual fee to wrap on their door before any self-respecting cockerel was awake. They appeared to have slept through it.

The cabbie guessed the situation correctly. He carried on the conversation through the door.

"Paid old Granny Brown a penny to give you a knock did you?" he shouted with joviality both the Nashes considered thoroughly inappropriate at this time of the morning. "She probably didn't turn up. I heard she's nursing some of her family. Her son and his wife have both gone down with the flu, so she's looking after them, a niece and the grandchildren."

"What's all this in aid of?" demanded Nash of his wife.

"You've forgotten haven't you?" retorted Ruby. "I'm off to the West End. I've got meetings lined up with Selfridge's, Marshall & Snelgrove, Liberty's and Gamages. You're supposed to be coming with me."

Nash *had* forgotten. He had no objector work on, and the wood factory didn't need him, so he had been looking forward to spending the day with his wife, while she attempted to get orders for the toy factory from leading West End shops.

The factory not only provided well paid jobs for local women and had an in-house nursery for their children, it manufactured products that were in short supply once relations had been severed with Britain's main foreign supplier of toys. Ruby was thus confident of getting some sales and was taking several large boxes of samples with her, so had dropped a hint that she needed a big strong fellow along.

Nash had offered his services as delivery man for the trip and his further offer of paying for tea at the Lyons Corner House in the Strand had been most cordially accepted. The café had a romantic element to it, having been where the couple had enjoyed tea together on their way to a Suffragette protest outside Buckingham Palace six years earlier. It had been quite a day, starting with Ruby kissing Nash for the first time, much to his surprise. And although it had ended with Ruby battered and bruised, and Nash being carted off to court for showing several policemen the error of their ways, the Strand retained fond memories for the couple.

But Nash was still getting over the shock of being rousted from his bed, so his mood was inclined rather more towards the early morning grump than the love struck romantic.

"What we got a taxi for?" he moaned. "Waste of money if you ask me, when we've got a perfectly good horse & cart in the wood yard."

"Well first of all, no one is asking you, are they darling?" He had walked straight into that one. "And you know that taxis are Sylvia's one little luxury. She's given up everything for the likes of us down here in Bow, and the one thing she likes to treat herself to, is a taxi. The toy factory can afford it. If I get an order from Selfridge's for some stuffed animals that'll pay for a hundred taxis."

"What's Sylvia got to do it with the price of fish?"

"Darling, we are dropping her off on the way, at the Whitechapel Art Gallery. She is hoping to persuade them to have an exhibition of our British, Japanese and African baby dolls. They are unique. Our moulded china heads are the first to include life-like foreign ones. Even German toymakers before the war never managed that."

"Horse taxi is it? Least that'll be cheaper."

Ruby was about to add a third darling to the conversation and some censure about her husband being such a grumpy old sod, when she remembered why he was so opposed to motor cars. Nash had only been in a motorised vehicle twice in his life. The first time was when, suffering from frostbite, an ambulance had transported him off the Titanic survivors' rescue ship to a New York hospital. The second was when a Black Maria had taken him to the cells of Bow Street magistrates' court and from there on to Brixton prison. Needless to say he did not have particularly fond memories of a horseless carriage.

She put her arms around her husband and kissed him before softening her tone.

"Oi grump. It's going to be a long day. We can't afford to hang about. I'm sorry but I've had to order a motor taxi. But once we've got to the first shop, we'll pay the cabbie off and get a horse-drawn for the rest of my rounds. I'll have given all my stock away to the shops as samples so we won't have anything to carry home, so we can get a horse-tram home from Lyons'. How's that?"

Nash's mood transformed in an instant. He nodded and smiled lovingly at his wife before producing a mock sneer.

"Since when were black and yellow china bonces art?"

Ruby pulled a face and poked her tongue out at him before changing into a warm smile.

"Never mind bonces, you've got work to do. Carry my crates out to the taxi for me and be quick about it my good man."

Nash pretended to be a shuffling lackey, touching his forelock as he scampered to pick up the crates.

******

The cab stopped outside Selfridge's. All other large London department stores had grown from smaller shops over time. Selfridge's was the first to be built from scratch as a large enterprise. It had been possible because the land and existing premises in the area had been cheap to buy up. This was the poor end of Oxford Street, with many tenements built for the needy opposite the store but hidden away discreetly behind Bond Street underground station.

And the great entrepreneur, showman, loyal Anglophile and war supporter that was Harry Gordon Selfridge, had huge war information sheets pasted up on his front windows, telling the populace everything the government and newspapers were willing to tell them about the war.

It was therefore not unusual for the area around the entrance to be crowded, and for many of the crowd to be members of the local poor. And today was no different.

On seeing the crowds, Ruby asked the cabbie to pull in fifty yards up from the entrance at the corner of the store, where it was less busy. It would be easier to alight and to unload her samples. When the cab came to a halt, Nash stepped out onto the pavement and started to pull the crate marked Selfridge's out onto the pavement. Ruby stayed in the cab and helped push out the crate. Out of the corner of his eye Nash spotted a group of four ragged teenage lads hanging about on the corner, doing what such young men did; hands in pockets, spitting on the ground, swearing and looking morosely at the cove who had just got out of a taxi cab. Had he been in the East End, Nash would have kept an eye on them but here in the West End, he didn't pay them any attention.

But he should have. Within seconds of the crate touching the pavement, they were on him. Two grabbed Nash while the other two made to pick up the crate. It was a mistake. All four of the thugs should have attempted to neutralise their victim before worrying about their prize. Nash grabbed an arm, twisted it behind its owner's shoulder blades and kicked the assailant to the ground, before stamping down hard on the foot of his other attacker. This had the youth hopping straight into an elbow to the throat. The lad collapsed to the ground as his Adam's apple turned to cider. His two mates dropped the package, and made for Nash. But they had no idea what they were getting into. They had been in many a fight before, but these had been fights between teenagers. Lots of posturing, swearing, throwing out of arms and legs like demented puppets, but few real solid blows struck, at least until someone was on the ground, and then they would wade in. But now they were taking on a man who was reaching inside his coat for something that was going to introduce a whole new level of violence to the proceedings.

It was at this point that Ruby stepped in.

"Leave 'em alone Nashey, they're only lads!" she said, throwing herself between her husband and his attackers.

Meanwhile one of the young men whom Nash had deposited on the pavement, had got back on his feet and joined his two friends. The three of them struck out at Nash around and over Ruby, while calling Nash every name under the sun.

Nash managed to multi task landing further blows on his attackers while answering his wife.

"They're old enough to get a bleedin' good hiding that's what they are!"

Ruby was receiving some of the blows meant for Nash, which was further inflaming her husband, but it was nothing more than she had received during her Suffragette years. She ignored the pain and wrestled with both sides in the conflict.

"Oi! Oi! Oi! All of you! Stop it. Now! Stop it I say!!!"

And much to her amazement, they did. At least, the physical side of the combat. The young men backed off a couple of yards. One of them went to attend his gurgling mate laying on the pavement, while the other two continued to hurl abuse at the man in front of them. Nash replied with East End violence of the tongue, much of which had been out of common circulation since the 1880's. Ruby continued to act as peacemaker, and eventually the abuse turned from threats of what each side were going to do to each other, to childish jibes. It was when the lads were telling the opposition to "fuck off and go and pick up your old age pension," while Nash retaliated by telling them they were nothing but "little titty babies who should go home to mummy," that Ruby knew she had control of the situation.

The young men eventually turned and disappeared round the corner, and the oasis of space which had appeared when Oxford Street onlookers had drawn back from the confrontation like a receding wave on the beach, was now absorbed as the tide came back in again.

******

Normally Ruby would have chosen her moment with more care. But here they were, she and her beloved, in their favourite café, with her glowing from the excitement of her success. She had got orders for baby dolls, some with wax heads, some with moulded china ones. And not just the British white dolls, but the much more difficult to sell oriental Japanese and black African ones too. She also had orders for various stuffed animals, and also wooden boy-scout and girl-guide toys. Nash was on good form too, as he was enjoying some reflected glory because as well as hiding objectors, he had once hidden a German toymaker friend of his, who had made the originals of all the toys, which were now copied by the women in the toy factory. And for the wooden toys, it was the wood yard in which Nash worked, that supplied the raw material.

The couple were chatting away merrily when a young waitress, immaculate in tight auburn bun, freckles and a uniform of black dress, white apron and cap, delivered their cups of tea. She set down the sugar bowl and a tea spoon, and then hovered. The couple had stopped talking for a moment while the tea was delivered, and then both peered up at the literally waiting young woman, asking her silently why she was continuing to stand there.

The waitress was used to this.

"Only one spoonful per person allowed I'm afraid. I have to wait till you've done see, then take it to my next table."

Ruby never had taken sugar in her tea, and war shortages had at least cured Nash of his three sugars per cup habit. After two years of drinking unsweetened tea, sugar in his cuppa would now have had him grimacing.

And in the good mood that he was presently enjoying, it tickled Nash's funny bone that the waitress was standing guard to make sure he and his wife didn't take a second spoonful from what was apparently the mighty Lyons' Corner House's only sugar bowl. He wanted to say something but appreciated that any joke he made was going to be at the poor waitress's expense, which wouldn't be right. He managed to keep a straight face while handing back the sugar bowl and spoon.

"That's all right duck, we're both sweet enough already. Let the next table have two lots eh?" he said with a friendly conspiratorial wink.

"Oh I'm not allowed to do that," she replied with great earnestness before shuffling away with the bowl.

The incident had not been especially funny, but the

married couple were in such a good mood and so much on each other's wavelength that they just looked at each other and burst into supressed chortling in any case.

This had Ruby wince.

"Ouch, I copped one in the ribs earlier."

"We'll have Dr Alice have a look at it when we get home. You did bloody well there girl. Saved them silly little sods from a good hiding."

"Saved my silly big husband from copping a few as well. Four against one weren't the best odds."

"It were down to three and I've dealt with worse," said Nash with a grim smile. "But yeah, I suppose I would have copped a few for me troubles."

"Funny though isn't it, when you say you've copped one. Do you suppose that's from the word coppers? When a copper whacked you one in the old days, it became known as copped?"

"Might be I suppose. Back when I were a lad the coppers used to roll their raincoats up as tight as they could and then use 'em as soft coshes. They used to pick on us lads. We'd be walking along minding our own business and they'd give one of us a backhander with their raincoat. Wallop, that's for nothing, now be careful."

"Always minding your own business were you?" queried Ruby sardonically.

"Well…"

The two shared a smile again.

And then Ruby just blurted it out.

"I was thinking. I wonder if I should consider becoming a woman police officer."

Fortunately Nash was not drinking his tea at that

moment. He would have made an awful mess of the nice white tablecloth.

There followed the inevitable conversation. Nash made it clear that he was horrified, and not just because of his history of always being on the wrong side of the law. He reminded Ruby of the amount of violence perpetrated on her, Sylvia and their fellow Suffragettes in the not too distant past by the police. Ruby countered that women police officers were different. She'd had a long conversation with her police woman friend in St Johns. Edna had told her that women police officers, or copperettes as they were nicknamed, were deployed to deal with the growing problem of juvenile delinquency. There were lots of young lads, now with no father, older brother or uncle figure to keep them in check, forming gangs and getting into trouble. Women could deal with them better than men. Look at what had happened earlier outside Selfridge's. A woman had stopped what was about to become a nasty incident.

Nash had to admit Ruby had done very well with those lads outside Selfridge's. It was the first crack in his defence. But he continued with his counter argument. The two of them were committed to the anti-war movement. Ruby's great heroine and friend Sylvia Pankhurst, was part of the international peace campaign. Surely being a policewoman was helping the government and therefore assisting in the war.

Ruby put the case that mere day to day living helped the government in some way. The reason going to the pictures to see Charlie Chaplin was so much more expensive than before the war was because of the entertainment tax levied on cinemas to help pay for the war. The entrance charge for that football match she had played in did not all go to charity. The match organisers had to pay a huge amount of tax on the takings to the government. And even watered down beer had gone up in price threefold, and you could guess where most of the increase had gone.

Ruby had originally only stated that perhaps she should consider becoming a police officer. She had just blurted it out without thinking it through. It was only a reaction to her success of a few hours earlier while the discussion with her policewoman friend was fresh in her mind. But the more Nash argued against, the more she came back with reasons for. She was talking herself round, as much as her husband.

One of the things that had so impressed her with Nashey, from the moment she had first met him on the Titanic, when he had gone below decks to look for female passengers and crew to rescue, had been his care and understanding of women. Ruby got on to this subject. A policewoman helped her fellow women. She patrolled near army barracks to quell prostitution and to ensure young girls did not get carried away with patriotic fervour. This in turn stopped pregnancies and the spread of VD. Nash had seen the horrors of unchecked prostitution and syphilis in his younger days. He had to admit anything that minimised it was a good thing. It was another crack in his wall.

Ruby continued by asking who was it who dealt with the air raids and the aftermaths? She immediately answered her own question. It was mostly Gorgeous Wrecks, policewomen and women fire officers.

Nash suggested she become a fire officer. He was weakening.

"There's worse things than fire now Nashey," said his wife. "Look at this flu…"

"Yeah! You look at this flu!" he interjected, his eyes bulging like organ stops to add emphasis.

Just when her little finger had a small piece of her husband starting to get wrapped around it, the mention of the new eff word had allowed him to escape his wife's grasp.

A rejuvenated Nash warned her that being a policewoman would inevitably bring her into contact with large numbers of the public, which was clearly a health risk given the new deadly flu they had heard about was bound to spread home from the trenches.

Ruby waved away his concerns. She had survived an ocean sinking; regularly being beaten up when a Suffragette; recently being bombed and knocked unconscious; lived for the past four years on scraps. If she could live through that lot she could certainly manage the flu. She had even survived Mrs Richmond's cooking! If she could do that she could do anything!

Nash retorted that the flu was no laughing matter. If big fit soldiers could be seen off by it so could a slip of a woman like her!

"Exactly dear husband! Slips of women like me, like Sylvia, Alice, Maud and every other woman you know. And all the woman you don't know. And every child and man as well. Goodness knows what might happen if this flu really grabs hold here. It might even end the war. One thing's for sure darling, the police are going to need all the help they can get. I can't stand by and let others do what I could do just because I'm afraid of catching the bloody flu."

Nash huffed. She always did this. Those clever women in the Suffragettes had trained her too well in arguing the toss. Back in those days when she had been shouting the odds from her soapbox, some wag might shout some abuse at her from the crowd, only to be cut to the quick by a rapier thrust of wit from his wife-to-be. He had always been very proud of her. The only trouble was now being married to such a woman, meant that when they argued he might say black and she could come back with white, and win every time, no matter how certain he had been that he was right. One minute he thought she had been joking about the flu, and the next she had turned the tables on him. Clever little cow.

He knew he was on the ropes. And there was no referee on hand to step in to stop an unfair fight.

The killer blow was delivered when Ruby mentioned Edna telling her about the government cover up of the Silvertown explosion. Police officers got to know things. Things that were kept from the ordinary man in the street. Working within the system could be very beneficial to those working outside it. Who knew what information she might glean that could be useful to her husband in his nefarious objector hiding business? She had not suddenly become Miss Warmonger. She was still the loyal wife of a man who believed this war was not theirs to fight. Nash started to show some enthusiasm, though he couldn't see how she would be accepted as a police officer.

"You've got a charge sheet as long as your arm; you know the cells at Holloway like the back of your hand; you attacked that copper outside The Monument when you were a Suffragette and that's all on record; and when that prison doctor came to force feed you, you bounced a prison mug off his bonce!"

He did not go on to say that she had also organised Emily Davison's doomed attack on the Derby. He didn't have to. That was always there unsaid, haunting her. He simply added his conclusion.

"They ain't going to have you as no copper are they darling?"

"Well that's just where you're wrong darling. Most of those things took place when I was working for Mrs Pankhurst. I got away with most of the things I did for Sylvia. I got beaten up by the police in Victoria Park right enough, and nearly got brained by a soldier outside Buckingham Palace, but I wasn't arrested either time. And Mrs Pankhurst is popular with the government these days. She's thrown herself into the war effort gaining support for it with her speeches, and a lot of the women handing out white feathers were her girls. Remember that girl who gave you a white feather that time? She was an ex Suffragette. They want women like me to become copperettes. Where do you think the name copperette comes from? Suffragette, that's where I'll wager. They know the ropes where crime's concerned. Takes one to know one, that sort of thing."

"I suppose you do realise Sylvia'll disown you," said Nash, with an air of resignation in his voice.

"She'll understand. I know we've always been on the opposite side to the police, and they gave us Suffragettes some right hidings, but we have to have coppers don't we? There'd be anarchy without them. And there's plenty who are decent men. Look at all the good work they've been doing in this war. Look how they helped out when poor

Hildegarde was killed." She then held up the cup of tea in her hand. "And we wouldn't even be able to have a cuppa if it weren't for them guarding the coal at railway depots would we darling?"

"That's all very well. But who's gonna look after the nursery and toy factory? And hold Mrs Richmond to account at the restaurant."

"I can be replaced sharp enough. There are lots of ways to get through this war Nashey. I just want to do my bit to help women. The toy factory, nursery and restaurant are running well enough. They don't need me anymore. Women are being attacked on all sides. By the government, the press, bullies in factories, pimps, gangs, soldiers and yes coppers. I can't stand by and watch it and not do something about it."

Nash nodded and smiled.

He had always thought that a fundamental weakness of the Suffragette campaign had been that they battered at the door of the castle, rather than having enough supporters inside to lower the drawbridge. Now he put his mind to it, having a wife inside the system was not such a bad thing.

"You'll be a bleeding good copper you will if I'm any judge," he said with knowing certainty.

And so it was decided. Ruby had talked herself into becoming a police officer. Nash looked forward without enthusiasm to the terrible stick he was going to get from everyone he knew about his wife becoming a police officer.

Chapter 17

"I soon realised that a great change in the mentality of the
people was taking place. They had lost their confidence."

Toni Seider, The Autobiography of a German Rebel

Fritz was intrigued by what he had read in the newspaper
that morning. A horse had collapsed dead in a Berlin
street. Caused by what? Nobody cared. Supposing it was
anthrax? Nobody cared. Within minutes anyone in the
area with speedy access to a knife or any other implement
with a cutting edge, had stripped it of its flesh to the
bone, quicker than any butcher could have managed. If
the ordinary German in the street was that desperate for
horse meat, imagine what wealthy restaurant goers would
pay for elephant steaks. Klaus had arranged a good price
at a Dresden slaughterhouse to have the carcass butchered,
and Fritz himself had appointments set up at several large
Dresden hotels who had all shown an interest in buying
steak from him. He had been a little hazy when it had
come to providing them with information on exactly
which cuts of meat were available, but he had assured them
that it was not horse.

But the smile was wiped off his face when he arrived

at Klaus' farm to find that the shortage of meat had led farmers to being ordered by the authorities to slaughter their entire milk cow herds. Thus Klaus now had neither the time nor inclination to assist further with the dead elephant escapade. Fritz would have to sort out the Dresden end of the operation himself.

With some slaughterhouses having been closed down due to the lack of work, the remaining ones were likely to be at full throttle now that so many cows were being destroyed, so Klaus warned that the Dresden ones were likely to be too busy to bother themselves with a solitary elephant carcass. He made a few telephone enquiries on behalf of his entrepreneur friend, to find his concerns were justified. The place that had initially accepted Klaus' booking for the elephant now reneged on the deal and he was unable to find a replacement venue.

Fritz could see his great enterprise failing miserably. Frau Burchardt had already wired the balance of the payment to the zoo. He would not be able to cut either the carcass or his losses. He was now the not so proud owner of one elephant – dead. And it had already been arranged with the zoo that it would be taken away within the next twenty four hours.

There was also the small matter of his forthcoming meeting with his moneylender at her bank, when she would be expecting him to be carrying a discreet but thick wad of high denomination bank notes.

In his panic, Fritz jumped on the next train to Dresden without a plan. An expensive taxi tour he could ill afford, of the hotels he had telephoned earlier, confirmed his worse fears. The more upmarket ones were not interested in elephant steaks, and the rest had no means of taking on a whole carcass.

He wondered whether the zoo had some form of deep freeze facility. Could they keep the carcass for him for a time?

The questions certainly needed to be asked, so he had started to shuffle towards the zoo when a large beer restaurant, not unlike the sort of bierkeller one might see in Munich, hove into view. Desperation took him through the front door. The shortage of decent food and beer to sell meant the place was quiet. He asked the man behind the bar if the manager was in, as he had some meat available for sale. Not surprisingly the owner was fetched in double quick time.

Fritz told the man what he had for sale and the logistical problems inherent in its supply. After the obvious shock and humour had dissipated, the bar owner said he might be interested at the right price.

On the train journey from Berlin some calculations had been made. The most expensive meat item Fritz had sold recently was a whole boiled ham, for which Frau Burchardt had paid him one hundred and forty marks. Klaus had advised that an elephant carcass would surely produce enough steaks for it to be worth at least a hundred times more than a ham. So Fritz asked for fourteen thousand marks. This was met with laughter. He was asked where he thought a bar owner could lay his hands on that sort of money. And to make it into an attractive dish, he would have to add sauerkraut. There was also the problem of refrigeration and storage, so he would have to sell steaks at a good price, no more than one mark thirty pfennigs per plate, to shift them quickly.

But this was all simple negotiation. The fact was the bar owner knew Fritz was in no position to haggle. He offered seven thousand marks, minus whatever it cost to have the carcass butchered and transported, take it or leave it. The former was chosen with a grudgingness that hid great relief as well as excitement at the profit realised.

Phone calls were made, logistics of butchery, transportation and payment sorted, and Fritz made the last train home with bulging pockets.

******

Aldo had gone down with flu and was in a bad way with it. Mrs Burchardt's doctor had been summoned but having seen the patient, had failed to impress when stating that bedrest was as good a treatment as any. And followed that by reassuring his usual client that she should not worry unduly if she should catch the disease, as it appeared to be attacking younger adults rather more powerfully than the mature person.

Looking at the condition her poor chauffeuse was in, Mrs Burchardt found it difficult to believe that if it were not wartime, simply doing nothing would have been the best prescription. She suspected that all worthwhile remedies were being used in the war effort. And the idea that the flu was less likely to affect her than a strapping young woman like Aldo, was absurd. She summoned her black market man, sending him a letter by messenger, confident that he would be able to get his hands on the sort of medicines that would help resist the disease in the first place, and also, should one capitulate to it, assist one to avoid suffering in the way that Aldo was doing.

Mrs Burchardt did not speak to Patemann personally about it. She thought that given people of his sort live so much closer together, they must surely be more prone to catch the flu, so for the time being the less contact she had with him the better. It was bad enough that she was having to meet him soon with regard to their elephant enterprise. Instructions were thus given to Frauline Emmerich, the cook, for her to relay to him when he came to the house.

Fritz had been his usual, your-wish-is-my-command self, and promised to return with the required medicines as soon as possible. But on making enquiries, it had become clear that there was no black market in flu remedies. There were too many cure-alls that one would could buy legitimately. But undeterred Fritz had managed to get hold of some bottles of medicine from Spain, which were apparently pretty much the same stuff that you could get in any German pharmacy, but crucially the advertising stickers on the front were in Spanish. This gave them a certain exotic air, and coming from the country from where the disease was apparently spreading, Fritz thought such medicine could be sold as the latest high quality product that the Spanish upper classes were successfully taking to stave off the disease.

When Fritz had received his orders from the cook, he had asked after Aldo, and was told she'd had the flu for a couple of days and was in quite a bad way. And during his asking around the underworld about the flu, he had been informed that many people started to make a sudden rapid recovery after three days. So two different Spanish remedies were sold to Mrs Burchardt at such an outrageously high price, it was obvious that this was the very best money could buy. One medicine was for her to take immediately to assist in keeping the flu at bay. But if she were to go down with the disease, she should start to take the other remedy on the third day of the illness. And of course, she could try it on Aldo immediately.

The timing had been perfect. Aldo, into her third day of illness, had been plied with the second remedy and had made a speedy recovery thereafter. Mrs Burchardt was impressed. She contacted her entire social circle about it, and soon Fritz was being contacted by the cooks and maids of many upper crust households on behalf of their mistresses.

******

Every Sunday the stations and trains overflowed with German city dwellers heading for the countryside. Berliners would sell whatever they had for whatever a farmer like Klaus might give them in return. A best coat for some meat; shoes for some eggs and half a pound of butter. And when they had nothing left with which to barter, they cadged or even begged for some dripping.

Klaus kept a secret supply of everything for which city dwellers were looking. But as far as he was concerned, this was done out of a sense of protest against the war. He was profiteering merely at the government's expense. He had no desire to rob his fellow Germans. It was why he was generous on Sundays. He did not drive the hard bargains that he knew other farmers extracted from the desperate. A man would offer him a suit for some meat; he would accept just the jacket, handing back the trousers telling the man he should keep them because the pockets were useful for carrying things in. The man would take back the bottom half of his suit, to find it rather heavier than when he had handed it over.

"As you know," said Klaus, "selling you potatoes is prohibited by the government, so I cannot *sell* you potatoes."

His placing of emphasis on the word 'sell' allied to the meaningful glint in his eye told the man that the extra weight he could feel was a potato in each of the suit's pockets. Slipped in there by the farmer, gratis.

It wasn't much. Not much at all. Certainly not enough to assuage the guilt he felt for being only the most grudging, minimal part of his country's war effort.

He had remembered an old classroom history lesson. A medieval English king had set up his own church. Not because he had wished to leave his faith. But because he did not agree with the running of his existing church. Klaus believed he knew how the man must have felt. Klaus did not wish to leave his country. He wished his country well and hoped it would win the war. But he did not believe in those stupid men who so unnecessarily started the conflict; the men who continued the war even after it was obvious it was a huge mistake; the men who had slaughtered all his pigs, all his cows, and taken away his livelihood and self-respect.

He could not start his own government as that Englishman had started a new church. But he needed to do something. He had written to Fritz. The reason he worked with him, rather than any of the other shady black market characters who had offered their services over the past few years, was that Klaus recognised Fritz had some element of respectability in him. He was breaking the law, but he was not a crook as such. He was a businessman. Just as Klaus believed himself not to be a crook. He was a farmer.

Fritz had even managed to feed many of his fellow countrymen in their hour of culinary need, thanks to that ridiculous elephant carcass escapade. And it must have left him flush with funds into the bargain. Money that perhaps could be used to help Germany in some way.

In his letter Klaus had wondered if there was something the two men could do together that was both profitable for them and also of help to their country, using Fritz's capital and Klaus' farm. He had an idea regarding photography.

Just before the outbreak of war, Klaus had started to make some money selling animal bones to a freight forwarder, who then supplied the Perutz camera film company with gelatin for the emulsion that was needed on camera film. With Klaus' farm and his slaughterhouse contacts, and Fritz's capital and business acumen, they could cut out the middle man and work directly with camera film companies. The profit the freight forwarder made was outrageously high. They could make good money. And with the profit there must be some way of investing in the flu epidemic. It was the fastest growing market out there after all. Perhaps they could go into gauze mask production or cleaning materials or drugs or something? And this would be how they could give something back to German people.

Could Fritz travel out to talk things over with him? Fritz replied that he certainly liked Klaus' ideas. The irony was that he was so busy at the moment supplying black market flu remedies that he would not be able to visit the farm any time soon. But he would certainly get out there as soon as he could.

******

Dorothea had sent word to Peter's family to let them know what had happened to him, and was only too pleased to have contacted the army to report that a soldier who had been struck on the head during a riot was being tended to by a professional nurse in her own home. Peter thought she must have laid it on a bit thick about the seriousness of the blow for them to have accepted he would not be returning to his post at the end of his leave. Admittedly the authorities had stated in their reply that they would be sending a member of the army's medical staff along to check on the story, but this had as yet not happened. With the flu taking such a hold on the Home Front and the war also suddenly starting to go so badly militarily, one more soldier falling through the administrative cracks was apparently neither here nor there.

But the information had not quite fallen on the death ears she and Peter had assumed. Someone must have passed on her details to the Kriegsrohstoffabteilung, the government department in charge of production. They had written, asking her to become a factory nurse in a large company employing mostly women.

Dorothea didn't know anything about the subject so had asked her more streetwise suffrage colleague, Ursula Wende, round for advice over a cup of ersatz coffee.

She felt a little awkward about having Ursula visit her home. They were more associates than real friends. Their relationship had only ever been one of shared beliefs being discussed at meetings. She regarded Ursula in the same way she did her tennis club acquaintances. She simply shared a love of a game with them. Chatting over a cup of tea after a political gathering or a glass of water after a set of doubles, was hardly what she considered a friendship. Dorothea liked to keep these relationships somewhat at arm's length. But now Ursula was going to see her rather comfortable home, complete with the antique furniture, soft furnishings and potted plants of a middle class lady. It was not the humble abode one might expect of a widowed ex-nurse. Dorothea wondered whether there may be some inverse snobbery issuing forth from her friend.

But she need not have worried. On arrival Ursula did not appear to register her surroundings at all. She didn't notice the well sprung sofa that she had been beckoned to sit on. It was just somewhere to sit while she got down to business.

Ursula was less than positive about the government's summons.

"Factory nurses are known as company midwives. Before the war they were a good thing. They looked after women in all matters relating to safety, health, hygiene, but these duties have been suspended now. They want us to work harder, longer and cheaper than men used to, but our health is not important. You are no longer a nurse. You have to deal with all the problems women suffer at home as well as in the factory. You have to deal with their childcare, food, transport needs. You even have to run their hostels."

"So what is your advice to me Ursula? Nursing Peter has made me realise that working on a market stall is a waste of my talents. I need to nurse."

"I am told the war is going badly," replied Ursula abruptly. "Curse the king, the king of the rich, who can't know our misery, who won't rest until he has exacted the last from us and lets us be shot like…"

"What shall I do?!" interrupted Dorothea, exasperated that her friend was prone to jump on her soapbox at every opportunity these days.

"I do not apologise Dorothea, but I am contrite, I forget myself sometimes," said Ursula quietly before continuing in a more business-like manner. "There are huge losses at the Front. The most serious injury cases are starting to be transferred back here to makeshift hospitals, where the army or Red Cross are setting up in schools, auditoriums, theatres and other large buildings. You should offer your services."

"Very well, I will ignore the summons and make enquiries about these hospitals as soon as I have Peter fully recovered. Until then I will remain at my post in the marketplace."

"Oh yes, you must look after Peter," said Ursula softly, conspiratorially, her tone completely changed from a moment ago. "For sure he is a good looking fish to have in your net."

The sudden change from barrack room lawyer to coquettish friend took Dorothea completely unawares.

She got up from her chair, turned on her heel and busied herself in the kitchen making coffee before the blush she could feel in her cheeks became evident. No longer having a servant to do the job certainly had its benefits.

Chapter 18

"Scandalous. It was time more doctors were sent home from the Front."

Doctor at an inquest, Manchester Evening News 1918

Ruby had started to feel unwell on the tram home from London. It soon became clear she was going down with something. By the next morning Nash was concerned that his wife might have caught the new deadly version of the flu.

Nash had never felt such panic in his life. He cared for his wife the best he could until Maud walked through the door having just finished her early shift at the munitions factory. She agreed to look after Ruby while Nash went looking for the doctor. On her way home Maud had picked up Rose at the nursery, so quickly popped her back there, partly so she could give Ruby her full attention and partly to keep her daughter as far away from the flu patient as possible. With his wife in safe hands, Nash rushed to Dr Alice's surgery, then her house, and when these trips proved fruitless, toured the streets stopping all and sundry to ask them if they had seen the good doctor. Some had, but each line of inquiry failed to track her down. By the time he had to get back to attend to his wife because Maud needed to pick up Rose at the nursery's closing time, he had left countless messages throughout Bow asking Alice to visit Ruby as soon as possible.

But with several local doctors now down with the flu themselves, Alice had spent much of the day and evening outside her usual jurisdiction attending patients in Mile End. She had not received Nash's message.

Having arrived home late at night, exhausted from a twenty hour duty, Alice had not even made it into her bedroom. She had slumped onto her kitchen chair, put her arms on the adjacent wooden table and within a second her head was resting on them.

The next thing she was vaguely aware of was someone banging on her door. She pulled her head up, straightened and immediately grimaced at the pain in her lower back. Her neck ached too. How long had she been asleep at the table? It was just starting to get light outside, which answered the question. She dragged herself to her feet and sloped groggily up the passage to the door.

On her way to another early shift, Maud had knocked on the off chance of catching the doctor in. On seeing the weary state of Alice, she apologised for the intrusion, but the doctor reassured her that it was probably just as well. Any longer sitting in that position and goodness knows what state her body would be in. The important thing was that she had managed to snatch some much needed sleep before she saw another patient.

Five minutes later she was knocking at a front door herself. Nash answered. He was carrying a candle, and nodded for Alice to come in.

"Good of you to come Doctor."

The formality in the greeting impressed upon Alice how worried Nashey must be. It was the first time he had ever called her anything other than Doc or Al.

"Take this here candle. I got the black-out going on in there. She just wants to sleep all the time but not before she kicked up a fuss about there being too much light."

He went on to tell the doctor that he was concerned Ruby's initial symptoms of headache, drowsiness, body pains, chills, feeling giddy and lack of appetite had changed for the worse.

"She's been coughing up green yellow puke. Reminds me of poor bastards I've seen coughing their guts up who've been invalided out the trenches 'cause they've been gassed. She won't eat nothing neither."

The doctor examined the patient and took her temperature. It was one hundred and two.

"Has she been sneezing Nashey?"

"No, funny enough that's something she ain't done. It's a rum sort of flu and make no mistake."

"The desire for darkness is photophobia. A fear of light," said the doctor. "Her symptoms suggest she has one of the new diseases which are cropping up. I've heard there are many cases of this in the trenches. It's rather indeterminate at the moment I'm afraid. I've tried to get some information about it from the local medical officer of health, but he tells me the higher authorities are keeping things under wraps. Don't want the Germans to think we're weakening, that sort of thing. But it appears to be a form of purulent bronchitis rather than influenza as we know it. One thing I do know, it gets worse if you try to shake it off. Now I know how tough Ruby is, but if she starts to fret about needing to get to work or anything of that nature, on no account allow her to get up."

"I'll see to it she don't get up, don't you worry", assured Nash with grim certainty.

"Good. Now I'd like to start her on steam inhalation to begin with."

The doctor gave Nash his nursing orders and said she would try to return the next day but with the proviso that she was so busy at the moment, that she could not promise anything. If Ruby's condition worsened he should attempt to contact her immediately.

******

As Dr Alice had expected, pressure of work had meant she had not been able to return to see Ruby for the best part of three days. But on entering the Nash household, all seemed well.

"She had a fever for a couple of days but she seems on the mend now right enough." said Nash, before adding with a hint of nursing pride in his voice. "I've managed to get some Lillian down her."

That was a new one on Alice. She tried to work it out. Lillian Gish − fish? She couldn't help but be amused by Nash's predilection to shorten everyone's names but also use rhyming slang which often lengthened words.

"She has eaten some fish? Excellent."

"*She* is awake you know" said Ruby, propping herself on an elbow.

Alice shot Nash the quickest of wry smiles before changing her expression to absolute seriousness as she turned to her patient to examine her.

"Cheeky little mare ain't she doc?" said Nash.

There was relief in the accompanying smile which betrayed the concern he had felt over the past few days.

Examination duly completed, the doctor diplomatically ignored Nash's comment on his wife, simply confirming that Ruby was indeed on the mend. Most importantly her fever had broken and her temperature was almost back to normal. She also had some news of the illness.

"I was off the mark with my diagnosis of bronchitis," she said. "It *is* a form of influenza. It's being called the three-day fever, because once the fever element has subsided after three days, one makes a full recovery within a week. So Ruby, I recommend you do not return to work for another week."

Alice knew full well that Ruby would return to work as soon as she could put one foot in front of another without keeling over, but she hoped that telling her to stay at home for a week might at least keep her indoors for one more day.

"I'll see she do Al, don't you worry," said Nash with a certainty that reassured the doctor but brought a sigh of exasperation from the listening patient.

He then changed tack to something that had been at the forefront of his mind during Alice's previous visit but only now could he bring himself to enquire about it given that his wife was clearly on the road to recovery.

"I've heard this here flu's killed some of the lads in the trenches Al. Quite a few of 'em as a matter of fact. That's why I was so worried about Ruby. How can that be?"

Alice looked at him like the workhouse beadle had young Twist after his inappropriate food request. She wondered how Nashey knew this. This information was not supposed to be in the public domain. It had only been relayed to her by the local medical officer a few days ago. The flu had apparently become a serious matter at the Front. Thousands had been infected. And many were dying. It was why, despite her just coming to the end of another appallingly long shift, she had made a beeline to see her friend Ruby. But a doctor exhausted from twenty four hours without sleep was not at her most considered, confidentially aware. She blurted out far too honest an answer.

"Well, just between you, me and the gatepost Nashey, the flu *is* very bad in the trenches. They are setting up flu infirmaries behind the lines. Many soldiers have succumbed I'm afraid; others are being sent back to Blighty to convalesce. It's initially being spread here by soldiers coming home, then munitions workers are spreading it further afield as they move between cities.

Nash pulled a face. He wasn't convinced he was getting the full story.

"Just ordinary flu ain't bad enough to kill loads of big hairy arsed soldiers is it?" he queried, with a hint of accusation in his voice.

No sooner had her words left her mouth and Alice had realised that she had lapsed in her level of professional conduct. She needed to get off the subject of soldiers and influenza as speedily as possible. Otherwise, in her tired state she might let slip something more. If it got out that the war had somehow created a mutation of the flu, producing a killer virus of epic proportions, who knew how the public might react.

She appreciated that throwing medical terms into a conversation with a layman served little purpose so she was usually careful to speak in a way that could be understood. But on this occasion she decided to retreat into medical-speak in the hope it would bring said conversation to a close.

"There is also a new disease which is initially being called war nephitis which has very similar symptoms to both flu and the broncho-pneumonic conditions that are usually associated with soldiers being gassed. The deaths you mention appear to have been caused by severe broncho-pneumonia caused by secondary bacterial infection. Mortality may have occurred from any or all of these conditions."

Nash had expected her to say something along the lines of, conditions in the trenches being so poor, with soldiers so weak from fighting, a few had inevitably succumbed to a disease which would not normally have carried them off. But her medical waffle made him think there was more to it than met the eye. He simply nodded and assured the doctor that he would try to keep his wife indoors, though given he had lots of work on he was going to have to leave her to her own devices, and they both knew what that meant.

Relieved the conversation about flu deaths was over, Alice ventured into a little levity.

"It would seem you got off lightly with steam inhalation Ruby. I have heard a rumour that some doctors have prescribed venesection. Blood-letting if you please! I thought those days were over!"

Neither Ruby nor Nash reacted or replied. Their doctor felt awkward. She said something about her needing to be off and Ruby needing to rest, gave her goodbyes and made for the front door. Nash followed to see her out. Alice felt the need to toss some small talk over her shoulder as she was about to leave.

"You mentioned having a lot of work on Nashey. Would that be war work?"

"When I asked you about the boys in the trenches you could have just said ask me no questions and I'll tell you no lies. Eh doc?"

He followed this with a wink, to reassure her that no offence had been either given or taken.

Chapter 19

"We took in bronchitis and rheumatism cases. Some of the bronchitis patients were as bad as the men who were gassed...It was pathetic to see the young men crippled... sometimes doubled up as if they were men of eighty instead of boys in their twenties. They suffered terrible pain with it."

Sister Mary Stollard, Beckett's Park
Military Hospital, Leeds.

Nash had visited the man who had collapsed in front of him outside the cinema. After a lengthy wait on the doorstep, his knock had eventually been answered by the man's wife, Elsie. She barely had the strength to stand and, from what could be seen of her face behind the handkerchief she had over her mouth, she looked awful. Nash saw past her into the living room. Her husband, slumped in an armchair by the fire, appeared even worse. Nash reciprocated with his own hankie and kept his distance while a short conversation ensued on the doorstep, which finished with him promising to pop by in a couple of days to see how they were getting along. He had asked if they were short of anything, and had been told they were running low on coal.

He had not been looking forward to returning. From what he had gleaned about the general severity of the flu, he felt sure his visit would end in a knock on the door going unanswered and a neighbour coming out to tell him that the couple had passed away.

Now he stood on the couple's front step, with a small sack of coal over his right shoulder, like a Santa from Newcastle. He used his spare hand to bang on the door. To his surprise it was answered within a couple of seconds, by the man of the house. A silent exchange between the two men had Nash lowering the sack, which was answered with a nod beckoning him inside.

Nash walked in to receive his orders from Elsie, who had been waiting just inside the door.

"Empty it down there duck," she said, motioning to the grate.

"You can keep the sack, save the dust going everywhere," replied Nash, dropping the sack deftly on to the tiles of the grate.

Elsie thanked Nash while her husband sank to his knees to empty some of the precious black stuff into the fireplace. It was time to warm the place and get the kettle on. The man set to work with some enthusiasm. It was not the house of death or suffering that Nash had expected.

Elsie told Nash to take the weight off his feet, which had him sinking in to an ancient leather armchair which was more arms than chair. It was so lacking any springs or upholstery that he felt his backside touch the floor. It was as if the furniture was consuming him, his shoulders pushed inwards as if he were in a straight-jacket, his weight seemingly forced back and down; he felt like a beetle stranded on its back. And the animal analogy did not end there. His head felt like it was disappearing into his neck, like one of those tortoise things he'd seen at the zoo. He couldn't remember when he had felt more small and vulnerable. At his scary granny's when he was a little urchin probably. He decided the next time he ever wanted to get some information out of someone who didn't want to provide it, he would place them in such a contraption. They would surely come up with the answers immediately.

Elsie spoke at Nash rather than to him, rambling merrily away ten to the dozen. It was the obvious over compensation of a woman whose husband was unable to verbally interact with her. Nash had known many such East End women over the years. Though usually it was because their husbands, exhausted from working long shifts in dock, factory or sweatshop, perhaps drunk from the escape of the pub, were too morose, bad tempered and dehumanised to bother to make any conversation with their wives and children.

Nash faded in and out of listening to the woman. He could not concentrate on everything she was spouting. When not listening, he glanced round the room of the slum, wondering how this couple had survived so well.

Elsie ended many of her sentences with a question.

"Didn't we Bert?"

But without seemingly drawing breath, or waiting for a nod in answer, she continued with her verbose diatribe.

Bert wheezed and clapped his hands with satisfaction when the fire took hold. He then got to his feet while Elsie disappeared outside to fill a bucket of water from a yard tap.

Nash took this as an opportunity to escape the clutches of the chair. With some difficulty he levered himself out of his captor, and offered it to the man of the house. Bert waved the offer away, but Nash stayed on his feet.

He tried to think of something to say that could be answered with a nod or a shake of the head.

"Good to see you both up and about. You both seem over the flu right enough."

Bert nodded. He took a step to a packing case that was the closest thing the house had to a table. On top of it, next to the tea cups which Elsie had already laid out in anticipation, was a battered old tobacco tin. He opened it and took out a shard of pencil and a scrap of paper. He licked the business end of the graphite, then scribbled something and handed it to Nash.

It said, 'I was up and about after 3 days. Else had it worse."

Nash remembered how badly the flu had struck down his fit, strong, normally healthy Ruby. And Elsie looked a good strong lass too. He was amazed a man with such weak lungs could not only survive it but actually recover quicker than others. Nash surmised that perhaps the poor little fellow had only had a cold. It was just coincidence it was at the same time as his wife had been laid low.

"Well you certainly seem more chipper than when I last saw you."

Bert nodded and started scribbling again.

This time he relayed how rationing had been a Godsend. Several inquiries from Nash and replied missives later, it was apparent that Bert's pension was way too low to be able to afford to cook and eat their full meat ration. But they bought their entire sixteen ounces of meat and five of bacon per person per week ration, and sold some of it off to more financially fortunate people. But they were able to keep some meat for themselves, and thanks to Nash's coal delivery would be eating meat tonight. Bert's final note told Nash that he now felt like a man again.

Nash nodded. He remembered how, when he was a lad and his family were barely keeping out of the workhouse, his father always got whatever meat they could afford, even when he was injured from a fall in the docks and out of work. Mother was the only one bringing in money and she needed to keep her strength up to do that, but it was father who got the meat. It had been, and Nash conceded still was, an important part of being a man.

The government had taken everything but his life from Bert, and then thrown him on the dust heap. But he had now recovered a modicum of self-respect. And he was grateful. If Ruby's desire to help people affected by the war had sewn seeds of doubt in Nash about his own role in the conflict, pathetic young Bert had dispelled those concerns.

"I might have a job for you," said Nash. "Only part time mind. Reckon you could make your way to Shoreditch and deliver messages for me as and when?"

Nash was becoming so busy he needed an errand boy to do trivial jobs. And since the Woolwich ferry incident he wanted to keep the level of contact he had with his objectors to a minimum just in case he was ever under surveillance. Why not use Bert and pay him for his time? He would get the No Conscription Fellowship to put their hands in their pockets to sponsor the arrangement. It was the least they could do. It would allow the poor young sod to keep a bit more of his meat ration for himself and his wife. And maybe gain a bit more self-respect into the bargain.

Chapter 20

"A sense of humour had kept me from any bitterness. I was quite as enthusiastically ready to work with and for the police as I had been prepared, if necessary, to enter into combat with them."

Mary Allen, ex-Suffragette and
British policewoman, memoir,
The Pioneer Policewoman

Deliverance from the grasping clutches of the flu had left Ruby more determined than ever to put something back. She ignored both her doctor and husband. As soon as the latter had not been around to keep her under control, she had got out of bed, washed and dressed. Her legs felt like jelly to begin with so she busied herself around the house for a while, holding on to a chair, kitchen table, sink or any other support, while she inadvertently did a mean impersonation of Charlie Chaplin's drunk routine. Once her legs started to behave themselves, she ventured out.

There was a bout of dizziness as she made her way along the street, which had her making a grab for a railing like someone trying to find their way home in a pea-souper fog. The virus was reminding her that it was not fully ready to leave her company just yet. But she managed to get along to Sylvia's house without too much risk to life and limb.

Sylvia was understanding. She appreciated that throughout her problems with the police force in the Suffragette years, it had only been following orders. If Ruby could introduce some feminine know how to the service, it had to be a good thing. And the fact that a woman could now become a police officer was all part of what the Votes for Women campaign had been fighting for. It was not just the principle of the vote that was important, it was the realities of what that tick in the box could bring. And this included wider employment opportunities for women. Sylvia wished her the very best of luck in her new position and, like Nashey, she rather hoped that having a police officer as a close ally might also provide some benefit on occasion.

Thankfully Ruby managed to arrive back home before her husband. She considered sneaking back under the bed covers, but given that she had already made up her mind to apply to become a police officer the following day, the sooner her husband appreciated that she was up and about the better.

Nash arrived home to find his wife sitting in the parlour while Maud was through in the kitchen making the tea. Ruby's friend had already been briefed. She was to do her bit.

"Ain't it fine to see Ruby up and about and doing so well Nashey?" Maud shouted over her shoulder.

"She ain't that up and about is she?" queried Nash. "I notice you're the one on your feet."

"It were my turn that's all. Ruby made the last cup."

Nash didn't answer, but gave his wife an old fashioned look to suggest he didn't believe a word of it.

"Good to see you're looking more like your old self Rubes," he said softly.

Ruby felt tired from her little excursion but she was not about to admit that to her husband. She took off her face mask and cast it aside with a flourish.

"I don't need this anymore. Give us a kiss," she ordered.

He was only too pleased to oblige but kept it to a peck given they were not alone. Maud duly arrived holding a teapot and a third cup for the man of the house.

"Shame her football career's over for my munitions team eh Nashey?" said Maud lightly. "Can't have lady coppers in the team pretending to be shells girls can we? At least I'll be able to replace her now I'm using flour and starch on me face to stop me looking yellow."

"Yeah, you're looking a lot better these days Maud," agreed Nash.

"Well, thank you kind sir," said Maud with accompanying mock bow. "Your fella's getting chivalrous in his old age Ruby."

"It's all them middle class gentleman he mixes with these days," said Ruby smirking.

Maud was the one person to know of Nash's conscientious objector work who did not know him from either his villainous or Suffragette days. She could be trusted. She had no love of a government that had treated both her and her husband as no more than cannon fodder. And living in the same house it would have been difficult to keep such work a secret from her in any case.

Nash had immediately noticed the saucy mood both women were in. Maud was obviously on a mission to have Ruby laugh for the first time in almost a week. It was good to see them both full of joy. He thought he would go along with it.

"I'm not too chivalrous to put the two of you over me knee if you should need it," he said mock seriously.

"Ooh, promises, promises," said Maud coquettishly.

"Oi, stop playing up to my husband you," said Ruby giggling. "Any way he prefers old firewomen, so your chances are slim."

"Is that right Nashey?" said Maud. "Take a shine to women in power do you? Or do you just like a woman with a helmet?"

The two women burst into full scale laughter.

Nash started to wonder whether he had made a mistake entering into banter with these two in the mood they were in. Although he had successfully dealt with the toughest of men over the years, he knew he could not cope with women once they lapsed into silly schoolgirl behaviour. He decided he would simply ignore the last few remarks. But he had assumed that Ruby had cried off from next Saturday's game because she appreciated the flu would have left her too weak to play.

"Never mind all that," he said, before addressing his wife. "Good to see you're being sensible about the football girl. No need to rush back to play."

His not rising to their bait simply had the women giggling even more. Excessive laughing when still in the process of recovering from the flu had Ruby coughing, excreting tears out from her eyes and dripping snot out of her nose. The latter, far from being embarrassing, simply had her and her ally giggling even more.

While Ruby pulled out a hankie from under her sleeve and blew her nose, Maud continued with the ribbing.

"She'll be too busy for football right enough. Still, you're in luck Nashey, Ruby'll have power and a helmet after tomorrow!"

More giggling from the women. Consternation from the man.

"What you on about?" he queried.

Once Ruby had pulled herself together she informed her husband that she was going to enrol at the police station the following day. Nash realised that it was not sheer chance that Maud happened to be downstairs having a cuppa at this time. His crafty wife had arranged it so she had some moral support at her shoulder when she told him the news.

Nevertheless, the chiding that she knew was coming, duly arrived. As far as her husband was concerned, Ruby was in no fit state to go anywhere tomorrow, let alone a police station.

Emboldened by Maud's presence, Ruby shot back that if he were that concerned about her being out of bed, he could cook the supper. She was both hungry and confident she could keep something down that was more solid than the fish she had managed thus far.

Being more hunter gatherer than chef, Nash popped back out and quickly returned with pies, mash and liquor. The sight of the latter, a disgusting green slime which passed for a form of parsley sauce in East London, had Ruby running for the kitchen sink. She wasn't going to make it to the outside toilet. When she returned, her husband made it clear that she was not going anywhere the following day.

How little the man knew his wife; he may as well have talked to the wall.

******

The ex-Suffragette walked into Bow police station feeling a little ill at ease. The last time she had passed through its doors, she had done so horizontal courtesy of a policeman dragging her by the hair. It had been six years earlier, after a riot when the police broke up a Suffragette rally in Victoria Park. Her uneasiness got worse after she saw the desk sergeant. She remembered him as the young constable whom she had rescued from the clutches of Mrs Arber.

Mrs Arber's husband was a printer. The printing press in the basement of his Roman Road shop, printed Sylvia's Dreadnought newspaper and all the East London Federation of Suffragette's leaflets. Mr Arber had to do this free of charge, much to his chagrin, because his wife, an ardent Sylvia supporter, said so. She was a big, intimidating woman and nobody argued with her, least of all her husband. And it was she who, during the Victoria Park altercation, had been holding a policeman below the surface of the Hertford Canal with a boat oar when Ruby had stepped in to save the young man.

Ruby wondered if he would remember her. She doubted it. The last time she had set eyes on him, he had been was far too busy kneeling on all fours coughing up water to notice the young woman who had knocked the oar away on his behalf.

He looked up as she approached the raised wooden desk above which he sat. Ruby was relieved to see there was not the slightest hint of recognition in his eyes.

She told him of her interest in becoming a police officer and expected him to warn her of the rigours involved, and follow this by having her fill out countless forms in what was bound to be the start of a long stream of red tape.

But the flu epidemic had left the police force seriously undermanned. Police officers appeared to have suffered from the outbreak more than most. And policemen had not been remunerated for the additional stresses in their work that the war had created. As a result there was low morale and growing unrest in the service. They were desperate for new recruits.

The sergeant supplied her with a form and while Ruby completed it asked her whether she'd had the flu. She thought she had hidden her wan complexion with a bit of subtle rouge shading, but obviously not.

She admitted that she had only just recovered from the virus. He looked at her with what appeared to be increased seriousness. She silently cursed herself. Perhaps he hadn't thought she looked ill. He might have just been asking her if she had *ever* had the flu. She should have pretended that she hadn't.

"Good. You're just the sort of girl we're looking for," said the sergeant with enthusiasm.

Ruby let out a breath of relief and relaxed somewhat while she listened to the policeman continue.

"If you've had it once, you won't have it again. Or

so our police doctors hope anyway. They reckon elderly people are not getting it because they have an immunity from the Russian flu epidemic that were here the best part of thirty year ago. So you should have immunity now see?"

It made perfect sense to Ruby. That was why Nashey hadn't caught it from her. She made a wager with herself that her husband was one of the 'elderly' who had previously suffered. She looked forward to asking him about it. She looked forward even more to calling him elderly.

Ruby lied about her age on her application form. That was standard practice. Everyone had done so when she had been on the ships, claiming to be older in the hope they would get a more senior, better paid position. But now she was passing herself off as younger. She was a young-looking thirty six but wondered whether there might be an upper age limit, in which case it might be thirty. It was pushing it a bit but she wrote twenty nine in the appropriate place. Given the scantiness of the information they needed about her, she was surprised there were also questions about one's father and husband. The former was easy. Deceased. She considered the latter a rather more difficult one to answer.

Goodness knew what the name Alexander Nash might bring up in police files. She followed the advice her husband had once given her that when lying you should keep the extent of the fib to a minimum so you were less likely to be caught out at a later time. She wrote down Alfred Nash, occupation: wood yard worker.

She hesitated about how much of her Suffragette experience she should tell them. They were bound to have her criminal record to hand, and Mrs Pankhurst was something of a hero with the government these days, so she decided to write down details of the work she had done for her which included going to prison for assault. She decided not to include her little known involvement in the Suffragette Derby, and also omitted her Suffragette work for Sylvia in Bow. This gap in her work experience was filled by saying she had returned to working on ocean liners for a time, before starting work at the local nursery. Edna had told her that they didn't check such things. Edna had originally assumed that it was because they didn't have the manpower to do the checks, but now having worked for the police, she had come to realise that they were simply too slapdash.

They may have been slapdash but they were also speedy. Only a few days later Ruby was called for interview. It was a perfunctory affair. She got the impression throughout that the job was already as good as hers. And her prison record was conveniently ignored by the two interviewers. At the end of the interview, the two men looked at each other, exchanged the briefest of nods to confirm they were satisfied, and she was promptly told her application had been successful and asked if she could start immediately. She confirmed that she could.

There followed a relatively short period of training during which time, amongst other things, she was shown how to put a restraining hold on someone. Her trainers had been amazed to see that their butter-wouldn't-melt new woman recruit, not only already knew the holds, but showed them a few others of her own. When her trainers had asked her the obvious question, she told them she had been brought up in a rough part of Southampton, down by the docks, and had learned the holds down there. The part about the location of her upbringing was true enough, but she had learned the grips from her ex-villain of a husband.

Having made a good impression throughout training, before she knew it she was picking out her uniform. When her husband saw her in the clothing for the first time he had to suppress the desire to smile. It was the most unflattering garb imaginable.

He had first met his wife on the Titanic, just minutes before it sank beneath the waves. Having thrown her into the last lifeboat to be launched, Nash later saved himself by swimming to an upturned lifeboat they had not had time to launch, and clambering on its hull. They had not then come across each other on board the rescue ship. The next time he had met Ruby, was well over a week later, when she was still in the uniform, an a la carte restaurant cashier's dress, in which she had left the ship. It had shrunk, was filthy, wrinkled and stained with salt. And her unwashed hair had been a mess too. But Nash still thought his wife had looked better then, than she did now in her crisp, clean, new police uniform.

There was a stiff shirt and tie, over which lay a jacket down to the hips, complete with four large pockets. A police whistle chain dangled out of the right breast before disappearing under a lapel. A thick belt did its best to show a waist, and there was WP insignia on each shoulder. A skirt appeared from beneath the jacket and descended to the ankles, where leather boots, shined to within an inch of their lives, took the eye. The whole thing was topped off with a glossy peaked cap and band, with a discreet WP police badge in the centre of it. And everything bar the white shirt was a sea of darkest Metropolitan Police blue.

Nash asked himself what was wrong with the clothing. The hat, shirt and tie were all right. The shiny boots were good. The skirt was plain and just hung limp, but what else would you expect? It was functional. It was the jacket that was the problem. It was just a mass of sagging wrinkles and creases. Nash had to admit that male police officers in uniform had a certain impressive look about them. The same could not be said of the new women recruits.

"I'm proud of you girl," he said and kissed her, before making the obvious joke that he never thought he would see the day when he would kiss a copper. He left it at that but his wife didn't.

"You should see the voluntary part-timers. They look even worse," she said before adding wryly with a raise of the eyebrow. "Mind you, I still look better than those little firewomen of yours."

Nash had not been very happily married for four years without knowing when to agree with this wife. A saucy smile was followed by a nod of agreement.

Chapter 21

"If the women in the factories stopped work for twenty minutes, the Allies would lose the war."

French Field Marshall Joffre

Granny Brown had lost a niece to the flu but the rest of her family had recovered. Although grieving, the old woman was back at work. Needs must. During the summer many of her clients preferred the free morning alarm of daylight and perhaps a cock crow to wake them, rather than pay for her services. So this was the last of her few calls to make this morning. Her pea-shooter and its ammunition were already in her mouth as she had taken up position beneath Maud Kemp's bedroom window. She crooked her neck up and let fire.

The short sharp piercing noise of hard pea on glass told Maud she owed Granny Brown a penny. It was five AM; time to rise, if not shine. Maud knew that if she tried to wake gradually she would simply fall back asleep. She shot to her feet, pulled back a filthy bit of curtain and put a hand up for the briefest moment as a thank you to her alarm, who turned and made her way out of the yard. Out of bleary minded habit she picked up her hat pin from the wooden crate that was her bedside table, to break the film of ice on her water jug. But even in this dark cold room, it was no longer necessary at this time of year. But it was still cold enough to have her throwing on her clothes in double quick time before running downstairs to the kitchen to spread some margarine over two slices of bread. She stuffed one in her mouth and left the other on the table while she popped back upstairs to wake her daughter.

Minutes later she was attempting the not inconsiderably difficult task of pushing a pram down the street while simultaneously attempting to ram a piece of bread into the mouth of a grumpy, crying toddler. And the little misery most certainly did not want to eat breakfast moments after being dragged out of bed and roughly dressed by a no-nonsense mother who had more important things to worry about than child psychology. It was not without a sense of relief, immediately followed by a mother's sense of guilt, that Maud left little Rose at the nursery, which had just opened its doors when she arrived. As she left she asked the nurse to make sure Rose finished the bread.

Maud took a dozen steps before stopping. She stood head down, staring at her shoes for a moment, hesitating. Then looked up at a nearby clock tower. It confirmed she just about had time. She walked back to the nursery and carefully took some creaking wooden steps which, care of some shrapnel from the last air raid, were a wonkily precarious route up to a side window. The Silvertown explosion almost eighteen months earlier had accounted for its glass, which had never been replaced. Now a bit of tarpaulin did a poor replacement job. But someone had had the bright idea of making a small hole in the material which enabled mothers to peer through the hole and check to see how their little ones were getting on, without the children being disturbed by seeing them. This was of particular benefit to local women who could pop by in their lunch break to check on their tots. Maud worked too far away to usually enjoy this luxury but now gazed down to see Rose sitting on what must have been a once beautiful rocking horse, which had had the stuffing literally knocked out of it. But the poor old thing was providing its jockey with a great sense of joy. Rose's tears had dried and she now giggled as she held the reins in one hand and a small sliver of bread and marge in the other. She urged Neddy to giddy up while her mother shed a little silent tear of her own.

A couple of minutes later Maud reluctantly began the three mile walk to the remote Abbey Creek munitions factory in which she worked.

She made sure that she was outside the factory gates a few minutes before her shift was due to begin. This gave her time to pop into a public lavatory to pluck out of her bag some leggings and rubber gloves, which she duly added to her uniform. And then out from a piece of cloth she pulled a flat, round, honed shard of glass, and just as she might have donned rouge before starting work behind a shop counter before the war, she now coated her face with flour and starch.

Her ghostly appearance was lessening the impact of the TNT. She felt better in herself. She smiled to herself when remembering that even Nashey had commented that she was looking better. And she had not had 'Chinkie' shouted at her by any young rascals for some time.

She and her fellow shell workers enjoyed a bit of friendly rivalry with the fuse girls to see who could come up with the most fashionable look. Rummaging in her bag produced some thin brightly coloured green ribbon, which she substituted for her existing government-issue shoe-laces. She and her shell girls wore green, the fuse girls yellow. The ribbon was more show than blow. It was not the most practical for the hurried three mile walk from home, hence the last minute change.

Then it was time to sort out her headgear. She was already wearing her munitions cap, which was a circular piece of material with a string round the edge like a pudding cloth. In her haste to get out on time she had plonked it roughly on her head before leaving the house. Now it was time to take out her hairpins and skilfully rearrange it. Royal Ascot, it was not, but great skill was used by all the women to make it appear that the authorities issued a dozen different types of headgear.

But fashion accessories could be withdrawn as well as added before starting work. Maud would not dream of appearing in public in her faded blue munitions uniform with the only decoration on it being a stencilled number on the back. It made her look like a prisoner. On leaving the factory at the end of a shift she would pin her shells workshop's flower emblem to her uniform, where it would stay until she had to unpin the posy before re-entering the factory the next day.

Maud was just attending to this task when she heard an explosion. It was not a large one but any explosion in a munitions factory was to be feared. She grabbed her things and ran out of the lavatory and through the factory gates to check her colleagues were all right. She quickly deposited her hairpins, posy and wedding ring with the security officers, some of whom were rushing to close the factory gates to ensure no prying eyes from the outside world could see what was going on.

Hundreds of women had just passed through the gates to start their shift. Waves of them in a sea of blue uniforms moved through the front courtyard. There was stunned confusion and inquiry in their faces; some voiced their concerns. But there was no crush or panic as they made their way to their workshops.

There was the smell of oil in the air. Slivers of what could have been anything were fluttering down. Maud trod on something soft, her foot skidding momentarily. It was a dead rat. Something that before the war would have had her screeching and rushing to the nearest stand pipe to wash any rat blood, real or merely perceived, off her shoes and trousers, now merited barely a response. She simply made a face. It was one of knowing acceptance. Even rats couldn't manage TNT.

She reached what had obviously been the building where the explosion had taken place. It was next to her own workshop. The building had a hole in the roof which was hardly surprising as workshops were built with weak roofs and strong walls so an explosion would go upwards but usually stay contained from spreading to other buildings. Women were standing outside, some coughing and spluttering. Others, unconscious or worse, were being dragged out. There did not seem to be any fire thank goodness but the water sprinklers didn't know that so were turning the place into a sodden mess. It reminded Maud of

186

a scene a couple of years earlier when a Zeppelin's bomb had hit a water main and turned a street into a torrent.

Maud recognised one of the women being attended to. Bea had a little one at Rose's nursery. Her husband was away in the army. She lived with her aged grandparents. She was on danger work because she had them to keep as well as a child. Although conscious she was badly dazed. Maud knelt down in a puddle by her side.

"It's Maud here Bea. You know, little Rose's mother. Don't worry girl, if the ambulance comes and takes you away and no one gets word to your grandma I'll pick up little Mabel for you at the end of me shift and drop off her at your place."

She wasn't sure the woman fully understood her but there was no time to repeat herself. She needed to clock in on time, otherwise she would lose wages. She made her way past the building to her own shop and was horrified by what was happening there. Or to be more precise, what was not.

Her colleagues were working away as if nothing had happened. The only thing out of the ordinary was that the male supervisors were standing over the women glowering at them. The deafening din of the machinery was such that the workforce working in total silence did not make any difference to the general sound of the place, but nevertheless you could clearly cut the tension with a knife. Maud suspected the supervisors had just laid down the law, telling their staff to get on with their work. She thought it reminiscent of what a Victorian sweatshop must have been like.

Along with scores of colleagues, she punched in

her attendance card, walked over to stand meekly at her machine and started work, head down. She exchanged the odd look, frown and use of eyebrows with a colleague when the supervisor's back was turned, but not a word was spoken. When women had to speak to each other as part of their work, they did so formally.

Maud got on with her work on what was nicknamed a 'monkey machine', because it had long arms with which to compress gunpowder into shells to get a greater payload of explosive into them. It was boring, laborious, dangerous work. A few hours passed before a supervisor called her into the office. Her hands were black with the warm thick oozing of her machine so she gave them a quick once over with some grease remover and a rag before following the man to the office.

She was offered a transfer from shells to fuses. To get away from the danger inherent in her present duties was certainly attractive. And there would be less contact with TNT. But she could not afford to give up the tuppence per hour extra wages she received for danger work. She explained this but the supervisor reassured her that she would retain her present pay level because the work she was going to be doing was categorised as danger work. So she agreed to the transfer.

Minutes later she was shown in to the very shop where the explosion had taken place. Women were working as usual with the walls around them splattered in blood. Four women had been killed and many others injured. This was why she had been offered the transfer. To walk into dead women's shoes. It was danger work all right

Chapter 22

"A soldier was so disordered while he was going down the stairs into the London tube ...mistaking the hollow space below for the trenches and the ascending crowd for Germans, fixed his bayonet and charged. But for the woman constable on duty... who was quick enough to divine the trouble and hang on to him...he would have wounded many."

Mary Allen, ex-British policewoman,
memoir, The Pioneer Policewoman

Given that her home address was in Bow, Ruby was allotted Aldgate as her patch. It was sufficiently distant so that she was unlikely to come across anyone she knew, but nevertheless only a tram ride away so an easy commute.

Ruby's first week on the job had her and another new recruit learning the ropes from an experienced woman officer who had joined the force three years earlier soon after women were first admitted to the service. It turned out that she too had been a Suffragette who had been to prison. It was a small world.

During this week Ruby impressed with her worldliness. New recruits usually suffered from being too naïve but that was not the case with Ruby. Having an ex-villain as a husband had certainly given her a head start.

She remembered him once telling her how he had used police rules to avoid Bobbies on the beat during his villainous years. Each policeman had a set beat of four streets, around which they were expected to walk round at exactly one and a half miles an hour, so they passed the same spot every twenty minutes. That way everyone always knew where to find a policeman. And of course it meant characters like Nashey always knew when and where to avoid coming across a copper. It was the shirker police officer who had always been his potential nemesis. The policeman who shirked off to have a crafty drag of his pipe, sitting down to rest his 'plates of meat' on a bench hidden in a dark spot somewhere. Then just when Nashey had been in the process of relieving some wretch of their valuables, a uniform could appear out of nowhere. He had been chased through Whitechapel on several occasions when this had happened. It was the main reason he had always kept himself so fit.

Ruby told her senior officer the gist of this story, though of course altered the narrator of it to being a friend of her father's. It made the woman smile. The two women then exchanged many a Suffragette anecdote from when they had both been on the wrong side of the law.

The following week the powers that be decided Ruby was ready to start as a patrol leader, in charge of part-time voluntary patrols. She was to be the link between these women and all authorities, civil and military, and direct the energies of these subordinates. Each patrol had the brief to befriend women they came across on the streets, warning them against unladylike, lewd behaviour. These patrols were to be at night, when the prostitution problem was at its worst. But being volunteers, members of the patrols could only administer such parts of the law that were the right of any private person to enforce, namely to make citizens' arrests. Only Ruby had the power to make any formal police arrest that may be necessary.

Aldgate, being close to the docks, and one of the places where the poor East End abutted the wealthy City of London, had, like the rest of Whitechapel, a long history of prostitution. It was a stone's throw from where Jack the Ripper had roamed only thirty years earlier. Ruby and her women were going to have their work cut out to keep things under control in the government's fight against the spread of VD.

This section of Whitechapel had been part of Nash's old hunting ground, and he had been able to give his wife some useful tips about the area. She deployed one of her groups around St Botolph's Without Church in Aldgate High Street, a renowned pick-up spot. Another group patrolled the dark Gower's Walk warehouse area just north of the Tower of London barracks.

Ruby and her patrols had a good week. They successfully curbed both professional prostitutes and young women who had become known as 'amateurs', for offering themselves for free to soldiers out of a sense of patriotic duty. The patrols were particularly successful in sending young soldiers on their way. In much the same way as the lads outside Selfridge's had responded favourably to a woman telling them the error of their ways, squaddies tended to accept what policewomen said to them in a situation in which a male police officer would have found himself embroiled in a punch-up. But Ruby and her colleagues were not so naïve as to think that these young men were not finding their pleasure up against a wall around the corner. So if she came across women who were amenable, Ruby would take the opportunity to hand out government leaflets giving advice about using sheath contraception. But amateurs were generally difficult to cope with.

Ruby's first arrest was of an amateur prostitute, who unlike the local poverty stricken professional wretches, had obviously had a decent meal as well as more unsavoury things inside her recently. She was strong and fought like a man. There was none of the usual hair pulling and scratching. This was real violence. She had already laid out one of Ruby's volunteers, and was about to put the boot in to another, when Ruby shouted at her to stop. The woman threw a punch her way but Ruby blocked it with an arm, then back-handed her truncheon so the tip of it smacked into the woman's throat. This was Nashey training. The woman collapsed gurgling, to her knees. Ruby picked her up. Police training said to put her in an arm lock but again she preferred to follow the teachings of her husband. She took the woman by the hand in what might have appeared from a distance to be a friendly gesture, but closer inspection would have seen her pressing a thumb hard into the webbing between the woman's left thumb and forefinger. It was painful for the recipient. She then heard herself repeating something that had been said to her in the past by many a policeman.

"Are you going to come quietly miss?"

The woman grimaced and nodded so Ruby released

her painful grip and simply held the woman by the wrist while she marched her to Leman Street police station.

Sergeant Granger at Leman Street was impressed. Though only grudgingly so. He thought this new WPC was rather too good to be true. Believing that 'leopards didn't change their spots' he would keep an eye on this ex-Suffragette troublemaker.

Chapter 23

"We want to have our husbands and sons back from the war and we don't want to starve anymore."

> Group of German soldiers' wives'
> letter to the Hamburg Senate.

Prisoners' Aid Society packages from England, and loaves from Switzerland arrived in Germany weekly. And the German authorities passed on the provisions to POWs with scrupulous efficiency. The local government official who accompanied the food to Klaus' farm considered it outrageous that British POWs were being fed better than many German people. The same man also kept the local farm's output statistics, and when he had first queried the farm's poor performance, the owner had simply shrugged his shoulders and told him the British were a lazy race compared to the great German farm hand at the best of times, and in captivity they barely worked at all.

He was telling the man exactly what he had always suspected. Consequently the official would unceremoniously dump the prisoners' packages off the back of a truck shouting 'schweinhund' at the lazy enemy as they gathered round him.

But once the farmyard dust from the departing food truck's wheels had settled, an air of reciprocity came over the farm. Tommies didn't care for the dark dry German bread that Klaus fed them as part of their official ration, so gave some of it to their guards in return for being allowed to forage on the farm for nettles and dandelions, which they boiled up to make soup. The remainder of the bread, which was at least filling, was thrown in to the soup as the heaviest of croutons. The arrangement also included that any old cabbages the Englishmen found were to be handed over to their hungry German counterparts. Klaus also had a deal going on with his captives. They were allowed to collect as many snails as they liked, which they cooked in their shell and ate like hot winkles. In return they passed on to the farmer as many acorns or chestnuts as they could find. The government were keen for people to collect these for use in ersatz foods, and Klaus was eager to provide as much of these as he could to keep the local official, who was becoming increasingly frustrated by the farm's poor output, at least partly happy.

Klaus also managed to keep the official off his back somewhat by feeding him an embroidered version of the truth about his business plans. With his farm doing so badly he was thinking of converting it into a factory for turning animal bones into gelatin for camera companies. As a farmer barely scraping a living, he had no working capital with which to do this, but a wealthy business associate would provide the funds. It was only the present flu epidemic which had delayed things. Once that had run its course, he and his business partner would be ready to proceed.

The official was aghast. One of the farms under his

watch providing such poor production statistics was one thing, but having the figures reduce to zero was quite another. His bosses would want to know why he hadn't been more proactive in helping the farmer. The POWs and the injured soldiers guarding them would need to be reassigned too. The official could see an administrative headache coming on. He promised Klaus he would look into providing him with more men to increase production. And given the way the war was going, they were more likely to be German than English.

******

Ursula climbed on board the back of the horse-drawn wagon and sat down in the only free space available on the crowded vehicle. There was a large urn on board and her two work colleagues were already in situ, their feet resting on a couple of the many large sacks of potatoes that took up much of the room. The driver was motioned to make a start. A crack of a whip and what sounded like a gypsy's guttural curse had the horse move off. Ursula greeted her friends in the usual way which included an oft used wartime motto that had become a casual form of address in Germany.

"Good morning Marita. Good morning Eartha. May God punish England."

Her colleagues responded similarly.

Their conveyance left the pleasant leafy area of Mitte and headed for a poorer part of Berlin. It could have struck out in any direction to achieve this, but on this occasion it was going to head towards the East End. But first it headed south towards what was to be its first stop, outside the Stettiner railway terminus.

Marita immediately set to work with the women's pride and joy, a-state-of-the-art electric potato-parer. Eartha got on with chopping while Ursula completed the assembly line by dropping the potatoes into the huge urn of boiling water.

The horse made slow progress carrying such a heavy load, which worked perfectly, giving the women time to get ready for what was sure to be a busy day.

Before the war communal soup kitchens were run by the Charitable Society for People's Coffee Halls, but this had now been expanded into the nationalised People's Dining Halls. Ursula was now in charge of this mobile version of one. She would be selling a quart of soup for forty pfennings and the clip of a ration card.

On arrival at the station, the three women shouted the colloquial name for their soup kitchen to announce their arrival.

"Gulasch kanone!" "Gulasch kanone!" "Gulasch kanone!"

That was enough. They were quickly surrounded. Women and children held up a tin or dish in one hand, forty pfennigs and their ration card in the other. Marita took their money and passed the ration card to Eartha to punch it. Ursula's long handled pale, now changed jobs from stirrer to ladle. She hauled it up and slopped its contents into the first dish of the day.

******

Even when he had first fallen into her arms in the marketplace and she had been the cool, professional nurse with him, there had been a frisson of chemistry between Dorothea and her patient. And once Peter had started to recover and his nurse had relaxed her guard with him, they had got on like a house on fire. She had even stopped wearing a face mask in his presence after a while. And one thing had led to another.

The first time they had kissed, the first words uttered while they were still in their embrace had been Dorothea telling Peter that, "I really like you."

Had it been spoken by one teenager to another after they had unlocked from their first hesitant grappling, it would have sounded gauche. But coming from an apparently sophisticated woman of the world, it appeared to carry a certain profoundness. Dorothea was telling the new man in her life that as far as she was concerned this was not the start of a mere wartime flirtation between two lost people. And he had agreed.

But there was one thing standing in the way of their relationship growing any further. The war. Or rather, how they disagreed about the relevance of the conflict. As far as Peter was concerned, it was the war that had brought them together, just as it had many lovers, and they should simply enjoy each other and see where things took them. They should ignore the war when it came to their romance.

Dorothea disagreed. The war was so all encompassing, it could not be ignored. He was a soldier. He could be dead next week. She could not bear to invest so much romantic capital in someone only to be made bankrupt a week later. It was not better to have loved and lost as far as she was concerned. And she was a nurse. If she became a nurse within the DRK, the German Red Cross, which someone with her skills ought to, she too could be dead in a week. Of the flu. She had heard through the nursing grapevine that huge numbers of soldiers were dying of a new, more virulent form of the disease, and presumably many nurses were as well. They agreed to disagree and waited to see what the future had in store for them.

Grenadier Fueschel's nurse had written to the army again, informing them that her patient had no sooner recovered from the blow to his head than he had contracted the flu. But the soldier always dressed in his uniform and kept his bags packed by the front door so should an army medic, or worse still a couple of military policeman, come calling, he would claim that he had finally returned to good health and was just about to report back to the Front. And there were his bags to prove it. The army were so desperate for men they might even choose to believe him. Or maybe they wouldn't. He was to all intents and purposes absent without leave, a deserter, hoping the war would end before it ended him.

He spent his days working from Dorothea's home, doing administrative work for her suffrage society. But cognisant of the fact that Peter could not simply do this all day, every day, waiting for the war to end, Dorothea needed to find him something more physical and manly to do. And she had. Her friend Ursula would not wish to admit it, but her mobile soup kitchen had become a fairly awful affair, feeding little more than slops to desperate people. But from the moment he had recovered enough to stand next to a boiling stove, Peter had impressed with his cooking skills, so Dorothea had decided he could help Ursula, hopefully turning her operation into something more akin to a military field kitchen.

And for his part, Peter thought he would rather be doing something useful, which gave him some sense of self-esteem, if and when the military police came calling, than be found simply cowering in his nurse girlfriend's house.

Chapter 24

"Dear mother, I'm in the trenches and I was ill so I went out, and they took me to the prison and I'm in a bit of trouble now."

Aby Bevistein, British boy soldier suffering
from shock, executed for desertion

Freddie Barber was fourteen years old when he lied about his age in order to get into the British Army. But after two weeks in France his young mind was already in a bad way. He told the authorities what he had done, and that he wanted to return home, but sympathy and understanding were in short supply. He was a soldier in the British army now.

The following day he was hit in the head by a piece of shrapnel. It knocked him unconscious and there was a fair amount of blood, but the wound looked worse than it was. He could have been up and fighting again sooner rather than later.

He was lying on the ground outside a tented casualty clearing station, a huge influx of gassed men having taken all the stretchers. A hopelessly overworked triage doctor worked his way through the copper coloured gassed men, their eyes swollen, bloodshot and streaming, a horrible discharge coming from noses and mouths, their breathing like that of bronchitis patients. When he arrived at Freddie, the doctor gave him only the most cursory of glances.

Head wound. Attention needed quickly.

He scribbled on a hospital admission card 'dangerously wounded' and 'head'. An ambulance was soon whisking Freddie away over shelled, pot-holed, dirt roads to a mobile centre for urgent surgical care. A doctor there took one look at Freddie's wounds and sighed. It wasn't his triage colleague's fault. How could any doctor make a proper diagnosis in such terrible conditions?

It would be a waste of the surgeon's precious time to treat him, so he was about to send the superficially injured, but temporarily 'unfit' man to general hospital 3 up the road, when he happened to look at his patient's face. He was not a man. Not even a lad. This was a boy. He stood and stared at the face. And then decided on a course of action.

Those badly injured but fit enough to travel were being shipped back to England. The doctor gave the boy an injection to bring him back to consciousness. While he waited for his patient to come round, he washed and dressed the head wound, then completed a postoperative recovery form that would have this soldier returning to Britain. He knew the hospital in England would give the boy a clean bill of health to return to France soon enough, but he hoped that once home, his parents or guardians would be able to get him discharged on grounds of age.

The doctor wrote 'ICT' on the form. Inflammation of Connective Tissue was an umbrella term that covered a wide range of conditions affecting the skin such as poisoned sores, tears from barbed wire or gangrene. The boy did not have any such condition, but the doctor wanted his patient to appear to be suffering from more than a mere bang on the head. He also wrote on the form 'childish'. It was a vague term that implied the patient was suffering from mild shell shock. If the boy turned out to be a lively sort, it would explain why such an apparently badly injured patient was so chipper. The doctor pondered the irony. To get a child home to his mother he was being termed childish.

As soon as the boy flickered into life, the doctor saw the fear and horror appear in his eyes like the illumination of a couple of gas mantles. It confirmed what the doctor had already assumed. This boy had seen enough. The doctor told his patient that he was to be put on an ambulance train to Le Treport, from where convalescents were being sent home to Blighty.

"You've had a nasty hit to the head. You will feel dizzy and generally bad for a while but that's all right," assured the doctor matter-of-factly. "You should stay on your feet. Best to be walking wounded otherwise you will find yourself back at a field hospital. Stay on your feet and you are going home. Lie down and you will not. This war may be coming to an end. Get home and stay home. Do I make myself clear young man?" barked the doctor brusquely.

The boy gazed up at the doctor, initially uncomprehending. Then his head cleared and he nodded. He immediately wished he hadn't, as seemingly a ton weight appeared to slip from inside one side of his head to the other. He winced.

"That'll teach you," said the doctor knowingly. "Now keep your head down in more ways than one."

******

Sergeant Granger explained to WPC Nash that her duties were being changed. There had been heavy casualties suffered in France during the German Spring Offensive. As a result there had been convoys of ambulances running throughout the day from Charing Cross station to the London Hospital Whitechapel. But they were not something the government wished the general public to see, so now the Germans were being pushed back and the volume of Allied casualties, though still heavy, had lessened, it was decided the ambulances could now be run safely at night. And it was thought that Ruby and her group of volunteers could be better deployed by keeping an eye on these convoys to ensure they ran smoothly.

There was no increase in rank or wages, but this was certainly extra responsibility on her shoulders and Sergeant Granger had informed her that it was a show of the high regard in which she was kept by their superiors. Her hard work helping to curb prostitution and its attendant problems had been much appreciated.

Ruby didn't believe that for a second. On the contrary, her sergeant was always rather off-hand with her, and she got the impression that she and her fellow copperettes were just a necessary evil as far as the police force was concerned. Especially now the air-raids had stopped and huge food queues were a thing of the past. Special constables could now be switched to dealing with juvenile delinquency, and Gorgeous Wrecks could keep prostitution in check. It was only the shortages of police manpower caused by the flu epidemic that was keeping her in a job.

No doubt this ambulance work would simply be 'women's work', liaising with nurses and chatting to the soldiers to keep their spirits up. She was disgusted by the cynicism behind her new duty. The government thinks it's acceptable to have such huge numbers of casualties just so long as the public aren't aware of it. Don't speed the ambulances to the hospital in daylight when you can wait for the cloak of nightfall.

This was not why she had joined the police service. She had joined to help women. To help the Home Front. And that didn't mean keeping everyone as ignorant as possible of what was going on in the trenches.

But she kept these feelings to herself. For one thing she knew she would get short shrift from her husband if she moaned. He would no doubt remind her that she had made her bed so she would have to lie on it. She accepted the new role in apparent good faith.

******

To keep the discomfort of the injured soldiers to a minimum, and because the semi-blackout made night travel by motor vehicle potentially hazardous, the ambulances trundled slowly through the streets of London. Most of the vehicles had open backs which allowed people to run behind them chatting to the less seriously wounded, while often plying them with chocolate, cigarettes and other goodies. The authorities had mixed emotions about this. They liked the idea of the men being comforted, and to stop good Samaritans from doing the decent thing would be a bad show. But the whole point of running these convoys at night was to keep the public ignorant of the appalling scale of the number of casualties, and the less the soldiers could tell the populous about their experiences the better.

Not that WPC Nash was informed of this. It was made clear to her that female police officers and their volunteers were to act as kindly overseers. Women were ideal for this sort of duty. Ruby was told that the injured men were not just in pain but terribly tired and must not be overtaxed by the public asking them any questions. Well-wishers could hand over chocolate and such, tell the men they were proud of them, wish them good luck, that sort of thing, but that was all. People running along the road at night, in the black-out, not watching where they were going, was obviously a public safety concern. And the last thing anyone needed right now was more people heading to the hospital, so WPC Nash's group were to ensure nobody ran behind the ambulance for more than a few seconds at a time.

Over the past four years Ruby, and everybody else for that matter, had seen more and more badly injured men come home from the war. Men hobbled about the streets on one leg and crutches; the no-legged pushed themselves about in wheelchairs; blind men sat about on the bench where someone had left them; and worst of all were the staring men with goodness knows what was wrong with them. Nash had also told her of some of the horror sights he had seen outside Queen Mary's Hospital. Bandages only hid so much. But now, not just seeing the soldiers in the back of the ambulances in their unpatched up state but hearing their groans of pain and despair, with the blood and dried mud of the battlefield still on them, was quite a shock.

The ambulances had a driver and a nurse sitting side by side in the open front section, with a thick enclosed dark green canvas behind, both sides of which had red crosses emblazoned on white circles. The vehicles were packed with injured men.

Ruby saw men laying in two tiers, with a single nurse sitting on a little stool amongst them, doing her best to tend to them all. The bloodiest men, with blood seeping from under their dressings, were on the bottom racks to prevent them dripping on to other men. But the worst were the ambulances that stank of gas. Gassed men had the smell of gas clinging to their woollen uniforms, greatcoats and the blankets they had been given at the aid posts in France.

There was also an unmarked grey ambulance, with its canvas fully down at the back so nobody could see in or out. Ruby had been told that on no account was this vehicle to be approached by anyone. The public or even police officers for that matter. This vehicle had the mental cases in it.

And although Sergeant Granger had used the word 'convoy' when telling Ruby what she and her group were to oversee, she had not expected the word to be quite so accurate. It really was a convoy of ambulances, one after the other, almost nose to tail. People running in between the vehicles was certainly hazardous.

Ruby's group would spread out from Aldgate to the London Hospital Whitechapel, with each of them patrolling a section of main road along the route. This left each woman on her own, with no other officer within several hundred yards, which was not ideal, but it couldn't be helped.

Ruby took the first section, outside St Botolph's Without Church through to Gardiner's Corner, from where one of her volunteers would oversee the section around Aldgate East underground station. Ruby had chosen the busiest area, which included many pubs, so it would no doubt be the most difficult to control.

Within minutes of the first ambulance appearing, as if on cue three men staggered out of a pub, saw the red crosses and immediately weaved unsteadily towards them. None had a bar of chocolate or anything else useful to hand. Nor did they retain the coordination to quickly roll up a cigarette. After a few drunken shouts of 'good ol' Tommies', 'God bless you boys', and phrases to that effect, the men changed tack.

"Here are boys have a fag on me," said one, before haphazardly throwing his tobacco tin into the back of an ambulance.

At this point another of the well-wishers lost his attempted grip on the back of the vehicle and face planted on to the cobbles with a terrible splat. The third man pulled out a handful of coins from a trouser pocket and was about to shower the injured men when Ruby's truncheon made contact with his wrist.

There followed the unedifying spectacle of slum dwellers coming out of the shadows to search for coins that had now been liberally scattered over the road. The next ambulance had to pull to a halt to avoid running down these people and the man who had splattered himself on the road. Ruby had to drag the latter out of the way and left him lying in the gutter. His nose was a bloody mess but he received little sympathy.

Ruby cleared the road with a few shouts and threats, then apologised to the second ambulance's driver and waved him on with a knowing nod of contrition. She gave the other two drunks a good talking to before venturing over to the pub with a view to informing the landlord of what had just happened and to make it clear she expected him to ensure it did not happen again. But before she could get a word out she was met with a loud chorus of sarcastic cheers and lewd comments about lady coppers from the lively clientele. But this was water off a duck's back to an ex-Suffragette.

"Never mind all that!" she shouted over the din. "Our injured boys from the Front are in those ambulances. Now bloody well show some respect or I'll nick the lot of you!"

The logistics of how, in reality, a single police officer, male or female, would be able to arrest a whole pubful of alcohol-infused rowdies without any back-up was neither here nor there. The little speech had the desired effect. As one, the men, mostly in the autumn of their three score years and ten, shut up immediately and lowered their eyes. Ruby walked out of the pub to the sound of her own footsteps on the wooden floor.

She took up position again outside the church and fumed silently to herself. Christ, it was going to be a long night.

But things settled down thereafter. Copious amounts of cigarettes, chocolates and anything else the public deemed a nice little tonic for a wounded Tommy, were handed into ambulances by eager, respectful fans. Short snatches of conversation were made with a soldier or two, before Ruby would intervene by saying that was enough and to let the men have some rest.

Throughout the night Ruby exchanged short snatches of information with her nearest volunteer, Patricia, outside Aldgate East tube station, and it appeared that things had gone smoothly enough in that section. Most of the people Patricia dealt with, appeared out of the Brick Lane slum area of Spitalfields. They were either too poverty stricken to offer the soldiers much, or simply too weak to run behind an ambulance for much of a distance.

When the final ambulance of the evening left Ruby's section she followed it towards the London Hospital, receiving a report from each of her group along the route before sending them home with a thank you for their efforts. She packed off her final volunteer at the New Road junction and headed for the hospital entrance to hand over to the male police officers in situ there. Despite the early hour, a fifty strong crowd had gathered outside the ambulance entrance, and were being controlled by a sergeant and a couple of constables. It was an easy duty. The crowd stood in quiet, orderly, respectful fashion.

The first light of a summer dawn was peeping out from below the horizon, allowing Ruby to make out silhouettes. Costermongers were starting to set out their stalls for the roadside market outside the hospital. She craned her neck to peer at a huge white canvas sheet flapping high above the main road care of a line running from the second floor of the hospital across to the roof of the Grave Maurice pub. In the improving light she could just about discern two of the four words written in bold black lettering. 'Quiet Wounded'. That explained why the costermongers were putting out their wares in such gingerly fashion, without the cacophony of clattering and ribald East End language that would normally accompany such a scene.

A queue of ambulances were waiting to turn right off the main road into the hospital grounds. A figure suddenly jumped out of the back of one. The ambulances were quite low to the ground. In normal circumstances it would have been an easy leap to make without falling, but the man had probably been lying prostrate in various transport vehicles since leaving the trenches. As he landed, his legs gave way under him.

The vehicle had hidden the man from the crowd and policemen outside the hospital. The costermongers were too busy to notice. The other men in the ambulance were probably either asleep or simply beyond caring about, or reacting to, someone leaping out of their vehicle. Ruby was the only person to take notice.

"Oi! What's your game?!" she shouted, from thirty yards away.

The man stared in the direction of the shout as he scrambled to his feet, slipping in his panic on the worn cobbles of a busy thoroughfare. Out of the murk he could see a policewoman closing in on him. He started to run. He deftly hopped between two costermonger stalls, and headed down the pavement back towards Spitalfields.

Ruby gave chase. For a moment she considered

blowing her police whistle but on second thoughts did not think it appropriate. Goodness knows what hearing a whistle might do to the poor wretch she was chasing. She had heard that in the trenches a whistle blown by your officer in charge was the last thing you heard before you went over the top. And besides it was not as if she was chasing a criminal. Just some poor chap who was probably suffering from shell shock or had perhaps just seen one hospital too many for his liking.

A foot race began. The noise of rumbling ambulances was quickly replaced with the eerie silence that a great city in the early hours can transmit. The echoing footsteps and panting of the two parties involved added a surreal touch to the scene.

The man was only a little fellow but quick on his feet. He was gradually pulling away from his pursuer along the Whitechapel High Road. Fearful that her recent bout of flu may have left her short of fitness, Ruby held something back and hoped that an injured soldier weakened from a spell in the trenches might run out of puff before she did.

The tactic appeared to be working when her target suddenly stopped to gulp air while he looked about him, hesitating as to what to do next. As Ruby closed in, he dived to his right down the poorly lit Vallance Road in a bid to shake her off.

Nash had recently walked Ruby around Whitechapel to ensure she knew all the courts and alleys of the area. Not the ones she was shown during her police training, but the dark hidden ones where strangers feared to tread. Not that he believed that such knowledge might help her catch criminals or anybody else for that matter. More, it was to ensure she did not end up in such dangerous places by mistake.

And now Nash's guided tour was proving useful. She knew that if the next time the soldier changed direction he headed west towards Spitalfields via the likes of Hanbury Street, she dared not follow him. A policewoman in such an area in the early hours would be asking for trouble.

And sure enough, the darkness of the alleys to his left dragged the man towards them like a black hole pulling him in. He stopped and grabbed another momentary breather before making a ninety degree turn towards the netherworld. Ruby, on the other hand, put on a spurt as she ran across the road at an angle without breaking stride. She cut him off just as he was about to enter an alley. The two of them collided, knocking the soldier off balance. He pitched forward next to the alley wall. Before he had time to recover, Ruby was pushing him against it.

"Behave yourself Tommy!" she said.

The soldier swung an elbow back at her, which she blocked with an arm. Ruby did not want to hurt the poor injured fellow unduly but she had to protect herself so grabbed one of his arms and yanked it behind his shoulder. She was surprised how easily she had blocked the attempted blow and got the man's arm up his back. If she could overpower a trained soldier this comfortably it just showed how weak these men were.

"Pack it in!" she shouted in his ear. "There's no need for this. I'm only trying to help you!"

But the soldier had clearly had enough of following orders. He executed a backward head butt which caught Ruby on her breast bones, causing her to lurch forward, her chin making contact with the top of his head, this in turn causing her to bite her tongue. The ensuing pain from the triple whammy had her lose her temper. She used a Nashey-trained technique, sweeping her right leg as hard as she could against her assailant's right ankle. A moment later he was lying face down on the cobbles, with Ruby having fallen on top of him.

It was only then she realised how slight of build this soldier was. He was quite a bit shorter than her, hence why it had been her breast bones that had taken the force of his blow.

He had stopped struggling. Was he feigning, hoping to take her by surprise again? Or had she knocked him out? No, she could feel him moving very slightly and he was making a barely audible noise. Christ, she thought, he hasn't swallowed his tongue as he?

She got off him, jumped to her feet, and took a step round to look at his face. It was difficult to see clearly in the gloom.

Was he crying?

She suspected it could be a trick so stepped behind the prone figure, then gingerly put the toe of her policewoman's sturdy footwear under his midriff and as gently as she could levered him over so he lay on his back.

A boy, barely a teenager, lay there sobbing. And there was something about the scared, pathetic expression on his face that made Ruby think that he wasn't crying with the pain of any injury she had just inflicted upon him.

The German Spring Offensive had caused the government to reduce the conscription age to seventeen and a half but this lad was far younger than that.

"How old are you son?" enquired Ruby.

She helped the boy up as she considered what she had just said.

Son! Blimey I'm getting old.

"For'een," the boy snivelled, cuffing a wet nose, while he looked down avoiding his inquisitor's gaze.

The glottal stop told her the boy had a strong London accent not dissimilar to her husband's. Perhaps he was not so far from home.

"Lied about your age to fight eh? Got yourself hurt and now you want to make a run for it off home?" asked Ruby.

She was eager for him to know he had a sympathetic copperette in front of him, so she was quick to add more.

"Don't blame you lad. I'd have done the same. Well done to you I say."

The boy looked up at her frowning. She didn't sound like a police officer to him.

"It weren't like I thought," he said.

"No. Daresay it weren't," agreed Ruby knowingly.

"I didn't..."

"No, nobody did, did they boy?" cut in Ruby to save the lad choking up any further.

******

Ruby was not looking forward to having to explain herself to her husband. She had never been on the end of his temper, but she had seen him dish out some fair old East End bile on many a man over the years. And she thought the time had come for her to receive not so much a flea, more a giant spider, in her ear.

She was about to bring an injured runaway soldier in to the house with a view to asking Nashey to squirrel him away amongst his objectors. But the army would no doubt be far more diligent in tracking down a suspected deserter than they were chasing after troublesome conscience objectors. And if the boy was caught, even though he would have the perfectly valid excuse of being a mere child, who knew what the authorities might do to him? And even if his age turned out to afford him some protection from the full wrath of the army, the same could not be said of the man & wife team who had aided and abetted him. In fact, any leniency the government were forced to show the boy, might have them looking to punish his partners in crime even more heavily than usual. An example always had to be made in such cases to keep the cannon fodder in line. She could also have put Nashey's whole objector operation, and the men in it, in danger.

And of course, there was the not inconsiderable little matter of her being a law-flouting police officer. The authorities would, with some justification, assume her becoming a policewoman had been done purely to assist her husband help men escape their duties. It was difficult to know which one of Mr & Mrs Nash would have the biggest book thrown at them. She could see keys to prison cells in Holloway and Brixton being thrown away.

******

Ruby had taken a circuitous route home, diving down every alleyway between Whitechapel and Bow that her husband had ever shown her, plus many others. The tour through some of the less salubrious parts of Stepney and Mile End was to ensure the boy got disorientated so that if he ever fell back into the hands of the authorities and was asked where he had been taken after his escape, he would not be able to help them. This might at least buy her and Nashey a bit of time to make a run for it.

Ruby motioned for the boy to follow her round to the alley at the back of her house. She was concerned that Granny Brown might still be doing her rounds, or some of her clients might be starting to venture out, so she was relieved to see the coast was clear. She and the boy walked quickly down the alley, across her yard and in through the back door of the house.

Cognisant of Nashey not being at his best first thing in the morning, Ruby had already explained to the boy that her husband was asleep in bed, so they had to be as quiet as church mice. The longer the young soldier's presence was unknown to the man of the house, the better. Ruby whispered to the boy to sit down and make himself at home. His glance towards what was her husband's armchair, had Ruby shaking her head and pointing towards her own chair. He did as he was told.

Ruby had made a point of not asking the boy his name when she had first tackled him. She didn't want him to think he was having his name taken by the long arm of the law. But now it was time. She crouched and quietly asked the question.

"Freddie, Freddie Barber."

"All right Freddie, you have a kip now. You didn't get much sleep on the way over from France I'll wager. Keep your boots on mind."

No explanation was offered as to the reason for this command. The fact was that she didn't want to hurt his feelings. He stank to high heaven, and she thought that if his feet were unfettered, the smell would no doubt increase.

"Don't snore do you?" she added mock seriously.

"No, no officer. I don't straight!" assured Freddie.

"That's all right then. We don't want to be waking up his nibs before time. He might have been up half the night. He often does night work. And before you ask, don't. Get me?"

Ruby winked. She had never winked in her life before she met Nash, but now it was a regular occurrence. The boy nodded so she continued.

"I'll know when he's stirring. He starts the day with a good cough. I'll then take him through some tea and breakfast in bed. He'll know something's up right enough. I've *never* taken him breakfast in bed!"

The boy smiled for the first time since she had collared him. Ruby changed the abrupt, no nonsense police officer's tone that she had adopted with him throughout, to a softer whisper.

"Now, when I speak to my husband, you may hear some shouting, swearing, a chair being thrown at a wall. That sort of thing. I'm sure you'll have heard the like in the army. And it might just take him a while to see things my way. So don't worry when he first sees you, if he's a bit, well, unfriendly. And I have to tell you, when the temper's on him, he is bloody scary and make no mistake. But don't take anything he says to heart. He'll be all right with you soon enough."

Freddie didn't seem unduly worried. After what he'd seen in the trenches, a man in a temper was the least of his concerns.

But there was a flaw in Ruby's plan. Her husband was not at home.

******

Nash was a little worried about Ruby doing a night shift alone in darkest Whitechapel, with none of her volunteers within shouting distance. It was no longer the no-go zone for a woman in the early hours it had been during the autumn of terror thirty years ago, but it was still a place where bad men could appear out of the shadows. In his villainous days he had only ever preyed on men, but there were plenty who had, and still would see a woman as an easy target. And a police uniform was certainly no protection. Quite the reverse in fact.

Not that Nash had conveyed these fears to his wife. She was the most independent woman he had ever known. And thanks to her years as an East End Suffragette, and her years living with him, she had also become one of the toughest women anyone might wish to come across. And he knew that any complaints from him would fall on deaf ears.

But having dropped off an objector in Shoreditch during the early hours, little more than a mile from where Ruby had told him she would be ending her shift at around the same time, he decided on a whim that rather than head straight home, he would make his way to the London Hospital and check all was well. He also hoped it would be a nice surprise for his wife to have her husband turn up unannounced to accompany her home.

He ducked down Brick Lane and through old alleys towards the hospital, before eventually taking a short cut through a tiny passage, Wood's Buildings, which led through in to the Whitechapel High Road opposite the hospital. He stopped at the exit of the passage to survey the scene. There was a line of ambulances waiting to turn into the hospital. Nothing much else seemed to be happening. He rubbed fingers along almost twenty four hours of coarse chin stubble growth, spat an oyster of spittle on to the ground and felt in his pockets to see if he had a sweet to suck while he waited.

A quarter of an hour passed before Nash noticed the ambulance queue was starting to get shorter. No more ambulances were coming along. The lights of the hospital were giving off just enough of a glow for him to see a woman in a jacket, skirt and hat was now walking up the main road. It wasn't a nurses uniform. Probably a policewoman's. There was a fair chance it was Ruby. Nash did not want to make himself known till she had finished her duties for the night so he stood in the passage arch and loitered, for once without intent.

"Oi! What's your game?!" came a high pitched, high volume enquiry.

Nash recognised that voice. Two figures started running away from him. The one closest was definitely his wife. She was chasing a young lad. What had the little blighter done?

Swiped some fags or chocolate as it was being handed to some soldiers?

Ruby had bragged to him about her ability to deal with juvenile delinquents. And now he was seeing it in action. He was rather excited by the situation and was eager to see his wife in full flow. He was confident she would be able to deal with the little Herbert. But if he turned out to be wrong and the lad started to get the better of her, he would have to step in, though he knew that would incur her wrath. But if it came to it, he would rather have her give him a tongue lashing than see her given a good hiding by some young scallywag.

Nash set off in pursuit but rather than follow them directly, used his local knowledge. He headed back down Wood's Buildings, then along Durward Street, which ran parallel to the main road. He came out into Vallance Road just as the lad turned and headed towards him. Nash stopped and waited. A moment later Ruby appeared, and cut across the road at an angle. The lad turned and ran across the road, allowing Ruby to cut him off and grab hold of him.

"Well done girl," muttered Nash with excited pride.

But then he saw the lad lash out. Nash noticed for the first time that the lad had a bandaged head and was wearing a soldier's uniform.

"Blimey she's caught herself a Tommy."

Nash did not like the idea of his wife trying to tackle a fully trained soldier, even if he was smaller than her. But he didn't want to get involved unless he absolutely had to. He slipped quietly across the road, and into an unlit spot to keep an eye on the grappling couple just a few feet away.

******

Nash was furious. Proud, impressed and furious. Of and with his wife. He had not been close enough to hear the conversation Ruby had with the soldier, but had managed to catch a sight of the lad. He was clearly well under age and scared out of his wits. And when she marched him off, not back to the ambulances but down side streets avoiding the hospital, Nash guessed what it his wife was up to.

The improving light allowed him to follow at a discreet distance for a short time. But once it was obvious that Ruby was indeed heading home with the soldier, Nash left her to it. He made his way back to the main road and stopped off at an early morning winkle stall, which was just opening up, to buy some whelks. He sat on a wall next to a strip of plane tree-lined grassland, incongruous amidst the urban Stepney slums surrounding him. It was known as the Mile End Waste, where William Booth had given his first speeches on his way to founding the Salvation Army a few hundred yards away.

Nash was aware of his surroundings and its history. He slurped down his rubbery breakfast while mulling over what his wife was playing at.

Ruby was the one who would need some salvation after he had finished with her. He rehearsed the fire and brimstone he was going to rain down upon her when he got home. He sat there until both his temper, and his great speech had disappeared from his mind. It took a while.

He understood why Ruby had done this. He guessed that she would want him to help get the boy away somewhere. It was the right thing to do, even if it did put them both at great risk. But just because he had calmed down, and had decided to go along with his wife's foolhardy adventure, he thought it best not to appear readily agreeable. He had accepted her becoming a policewoman far too quickly. Ruby had wrapped him round her little finger. But he was not to be taken for granted. It would not do his wife any harm to be taken to task. He would therefore pretend to still be in a temper when he got home, and give her the ear-bashing she should know she deserved.

******

Ruby had changed her mind about having Freddie sleeping in an armchair when her husband surfaced. The boy was out on his feet and the longer before Nashey saw him the better, so she had removed various tins, pots and pans from the scullery floor, and had just finished tucking Freddie round the corner of the l-shaped room.

It was Maud's day off from the munitions factory, but she was up and about early as usual so Ruby had asked her down for a cup of tea. She was not going to be able to keep Freddie a secret from someone living in the same house in any case, so the sooner Maud knew the situation the better. And having a friend there when she told her husband what she had been up to, might keep a lid on his anger. He tended to only lose his temper momentarily, so she just needed to keep things under control for a minute or two. The air would be the darkest of blue of course, with old Victorian oaths almost withering the wallpaper, but hopefully everything would settle down soon enough.

The tea was brewing. Ruby was just rearranging the scullery so she could find a new home for her only frying pan, when the front door suddenly banged open.

Nash stormed in with a face like thunder ready to read the riot act. But the first woman he saw was not his wife.

"Hello Nashey," said Maud, with obvious surprise in her voice. "Just about to have a nice cup of tea with your beloved."

Nash ignored his visitor, glaring around the room, hands still stuffed in the pockets of the greatcoat he always wore at night, even on the warmest of summer evenings. He did not say a word. The feeling of surprise turned to one of awkwardness for Maud. She took Nash's silence as her cue to inform him of where his wife was located.

"She's just out the lav Nashey," she lied.

Ruby was still in her police uniform. Talk about a blue rag to a bull. She had heard the one-way conversation. Her husband's silence was deafening. She was for it all right. She was about to walk out to face the music, when a thought struck her. Where the hell had he been till this time of the morning? And why had he crashed through the door like a man possessed and then given Maud the silent treatment. It was as if he already knew what she had done. Hmmm.

Ruby walked into the parlour with a face to match her husband's.

"Where you been?!" she demanded with menaces, before immediately answering her own question. "Spying on me that's where!"

If Nashey was innocent of all charges, she could apologise quickly enough. Some of their loveliest moments together had been those immediately after an apology had been tendered by one or the other, or often both, of them. And she would soon have to tell him about the boy, so a little bit of attack being the best form of defence, might not go amiss.

Her husband looked at her astonished. He was not the only one. Maud decided pre breakfast tea-time was over.

"I'll just er…" she said nodding in the direction of the stairs, as she started to get up from sitting in Nash's chair to escape to her half of the house.

"Stay where you are Maud!" barked Ruby, like a policewoman giving someone an order, though this was no simile.

Maud did as she was told. Her eyes flicked between the two soon to be warring factions. Ruby and Nash stared at each other. This went on for several seconds. It was like a stand-off in a Tom Mix western. But which one of them would turn out to be wearing the white Stetson of the hero, and which one the black of the soon to be outgunned villain?

Nash cracked first. Ruby had taken him by such surprise that the wind in his sails suddenly dropped completely Not that this left him in the doldrums. Quite the reverse. He burst out laughing, shaking his head with amusement.

"You cheeky little mare!" he chuckled, shaking his head. "You've got some bleeding neck on you. I'll give you that. Come here!"

Nash motioned with both arms for his wife to move towards him. Ruby then cracked into laughter too, did as she was told, and the two of them encircled each other in reciprocal bear hugs.

It was Maud's turn to shake her head in amusement, not to say relief.

"Can I go now constable?!" she said over her shoulder with sarcastic mock effrontery, as she left the room without waiting for an answer.

In due course Nash told his wife how he had come to see her in action outside the hospital, and Ruby confirmed where their lodger was sleeping.

Chapter 25

"All this madness, all this rage, all this flaming death of our civilisation and our hopes has been brought about because a set of gentlemen living luxurious lives, mostly stupid, and all without imagination, or heart, have chosen that it should occur."

Bertrand Russell 1914

Peter made his way into the marketplace to take up his duties. A middle aged man entering the square, who looked better fed than most, spotted the uniform and made a beeline for it. The man was keen to ingratiate himself with a member of the armed forces.

"It's good to see you soldier," he said officiously, his neck and back straightening him to his fullest height. "The German armies have not lost the war yet. The soldiers remain in the field, valiant and in good order."

The man then overacted for dramatic effect, looking round the marketplace, nose in the air, before he continued his diatribe.

"But the Home Front has collapsed amid a bitter harvest of subversion and agitation by pacifists, socialists, slackers and Jews. The German army has been stabbed in the back."

If there was one type the German soldier resented almost as much as the businessman profiteering from war contracts, it was the loud, arrogant, patriot who failed to understand the experience of fighting in the trenches.

Peter was therefore not tempted to reply. His mind raced to the trenches, but for once not their associated horrors. Rather, the camaraderie, friendship and even a perverse feeling of belonging, overwhelmed him. When back there the welfare of the Home Front had been the only compelling reason to keep going once the Spring Offensive had failed, the flu had hit and exhaustion had set in. But it had become clear to him that the Home Front was lost too.

This was not the place for him to see out the war. He would report back to the trenches first thing tomorrow morning.

******

Ursula, her team and cart driver had been laid off by the Berlin authorities, who were too busy dealing with the flu and its effects, to provide funds for feeding the very poorest, least productive members of society. Her ex-employers were also fighting too many other culinary fires to worry about retrieving their now redundant cart and its soup production equipment any time soon.

But Ursula had recently received an offer of help from her friend Dorothea. Her soldier friend was apparently keen to help out while he waited to be called back to the Front.

And thanks to the blight, there were still plenty of potatoes left in stock. So Ursula concluded that it was no good crying about her sacking. With help from Peter she would take out her mobile soup kitchen as usual. The authorities had not expected her to have any takings from the past week but careful potato paring had meant she and her girls had managed to sell some soup in the past few days, albeit fairly grim fare. But the potatoes were now beyond even this usage. So with the cash, Ursula had bought some ersatz sauce, with which she had smothered any of the sweet greenish potato pulp that had not turned completely into stinking mush. The sauce was foul but it covered something worse. She had also, out of her own pocket, bought the ingredients of turnip & bones salad and turnip marmalade.

It had been arranged for Peter to meet her in the main square, where Dorothea would be selling food from her own stall. Ursula would set up next to her to begin with before she and Peter headed for Zentral Viehund Schlachthof, a particularly poor area where any food would be welcome. En-route Peter would see what he could do with her turnips and assorted other purchases to make them into something more palatable than her ersatz and pulp concoction. It wouldn't be difficult.

As she pulled the reins to bring her vehicle to a stop, Ursula noticed quite a crowd had already gathered in the square. It was not surprising. It was lard day after all. Dorothea was already hard at work feeding people. Ursula's chest swelled with pride. She announced her arrival, shouting out with spirit to the people queueing at the stall.

"My friend is feeding you to help the Fatherland to hold out!"

Dorothea did not share such blind faith and patriotic fervour. Ursula knew very well her friend's stall was being run for women's suffrage, not the Fatherland, but nonetheless she received a cheery smile and wave of acknowledgement.

Ursula was just about to call to the crowd that she too would have food for them as soon as she got set up, when a very expensive looking motor car appeared out of the street that led into the square, and rumbled over the cobbles to pull up next to her friend's stall. A woman in trousers, presumably a chauffeuse, jumped out and went straight to the head of the queue. Whether out of deference or simply shock, Dorothea appeared to welcome the woman and gave her some lard, telling her she had better take some now, in case they ran out later. Ursula was puzzled, perplexed and most of all angry.

And if anyone required evidence as to the bitterness felt by working people for the wealthy classes who always seem to go well fed in their large houses and plush restaurants, it was about to materialise. A metamorphosis took place as hitherto law-abiding people in the queue became an angry mob within seconds. Initial shouts, oaths and swearing soon gave way to violence. The chauffeuse was set upon but with the help of Dorothea managed to extricate herself from the crowd and climb back into the driver's seat of the car and shut the door. A couple of women then tried to get a grip of her through the open window while others had opened the back door expecting to find Lady Muck. They were disappointed. The chauffeuse was on her own. Some men started to rock the car as violently as they could from side to side in an attempt to roll it over. This at least had the effect of stopping the women who had been trying to drag the chauffeuse out of the car. A lone policeman overseeing the marketplace queues drew his sword. He had a full scale riot on his hands.

Ursula may have shared these people's anger but this was no way to behave. She clambered on to her cart and shouted.

"Are Germans on the Home Front still the people they were at the war's beginning or have every day concerns taken over? Do not jeopardise our great country, the lives and future of every German, with your petty discontents!"

It was far too wordy an appeal to which a mob might listen. Many continued to rock the car. A few attacked the policeman. Others were already marching on the police station to break its windows.

******

Frau Burchardt had finished her business with Fritz inside the bank a quarter of an hour ago. She had waited a discreet period after he had left the premises before she had ventured outside, by which time her chauffeuse should have already arrived. But now here she was, waiting around on a street corner like a woman of ill repute. She was furious.

Where is that blasted driver of mine! Just wait till I see that wretched girl! I made it quite clear what time she should arrive! I suppose she is having too much fun talking to every working person to whom she is selling lard, and has forgotten the time! Lard! When I am standing here!

She hailed a passing horse taxi coming from the direction in which she wished to head. She had not been in a horse drawn vehicle for years but what could one do? The petrol shortage was obviously having its effect. Thank goodness for her chap Patemann. He might be a rough diamond, but at least you could rely on him. But having a nice new deposit sitting in one's bank account, the best flu remedy around, and a car with a full tank of petrol, was not of much use standing on a street corner if one's driver forgets to pick one up!

The cabbie swung his horse across the road and asked his potential new fare for her intended destination. When she told him it was the marketplace, he pulled a face and immediately hit the accelerator by use of his whip and a curse. She was not sure whether the curse was aimed at her or the horse but one thing was certain, manners were yet another victim of this terrible war.

There was nothing for it, she would have to walk. It must be at least a couple of hundred metres, crossing at least one filthy street. It would not surprise her one iota if her skirts were ruined!

Little more than five minutes later the square hove into view. There appeared to be a riot going on. People were streaming out of the marketplace and into the surrounding streets to get away from the melee. Now she understood the cabbie's lack of enthusiasm for her requested destination. She found it difficult to make much progress up the narrow street against the tide. But she eventually reached the square, and there amidst the crowds lay her motor car. On its side.

Where is poor Aldo? She ran forward, looking round the crowd, asking them what had happened to her driver.

The mob didn't hear the question. They only heard the cut glass accent and saw the clothing of an extremely well-heeled woman. Not something they would usually come across in this part of town. She must be the owner of the motor. An old woman rushed out of the crowd at her. She grabbed the wealthy car-owner by the hair for a moment, before Ursula pulled her off and pushed her away. Not just to be heard over the din but to emphasise the seriousness of the situation, Ursula shouted at the woman she was attempting to protect.

"If you are the owner of this motor, your driver is injured! She is being tended by a nurse! Come with me for your own safety!"

******

Ursula had run forward to try and remonstrate with the mob while they were still attempting to turn over the car, so she had been the first on the scene when they succeeded in their crime. Dorothea was there a few seconds later, having quickly told her colleagues that they should pack up the stall and get out of the square as soon as possible. She explained to Ursula that she knew the injured girl and would attend to her. It was agreed that Ursula should head off to get assistance.

Being a top of the range motor, Frau Burchardt's car had windows. The passenger side ones had smashed against the ground when the car had been tipped over onto its nearside. Aldo had been holding on to the steering wheel for grim life during the mob's rocking of the car, but she had lost her grip when it had been turned over, gravity plunging her towards the window glass as it shattered against the ground. Dorothea laid down on the cobbles and peered sideways into the car. Aldo was lying head down along the full width leather front seat, with one of her legs awkwardly wedged against the steering wheel. It was difficult for the nurse to see the extent of any injuries, but the peak of her cap appeared to have protected Aldo's face to some degree, notably her eyes, from the glass. Nevertheless she had lacerations on at least one cheek, and her lips were a little bloody.

There was movement and groaning blasphemy issuing forth which made it clear the patient was conscious. Dorothea was concerned that in Aldo's dazed state, her new patient may not remember who she was, so told her who it was speaking; the woman whom she had originally met at Frau Ute's house, and whom she had just met again at the lard stall. Dorothea didn't remember mentioning during their previous meetings that she was an ex-nurse, so she did so now, hoping that would give some reassurance.

She told Aldo to keep her head still before asking her if she could speak. A muffled affirmative came from the car seat, so Dorothea asked how her head and neck felt, and whether she felt pain anywhere else. It was relayed that although she had hit her head she felt all right apart from a sore mouth. And her neck was fine. To which her nurse replied with a request that Aldo wiggle her toes, which she was able to do without discomfort.

Although she was satisfied that her patient may not

be too badly hurt, Dorothea decided it was best to tell her to stay still. Those responsible for the young driver's predicament had, temporarily at least, backed off. But the promise Dorothea had made of help arriving was more assumption than fact, and the baying crowd were still having plenty of negative things to say about the woman in the car. She was probably safer inside the vehicle than out.

The height, which was now the width, of the car plus two spare wheels attached to its side, made it difficult for a petite woman to reach up and over to the door handle, so Dorothea altered her attention to the front of the car lying on its side. The front window would have been a two sectioned affair, with the top half movable by way of a hinge, but the whole thing had buckled and its glass now lay in shards on the ground. If need be Aldo could be extricated through the space.

Ursula returned and bent down to relay to Dorothea in little more than a whisper, so she could not be overheard, that her attempt at going for help had been thwarted by the need to stop and protect the owner of the car, who had just turned up in the square. The two women agreed that surely the police would arrive any moment to clear the crowds and call for an ambulance. It was decided that Dorothea would stay and look after Aldo while Ursula would escort the wealthy woman out of the area before there was any more unpleasantness.

"What the hell is going on?!"

It was a man's voice. The two women looked around to see who owned it.

"Peter Fueschel!" shouted Dorothea in delighted

surprise before recovering her poise. "I see you have arrived for work at last! Better late than…"

That was as far as she got before she was interrupted.

"There's fuel on the ground!" shouted Peter. "Is there much in the tank?!"

Dorothea looked back at him bemused.

"Can I ask you what business it is of yours young man?"

Necks were craned to stare at the woman who had asked the question. Ute Burchardt was now the centre of attention. Peter snapped back at her.

"It will be everyone's business if the fuel tank explodes! Which it could if it has plenty of petrol in it. The tank has been ruptured as you can see!"

"The tank is full as a matter of fact," came the inappropriately haughty reply.

The soldier was not sure whether even the army's tanks were able to be completely filled with fuel these days. He was about to show the woman his disgust when his eye was drawn by the other two women running towards the car.

"You will look better without eyebrows perhaps!" he shouted sarcastically after them.

Dorothea shouted over her shoulder back at him.

"There's a woman in the car!"

Peter sprinted to join them, shouting at and waving away the crowd as he did so.

"Get back! The car is full of petrol and is leaking. It will go up like a bomb!"

For the first time that day, the mob listened. The riot was over. The crowd still lingered, but from a distance. They were now just an audience.

Dorothea pointed Peter to the front window.

"Go in through there!"

Without breaking step the soldier dived on to the side of the bonnet, which was now its top, crawled along it, and was about to throw himself into the car when he saw Aldo lying on the front seat. He wedged himself into the front window space, stooped down and pulled her up by one arm to begin with, before reaching to grab her more securely under both armpits and levering her up. She found one leg a little difficult to unfurl from the clutches of the steering wheel but eventually her rescuer was able to yank her out of the car. A moment later they slid off the side of the bonnet and on to the cobbles.

Ursula and Dorothea ran forward to help Aldo up to her feet. She was now bleeding from her hands and knees as well as her head, having landed on smithereens of glass. Dorothea asked her if she was all right and received a nod. A moment later all five cast members in the drama were running.

Chapter 26

"In war-time the word patriotism means suppression of truth."

Siegfried Sassoon,
Memoires of an Infantry Officer

When Ruby had reported back to Leman Street police station for her next shift, she told Sergeant Granger that earlier in the day, just before the end of her previous duty, she had taken off in pursuit of a soldier who had leapt out of the back of an ambulance. She managed to grab him for a moment at one point, but he had elbowed her on the jaw and made off. The bruise on her chin bore testament to this. She chased him down various courts, alleys and passages. By the time she lost him, she was somewhere in Bethnal Green. She was in pain and feeling a bit sorry for herself so made her way home, forgetting her orders to formally hand over responsibility for the ambulances to the sergeant in charge at the hospital entrance.

Granger had reprimanded her for not following correct procedure, but also somewhat grudgingly praised her for her efforts. He would pass on her report to the army. They would no doubt ascertain in due course who the missing soldier was, and might want to speak to her at some later date, but he doubted it. He had then informed her that a police strike was about to begin so she should go home.

A tram ride later, Ruby walked through her back door with a spring in her step. Nash looked up from his battered old armchair and shouted through to the kitchen.

"What you doing home? Thought you were on late turn?"

"Hello duck, this *is* a nice surprise," replied Ruby, sarcastically suggesting that her husband could have shown a little more enthusiasm for his wife's unexpected arrival. "Fancy seeing you home so early. What a treat. You're a sight for sore eyes and make no mistake. Is everything all right? How has your day been?"

"All right, Funny Cuts, come here," he said, beckoning for her to join him on the chair for a cuddle.

She sat on his lap, put her arms round his neck and gave him a hello peck on the lips.

"This *is* a nice surprise," he confirmed, which had his wife pull a face and poke her tongue out at him.

They smooched and shared their usual array of leg-pulling, giggles and silly talk, interspersing it all with more serious chat about how their day had gone.

"So what *are* you doing home?" was eventually repeated.

"Well, I am on strike would you believe."

She had expected a wide-eyed reply from the recipient of the news. But she was disappointed. Nash assumed his wife must have downed tools for a good reason, which could well be an unpleasant one.

"Why, what's happened to you?" he said, with a

concerned frown, looking her up and down, inspecting her for a sign of injury.

Ruby immediately realised he had misunderstood.

"Nothing. I'm all right you silly sod," she reassured. "It's not just me. It's the lot of us. The whole bloody Met Police and loads of prison screws have all gone on strike! Well the majority of us any way. Twelve thousand they say. And by all accounts we've also got six hundred what they call mobile pickets who are organised to move about to trouble spots as and when, to keep the strike solid."

The wide-eyed response now came.

"Blimey! Good times! What shall I go out and nick first?!" he said with a broad grin on his face.

"Oh yeah, as if there being coppers about ever stopped you from doing anything you wanted, you old villain," Ruby countered. "And besides we've already heard the government are rushing in soldiers to guard public buildings, and no doubt the Specials and Gorgeous Wrecks will be asked to do more hours. But, dear husband, wouldn't you like to know *why* we're on strike?"

"Go on then."

"Some bolshie police and prison officer union rep called Tommy Thiel got the sack over at Tower Hill nick. He's a right East Ender by all accounts. Don't take any flannel from anyone. They gave him the boot off the force because he was kicking up a storm about our conditions. Pay and pensions and the like. Well, you've got to admit, we are paid terrible."

"You're getting paid more than Sylvia used to pay you," said Nash with a whiff of effrontery which betrayed his lifelong antagonism to all things police.

"That's different, that were charity work. And besides, when working for Sylvia I didn't have to run through the streets of Whitechapel chasing and apprehending all and sundry in the early hours did I?"

"One fourteen year old lad who can't be more than seven stone soaking wet, don't make up all and sundry," said Nash, putting his wife in her place as far as he was concerned.

But before he received a volley of well-earned abuse and an elbow in the ribs from said wife, he wisely became more conciliatory. He held up a hand.

"But I get your meaning girl. Looking after them ambulances and soldiers and the like should pay decent. I'm proud of what you did there."

"Saved by the bell," she said, looking up at him with a knowing smile.

The mention in passing of their new fourteen year old lodger, who was having his second sleep of the day in the scullery, brought the conversation around to their most pressing problem.

Ruby believed the police strike was an ideal time to get the boy away somewhere but her husband surprised her by saying he was not so sure about that.

He told her that a company of Scots Guards had just arrived in the East End as a show of force against picketing rail workers because the police were not the only ones on strike at the moment. The area was already teeming with soldiers, and within the day no doubt they would be joined by every jumped up little stickler for law and order that the Special Constable and Gorgeous Wreck fraternities could muster. And these stand-ins were likely to be more officious than regular police officers, at least in the short term, when they would be keen to impress and would have the twitchiness of the raw recruit.

Throughout the war Nash had heard stories of Specials arresting people in the vicinity of bridges, tunnels, canals and water & gasworks, in the belief London was being overrun by spies and saboteurs. And the problem was Nash and Ruby's part of the East End was full of such infrastructure. Nash had also heard that a Bethnal Green tailor with a German name had got six months in prison for being caught by a Special three yards from a pigeon! The suspicion being that the bird could have been used to send a message to the enemy. As far as Nash knew, there had not been a single act of sabotage in the whole war, but that hadn't stopped officials looking for it. All this considered, Nash had already suspended taking on any new objectors for the time being, and had sent Bert out to warn all his existing objectors that they should keep their heads down even more than usual for the moment.

He thought it would be safer, not just for Freddie but the two of them, to keep him under their wing. Nash also had to admit he had been rather taken with the boy. He remembered how, on leaving the workhouse when he himself was fourteen, he had vowed never to return. He could appreciate how the lad was determined not to go back to the trenches. In many ways Freddie reminded Nash of his fourteen year old self, with the exception that when he was that age no slip of a woman copper would have been able to get the better of him. Not that he would ever tell his wife that.

"No, let's keep him here with us," said Nash. "He

can help young Bert. That poor sod can't cope with the work I'm giving him, if truth be told. You need a proper set of lungs to hop backwards and forwards to Shoreditch. Trouble is I have to pass him some work, otherwise he'll think the money I'm giving him is charity, and he won't take that. Pride's the only thing the government ain't taken from the poor little bleeder."

"That's good of you, Nashey," said Ruby softly. "And Freddie being fourteen, and to look at him you'd think he were even younger, there's no reason for any Special, Wreck or soldier to take a blind bit of notice of him. We'll have to be careful though, his description went out to every copper before we went on strike. And I suppose the Specials and the rest will have it too."

"Can't be helped. I had a talk with the lad whilst you were at work. Told him what I had in mind for him. Told him about my name being Smith as far as the conchies are concerned. He was all right with it. I told him you'd be really for it if we all got pinched. I think he's got a bit of a soft spot for you. He promised me if he got buckled he'd keep his trap shut. Reckon he will an' all."

"Soft spot indeed," said Ruby dismissively. She knew her husband all too well. "More like you told him what they did to informers in the East End. And you had your scariest Victorian villain face on when you told him I'll wager."

"I'm telling you he's got a soft spot for you," repeated Nash in protest.

Ruby noticed that her husband had not denied threatening the lad.

"Never mind all that," she said. "We'll have to get a

message to his mother to let her know he's all right, but he daren't come home, even for a visit."

"He told me he were from Hoxton," replied Nash. "It's only up the road from Shoreditch. Next time I'm there on conchie business I'll go and tell her."

Ruby nodded. She wondered what else Freddie had told her husband.

"Did he tell you anything new about the war?"

"Yeah. He says as how our boys are dropping like flies with the Spanish flu. All kept on the q.t. of course. But the Germans must have it just as bad otherwise we wouldn't have been able to push 'em back like we have. That's why we're shipping so many walking wounded back here. Patch 'em up proper while the Germans are in retreat, ready to send the less injured ones back when needed."

"*Spanish* flu?" queried Ruby.

"That's what they're calling it now," said Nash. "Remember Sylvia told us as how Spain had the flu bad. There's thousands dead there by all accounts."

"And remember how she told us Spain couldn't be the only ones," reminded Ruby sagely. "And now she's being proved right. And if there are so many dying of it in the trenches, there must be even more of the injured being shipped back here with it. There must have been thousands just in the convoys I've seen, and that's just to one hospital. We'll be like Spain soon enough, you mark my words."

******

244

Ruby was back at work within forty eight hours. An emergency meeting of the Cabinet had brought about a pay rise and improved pensions for the police.

She had expected to be quizzed further by Sergeant Granger about the incident with the soldier but on walking through the doors at Leman Street she was told there was no need to worry about it because the Met now had bigger fish to fry.

Cities and towns throughout the country were now competing with each another to see who could raise the most money for the war effort from their 'Tank Bank' weeks, during which huge numbers of government war bonds were being sold. Tanks were being deposited in main squares as a means of publicising the event, attracting large numbers. London was not in competition with anyone given that its huge population would obviously raise the most, but crowd control on the narrow old streets of the capital was a concern. There had already been a dangerous crush at one London war bond event that had ended with casualties in Fleet Street and Ludgate Circus. And the Selfridge's war bond scheme had been such a success that the resultant throng had brought the whole of Oxford Street to a claustrophobic squash.

Consequently, all the East End divisions of the Met Police had been asked to provide assistance to their Westminster colleagues. Ruby was told that as from next week her presence was needed up at Trafalgar Square to help control the crowds for the forthcoming 'Feed the Guns' war bond event. The square was apparently being turned into a mock-up of a ruined French village. And in the middle of it, as the centrepiece for the event, was to be a tank. It was going to be quite a sight. And no doubt quite a crush.

In the mean time she and her volunteers were to carry on escorting the ambulances for a couple of nights. She would get Friday off, as she needed to transfer onto days, not just in readiness for Trafalgar Square but because on Saturday afternoon she was required to help out on crowd control at a women's football match. Granger had heard through the grapevine that she was something of a local women's football expert, so her expertise might be useful.

The best, most renowned women's football team in the country, Dick Kerr's Ladies FC, were going to play at West Ham's Boleyn ground. A record attendance for a women's football match was expected, so it would also give her some useful crowd handling experience before tackling the Trafalgar Square hordes.

******

Freddie and Bert had started their partnership. Freddie was staying at Bert's, sleeping in a chair in the parlour. This way Nash had been able to get the No Conscription League to increase Bert's wages to compensate him for the cost, inconvenience and danger of housing the lad.

The two ex-soldiers could not have been more different. Years apart in age; single and married; lively and quiet; able bodied and disabled. Like all teenagers Freddie would never stand when he could slouch somewhere, whereas Bert was always on his feet, his bullet ravaged lungs being much better when they were in a vertical position. He even slept sitting up at night.

The man and the boy had quickly formed a successful symbiotic relationship. Nash had put the older man in charge, which had given him the most sense of self-respect since being invalided. For his part Freddie enjoyed being the stronger of the two. Having been a boy in a man's world while in France, he was now able to regain some of the confidence he had once had as a brash young East End tearaway eager to go to war. And both of them were, if they were honest with themselves, rather afraid of Mr Nash, so they found some comfort in no longer having to deal with him on a one to one basis.

The two of them sat in the parlour awaiting, with their usual trepidation, a visit from their boss. Nash still retained his old villainous ability to move silently across cobbles when it suited him. He arrived at the back of Bert's house without making a sound. Bert's wife Elsie came out of the scullery and almost leapt out of her skin when she saw a huge man standing at her back window, looking at her. Nash gave her a grim smile and a wink. She quickly recovered her composure and beckoned him in with a wave.

"Hello Nashey. You gave me a right old start there you did, and that's the truth."

Nash didn't want to stand and listen to Elsie ramble on so he cut in.

"They through in the parlour are they Else?" he said, walking past her.

"That's right Nashey, you go on through and I'll get the kettle on. They're gasping. I wouldn't make them a cuppa till you arrived. I told 'em I'm not making you tea and then have to make another lot when…"

At this point Nash closed the door to the parlour behind him, having just previously given Elsie a wink down the passage so she did not think him rude. He looked down at his two seated cohorts. He was always terse with them. Nash was abrupt with any men he did not know well, and being ex-soldiers he thought they would probably respond best to being told with fierce certainty what was required of them. He also believed that it was good to make Bert feel that he was still a soldier of sorts, and it was always best to keep fourteen old lads up to the mark otherwise they might take any sign of kindness as weakness. The first time they had met, Freddie had been petrified when Nash had shouted at him to come out from skulking in the scullery. And the boy had been kept on his toes ever since. Thus there was no word of greeting from Nash, just a nod, before he went straight to business.

"What you two got for me?" he barked. "And hurry up before Else comes back in with the tea. I ain't got all day."

Freddie jumped out of his chair to speak with the enthusiasm of youth.

"You're never guess what Mr Nash. One of the conchies has heard on the grapevine that the government's only gone and put four battleships in the Thames! But that's not the all of it. The rum thing is as how they ain't for no military purpose. What do you reckon to that eh Mr Nash?"

"They ain't conchies, they're conscientious objectors to you boy," corrected Nash morosely.

He then considered for a moment before answering the lad's question.

"Sounds like one of four things to me. First, there's so many people doing time now, what with all the aliens interned, people caught nicking stuff for the black market, objectors and the like, prisons are full up so they're gonna go back to having prison ships in the river. I heard they did something like it with ocean liners down in Pompey harbour for the aliens at the start of the war. Prison hulks they were called back in the old days. Terrible things by all accounts. Worse than Victorian East End slums if you can imagine. I can't. They got rid of 'em about the time my mother had me."

"Back in Oliver Twist days eh?" said Freddie, his earnest interest being greater than his historical or literary knowledge.

There had not been any hint of sauciness in his question but he got a cuff round the ear for his trouble in any case. And a cuff from Nash was a painful one.

"I'll give you Oliver bleeding Twist! Now, second reason might be 'cause the flu's got worse. Suppose they might be going to have 'em as hospital ships. Quarantine ships to stop it spreading see. *Like they used to in the old days.*"

Nash looked at Freddie pointedly, silently asking him if he wanted another cuff round the ear for his trouble. Freddie might have been as thick as two short planks but he was not completely stupid. He kept quiet, so Nash continued with his theorising.

"Third up. The papers keep telling us as how our army has driven the Germans back across the Marne River, got back most of the territory we lost in their Spring Offensive and we've taken loads of prisoners. If that's true, perhaps these battleships are going to be prisoner of war camps. Same sort of thing as hulks were to start with.

"Last and by no means least, the government's lost their arse. Police and screws on strike, mobile pickets, rent strikes, munitions factory strikes, army rebellions in France. They've already sent troops here to the East End. And I know this cove called 'the bolshie' who tells me there's trouble brewing down at the docks an' all. Russia's gone. The papers tell us they're looting and all sorts in Germany. Perhaps people all over have just had enough. Maybe them ships are full of soldiers ready to shoot at us if we get like the Germans."

There was the sound of chalk scratching on blackboard. It was Bert.

When Nash had first taken Bert on board he had asked Sylvia's toy factory to make a mini blackboard and supply him with chalk, which he had passed on to his new recruit so they could communicate more securely. Nash believed this was a safer option than notes being written all the time. They could always burn whatever he wrote, but such a chore could easily be forgotten, and who knew who might end up scavenging through the screwed up paper in a bin.

'Its number 2 I say. Feller down the frog just passed away', said the chalk.

"Better getting the flu than getting shot at Bert," interjected Freddie. "Let's hope you're right."

Nash wasn't so sure about that but kept his thoughts to himself.

Chapter 27

"I had a little bird, Its name was Enza, I opened a window,
And in-flu-Enza"

Children's Skipping Rhyme 1918/19

Ruby reported to Leman Street prior to starting her final
night on ambulance protection duty. Sergeant Granger had
some news for her.

"Your duties have changed. You will be staying on
nights for another twenty four hours. The Boleyn ground
can't hold Saturday's football match. The lease of the
ground is owned by the church and they have complained
about the match being played by women...."

"Bloody cheek! It's for wounded soldiers! Who do
they think they...."

What was about to become a rant, which would have
betrayed both Ruby's feminist credentials and her less than
enthusiastic views of the Church, was cut short by her
superior officer.

"WPC Nash! Less of your lip! I've told you about this
sort of behaviour before. It's not your place to comment on
orders. We are public servants. Ours is not to reason why.
And you do not swear in this police station! Or anywhere

else for that matter when you are wearing that uniform. You must respect your office. Do I make myself perfectly clear my girl?!"

Ruby stared back at him. My girl indeed. I'll give you my girl.

But she bit her tongue and nodded. She expected him to carry on with his lecture but he just stood and glared at her for a few seconds, radiating his most intimidating stare to add gravitas to his words. It failed to impress its target audience, but Ruby played the game.

"Yes sergeant," she barked officiously, like a squaddie on parade.

"Yes sergeant," aped Granger softly, while giving her a knowing look that told her he knew full well that his words of censor had fallen on deaf ears.

He had heard that this WPC had been a Suffragette and was married to a man with an infamously villainous reputation throughout the East End. But beggars could not be choosers so the Force had taken the woman on. The sooner this war was over and these women could be packed off back where they belong, the better, as far he was concerned.

"Now, as I was saying when I was so *rudely interrupted*, the Boleyn ground cannot hold the match because the East End munitions factory whose team is playing against this Preston lot, needs all its women to work all day on Saturday. We need every shell we can get, to carry on driving the Hun back. As you know we've nearly beaten the so-and-sos at last, so it's no time to shirk now. Our boys in the trenches have got to ram home the advantage. But as you so correctly stated WPC Nash, the football match is to raise funds for charity. So it will still go ahead. The match is going to be held at night. The first ever football match at night. Using searchlights would you believe. But the church, and their tenants West Ham United have, *quite reasonably I would say WPC Nash*, expressed concerns that their ground may be damaged by what would obviously be quite major construction, all for just one game. But Clapton Orient have agreed to the lights being installed at their ground instead."

Ruby was delighted to hear that the game was still going ahead. A match at night! How exciting!

But she kept her enthusiasm to herself, maintaining a professional straight face while the sergeant proceeded to tell her all the details she needed to know for her night's duty.

******

The Dick Kerr's Ladies football club had started life as a Preston munitions factory team. They had recently attracted 10,000 paying spectators to watch them play at Preston North End's Deepdale ground in a local derby against their biggest rivals, St Helens Ladies.

But Ruby had been told that Preston wasn't even as big as her home city, Southampton. How many would the mighty Dick Kerr's team attract in a place the size of London? West Ham's massive Boleyn ground might have been able to handle the crowds, but Clapton Orient?

Ruby had piled into a police van outside Leman Street, along with a dozen colleagues. It was an old Black Maria, with the single person wire cages removed. She remembered sitting in such a cage with her knees forced up against her chin in her Suffragette days, on her way to Bow Street Magistrates court. Goodness how her life had been changed by this war.

On alighting from the van outside the stadium, Ruby saw that while it was no Boleyn Ground, Clapton Orient was a far bigger stadium than the one in which she had played in that inter-factory match. Perhaps it would not be so bad after all.

She and her fellow officers flooded through an entrance gate to be met by a sea of further policemen. It was two hours before kick-off and still daylight. They had all received orders before setting out from their respective police stations, but now it was time to get themselves acquainted with the topography of the ground and receive specific logistical information from a team of sergeants.

The majority of constables were to be deployed outside the ground, to keep the turnstile line-ups orderly, stamp out jostling and queue-jumping, and keep an eye out for other problems associated with crowds such as pickpockets. Others were to head for the local train and tube stations to help railway porters and underground staff keep things orderly there and to stop fare dodging. But the biggest potential problem was going to be when the ground capacity was reached and the gates were locked. It was expected that many thousands outside might be turned away disappointed, and this had the potential for a dangerous crush to occur.

Sergeant Granger was there. He beckoned Ruby over to him. He made it clear that as a slip of a woman, he considered her usefulness in crowd control to be limited, so he had appointed her to a team looking after the security of the searchlights. The things had been rigged up on top of stanchions in each corner of the ground and angled down on to the pitch. She was assigned to one of the four of them. She was to deal with any likely lads seen throwing things up at it and ensure only people with the correct pass gained access to the searchlight operator's hut. And most important of all, keep everyone away from the area where its generator was installed.

Ten minutes before kick-off the ground was full and the turnstiles closed. It was mayhem on the streets outside as seemingly the entire population of London had descended on the place. Thousands were locked out, and there were not enough police to control the situation.

Ruby was exasperated to be standing about doing nothing while all this was going on, with not a stone throwing lad or suspicious character roaming the searchlight area, to worry about.

Her generator was humming away and it was now dark. Time for the searchlights to crank in to life. One by one each segment of lights came on. It was now as bright as day. More lights flickered to life. It was now brighter than day. By the time all the lights were on, it was glaringly bright. The teams took this as their cue to run on, to a huge roar of approval from the enthusiastic, packed crowd.

Ruby could see part of the pitch from her assigned spot. She noted that the footballs being kicked around during the warm up had been whitewashed. They were going to play with a white ball. Ruby thought this would surely add weight to the already heavy leather. She remembered the last bit of action in her football match. She thanked goodness that she was not playing tonight. If she headed a powerfully kicked whitewashed ball on the top of her head she'd be knocked over for sure!

The match kicked off but no sooner had it started than her searchlight went out completely. A quarter of the pitch was now in darkness, which made the other three-quarters seem even brighter. Like the best thespian troupers, the referee, linesmen and players carried on regardless. And the crowd were greatly amused. Above the hubbub Ruby heard a wag close to her shout out to a player chasing the ball into the darkness to stuff it up her shirt while no one was looking and smuggle it in to the goal!

But Ruby wasn't laughing. It was all well and good, but if another searchlight went out, the game would surely have to be called off. And then what would happen if all those inside the stadium suddenly made a dash for the exits? The exit gates would probably not get opened in time. And even if they were, the streets outside were probably still badly overcrowded. It was clearly a potentially hazardous situation.

Her searchlight operator's hut was only a few feet away so Ruby took it upon herself to see what was happening. As she burst through the door and into the hut, a guilt-struck young operator stared back at her like Guy Fawkes caught in a cellar. She didn't have to say a word. The man shouted an abject apology the moment she entered, followed by an explanation. The searchlight had got an airlock.

Ruby asked what could be done. The man nodded at his field telephone. He could call the operator of the opposite searchlight to tell him to boost his wattage to maximum. It should be able to provide enough light to illuminate the dark side of the pitch. To a police officer with no knowledge of electric lighting whatsoever, it seemed like a good idea. She told him to go ahead.

The telephone call duly made, the other searchlight went into overdrive. It became so bright that people in the crowd were momentarily blinded. Some fell to the ground. The Dick Kerr's star player, their left winger, Lily Parr, was dribbling the ball along the touchline when she had to stop because she could no longer see the ball or anything else for that matter through the glare. The ball came to rest near the corner flag. Nobody on the pitch could see it. The game stood still for a moment. At which point an enterprising little urchin with his back to the light, ran on to the pitch and stole the ball. Chaos duly ensued.

Ruby had seen all this through the window of the operator's hut. It was time to cover her back. The operator received as grim an expression as she could muster.

"You didn't know for certain it was an airlock. You never told the other feller to turn up his light. You told him you would turn up your light to see if it cleared. He must have misunderstood. I'll back you up. No point in either of us getting in to trouble is there? You got my drift young man?"

The man's expression changed from stressed woebegone to stressed enthusiast. He nodded his acceptance of the arrangement.

******

If it had been any of Sergeant Granger's other constables, man or woman, he would have believed them. But odd things seemed to happen when WPC Nash was about. He did not believe a word of what he considered to be her cock and bull story. But the tall tale had been supported by a suspiciously sheepish looking searchlight operator, and despite the mayhem that had occurred, no damage had been done.

The brightness had stunned half the people in the ground, causing them to turn their backs away from the most powerful light, and stay where they were. They were too dazzled to make for the exits. This had allowed the police time to liaise with ground stewards to get the exit gates opened speedily. The Pathe News film crew were some of those caught in the glare so, much to the relief of the local authorities, they didn't get any footage of the fiasco. And the government were delighted to hear that the crowd had numbered many thousands, who had paid a healthy admission charge, a percentage of which was going into the war chest in the way of entertainment tax. But because the match was, partly at least, in aid of war charities, there had not been too much fuss kicked up by people wanting their admission money refunded.

Nevertheless, Granger had begun to wonder whether WPC Nash's report of her chase after the young soldier outside the hospital was all it appeared to be. Could she have actually caught him? Did he have some way of bribing her to let him go? And the searchlight operator did likewise? This woman Nash was, after all, the wife of a known villain. Perhaps that was it. She had become a police officer simply to make a few bob on the side from nefarious means? She was not merely disrespectful, but crooked.

Chapter 28

"I know of men who did themselves in…soldiers weary of
sitting in the trenches who cut their throats during leave."

Gaston Boudrey, Belgian writer,

Van den Grooten Oorlog

Dorothea had been proud of the way Peter took control
of the situation and rescued poor Aldo. On arriving home
she had been looking forward to sharing a meal with him,
followed by passionate love making. It had made his sudden
declaration, almost as soon as he had walked through
the door that he was reporting back to the trenches the
following day, all the more shocking.

She had initially exploded into mere temper at his
stupidity, but the longer she railed against his decision, the
more she realised how much she cared for this man, and
so the greater her rage increased, transforming into quiet,
trembling, incandescent fury. How *dare* he do this to me?
To himself!

Words were said which both sides regretted the
moment they spoke them, not that anything was
retracted. Quite the opposite. The argument escalated
the way only arguments between lovers can. There was

no sharing of a meal, and Peter spent the night sleeping on the floor.

"Sleeping there will get you used to the trenches again!" being answered by "except the trenches are a good deal warmer I think!" was the level of name calling the argument had descended in to by the end of the evening.

The next morning, Dorothea was accompanying Peter back to Supreme Army Command headquarters, where the soldier was to explain himself. His nurse was to be there as his physical sick note, confirming that the man she had been attending could not have reported back any sooner due to a blow on his head received when the soldier was heroically doing the police's work for them during a riot. He was just about to return to his army duties when he caught the flu. Of course this did not last long, but it was her professional opinion that had he reported back sooner, he would have been at risk of passing the illness on to other soldiers. And surely that was the last thing the Fatherland needed right now.

No doubt both of them would receive a severe flea in the ear for their tardiness, but it was hoped that was all. And if there was anyone the army needed almost as much as soldiers right now, it was nurses. Surely there was little point in either of them being disciplined further.

The obvious friction between the couple would at least have any army interrogator mistakenly believe there was no love lost between the two. The frosty nurse was clearly annoyed that she was having her time wasted by being dragged along here by this soldier. She was there on sufferance, doing her duty.

But their tram from Mitte soon became stuck in a

traffic snarl up which, given the non-existence of petrol to all except public transport vehicles and those who could afford black market prices, meant it was mostly trams. Peter was not in the mood to be patient. He glared at Dorothea and nodded in the direction of the street that was a hint that he was going to jump off and she could follow him or not. Her choice. The two of them alighted on Leipzigerstrasse, just short of the Kaiser-Wilhelm Bridge spanning the Spree River near the Imperial Palace.

They strode along at the fastest pace Peter's legs could carry him. Dorothea was not going to give him the satisfaction of asking him to slow down. She marched, and occasionally shuffled to keep up, alongside him.

They passed close by the royal palace and continued to head west towards the Reichstag before coming to a halt at Charlottenstrasse. It was now clear what had caused the traffic problems. A wall of police, stretching along the street, swords and pistols in hand, were a great dam holding back a torrent. A huge protest march, many thousands strong, had been stopped from heading towards the home of Kaiser Wilhelm. The wording on the banners and in the aggressive chanting made it clear that this was a demand for an end to the war.

"Your English is better than mine Peter Fueschel," said Dorothea sharply. "Charlatan is an English word for hoodwinker, is it not? The greatest hoodwinker of them all is protected on Hoodwinker Street. Apt yes?"

Peter thought it quite a caustically witty remark, typical of his girlfriend. The ice was broken.

"You have turned in to your friend Ursula I think." he said with a smirk on his face to let her know he appreciated her comment. "And of course your English is better than you let on actually. He is saved this time but Kaiser Hoodwinker is finished. The war is over! Let us go home."

Chapter 29

"Depression on faces very marked in trains and trams. People very full of sad cases of death from influenza. A great sense of dread about everything."

Caroline Playne, diary entry,
October 1918

WPC Nash was informed through Sergeant Granger's gritted teeth that due to her brave work chasing the soldier through Whitechapel, and her quick thinking in preventing what could have been a serious crowd control problem at the football match, she was considered by the powers that be, at least, to have a bright future.

Assuming the sergeant had made a double pun, when immediately after mentioning the floodlit football match he had stated the 'powers' that be said she had a 'bright' future, Ruby laughed.

"Oh, very good sarge."

Granger did not allow female constables to call him 'sarge'. Too intimate by half. And why on earth was this disrespectful young woman laughing at him? Normally he would have given her a severe dressing down, but he had other things on his mind.

"It's sergeant to you, WPC Nash," he rebuked pompously, and left it at that.

Ruby realised she had misunderstood, and was pleasantly surprised by not receiving more severe chastisement.

"Sorry sergeant."

"Now, I have a new recruit. PC Cyril Pemberton. He's as green as grass. So given the ability you have shown recently, I would like you to take him under your wing at Trafalgar Square this morning. All my other male police officers will have their hands full, so won't have the time to show him the ropes. I thought it would be a good job for a talented woman police officer."

"Yes sergeant," said Ruby.

An hour later Ruby's thoughts turned once again to her Suffragette days. The police van was dropping her, Pemberton and several other constables outside Charing Cross Hospital, around the corner from Trafalgar Square. She had been involved in many a Suffragette rally or protest in the square, many of which had degenerated into scuffles with the police in Whitehall. And some of those had included acts of police brutality. When she had become a policewoman she had made a vow both to herself and her husband that she would never allow herself to be used as a government thug against people who were merely protesting. If, or more likely when, given the way people were starting to turn against the government, she was ever asked to be a thuggish pawn of the state, she would shed her uniform and tell her sergeant where he could stick it. She had joined the police force to help people. Women in particular. Not abuse them. She doubted Granger would be advised today into which part of his anatomy he could painfully insert her uniform, but if it came to it, so be it.

But these considerations were driven quickly from her head. Once she and her colleagues had walked around the corner, she stood wide eyed in amazement at the scene in front of them.

Trafalgar Square had been transformed into a ruined French village. From their vantage point on the steps of the National Gallery, looking down on the square, Ruby had a great view. To her right was a battered windmill; immediately in front of her was the ruin of an old white church; and to the left of that were a couple of what she assumed were French style cottages with parts of their roofs missing. Around these buildings were clods of earth and sods of grass to make the place look suitably battle ravaged. There were also various wooden and canvas huts, several field guns and a couple of mock shell holes to complete the image. And behind the windmill and church ruin stood a massive four-sided poster encircling the base of Nelson's Column which read 'Feed the Guns with War Bonds and help to End the War'.

Ruby and Pemberton had been given orders to keep an eye on the crowd forming at the top of the square by the foot of the National Gallery's steps. The crowd was already twenty deep behind the stone balustrade above the square, which was the only thing stopping people tumbling ten feet down into the French village below. There was the potential for those at the front to be crushed against the stonework or pushed over it by a forward sway if numbers got too densely packed. But there were plenty of other officers on crowd control duties. Ruby and Pemberton were there to keep a watchful eye out for pickpockets, some of whom were sure to be in attendance.

Pemberton was there supposedly to gain experience but Ruby was not so sure this was true. This suspicion had grown from the moment she had been introduced to him at Leman Street. Given Sergeant Granger's 'green as grass' comment about his new recruit, she had expected a wet behind the ears young fellow. But this man was close to her own age.

And then there was the police van journey. There was the usual banter between excited young men. And of course having a woman in the mix, and a slightly older one at that, only added to the ribald humour. Especially when that woman could put any of them in their place with a rapier thrust of her tongue, which had the naïve scamp who had made the mistake of making a remark against women, age or both, ruefully having to listen to the jibes of his mates after he had been verbally knocked down. And Ruby was quite happy to go along with all this. She was not averse to adding fuel to the conversation fire by calling her fellow constables 'boys' in a mock contemptuous way. And if anyone was bold enough to mention she ought to be kept under control by her 'old man', they were told with some little certainty that her husband 'could eat you boys for breakfast'. Cue much laughter and further ribbing, though if the rumours about her husband were true, they knew that behind that claim lay a terrible accuracy.

But Pemberton had kept out of all such social interaction. He had been monosyllabic when Ruby, or any of the other constables, had attempted to bring him into the group dynamic. Ruby had got the feeling that it wasn't him being morose, shy or aloof. It was not the lack of confidence of a raw recruit or even a desire to simply concentrate on the task about to be tackled, which had brought the one word answers. No, she thought him guarded. And on arrival at the square, he did not seem at all overawed by the crowds or the extraordinary sight that had befell them. It appeared to be water off a duck's back, as if he were a seasoned professional.

Perhaps he was actually an experienced officer who was there as muscle because Sergeant Granger thought a mere woman would not be able to bring in a villainous pickpocket single handed? And given that pickpockets often worked in gangs rather than as individuals, it would be a reasonable precaution. But if that were the case, why the subterfuge? No, there was more to PC Cyril Pemberton than met the eye. Pickpockets were not the only ones on whom she would be keeping a wary eye today.

Ruby noticed the hedonistic atmosphere around the square. Everywhere she looked the usual expressions of misery and gloom that the war had imparted on people, had been replaced by a level of jollity. People were laughing, joking, mucking about. Yes, you could always see a level of alcohol-fuelled gaiety in a pub, but this was the first time in three years, since the excited novelty of the war had worn off, that Ruby had seen such mass levity in an outdoor crowd.

She wondered whether it could simply be due to the good news coming from the Front. Allied tanks had pushed the Germans back further; with thirty thousand enemy soldiers captured. But the news of the first great counter offensive victory at Amiens had come through some time ago, and since then she had not detected any great improvement in the war weariness of the public. She knew the newspapers never had fed the populace the true story of how appalling the war had been going. The news reports bore little relation to what she knew to be true thanks to the stories she had received via Sylvia's and Nashey's grapevines. So the news, though very positive, was not so markedly different from what had gone before. According to the press, it had always been just a matter of time before the reported acute food shortage of 'the Hun' came back to haunt them, and now, sure enough the inevitable Allied gains were taking place. In minimising the bad news to date, the newspapers were unable to make as much impact as they would have liked with their new supremely positive headlines.

Perhaps the atmosphere was merely created by the excitement of seeing the impressive mock up French village? After all, it was one thing to see a poorly reproduced black & white image of a war torn village in a newspaper, it was quite another to see it in the flesh as it were. It brought you closer to the war somehow. And the fact that it was Allied tanks that were turning the war our way, and here was such a tank, in Trafalgar Square of all places, for all to see, was certainly impressive. And there never had been any loss of patriotic fervour when it came to excited crowds coming out in droves to buy war bonds.

She made a mental note to keep an eye out for anti-war protesters. Now things were on the up, any anti-war sentiments were liable to be met with even more fierce resistance than usual. She thought the atmosphere in the square was reminiscent of a pub on a Saturday night.

Crowded and full of cheerful bonhomie, but such a scene could turn ugly in a heartbeat. A wrong word here, a knock of someone's drink there, and suddenly there were men throwing fists at each other. And both the ex-Suffragette and present day police officer in Ruby made her well aware that Westminster could become one big punch up at the drop of a hat, or the raising of a protest banner.

Her gaze eventually fell on a small knot of soldiers, whose hands were wandering up, down and beneath the clothing of star-struck young women who appeared only too keen to allow it to go on. Ruby glanced at her colleague to catch his eye, then nodded towards the cavorting group.

"Let's go and break up that little love nest."

Just for a moment Ruby saw argument in Pemberton's eyes, but he kept his thoughts to himself, merely nodding in acceptance of her idea.

"Keep your wits about you," she advised. "Soldiers can be nasty bits of work. Especially if they've had a few like this lot probably have."

For once, her colleague made a bit of conversation, based on the fact that earlier in the war, as soon as a man in army uniform walked into a pub, everyone offered to buy him a drink. It being rude to refuse, too many home on leave soldiers rather overindulged. The government had responded to the situation by, controversially, putting a stop to the practice.

"We should thank our lucky stars they've made it illegal to treat soldiers eh Ruby?"

Ruby was immediately on her guard. Was he pumping her to see if she would say anything contradictory of the government?

"They had to," she replied tartly. "You can't have half the British army rolling around drunk as lords can you?"

"Yes, but you've got to admit, it's coming to something when you can't buy a lad home on leave a pint when he walks into your local," he complained, before continuing with an accompanying sly smile. "And you must like a drink yourself I'll wager!"

"No more than the next," said Ruby abruptly, keeping her tone reminiscent of the clipped, professional one she used with the public when in uniform. "But there's a pub on every corner where I live. And my husband likes a plate of whelks. And I like a cockle or two. You can find us with a glass in our hand, chatting to all who'll listen, at the stall outside our local when we've a mind."

"But I can tell from your accent you're no East Ender. What were you doing before you were a copper?"

"I was a Suffragette. Last time I was on a protest rally here in Westminster I got a good hiding from a soldier. Not a copper mind you. A soldier."

"Up to something were you?" asked Pemberton knowingly.

"Yes, you're right there. I was up to minding my own business."

This was said in an off-hand tone that told him their conversation was over and to make of it what he wished.

Ruby then moved in on the group of uniforms, and the women whom they were groping.

"That's enough of that," she said. "There's women and children here in the square. They're here for a nice day out. They don't want to see all these carryings on."

The soldiers were taken aback and suitably shamefaced.

It was the women who were the problem. They laid into Ruby verbally, before the policewoman paid them back with interest, informing them that girls who gave it away were known on the streets as 'amateurs'. Whores looked down on them with contempt.

This cut the young women to the quick. There was no greater snob than those within the complex multi-strata that made up the English working class. For these women to be told that they were looked down upon by those whom they themselves considered the lowest of the low, was a shock. All but one of them now looked very sorry for themselves. But there's always one. A tall thin young beauty threw back her long brunette locks to show her contempt. She was not about to take any advice from anyone, least of all from some copperette.

"Why don't you just leave us alone copper? We're all just enjoying ourselves while we got the chance. We could be gone of the flu next week. There's enough as has already. My friend Joanie's dead and buried. Fit girl she were. Played tennis only a fortnight since. Didn't do her no good though when the Spanish Lady came knocking in Lambeth."

Now it was Ruby's turn to be shocked. She had been expecting an argument along the lines of the girls wanting to 'do their bit' by giving 'our boys' a last moment of happiness before they returned to the dangers of the Front. This was the first time she had heard the flu being talked of in such a way. As if it was just as deadly as the fighting. And now it even had a nickname.

Ruby thought it typical that something bad had been given a woman's name. Couldn't be the Spanish Lord could it? She wagered to herself that a man thought that one up. But now was no time to dwell on such things. She had to deal with this tricky young woman.

"Never mind all that," she said defensively before regaining her police officer composure. "Khaki fever is what you need to worry about my girl! Dizzy…"

"Your old man don't let you speak to him like that I'll wager!"

The shout came from behind her. Ruby stopped what she was saying and whirled round. A section of crowd were laughing at the man's comment on her marital arrangements. And as was usually the case, once one man in a lively crowd had found the gumption to shout the odds, others followed.

"Perhaps he does! But she won't get any if she do! No wonder she's jealous!"

"Everyone's taking the rise out of you copperette! You've got more on your plate than a spinster at a wedding!"

"She *is* a bleeding spinster! But don't worry girl. Get one of them soldiers to sort you out!"

"Yeah! You'll be doing your bit and he'll be doing his all right!"

Ruby had heard it all before in the Suffragette days. She knew that if she responded in the obvious way, namely to threaten to nick the lot of them, it would just bring more ribald comments. She decided not to feed them the ammunition. She simply turned back to face the young woman who had engaged her in conversation in the first place.

"As I was saying", started Ruby, lowering the tone of her voice and speaking slower to add gravitas to what she was saying. "Dizzy girls with khaki fever like you lot will find yourself in a mustard bath with the Epsom salts next month if you're not careful."

There was a gasp from everyone within earshot. While unmarried pregnancies were a fact of war life and Marie Stopes' new book was a best seller, talking of abortion attempts in mixed company, in public, was beyond the pale. It just wasn't done. And certainly not by a woman police officer in uniform. Even Ruby was embarrassed once she realised what she had said. But it certainly had an effect. The soldiers and their groupies shuffled away together, looking askance at her.

Ruby feared that she had simply moved the action on to somewhere else, probably that narrow alley on the other side of the square behind the Edith Cavell memorial. She could only hope that perhaps one of the young women at least would think twice.

Her fellow police officer should have come to her defence when the crowd had been laying in to her, but he had kept quiet. Now he spoke up with a wave of his truncheon.

"Move along there now, you men," he said to the crowd.

Most of the wags and their audience had already turned their backs once the copperette had not risen to their bait. They'd had their fun, and why waste time on a lady copper when there was a tank and a ruined French village to see and war bonds to buy.

"I don't think we'll have any more trouble from that lot," he said with the pomposity of the know all, erroneously taking credit for the crowd's loss of interest in his colleague.

He didn't receive the thanks he was expecting. Ruby was looking out over the square, gazing into the crowd, deep in thought.

Pemberton looked around and soon spotted something.

"I think that fellow in the straw boater up at the top of the steps there might be a dip," he said nodding in the direction of the man. "Just saw him deliberately bump into a wealthy looking chap. Wouldn't surprise me if the fellow's now missing a wallet. Let's take a look."

Ruby absent-mindedly agreed. As she followed Pemberton up the steps she was still thinking about what had just happened.

Even the crowd who made jokes at her expense, did so in the most good natured of ways. It was just good old ribald, slightly cruel London humour. There was none of the anti-authority feeling that might normally have sprung up from an altercation with the police. All the insults were against a woman who was stopping others from having fun, rather than against a policewoman as such. Why was everyone in such a devil-may-care good mood? She thought back on what that young woman had said. It was not a good mood. In a way, it was quite the reverse.

Chapter 30

"It would have been better to lock the stable door before the escape of the horse... the chances of achieving its (the precautionary instructions') purpose would have been enhanced had it been published at the beginning instead of in the middle of the outbreak."

The Times, 1918

Maud's munitions factory had been on strike. And they were not the only ones. Munitions workers throughout the country had been downing tools. They had been driven to exhaustion and beyond. Enough was enough.

The explosion which killed several women at Maud's shop had not been the final straw for her and her fellow workers, but the donkey's back was certainly in great pain thereafter. It had been the refusal of the factory owners to allow the women to wear their fuses' team posy for the day to remember their lost colleagues that had the poor creature collapsing with a snapped vertebra.

So Maud had been at home for a while, doing what strikers did, worrying themselves silly thinking about how they were going to pay the rent and feed their family. But the factory had warned the strikers they would bring in blackleg labour, so given many of the women were in a similar predicament to Maud, the threat of eviction making their grumbling stomachs seem minor in comparison, they had conceded defeat and were about to return to work.

Unfortunately Maud had been feeling increasingly ill throughout the strike, and as she was leaving the house for her first day back at the factory, a wave of dizziness came over her. It had to be ignored; there was no time to hang about. Being late for work was greatly frowned upon by the supervisors at the best of times, and the factory owners were sure to be in the foulest of moods given the recent behaviour of their workforce. She could be put back on lower paid work if she wasn't careful, and she could not afford that. Rose was thus bundled into her pram and Maud rushed out of the house. As she closed her front door and turned to head off, she wobbled and had to lean back to put a hand on the door to steady herself. Through her spinning head she cursed at the realisation that she had the flu coming on.

When Ruby had been ill, Maud had stocked up in case she was the next to get it. There was some Veno's Lightning Cough Cure in the scullery. She left the pram outside, let herself back into the house and within seconds was taking a swig of the concoction.

******

Nash was just returning from a visit to Kosher Bill, when Sylvia's assistant Norah Smyth hailed him from across the street. There were few women Nash respected more than salt-of-the-earth Norah. They had become friends soon after Nash had joined Sylvia's Suffragette organisation.

Norah was from a very wealthy background. She had spent most of her considerable inheritance sponsoring first of all Sylvia's East London Federation of Suffragettes and then her friend's Great War work in the East End. Without her, the Cost Price restaurant would certainly, and the nursery possibly, have not existed. Norah had also been the official photographer of the Federation, capturing many memorable images of the campaign. If Sylvia was the most loved woman in Bow, Norah Smyth was a very close second. Almost everyone in the area called her Miss Smyth out of respect. Only her friends called her by her Christian name. And only one person had the temerity to call her anything else.

"Nor!" bellowed Nash across the street, when he heard her call after him.

With some relief evident in her voice that she had found a member of the Nash household, Norah informed him that she needed to contact Ruby urgently, but she wasn't at home. She had spoken to Maud but she had seemed a little preoccupied and had not been able to help. The problem was that one of Sylvia's helpers on the Dreadnought newspaper, had gone down with the flu. She was supposed to have picked up an article last night which Ruby had written under a nom de plume, ironically enough about the Spanish flu. Could Nashey pop home, pick it up and bring it to Sylvia? It was needed within the hour because the government were threatening to close down Mr Arber's printing press because Sylvia was printing things about the flu that were far too accurate for their liking. It was a chance to get one last newspaper run out before the inevitable happened.

Norah started to apologise, not only for any inconvenience but for asking him to do something which carried a level of risk, but Nash cut her off.

"Leave off Nor. Be a fine thing if I couldn't help the likes of you out when you needed it. I saw Ruby writing something the other night as it happens. Think I know where she left it. Don't you worry, I'll have it round to Sylvia in two shakes of a lamb's."

After passing the time of day for a while, Nash wished his friend all the best, and headed for home. He was almost there when he saw Maud standing still on the pavement ahead of him, head down, hands on the pram, with her weight bearing down so the little contraption was standing on just its back wheels, like a tiny black stallion rearing up on its hind legs.

Nash flew into a panic. Christ, the baby'll fall out!

He rushed to her side, but had underestimated how well Rose had been tucked in by her mother. He didn't bother to ask the obvious question. Maud was clearly ill. Nash took the handle of the pram in one hand and put the other around her waist. The ground was thankfully flat so he was able to leave the pram where it stood. It had only been the mind over matter of a mother with a child to care for that had kept Maud upright. And now, with help having arrived, she was able to let herself go. Nash lowered her gently to the pavement and propped her sitting against a wall, reassuring her as he did so that he would get Rose home and then return. Moments later he was running at full tilt, pushing the pram in front of him, like a bobsleigher at the start of a descent, to deposit its precious cargo home. He then returned to Maud, picking her up off the ground, and with one arm round her he half walked, half dragged her home. She was soon laying on her bed, next to her crying child.

******

Ruby had popped along to the munitions factory to let them know of Maud's predicament. The supervisor gave Ruby a message to pass on to his stricken member of staff.

"Tell her not to come back. There's no job here for her now. I'll see she gets sent what she's owed."

Ruby looked at him as if he was something stinking and squelchy she had just stepped in while crossing the street. But she left it at that. Why waste your breath? She knew what the answer would be to anything she said. If Maud could not get to work, there were plenty of people ready to jump into her place. And the war didn't wait for anyone.

Not that Maud was in any condition to worry about her job. But she was reassured by Ruby that Rose was being looked after. The nursery childcare was cheap but it was not usually free, so Ruby had spoken to Sylvia and it had been agreed that Maud would not have to pay for the nursery place until she was back on her feet and earning a wage again.

The next door neighbour, a woman called Billie, was looking after Rose outside of nursery hours. While picking the little girl up she had told Maud that she had heard a rumour that the new wave of illness was different from normal flu because it was a form of Hun germ warfare put ashore by their u-boats. This nonsensical scaremongering was not the best bit of bedside manner. It had made the patient feel worse, if that were possible. Flu, however bad, she might eventually overcome. But germ warfare? She wondered if the rumours could be true. That would certainly explain why it was such a killer and why there was so little mention of it in the newspapers.

Everyone was doing their bit as best they could. Ruby was popping her head through Maud's bedroom door whenever she got the chance, but a rail strike for better pay and shorter hours had now paralysed the nation, and this was producing a lot of extra work for the police, so she was working double shifts. Maud's cousin had sent round some soup and half a loaf. Billie was doing Maud's washing. Norah was picking up the little girl from Billie's in the mornings and taking her to the nursery. Nurse Drebbes was dropping her back when the nursery closed. Dr Alice had waived all her costs. The woman next-door-but-one had popped along to the corner shop and asked for credit on behalf of her neighbour.

And now the vicar's wife, Jenny, had brought round some porridge. Nash opened the front door and on seeing who it was, and what she was delivering, couldn't resist some decidedly cruel, inappropriate humour.

The previous year, when German u-boats had been threatening to starve Britain into defeat by sinking a high proportion of its imported foodstuffs, the British government had asked its people to start an allotment campaign to grow and eat as much of their own food as possible. The vicar's favourite dessert, tinned rhubarb, had been unavailable for some time to all but those who could afford to dine at the best West End restaurants, so he had decided to grow some sticks. But he had been born and bred in the East End, where if you saw something pink, thin and a foot long, it had Blackpool or Brighton printed through it. And waste not want not; those huge leaves could make a decent soup.

The poor man had swopped his dog collar for a hospital gown in the critical ward for several days. The poisonous leaves had almost killed him. But he was fully fit again now, and therefore it was open season on him as far as Nash was concerned.

"Porridge Jen? Thought you might have brought round some nice soup. Or better still some custard. We were just about to give Maud some rhubarb for her tea."

"May I have say that is in extremely poor taste Nashey," scolded Jenny.

"Not as bad a taste as…"

"Yes, yes, yes," interjected Jenny with a hand up, stopping the obvious joke in its tracks. "Now, see Maud gets this while it's still hot will you?"

Nash winked at her and despite herself she gave him a little look and shake of the head which hinted that she had not taken offence. If it had been anyone else it would have been a different matter, but there again nobody else would have dared make such a joke to the vicar's wife in the first place. Jenny bid the reprobate a curt good day and left him to do as he was told.

Ruby was at home so Nash took her with him into Maud's bedroom. They had devised a little one scene play for their captive audience.

Perched awkwardly on a bedside crate, Ruby spooned porridge through Maud's lips as she told her husband matter-of-factly that an enemy plane had been shot down nearby. It had landed in a lake and its fuselage had survived the impact. It had been fished out and was going to be on display at The People's Palace in Mile End tomorrow. But there wasn't a large enough motor vehicle available to take it, so it was going to have to be taken to Mile End by horse & cart. She and Pemberton were to guard it later today along the route and then at the Palace tomorrow morning when a big crowd was expected to see it.

Ruby then asked her husband how his day had gone. Nash equally matter-of-factly told his wife that he had been laid off at the wood yard but he had heard Charlie Selby was so snowed under that he needed another pair of hands at his undertakers firm in Bow Road, so he went round there and got himself a new job, starting on Monday.

So far, so mundane. The chit chat of a married couple discussing their respective working days. Nash then went on to mention that he had passed through Roman Road market on his way home, and they were selling stuff off cheap so he had bought some food for their supper.

"Since when did you go marketing?" asked Ruby. But she didn't give her husband time to answer before continuing. "I've already got food in for us. And if they were selling it off cheap it'll be on the turn for sure. It won't keep. We'll have to chuck it."

"That's the last time I help with the marketing, I only did it because I knew you were on late turn, and were back on again tomorrow morning," said Nash, appearing to bristle at his wife's lack of appreciation for his efforts.

Ruby became more conciliatory, no doubt feeling some remorse for her behaviour.

"Sorry Nashey. Your heart was in the right place. What did you get anyway?"

"Spuds, cabbage, scrag of lamb, hearts, bacon, fruit."

"That all?" said Ruby sarcastically, before she softened her tone again. "Well, you did all right as it happens. I can make larded potatoes and cabbage mush. That'll keep. I can do lamb and sugar pie and I can do stuffed hearts and candied peel. The sweet will keep the meat for a while if it's not too far gone. I'll make bacon pudding and fruit junket. That might keep. That's good meals there. We might be able to save our ration cards till next week now."

"Good," said Nash brightening. "Mind you, we won't be able to eat all that lot before it goes off, will we Rubes?"

"No, Maud here and little Rose will have to help us out," said Ruby, as if she was asking for a favour. "You'll need to eat to keep your strength up Maud. Nashey made me eat when I had it and I was up and about soon enough. And don't listen to any of that old codswallop Billie told you. U-boats indeed. It'll be over soon enough, you mark my words."

Her head may have been spinning, making concentration difficult, but the little play had not fooled Maud for a moment. If she had not felt so terrible she would have been amused that Ruby and Nashey did not realise that when they were really having an argument, hardly a sentence went by without them calling each other 'darling'. There had not been a single darling throughout their apparent argument. Nashey had also been far too timid. He would never have let Ruby get away with speaking to him like that without giving her as good as he got. And since when was Ruby able to think up four recipes just like that? You would never find her in the kitchen if the oyster man or pie man had just been round. No, she concluded, it was clearly a put-up job they had rehearsed for her benefit. They obviously didn't want her to think she was being offered charity, especially from people who were not doing too well themselves. She knew Nashey didn't make much out of either of his jobs, and from what she had heard Ruby was not really cut out for being a police officer, and surely wouldn't last in the job. So they couldn't spare much. And normally they would have been right that she would not have been prepared to accept charity. But this illness had knocked her for six. And Rose could catch it too. She knew she needed all the help she could get. But there had been a half-truth in what Ruby had said. From what Maud had heard about this new flu, it would be over quickly, one way or the other.

"That's kind," she wheezed, before passing out.

Chapter 31

"Lives might have been saved, spread of infection diminished, great suffering avoided, if the known sick could have been isolated...but it was necessary to 'carry on' and the relentless needs of warfare justified this risk... and the associated creation of a more virulent type of disease."

Sir Arthur Newsholme,
Chief Medical Officer,
London Government Board 1918

Dr Alice had never felt so helpless. Almost all of her large number of house calls today had been to minister to patients with influenza. She was dolling out quinine for relief of fever; morphine for the pain and in one house digitalis to strengthen the heart. But her experience of this new wave of flu told her that bed rest was as good a treatment as any. One thing was for sure, none of the treatments were to actually cure her patients. And when a sufferer mentioned that they had been recommended some remedy or another by someone who knew someone who had recovered, she was loathe to reject it. If a patient had been recommended cinnamon, camphor, ammonia, eucalyptus or an alcohol rub, the doctor of medicine simply agreed that it could not do any harm. She was becoming increasingly concerned that medical science was simply providing palliative care to many.

At the end of her rounds, Alice sloped home depressed. Her shoulders were not the only thing which drooped. Her purse was laden with cash. She felt such a fraud taking money from people for achieving so little, but most of them insisted. They would not take charity. She had managed to reduce her usual shilling fee to a threepenny bit, telling people a little white lie that it was a government initiative because of the wide spreading nature of the flu. But despite only charging a quarter of her usual fee, today had seen her take home her highest ever day's takings.

She usually bought a newspaper on her way home from the newsboy at the top of her street to get the latest news of the war. The lad was always there, in all weathers. But he wasn't today. She guessed where he might be. She would be seeing him soon enough no doubt.

There was another newsboy across the street. He sold a different newspaper, one which she did not usually buy, but since the war had started one newspaper seemed pretty much like any other, so she crossed the cobbles to give the lad her custom.

A minute later she was inside her home putting on the kettle. A further minute and she was slumped in a comfy leather armchair, in a position she knew was bad for her back, smoking her first, much needed cigarette of the day. But backache was the least of her worries.

Alice looked at the front page of the newspaper. It was festooned in advertisements relating to the flu. The manufacturers of Oxo were claiming it 'fortified the system against influenza action'. There was a proliferation of ads for meat substitutes and tonics, while cleaning companies suggested that keeping a spotless home was the way to defeat the illness. Jeyes fluid and other disinfectants had never seemed so enticing.

She turned to the main news pages and read every report pertaining to the war. The Hun, as the newspaper referred to the enemy throughout, were in retreat. As well as news from the Front, there was an awful lot from foreign correspondents reporting on conditions in Germany. The enemy were apparently running out of food, and their Home Front appeared to be collapsing. She then scanned the newspaper looking for medical matters. By the time she had run out of tobacco and her eyelids started to close, she had speed read every word of the newspaper. There was the occasional article that mentioned the flu, but no critical analysis of what exactly the Spanish Lady was, or how it was effecting the war.

"It must be worse than I thought," she muttered to herself.

She leaned back, rubbing her eyes, pulling fingers down over her closed eyelids and onto her cheeks. The last thing her brain managed to process before sleep overtook her was that the flu pandemic was ending the war. One side or another would collapse under its weight. People cannot fight each other, starvation and a deadly virus all at the same time. Something had to give.

******

The following day Alice was craning her neck at the palatial splendour of the Poplar Board of Works building. No expense had been spared on constructing the gothic pile, with Portland stone and polished granite much in evidence. It had been built in the late nineteenth century, at a time of great deprivation in the surrounding area. She wondered how the Victorian mayor and his cronies could have been so detached from the realities of the local people they represented, that they could justify such opulence.

The good doctor had been called there for a meeting with numerous dignitaries; the local medical officer, the Chief Medical Officer of the London County Council, the mayor, local councillors, and representatives of the local sanitary authority, the Board of Education and a life assurance company. It was an emergency meeting forced upon them by the severity of the influenza outbreak. Though it was only pressure applied by local people's champion Sylvia Pankhurst, which had actually got them to the table.

Alice did not have to wait long before she started to appreciate that the attitude of the people in the building had probably changed very little in the past three decades. The pomposity which must have been in evidence back in the last century, lay as thick in the room as the carpet and cigar smoke.

The local medical officer was the first to speak. He advised against piecemeal attempts to stop contagion.

"Drastic action is impossible and tinkering is not worth the price."

Alice suspected that she had only been invited to the meeting as window dressing to keep her friend Sylvia happy.

No doubt she was not expected to actually contribute. So it was somewhat of a shock to everyone when she cut in to the medical officer's diatribe.

"We have to shut our schools. I have been told that schools outside London, which haven't as yet been as badly affected, have already been closed. I believe the worst hit areas of all are Bermondsey, Lewisham and Lambeth, areas close to London Bridge and Waterloo stations. Alighting points for soldiers returning from France. It is clear that this is where the infection is being spread from. We're just across the river from these areas, and Whitechapel's London Hospital is now full of infected soldiers, so it would seem only a matter of time before the situation becomes equally dire here. And now, due to the shortage of teachers in our areas because so many have already been struck down, children are having to congregate in ever more crowded classrooms which amplifies infection. We must..."

At this point the Chief Medical Officer cut in. He had heard enough. Who on earth did this woman think she was?

"My good woman, we do not close schools in London as a matter of routine on account of influenza. Closing schools is simply impractical." At this point he turned to face a local councillor whom he now addressed. "I believe the council has taken measures?"

The councillor took up his cue.

"Yes indeed. We have distributed powerful electrolytic disinfectant with instructions to gargle and rinse the throat daily. And council workers are now disinfecting the streets with Jeyes Fluid."

The local medical officer realised that this sounded just

like the piecemeal tinkering he had previously criticised so he re-entered the conversation.

"And furthermore we have printed handbills advising people to prepare their own gargles using permanganate of potassium and table salt. And we have also festooned the streets with placards and posters advising people to avoid crowds and keep bedrooms well ventilated."

"Excellent," said the Chief Medical Officer. "And of course for the very worst cases, doctors and chemists have quinine."

Mentioning doctors was a mistake. This brought Alice naturally back into the conversation.

"Quite so. My surgery is besieged by people demanding quinine. I exhaust my supplies as soon as I receive them. But quinine simply relieves the pain. It is no cure. I have been told there were recently ninety five deaths of children in London in one week alone. And one assumes such statistics take some time to collate. The situation must be worse by now."

The Chief Medical Officer was furious at such alarmist talk. And where on earth was this woman getting her information? It was far too accurate by half. That Pankhurst woman no doubt. But it was his job to allay such fears.

"You have been told have you? By someone who knows someone who knows someone ad nauseum no doubt. I for one, and am I not surely the first who would know, have not heard anything along these lines. One hears many tall tales in these circumstances. Rest assured, the situation is under control."

"But the children…" was as far as Alice got with her

reply before the Board of Education representative finally spoke up.

Alice had hoped for support from this quarter. She was to be disappointed.

"Ilford have closed their schools and now tell me they wished they had not. Eleven thousand children have been left to kick their heels. Most have flocked to cinemas. A corrupting influence I think you will all agree. And of course, they are more crowded and lacking in good ventilation than any school."

And so the argument went on. The life assurance man was Alice's only ally. At one point he put forward an idea to issue instructions to reduce crowds on public transport, but this was shouted down even quicker than anything Alice had proffered. It was the general consensus that workers must not be impeded by any travel regulations. The war took precedence.

The Chief Medical Officer had the final word.

"It is not expedient to spend energy to reduce the impact of the flu. We must ignore the disease lest fear open the way to infection through the weakening of nerve power known as war weariness. Our major duty is to carry on."

Alice trudged home in low spirits. She had promised to inform Sylvia of what had occurred at the meeting. Not that she was going to find the time to see her friend any time soon.

Chapter 32

"The coffins were stacked one on top of the other. It was at that moment at the age of ten that my boyhood ended."

B.E.Copping, letter regarding
his father's funeral

Nash started at Selby's Funeral Directors on a Sunday. He had been due to start the following day but pressure of work had meant the firm were working on a Sunday for the first time, and he had been called in for a morning's work. It had been depressingly busy. Mr Selby himself had come out of retirement to deal with the huge increase in administration. Timber for coffins was now rationed; forms needed to be filled in and presented to a timber controller for permits to be acquired. The manager, Mr Napier, was busy offering the relatives of the dear departed a cut price deal on cremation, but funeral insurance did not run to such expenditure. The other office worker, young Horace Wilkins, was spending his time trying to acquire the use of additional black horses, their own being close to exhaustion from so many trips to the cemetery.

Nash soon heard why he had been employed. Not only was he to use his wood yard connections to get hold of any timber he could without the use of permits, but it was also hoped he might be able to acquire from underworld associates the odd horse. And like Napier and Wilkins, he was to double up as a coffin bearer too.

On finishing his shift, Nash decided he needed to lift his spirits, so given he had a little bit of time to kill in any case, the local café beckoned. He thought he would have a cup of 'River Lea and two of toast' at Milo's, before getting himself along to the People's Palace in Mile End to meet Ruby at the end of her shift guarding the on-display German plane.

Nash came out of Selby's and crossed the Bow Road to a greengrocer's shop opposite. The place did not look right. For one thing there was no display of fruit and veg outside. He peered through the window to see that what little stock was on display inside had begun to shrivel and discolour. The till was empty; it had been left open to deter burglars. A message read 'Closed: All Sick'.

Earlier in the war Nash had seen shop owners who had been bombed out, still opening to trade as a stall amidst the rubble. It was business as usual. And normally when a proprietor had an illness or injury, there was a sibling, cousin or mate who would help keep a shop open. Nash thought things must be bad to have come to such a pass. He turned and headed in the direction of the neighbouring café.

A queue, made up exclusively of children, was spreading along the pavement outside Milo's Dining Rooms. The queue was for the shop next door, Bailey's Chemist. Nash's curiosity was aroused. Instead of pushing through the queue to reach the front door of the café, he sauntered along the line to have a look in the chemist's double bay windows. In both of them was a fine display of traditional apothecary jars, but that was nothing out of the ordinary. He asked the oldest looking lad in the queue what was going on.

"They've got Dr Collis Brown's chlorodyne in. Best thing there is for the flu they say," said the boy. "Cheaper than getting the doctor out as well. They can't do nothing for you no how."

That didn't fully explain to Nash what was occurring.

"So why's it all you nippers in the line up?"

"No Sunday School 'cause of the flu," said the boy. "So the old dear sent me up here. And the others here are the same I shouldn't wonder."

"What about during the week?" asked Nash. "Schools staying open are they?"

"Yeah, but so many teachers are down with the flu, classes are just sent home a lot of the time. I'm a half-timer anyhow so as long as I get me name ticked off the register in the mornings, it counts as me being there half a day even when I get sent home. Suits me. I can get off to work sharp see."

Ruby had recently mentioned to Nash that the shortage of labour had led to children aged twelve to fourteen being allowed to work for up to thirty three hours a week so long as they attended half their school lessons. At the time Nash had thought cynically that if thirty three hours and half their lessons were the official limits, blind eyes would no doubt be turned to allow it to be more like forty hours and a quarter of lessons. But it was clear to him now that children could work for as long as their parents or guardians needed them to, with no censure.

Some of the other children in the queue had overheard the conversation, so being bored with queueing decided it was time to serenade Nash with their rendition of a popular song, the words of which had been changed to reflect the times. A few likely lads started singing, but by the time the second line was being sung, pretty much the whole queue was joining in.

"Don't cry-ee, don't sigh-ee, there's a silver lining in the sky-ee. Bonsoir, old thing, cheerio, chin-chin, nah-poo, take the flu and die-ee."

Nash didn't know how to react. Should he give them all a clip round the ear followed by a good talking to? No, one of them no doubt learnt it from a parent, and quickly passed it on to their mates. It's probably being sung in every factory and school. It was like the odd cheeriness Ruby had told him about in Trafalgar Square.

People seemed to be in a good mood but read between the lines and there was sad resignation. There might be strikes everywhere, but the government needn't have put those battleships in the Thames. Resignation did not lead to insurrection. Maybe Bert was right after all and they were there to help out with the flu. But the government didn't seem overly bothered by the Spanish Lady so he doubted it. He turned on his heel and made his way into the café.

******

Nash did not enjoy his visit to look at the captured plane. It reminded him of the last air-raid. Of that poor woman being sliced through by that piece of shrapnel. He wondered how on earth what was clearly not much more than a box with wings and an engine had caused such carnage.

Ruby soon spotted her husband in the crowd. The two of them had agreed that he would come to see the plane just before her duty was due to end. A police van was then due to pick up her and Pemberton and drop them at Leman Street. Ruby would quickly change into her civvies while Nash was making his way by tube from Mile End to Aldgate East, a stone's throw from the police station.

The two of them were then going to spend a much needed Sunday afternoon at leisure together, enjoying the street theatre of the always very crowded Club Row animal market, and in particular the Sclater Street bird's section.

But first of all Nash had a little bit of work to do in the vicinity. The market was only a hop, skip and jump from Shoreditch railway station, inside the entrance of which Nash had agreed to meet briefly with one of his objectors. He was to give the man details of a job he had procured for him, as a grave-digger at Bethnal Green cemetery. It was not the sort of position that Nash would normally have been able to secure for one of his men, but the local authorities were struggling to keep up with the demand for six feet deep coffin-friendly holes in the ground.

It would be too dangerous for a local off duty police officer to be seen anywhere near such a meeting so while her husband met the man, Ruby would make herself scarce by popping along to Nash's favourite Jewish beigel shop at the top of Brick Lane, to pick them up a late dinner.

The couple made their way through Spitalfields, heading past the Ladies Swimming Bath & Recreational

Hall in Old Castle Street where they had once seen a Charlie Chaplin film. Nash then showed off his knowledge of the area by taking them down a series of alleys so claustrophobically narrow and high walled that they were dark even in the middle of what was a bright autumn day. And after passing through Spitalfields market, they crossed a run-down area of filthy old silk weaver's houses, and in no time at all were approaching Shoreditch.

They smelt and heard the animal market before they saw it. It would be very crowded so this was a cue for them to don their face masks. A cacophony of whimpers, yaps, yelps and barks soon informed them that they were arriving at the dogs section. New-born litters of puppies tumbled over each other in the window display of choice, which in an earlier life had been children's cots. Older pups cowered docilely together in laundry baskets. Dangerous looking men had furry little faces peering nervously out from the inside of their jackets. On the cobbles stood lively sheepdogs, alert greyhounds, and strong bulldogs pulling at their leads. Some were the property of hawkers and dealers, others were the single animal of a poverty stricken pet owner eager to make a bob or two to keep their distance from the workhouse door.

Pushing their way through the packed crowds, Ruby and Nash passed chickens in cages, cats in boxes and women selling bunches of cut flowers from baskets. They eventually reached Sclater Street, where the yelps were replaced by birdsong. There were cages of pretty birds to liven up the dullest of homes. Songbirds to lift the spirits; larks, thrushes, canaries, blue tits, minor birds. There were also pigeons, though the wartime ban on racing them due to concerns that enemy agents could use them to send messages, meant these birds were likely to be bought with a view to them joining some cabbage beneath a nice pie crust.

St Leonard's Church rang out the hour. It was time for Nash to get to his meeting. Ruby was so taken with the birds that she decided to stay in the market to decide which one they should buy to take home with them. She thought that after finishing his business Nash could return to the market and then the two of them could go together to the beigel shop. But her husband suggested that meeting up again in such a densely forested bit of humanity was easier said than done, so Ruby agreed to meet him outside St Leonard's Church, just across the road from Shoreditch station.

Nash's meeting took somewhat longer than planned. He had expected to simply give the thankful objector the details of where and when to turn up for work, rates of pay etc. But he was met with less than enthusiasm. The man was the most extreme type of objector; an Absolutist. Such men refused to have anything to do with the war. Nash's charge suspected he would end up digging graves for the bodies of soldiers.

It was explained that ordinary people were dropping like flies from the Spanish Lady, so Nash could assure him that it would be the graves of these poor unfortunates he would be digging. The man countered that it could be the war that had caused the flu to mutate in to such a killer, and it was clearly the war that was spreading the disease, so why should he help perpetuate such a thing? Nash replied that the quicker bodies were under the ground, the quicker the disease was stopped. Grave digging could save thousands of lives.

More umming and ahhing followed, with the man changing tack to state that he simply did not like the idea of digging graves. It was all rather too Burke & Hare for his liking. This had Nash start to lose his temper.

He told the man with ferocious conviction that some poor bastard had to dig graves, and it might just as well be him. Was he too high and mighty for such work? Who the bloody hell did he think he was?!

Nash was not a man you argued with when he was in a temper. And besides, his comments had hit home. The man also appreciated all the work Nash was doing for him and his fellow objectors, and the risks he was taking. So the man grudgingly agreed to start work as a grave-digger.

All this meant that Ruby was left waiting outside the church, like a jilted bride. And her trousseau was a recently bought, caged canary. She had been excited with her purchase and had looked forward to showing her husband the latest, beautiful yellow addition to their household. But her mood had turned somewhat less bright than her bird's plumage.

Where the bloody hell is he? It doesn't take half an hour to tell some feller he's got a new job. She wagered that the man was so pleased he took Nashey down the pub. It was funny how even the strongest willed of men simply couldn't refuse such a request. She could hear the excuse coming.

"He insisted. Wouldn't take no for an answer. Pub was packed. Took an age to get served. Had to get him one back didn't I? I drank up as soon as was decent."

Enough was enough. So much for her keeping her distance from an objector. She crossed Kingsland Road and headed for the station entrance. If her husband wasn't there, there were pubs on the surrounding street corners. He would be in one of them, and she would be joining him and his drinking mate there to give them what for.

At the entrance to the station Nash nodded a curt goodbye to his objector, who started to make his way towards the market. Nash hoped his wife had taken longer than expected to decide which bird to buy. If she hadn't, she would have been waiting outside the church for quite a while. A peace token might be in order. A flower girl was standing just outside the station. He paid for a bunch of her stock, and was about to head in the same direction as his objector towards the main road traffic lights opposite the church, when he saw Ruby waiting to cross towards him. She had not spotted him, so he was about to wave when he saw something odd. He quickly turned on his heel and ducked back out of sight, inside the station.

He had seen the copper Ruby was showing the ropes, Pemberton, dressed in his civvies, skulking behind one of the pillars of the church. It would have been easy to follow Ruby in a crowded market. The fellow must have followed the two of them all the way from Leman Street.

Ruby had previously told him of her suspicions about this man but Nash had not given too much heed to her concerns. He had concluded that the fellow was probably just a rum cove. Now he knew she was right. But was Pemberton following her on police business or was he simply a wrong 'un, interested in Ruby as a woman? If the former, could it have anything to do with Nash himself; his objector work? If it was the latter, the worry was that wrong 'uns could turn violent against women. A quick punch on the nose might sort out the problem. And Nash would impress upon him that he had better tell his employers that his squashed nose was due to a nasty fall. If the police came after Nash, there would be more trouble than any pipsqueak copper could handle.

Nash did not have time to ponder any further. Ruby walked into the station, spotted her husband and started to walk towards him with an expression on her face that told him that she had bought the canary she was carrying in double quick time and had been outside the church ever since.

Nash gave Ruby a serious look and put his left index finger to his lips, then beckoned her with a nod over to the booking office. She immediately realised something was wrong and did as she was bid. Her husband quickly bought two platform tickets, and moments later the couple took the stairway up to the two platforms. Nash spotted some luggage trolleys so rather than go on to a platform, which would have left them exposed, he motioned to his wife to follow him.

The couple spent the next minute or two crouched behind the trolleys, in whispered discussion, keeping their eye on the top of the stairs. As if on cue, their pursuer soon appeared. Nash looked at the tiny yellow new addition to his family which was hopping about in its cage inches from his face. He doubted making a shushing noise towards it would have the desired effect.

Their pursuer spent a few moments scanning the platforms, before showing something small cupped in his hand to a ticket collector, who stood aside and allowed him to pass through. It was obvious the porter had been shown police identification.

Ruby whispered to Nash that her colleague would not do that if he was there off his own bat. He would be loath to break police regulations by using his ID just to avoid paying for a rail fare or platform ticket. He was there on police business.

A train pulled in. Pemberton slid behind a pillar and watched, no doubt hoping to see them get on. He was out of luck. He then seemed to decide he had lost his quarry. He grimaced, said something under his breath, and ran for the station exit.

Ruby and Nash straightened up. Trains ran from Shoreditch to their local station, Old Ford, every fifteen minutes. The route was a leisurely multi stopping affair via Hackney. The train would probably be too crowded for them to discuss what had just happened, but there would be time for them both to think before putting their heads together at home. They knew one or both of them were in trouble.

Ruby looked at her little bird, and then at her husband to ask him something.

"Didn't canaries used to be sent down mines to see if there were trouble brewing?"

Chapter 33

"We're telling lies; we know we're telling lies; we don't tell the public the truth."

Lord Rothermere, proprietor of the Daily Mail,
Daily Mirror, Glasgow Record & Sunday Mail,
and Sunday Pictorial

With the People's Palace security work finished, Ruby had been given a new duty. The military authorities had declared cinemas and music halls were off limits to their personnel due to the flu. The soldiers would have been informed of the restriction by their sergeants back at the barracks but most of them were bound to ignore the instruction. Ruby and Pemberton were to tour round the queues and turf out any uniforms they saw. She was not looking forward to it as the soldiers were sure to kick up a fuss, and the public would then wade in with their four-penny's worth in support of the men.

The only saving grace was that she had a guardian angel watching over her. Nash had given Freddie the job of following the two police officers from a discreet distance, and keeping a close eye on Pemberton.

Backyards were no longer sufficient to contain the

increased passion for the national pastime of washing and scrubbing. The streets were now full of pillow cases, shirts, bed covers and the like, hanging from lines strung between lampposts or anything else suitably high. Water, a cleaning agent and billowing in the fresh air were all this linen needed to recover its past glory, which was more than could be said of its owners.

It made good cover behind which Freddie could hide. The fourteen year old was terribly excited by such clandestine work. It was just like being a spy. He was to report back to Nash if and when anything out of the ordinary occurred.

Ruby stood outside the local cinema, where she and Nash had first met Bert. Two scruffy looking men, complete with brushes, rectangular metal buckets and satchels of advertisements, were busy pasting posters on to walls. They pasted over some of the inducements to go to see the latest Perils of Pauline film. Ruby looked on with idle curiosity, hoping Charlie Chaplin's image would appear. But she was surprised and disappointed when, rather than the Little Tramp emerging, an ad campaign for the cinema itself started to take shape.

'Best ventilated theatre in London without draughts', read the new posters.

Ruby lost interest. A nearby screech of brakes took her attention. A motor driven van had come to a sudden halt on the street corner. A big bundle of newspapers was thrown out of the back of the vehicle onto the pavement. The paper shortage throughout the war meant newspapers had got thinner and thinner. Such a large bundle had been a thing of the past.

A newsboy was beckoned over to the van. He put his head in the back to be told something. Whatever it was had him rushing to unwrap his new delivery. He stopped and gawped at the top copy for a moment. The three other newsboys waiting for their deliveries read over his shoulder. Another newspaper van approached at speed. This was a prompt for the fortunate first with the news to exercise his lungs. He grabbed a pile of newspapers from his pile.

"Turkey surrenders! Hun fleet mutinees! Hun appeal for armistice! Read all about it!"

Apparently the war was over. The newsboy was quickly besieged by those eager to indeed read all about it. Yet there were some who walked past him with little more than a sideways glance.

Ruby thought it not so surprising. The end of the war had been coming for a while. And for over four years the populace had chosen to believe almost every word the press had printed about the conflict. Even when they knew the newspapers were being less than accurate with their reporting, people accepted that such things were all part of the war effort. But now, with the flu-drenched streets of London bearing no relation to the self-satisfied victorious country painted in the newspapers, people had grown contemptuous of what they were being fed.

True, the devil may care attitude Ruby had experienced in Trafalgar Square was still about. There were queues at popular restaurants, the shops were busy, theatres and music halls were booming. Because after all, the flu could kill you tomorrow. But elsewhere, on the streets, outside the factories, amongst the majority, Ruby saw depression. Because yes, the flu really could kill you tomorrow. It had killed. People you knew. Loved ones, neighbours. People had become preoccupied with something other than the war. The Hun may have been beaten, but the Spanish Lady was proving just as great an adversary.

Ruby's deliberations were interrupted by a little wave of people creating the start of a queue outside the ticket office of the picture palace. Soon enough they were joined by a couple of soldiers with young women on their arms.

"Here we go," said Ruby, with weary resignation.

She nodded to Pemberton to join her. But what she had assumed would be the inevitable altercation failed to materialise. The soldiers accepted that they had already been told they were not allowed in cinemas, and had been caught trying it on, so they simply slunk away with their tails between their legs. And as they did so, a voice from the queue spoke up. But it was not in defence of the soldiers. It was a quiet "thank you miss" to Ruby for moving the army boys on. Other people in the queue had kept themselves to themselves. Passing bystanders had not so much as cast a glance their way. It was clear that people no longer wanted to be in close proximity to soldiers. The word was out.

Ruby noticed that Pemberton had left her to deal with the soldiers. He had stayed very much on the periphery of things. She suspected the reason was that he was afraid of catching the flu himself.

It was understandable. Dr Alice had recently confided to her that a high number of the people suffering most from it were not, strangely, the young and old, as you would expect, but fit adults in the prime of their lives. Ruby had replied by telling Alice what she had heard from a police sergeant about the Russian flu epidemic of thirty years earlier having left older people with an immunity. Alice had agreed that could be a factor, but it didn't explain why younger people were also less effected. It was her belief that the mutated virus was causing the immune system to attack its own body. The stronger one's immune system, the stronger its reaction to the virus. One effectively drowned in one's own juices. It was thus a disproportionate number of people aged between twenty and thirty five, those at the height of their body's physical powers, who were dying. People like soldiers. Like police officers.

Chapter 34

"The doctor is not unsympathetic but he has seen it a hundred times. He is hoping it will all end quickly so that he can sign the death certificate and get back to bed in time to catch a few more hours' sleep before dawn brings the next round."

Melanie McGrath, Silvertown
– An East End Family Memoir

There were now fourteen hundred Metropolitan police officers ill or worse with the flu. Having two officers working together had become a luxury the force could no longer afford. The shortage of personnel meant those who were still fit had to become Jacks of all trades. Pemberton now had to tour the local picture palaces and music halls, not just to keep military personnel out, but to ensure that everyone left at the end of each performance, as councils now insisted that such places were emptied every four hours while all windows were opened to aerate the halls.

Freddie's surveillance of him while he was working with Ruby was thus short lived, much to the boy's chagrin.

And Sergeant Granger had to admit that WPC Nash had always shown great ingenuity and an ability to respond well to any unforeseen circumstance that came her way. Consequently she had been given a wide range of new duties to perform alone.

She toured the chemist's shops and doctor's surgeries in the area, to maintain a police presence in an attempt to ensure no rioting or looting broke out. She also had to patrol near funeral directors, to keep an eye on rows of newly arrived unpolished empty coffins lined up along the pavement. There was such a shortage that other funeral directors might be tempted to swipe a few.

When told this, Ruby immediately thought of her husband's duties at Selby's. She wagered that was exactly what the old devil was getting up to.

The shortage of wood meant that she also had to show her presence one step down the chain, outside wood yards and carpenters' workshops. And if she happened to pass a window through which she could see someone on the telephone, she was to tap the glass to grab their attention, and then give them the sideways thumb as a hint to hurry up and finish their call. If they ignored her, she entered the building and told them brusquely that London had a thousand telephone operators down with the flu so get off the line so others could have a go. She was also under orders that if a fire broke out anywhere, she was to attend and then ask any passing man in the vicinity to help the sparsely manned fire engines.

All these duties she did with enthusiasm but the one she faced with dread was in helping the overstretched London Ambulance Service. There were occasions when bodies had to be recovered from houses in which they had lain unattended for days.

******

Dr Alice had seen Maud when she had originally collapsed, and again yesterday. On that occasion her patient had felt severely exhausted, weak, short of breath, dizzy, had a throbbing headache, chest pains and hacking cough. The advice had been to stay in bed, keep warm and ask Nashey, Ruby and anyone else who was willing to enter, to bring hot poultices to prevent the lungs from becoming congested.

But today Nash had tracked Alice down and asked her to come as soon as she could, as Maud's condition had deteriorated badly. On entering the bedroom Alice's worse fears were realised. Maud's hair had turned white overnight and she had slipped into trembling, shouting, confused delirium. Her head was back, mouth half open and dribbling the blood-stained greenish yellow sputum that had been coughed up. Her cheeks had turned from the sallow pallor of yesterday to a blue discolouration, her lips and ears purple. They were the usually fatal signs of cyanosis. Nineteen of every twenty 'blue' cases died.

Alice stayed with her patient. In normal circumstances she would have had to use a triage method whereby she would leave to attend someone who had more of a chance of survival. But the fact was that survival appeared to be largely dependent on one's age and sheer luck. There was nothing she could do as a doctor. She was simply a palliative nurse.

She stayed with Maud and watched her skin start to turn the colour of mahogany. Maud made one last fight for breath, gurgling horribly. It was as if she were drowning.

She reached out and grabbed at her doctor as if Alice were a lifeguard proffering a life belt. And then she was gone.

Alice did not feel a thing, other than horror at her own numbness. Was this what the war and this disease had reduced her to?

******

The Nashes were fed up with paying a good slice of their income to the avaricious owner of their near-slum property. The last time Nash had found a new cockroach lodger in the place, he had carefully gathered it up into a matchbox and taken it round to the landlord's rather more salubrious home. On the front door being opened by a maid, he had barged into the hallway and set the insect free from captivity. The maid's shrieks soon had the man of the house arrive on the scene, where Nash told him in his most intimidating voice, that he would only be paying half the rent from now on unless the house was kept in better condition, and woe betide the man if he sent round any of his bully boys to get the balance.

The landlord, a man called Sharples, had threatened eviction from the safety of a letter. And there were plenty of hours in the day or night when neither tenants were about, when the first one of them home could return to find all their worldly goods and chattels thrown out on the street outside, and the locks changed. But Sharples was well aware that Nash's threats were not to be taken lightly, though it was the lady of the house who concerned him most. Evicting a police officer, even one who was only a woman, could have repercussions. The police force were not an organisation with which you wanted to fall out.

Consequently, relations between Mr & Mrs Nash and their landlord were somewhat tense. But Sharples had every right to get Maud's half of the dwelling ready for a new tenant. That said, he was not unwise enough to use his set of keys to let himself into the house unannounced.

The front door was open but the landlord knocked on it in any case. Nash appeared and nodded unenthusiastically for him and the two heavies he had astutely brought along, to enter the house. On walking in to the passage, the three strangers wrinkled their nose. Sharples took the stench to be evidence of a business involving death being in progress. The slaughter of animals in the backyard for the cats' meat trade, most likely.

"May I point out to you Mr Nash that it is a requirement of your tenancy that no noxious trade may be entered into in these premises or in the yard without," said the landlord pompously.

The suspicion that Nash was involved in animal slaughter was quite ironic given that he was looking at his landlord as if the man was a piece of offal that had become trapped under his boot. But when Nash answered, he sounded surprisingly conciliatory.

"It's not me guvnor," he said. "You'll have to take it up with the other tenant. It's her fault."

The landlord looked perplexed.

"I was given to understand that Mrs Kemp had, sadly, passed away. It is the sole reason I am in attendance here today."

Nash turned and headed up the passage to the foot of

the stairs, giving the men a nod for them to follow him. They all trundled up to the first floor, and followed Nash into Maud's bedroom.

"There you are," said Nash. "Take it up with her."

Maud's body lay there on its deathbed, looking at them through pennies over the eyes. The stench was overpowering.

"You boys have been a bit too quick off the mark," said Nash. "It's not been two days. Ambulance ain't been round yet. My wife says as how she could use her uniform to get 'em round sooner but I said no. Why should we be treated any different from any other poor bastards?"

It had the desired effect. The three men rushed out of the room and tumbled down the stairs in varying degrees of distress. Nash noticed that the landlord had turned out to be tougher than his two henchmen. He was the only one not retching in the gutter outside.

"Now fuck off out of it!" shouted Nash as he slammed the door on their backs. But point made, the need for fresh air soon had him reopening it.

******

When male workers had gone off to war and many of their jobs were filled by a new female workforce, one job women did not take over was street cleaning. It was non-essential, non-war work. Streets were left to their own devices. As a result, the streets of Bow, not the cleanest at the best of times, had reverted to the filth of a bygone era. But November 11's yellow autumn morning sunshine turned the dirty streets of Bow aptly golden.

Many people had stood vigil all night waiting for the big day to dawn. At half past ten the Union flag was raised on Bromley by Bow Town Hall. By noon there were flags flying from nearly every building. Hundreds of thankfully redundant munitions workers streamed out of the factories at which they had gathered for one last time, and marched down Bow High Street singing patriotic songs. Trolley bus guards left their posts, their vehicles now marooned in the crowds. Stranded passengers cheered as soldiers broke into foxtrots. People packed into cinemas, but didn't wait for the professional entertainment to begin. They serenaded each other with singing and flag waving. Come the afternoon the main thoroughfares were so packed that the tram system was at a standstill. Crowds linked hands across the road behind bugle bands and drummers.

Their joy was literally infectious. Had the influenza bug been a predator lying in wait, it would have licked its lips.

One of its recent victims was taking her last journey. Maud's cortege was on its way to the church, surrounded by the sounds of bells, hooters and whistles. She had always religiously paid her funeral insurance even when things were tight, and now she had beautiful black stallion horses with ostrich plume feathers and a marked grave to show for it.

Nash was a pallbearer. Ruby was wearing her police uniform. Not because she believed it looked suitably formal or smart, but because all police leave had been cancelled for what was sure to be a busy day. She had told her sergeant that she was going to the funeral. He could sack her if he liked but she was going. Granger would have loved to have called her bluff and finally got rid of WPC Nash, but with such staff shortages he was not in a position to do so. He agreed that she could take time off mid-shift to attend the funeral, and could work till midnight to make up for it.

Along the route to the church, revellers fell silent, removed their headwear and bowed in respect.

Chapter 35

"It was a grievous business having to listen every morning to the chief of staff's recital of the number of influenza cases, and their complaints about the weakness of their troops if the English attacked again."

General Erich Ludendorff,
German Quartermaster General:
My War Memories

Frau Burchardt had been shaken to the core by the car incident. She had dwelled on it at some length, and was no nearer coming to terms with the event, when the war had ended. This shock had jolted her out of her self-pity. It was time to receive some education from ordinary people about the conflict.

She had asked those who had rescued her from the riot, to visit her. Considering it rather inappropriate to receive these guests in her opulent drawing room, an additional hard backed antique chair had been placed in the parlour. She sat in it surrounded by her injured chauffeuse, the soldier and nurse who had rescued them, and a woman called Ursula, who appeared to be something of a socialist firebrand.

Social niceties having been observed and tea cups drained, they were now well into a conversation about the war, with Ursula holding court as to the need for equality in German society. And not just between the classes. She believed that the sacrifices of Berliners were ignored by the state compared to the rest of the country. As Prussians they suffered relative to Bavarians. She claimed that it was inequality that had cost the Fatherland the war and had led her to join the Spartacists. She had believed that if the Spartacists had taken over the government, the German people could have fought back against the English devils. Once Germany had better organised its agricultural requirements, it could have reduced the effects of the Allied blockade. But it was all too late now.

The rant finished with a dig at royalty.

"Had Wilhelm stood in the crosshairs, or stood in a line for potatoes, the Home Front would have been arranged differently," she said knowingly. "It was not merely inequality but the black market which was the greatest pestilence of the people in this war."

This brought Aldo into the conversation.

"Whoever doesn't follow food regulations, belongs in prison. Whoever does, belongs in the nuthouse."

"Oh, do be quiet Aldo," barked her tired, confused employer.

Peter had taken a shine to the young chauffeuse, though not in any sort of romantic way. He was keen to have her now red cheeks return to a lighter shade, so went to her defence against her employer, whom Peter had down as a hypocrite. One moment the woman had been telling everyone to call her Frau Ute and the next she was lording it over them all, arguing that there had been nothing wrong with paying a little extra for things if one could afford them. Surely it was all good for the war economy.

"Aldo is right of course. We did what we could to get through the war. We have fought for four years without enough food to go around. With farmers, the black market, factory owners and other crooks making their fortunes. But we kept going. It is the flu that beat us in the end."

He went on, stating that he knew nothing of what Ursula was saying but speaking purely as a simple soldier he was certain that once the German Spring Offensive had been halted and pushed back the war had been lost. The German army had been exhausted. The German Home Front had been decimated by the flu. The English must have been too, but managed to keep going somehow. They clearly coped with the lack of food and kept up their morale. Morale is everything in war. That is what won the English the war.

Dorothea agreed with her soldier and was better able to articulate the point he was making. She appreciated that Britain must have better organised its rationing system, which had resulted in the enemy being better fed than the German people. English morale had received a boost from rationing that enabled them to withstand the terrible effects of the killer strain of the flu, just as morale in Germany had collapsed under the stresses and strains created by the virus. And once the war was won and lost on the Home Fronts, the military conflict soon followed suit.

Ursula had not thought of this before but it fitted with her. The German people, the German army, had not been defeated by the English per se. It was a mix of bad luck that the flu had hit, and the capitalist government's fault in failing to deal with it.

The conversation ebbed and flowed for hours. Real coffee rather than the ersatz variety her guests would usually imbibe; and cake that was both Black Forest and black market, was consumed. Much of the talk educated Frau Burchardt about the ways of the world at war. The longer the chat went on, the darker the wealthy woman's mood became and the greater her sense of guilt. She had been naïve, ignorant, and she had to admit greedy, as she had turned a blind eye to the horrors of the Home Front.

Out of this naval-gazing came an epiphany. Whatever the reasons, whoever was to blame, it was clear to her that the German people had hit rock bottom. They could not continue like this. But despite the war ending, the English were not ending their blockade of German imports so things were only going to get worse in the short term. If the English would not take their boot off their throats, Germans had to find another way of getting their breath. Something had to be done. And she would be one of those to do it.

Chapter 36

"All the girls in the village…prayed every night for the war to end, and for the English to go away…as soon as their money was spent. And the clause about the money was always repeated in case God should miss it."

Robert Graves, Goodbye to All That

The present socio political upheaval in Germany had put at the very least a temporary hold on Klaus' entrepreneurial venture with Fritz. It was no time for them to be starting a new business. Klaus would remain a traditional farmer and Fritz would no doubt have plenty of black market duties to perform during such a period of shortages.

And though the war might have been over, the Sunday ritual of city dwellers crowding on to trains heading for the countryside looking for food, would not abate until the Allies ceased their blockade.

One of the latest bits of the German language Klaus' POWS had learnt was 'hamsterfahrt' meaning foraging jaunt. They found the word highly amusing and would shout 'hamster fart!' towards city dwellers when such people had indeed made their way to the farm on a foraging mission. If this was next shouted on Sunday, some bright spark

Berliner would surely shout some sarcastic congratulations or abuse at them in English about the Armistice.

The problem for Klaus was that he had chosen not to tell his British workforce that the war was over. As soon as the news had come through, he had astutely bribed the guards not to tell the enemy that they had won the war. He did not have to bribe them with very much. A few eggs and an appeal to their patriotism, telling them with a wicked sneer that the pig dog Englishmen could give the Fatherland some free labour. It was the least they could do.

He had initially believed that with a bit of luck he could get away with this for a few weeks. From what he had heard, the repatriation of troops was going to be a slow process. And the local area's Corps Commander in charge of organising the POWs in the district was in a spat with the head of the local Spartacist revolutionaries, which was going to ensure things proceeded at a glacial pace.

But it was inevitable that his POWs would find out about the end of the war as soon as they came in to contact with anyone from outside the farm. So the plan was to have all the Tommies work in the top field on Sunday. This would keep them as far away as possible from visitors who arrived by walking up the lane to the farmhouse. But such people were becoming increasingly cheeky. Some were circumnavigating the entrance to the farm so they could sneak in to the fields to steal any vegetables they could lay their hands on. Klaus simply hoped that any such characters would be too busy stealing and running off with their loot to engage in conversation with men of the victorious enemy.

A Danish Red Cross vehicle turned up at the farm,

laden with a truck load of bread, tinned beef, pork & beans, dried apricots, cocoa, bars of Sunlight soap and good news. All for the British prisoners of war. They were to be repatriated from Danzig or Hamburg. They would be taken by ship to Rotterdam, from where the British authorities would be sending them to Hull. Accompanying the Danes was the local official whom Klaus usually liaised with, and an English-speaking German army officer, who was to formally tell the men of all this.

Klaus' plans lay in tatters. And who knew what the penalty might be for having kept the news of the Armistice from the POWs. He decided to play the stupid, frightened country bumpkin card. He told the officials that he had not told his POWs that the war was over because he feared they would overpower his poor injured soldiers and attack him and his wife. He claimed the Englishmen were a surly bunch, who had done as little work as possible. He looked knowingly at the local official, encouraging him to back him up on this.

This he did, and the German army officer appeared too exhausted to be bothered one way or the other, so although the Danes were exasperated by such behaviour, the old farmer got away with nothing more than a verbal slap on the wrist.

The POWs knew something was up when, instead of being called 'schweinhund', a German army officer whom they had never seen before, addressed them as 'gentlemen'.

"I don't want you to make much noise, but Germany has lost the war and is finished," he said in strongly accented English.

He said this so quietly and matter-of-factly, as if he were

chatting to a friend in his sitting room, that the obvious cheers and screams of delight were not immediately forthcoming. The men had been captured at a time when it was the Allies who were losing the war.

Had the Hun got his English language arse about face? Why add that his country was finished? Did he mean England had lost the war and was finished?

The silence that followed had a member of the Danish Red Cross step forward to emphasise in rather better English that Germany had surrendered. The war was over.

It was the last sentence that did it. The men collapsed into delirium. Five minutes later, 'knees up Mother Brown' was in full flow. But the men were so weak from their deficit of work over calorie intake that the singing and dancing did not last long. And they were soon boiling up cocoa and stuffing their faces with food.

Within the hour reciprocal arrangements were in evidence between soldiers no longer at war with one another. Germans cut off epaulettes from their uniforms to swop with their souvenir hunting English counterparts. Not that there was any desire for scraps of British tunics in return. Food was handed over as the British side of the bargain.

The guards received further Red Cross proceeds in return for escorting all but one of the Tommies into the nearby town where, armed with a large tin of cocoa and a couple of bars of soap, they descended on a bar which supplied the men with ersatz beer until they were nicely drunk. In their weakened, excited state, it didn't take long.

The teetotal conscientious objector Albert Walker was the exception. He paid a German soldier with food to take him into central Berlin for some sightseeing. They wandered Unter den Luden, the Reichstag and the Teirgarten. They also followed a crowd to see a Spartacist leader; a gesticulating, volcanic figure with a vivid face, wild eyes and the distorted mouth of a Greek tragic mask, address a mass crowd with red banners. The Englishman had no idea what was being said but the atmosphere was intense, and he thought that a British uniform, albeit one so filthy from farm work to be barely recognisable, was not the ideal attire to be on display at such a meeting, so he and his guard-turned-guide started to make their way home.

The two men were not the only tourists in town, and hawkers had been quick to respond. Emaciated women dressed in rags, selling albums of views of Germany, spotted the British uniform and headed towards it shouting 'Engleesh!'

It flashed through Albert's mind that perhaps he ought to buy something. After all, it was the least he could do. But then reality hit him. Some of the sights in those albums probably no longer existed, courtesy of the British or French armed forces. And what would he do with such an album? Have it as a keepsake of the war? Show his friends back in Blighty what Germany used to look like? What German people used to look like? Before the war reduced them to what stood in front of him now. He had decided it would be the height of bad taste to buy something, but was toying with the idea of simply giving one of them money. But which one? There were a half a dozen women surrounding him, but he only had a single coin in a breast pocket of his army tunic, given to him by his guide in return for a few dried apricots.

He saw how the women tugged at their clothing to stop it from falling off them. Even their rags were too big for their thin bodies. They were clearly white German women but could have been from the streets of Cairo or Baghdad, their weather-beaten wrinkled faces, billowing clothing and head scarves could have them passing for Arabs. But they had nothing of the exotic tales of A Thousand and One Nights about them. There was nothing romantic in starvation.

As they gathered closer to him, their bony hands thrusting their merchandise his way, he found these insistent, desperate women strangely intimidating. They should be shouting insults at him, at this Englander, not begging him to be their client.

"Eengleeshman! Kekse! Shokolade!"

The shouts had come from the opposite direction to the one from which the women had arrived. In high pitched, excited voices. Albert whirled round to see a gang of children running towards him. Within moments the urchins were elbowing their way through the entourage of women encircling him to get to their target. Demands for biscuits and chocolate were repeated. But the Englishman had not thought to bring any of his Red Cross parcel fare with him, so he had to splay both his empty hands in guilty submission to show he had nothing to give them. He pulled out what little was left of the lining of his trouser pockets, complete with holes, to add emphasis.

He wanted to turn on his heel and quicken his pace to get away from the children and women alike, but believed his German soldier guide, who had a heavy limp courtesy of a Somme shrapnel wound, was in no condition to make any sort of a run for it. But just as he considered this, he saw the soldier scuttling away as quickly as his heavy limp could take him. To see such a badly disabled man moving with such jarring difficulty had something of the grotesque about it. Albert wondered what on earth the man was doing.

The question must have been written in his face as he looked towards the soldier. He received a speedy reply by return of glance.

"Grippe!" shouted the soldier.

As a child Albert had been a bright boy. Top of his class or close to it in all but one subject. French. He found learning a foreign language incomprehensible. And when, last year, he had been captured and sent to the farm, the stream of German words that had come his way had gone in one ear and out the other. All but one. Grippe. The German, the French, the international term for influenza. It seemed such a horrendously perfect, ironic word for this new strain of a virus which was gripping the war by the throat and slowly increasing its grip to throttle the life out of it. The word had stuck immediately.

The soldier was clearly concerned that having such a large group so up close and personal was a recipe for catching the deadly virus. The Englishman ran to catch up his German minder.

Chapter 37

"The Germans... are going to be squeezed, as a lemon is squeezed – until the pips squeak."

Sir Eric Campbell-Geddes,
Minister without Portfolio,
Cambridge speech, 1918.

Having a telephone was all very well but the problem was that few people of her more recent acquaintance were equally blessed. Frau Burchardt therefore summoned Fritz Patemann by messenger delivered letter. You could not call it a request that he present himself to her as soon as possible. It was more a demand, and Fritz noted that his client had used her surname rather than her usual Frau Ute. The messenger was sent back with a missive asking if he might have the temerity to ask Aldo to pick him up in the motor, as he was feeling poorly. The messenger's foot leather had more miles put on it, Frau Burchardt agreeing that such a request was indeed the height of temerity, but it could not be accommodated as she no longer owned a motor car. She would expect him within the hour.

Despite the tidy profit he had made from the flu remedy and elephant deals, he was too tight with his money to hail a taxi. He wanted to keep every penny he had, in case his business venture with the old farmer could be resurrected once the present turmoil ceased. So he crammed his aching limbs on to a crowded tram and then had a fair walk to his client's house. By the time he got there, he was feeling terrible.

He had seen Frau Burchardt's cook quite a few times of late, having used the tradesmen's entrance to take his orders from her in the kitchen, and returning with the requisite items within the day. But the last time Fritz had met the mistress of the house had been some time ago, at her bank, when he had handed over the considerable return she had made on her investment in elephant steak. His investor had ushered him into a discreet little wood panelled private booth inside the bank, where he had been encouraged to pass over the money speedily and be on his way. There had been very little social chit chat, though it had been evident that Frau Burchardt had assumed that a well-to-do restaurant, of a five star hotel perhaps, had bought the carcass and Fritz was certainly not going to disavow her of that assumption.

He had smiled to himself. He would have liked to have seen the look on her face if she ever walked through the doors of the huge Bavarian style bar restaurant that had bought the beast. Not exactly the sort of establishment to which she was accustomed. And a cheap plate of steak and sauerkraut washed down with a disgusting ersatz beer was probably not what she would have in mind as her meal of choice.

But despite the brevity of their meeting, they had parted on good terms, with her requesting that he contact the restaurant owner in Dresden to keep a couple of steaks by for her. She intended to have Aldo drive the two women all the way to Dresden to enjoy an elephant steak meal.

The terse nature of her summons had him thinking that perhaps she had indeed driven to Dresden. He had contacted the owner to keep a couple of steaks back for her, but perhaps the man hadn't. Or perhaps he had. That might actually have been worse. Another possibility was that she had found out somehow that he had sold the carcass to a bar rather than a plush restaurant, and for less than she believed he should have. Perhaps there was a suspicion he had fiddled her out of some of her profit?

Then it dawned on him that the summons could be about something far more serious. Could someone in Mrs Burchardt's circle come to realise that they had all had been paying way over the odds for cheap Spanish medicine, which was no better at staving off the flu than anything else? Supposing one of her friends had contracted the disease and died? Fritz felt a sudden terrible realisation that he could be in big trouble.

Aldo, wearing a face-mask, met him at the front door. She was far more formal and serious than usual. And did not thank him for the medicine that he had provided when she had suffered the flu. A further sense of foreboding swept over him. Was her mood simply governed by the considerable events that she had been through recently? Flu, then attacked in a riot, then Germany surrender. Or was he in big trouble with her employer?

She took his hat and as she ushered him in to the house, asked if he would like some ersatz coffee. Fritz was confident that, despite Aldo's straight face, she must be joking. She wasn't in such a dull mood after all. He chuckled, thanked her politely and confirmed with mock delight that of course he would love some.

He was shown in to the parlour and motioned to sit. Frau Burchardt was already in situ. She was not wearing a face-mask but Fritz noticed that their two respective chairs could not have been further apart. They would have to contact their business in slightly raised voices. Aldo busied herself pouring, and then serving coffee for two, before leaving them alone.

Fritz looked at the liquid in his coffee cup. It really was ersatz. What on earth was going on?

Ute Burchardt looked at him with no hint of the usual smile of welcome. There was a hardness; a coolness to her. Fritz braced himself. He was convinced that whatever she was about to say, he was not going to like it.

The conversation began as he might have expected with her asking him about the trip to sell the elephant. Their previous rushed meeting at the bank had not included any great debrief about the Dresden deal so Fritz gave an accurate, honest account of the trip and transaction, but his questioner did not appear overly interested in the answer. She just nodded rather absent-mindedly and confirmed that is was good that things had gone so well.

"Are you still planning to have Aldo drive you to Dresden to partake?" he asked lightly.

"No I am afraid not," she replied. "I no longer own a motor car. My motor was turned over and later set on fire by protesters. It was insured of course, but I have no desire to replace it. I will no doubt purchase a small vehicle in due course. What would poor Aldo do without a motor to drive eh? But my previous great motor was a frivolous luxury in this day and age don't you think?"

Fritz did not know whether to answer or not. It was his experience that wealthy people often ended sentences with what sounded like questions, but were not at all, and they were certainly not expecting answers. He took a sip of what he considered disgusting coffee and hoped his client would get to whatever point she was planning to make.

"I see you do not enjoy my coffee," she said, with perhaps a touch of humour in her voice. "I have something of an economy drive going on here at the moment. Not to save money you understand. I want, no, I *need* to do my bit for the German people. I am no longer living in my ivory tower. It is the principle do you see?"

There's another of those sentence ending questions that weren't questions. Annoyed with himself for not having hidden his disdain for the coffee, he thought he should say something.

"No, no, not at all Frau Ute er Burchardt, the coffee is most fine. It is just that I am feeling rather under the weather today."

"Oh yes, indeed, you mentioned that in your note. I am sorry to hear of it," she said without any hint of sincerity. "Let me cut to the chase. I would like to ask your advice on something. You clearly have farms supply you with some of your black market produce. And I know farms are struggling, what with the government's demands, the loss of men and horses to The Front and so on. Would you know of one that might wish to go into partnership with me?"

Fritz was completely taken aback. He had certainly not

seen this coming. What on earth had happened to cause this? But his was not to reason why. He tried to think quickly on his feet. How could he make something out of this?

Frau Burchardt was a step ahead of him. She spoke again.

"I would pay you a commission of course. You negotiate the right deal for me at the right farm and I will return to you my share of our elephant escapade. It needs to be a farm with expertise in dairy. Perhaps one that has just lost cows in the latest slaughter."

"Klaus Winterhager!" Fritz had blurted it out as if his host had thumbscrews on him. "He's the farmer who advised me about the slaughterhouses for the elephant carcass. He has just lost his dairy herd due to the government's demands. He's perfect."

"He is indeed," agreed his benefactor. "The idea is that I will pay for a new dairy herd to be introduced to the farm. And all milk produced will be given away free to the German poor."

She knew Patemann was sure to interrupt her to point out that no farmer would agree to such a thing, so she had a flat hand raised like a policeman directing traffic before he could do so. She fixed him with a steely stare, dropped her hand and continued.

"I will pay this man Winterhager the going rate for whatever income he would normally have received from the milk. I will also send him a woman to work free of charge on the farm. Her name is Fraulein Wende. She will oversee the production and transportation of the milk and be my representative on the farm. I am sure you understand what that means? And when the present food shortage ceases, presumably sometime after the Allied blockade ends, I will end my control of the milk production, and sell or if he cannot afford this, rent the cows to the farmer. I expect you to earn your commission by negotiating the rate for this on my behalf. Of course, if I find out that you have negotiated a deal that is more beneficial to your friend Winterhager, than it is to me, I do not think I need to tell you that a woman like me has friends in high places, who can make things difficult for someone like you. After all, some people believe the black market contributed to our losing the war. Emotions run high on the matter. I am sure you understand Herr Patemann?"

There was the question to end the speech again. But this time Fritz knew it was a question he did need to answer. He had not taken offence at the inherent threat. It was just business. And yes, he did understand what she meant about the woman Wende. She would be there on the farm to make sure the farmer did not get up to any fiddles at her employer's expense.

"It would be an honour to serve you in this capacity Frau Burchardt," he said, formally bowing his head slightly. And he meant it.

******

Once the initial shock of what Fritz had to say to him had subsided, Klaus could not help but be delighted by the proposed business venture. It was a far better idea than his had been to have camera film and the influenza outbreak as the basis of a business. Not just because it was an opportunity to become a dairy farmer again and earn money that was guaranteed by a benefactor rather than rely on the vagaries of post war entrepreneurship, but because he saw it as a chance to do something positive for his fellow Germans.

This free milk idea would give him a chance to give something back. He would throw himself into the project. He did not like the idea of some busybody woman coming to supervise him, but he had to admit that he was a dog which had quite fairly been given a bad name.

The finer points of exactly how this project would work, were then thrashed out by the farmer and the black marketeer. But progress was becoming slower and slower as Fritz had to continually stop to clear his head. Flu was getting on top of him. Eventually the discussion was done with Fritz slumped in an armchair, eyes closed. And when a question by Klaus went unanswered, and the farmer shook the man without success, it was clear no answer would be coming forth that day.

Chapter 38

"Allerlei Ersatz!..If there must be a substitution, then to me you are the dearest."

Soldier holding a nurses hand in
Kriegszeitungder 1. Armee,
(German pictorial newspaper) 1918

While she had been visiting England before the war, Dorothea had been invited to attend a Women's Social & Political Union medal ceremony at the Royal Albert Hall for Suffragettes who had been on hunger strike in prison. She had been introduced to some of the medal winners, including Kitty Marion, a woman a little older than herself, whom she detected had a slight German accent.

Was there a trace of Westphalia in that voice? Kitty was asked about this and it transpired that she had been born and brought up in Germany, and yes it was in Westphalia, until she migrated to Britain as a fifteen year old, a quarter of a century earlier.

Kitty's German was better than Dorothea's English, so she had enjoyed using her mother tongue for a change. The two women had hit it off immediately.

Her new friend had gone to see Kitty, who was an

actress, in pantomime. She had also visited her at her home in Brighton, where they had put the world to rights as they marched along the sea-front promenade arm in arm. Kitty had also confided that her allegiance to the Suffragette cause had led her to be force fed over two hundred times, which had both appalled and impressed Dorothea. Their friendship had quickly blossomed and they had stayed in touch until the Allied blockade ensured that not only did foodstuffs not get into Germany, but such things as letters did not get in or out.

The last correspondence that Kitty, or Katherina Schafer to use her real name, had managed to get to Dorothea in 1914, just as war broke out, had mentioned that she had been under threat of being interned as an enemy alien and deported from Britain. But some old Suffragette allies with contacts in high places, had managed to arrange for her to be allowed to emigrate to the United States.

But with the war, if not the blockade, now over, postal services were less disrupted and Kitty had managed to get a letter to her friend via a contact in Sweden. The letter had informed its eager recipient that Kitty had not, as one might have expected, joined the American women's suffrage movement, which was still fighting for the vote, because she had been drawn into another fight for women's rights. She had joined the movement to change America's birth control laws. The long term plan was to set up the first American birth control clinic. This had led her to seeing the inside of an American prison. She had just been released, having served a sentence for breaching obscenity laws.

Kitty invited her friend to her adopted home city of

New York as soon as she was able to travel out of Germany. They could see all the sights. Times Square, the Statue of Liberty, Coney Island, Grand Central Station, and perhaps they could sell a few copies of Birth Control Review while they were at these places. They attracted good numbers after all.

The two women swopped further letters, and as travel plans were formulated, it became apparent that no transatlantic liners were as yet leaving Germany for America. If she wanted to travel sooner rather than later, she would need to get a ship to England and travel to the US from there.

This was no hardship for Dorothea. England may have been the enemy for the past four years but it had been a war between politicians, not peoples. Visiting England would also give her an opportunity to meet up with her old Suffragette friend Emmeline Pethick-Lawrence.

******

Peter was in a quandary. He wondered whether he was in love with Dorothea. He was certainly in love, but was he in love with a nurse, rather than an actual woman? He had heard how it was quite common for soldiers, even happily married ones, to fall in love with their nurses. It was a natural occurrence. One moment you're in a filthy foxhole up to your waist in water, wondering if the next bullet propelled your way had your name on it, when suddenly there's an explosion, and the next you know of anything you're in a warm, clean bed being attended to by a nurse in her attractive uniform. She is your mother tucking you in at night as a small boy; your favourite sister in whom you confide the most innermost secrets and concerns; your saviour taking away all that terrible pain with her drugs and care. She is the perfect woman. Why would you not fall in love with her?

He and Dorothea made each other laugh. Both had a sardonic, sarcastic sense of humour. And they had the same outlook on life. They shared a similar political view, not just in general terms but in their scathing opinion of how their government had run the war. They also agreed that it was the flu that had finally defeated Germany and that but for the deadly outbreak the war would have continued ad nauseum. There was also a shared cynicism about the economic forces that had caused the nonsensical war in the first place. And Dorothea had been impressed that this new man in her life agreed with her on what could be the thorny subject of women's rights.

But could Peter trust his feelings? Or were they a wartime substitute for the real thing? An ersatz?

Peter was a thirty year old upper working class divorcee; Dorothea a thirty six year old lower middle class widow. He was bright, but she was brighter. Not a huge age, class or intelligence gap, but gaps nonetheless. The war had highlighted the huge differences between the classes. And an age gap was unusual when the woman was the older one.

And while he had been relieved to escape the mistake of marrying his first girlfriend, and was now keen to have a relationship with someone more suitable, he was unsure whether Dorothea was so eager to have another man in her life. She had been remarkably open with him about the huge mistake her marriage had been. She greatly enjoyed Peter's company, and was quite gushing with her sentiments towards him. She had told him that "I adore you," but while the verb could be used in a profound manner by some, he appreciated the expression was more of a throw-away line when coming from the overly dramatic Dorothea.

They had made love unusually early on in their relationship, at her bequest. She was clearly enjoying the freedom that first widowhood, then the war and in turn the end of the conflict had afforded her. She was certainly in love with life as it was now. It was a different world from the one she had left behind. But was she in love with him as well as her new life?

There was also the fact that he was a toy-maker by trade. Admittedly a very good one; there was none better, though he said so himself. But his life living in the working class East End of Berlin before the war was a world away from Dorothea's. She may have trained as a nurse, and certainly retained the common touch, but she had spent much of her adult life as a lady of leisure living in the leafy suburbs.

And there was one final subject of concern. The very basis of their mutual attraction. They were opposites who had attracted. He was down to earth; reliable; stoic; and before this war came along at least, mentally strong. Dorothea, for all her veneer of knowing worldly wise sophistication, was flighty, erratic and presumably due to her previous family problems, lacking confidence in her inner self. The war had left him in need of a nurse; she in need of a patient. Just the one patient. Despite much talk of her joining the German Red Cross nursing effort, she had never done it. He suspected that even if the war had dragged on longer, she always would have found some reason for not donning the uniform. Not that he had minded. It was good to have her all to himself.

But could these magnets keep their positives and negatives facing in the right directions now that the very thing that had brought them together had finally ended? Could two such mismatched people settle down to a life with each other?

He thought this would not normally be a pressing problem. The whole thing would work itself out, one way or another, over time. If they were to be simply ships which passed in the night, it would become apparent soon enough.

But before they had become seriously involved, Dorothea had arranged to travel to America as soon as she could, to visit an old friend of hers. And Peter's usual self-confidence dissolved when it came to the subject of Dorothea and him. He liked to think that he was not being paranoid, but he had to accept that he was at the very least concerned. Would she return to Germany? Would she fall in love with America? Worst still with an American?

Perhaps she understood his unsaid concerns because out of the blue, she addressed them.

"I do not want you to come to America, Peter," she said with her usual cool frankness. "Listening to two old girlfriends chew the cud would hardly be fun for you. And it would not be fun for me worrying about you. And besides you cannot afford the fare and you would not want me to pay for you would you? But why don't you come to England with me? I need a bodyguard and translator. I doubt my German accent is something that will win me many friends over there after all. I have forgotten much of the English I learned before the war. You speak it better. You were obviously a good boy at school and listened to your English teacher. I did not. I have to get two trains and a boat to reach London. I have taken a room in a hotel there for one night before I get an underground train across the city and then a train to Southampton for the ship to America. It is quite a journey from Berlin to Southampton I think. It would be very nice to have you with me on it. You see me off to America and then come home here."

Peter's initial reaction was to be horrified by the thought of visiting the land of the enemy. True, he shared with Dorothea the belief that the people of Germany and England had been used as mere cannon fodder by their politicians, and the two peoples themselves had nothing against each other. But nevertheless, the English had killed many of his friends and starved his nation to defeat. It was not something one could forgive or forget very easily.

But he kept these concerns to himself. From the moment she had told him that she was having to travel to America via England he had been concerned about Dorothea's safety, and had told her so. He had heard that during the war German shops in England had been looted; German people who had lived in England for decades, abused. Even dachshund dogs had been kicked, and Schweppes, the Swiss lemonade people had been boycotted just for having a German sounding name. She had initially waved away such stories as a mix of the inevitability of war and propaganda nonsense, and that his concerns were unwarranted in peacetime. But perhaps she had reconsidered. Or perhaps she just wanted to spend some more time with him? Perhaps she too felt time was against them? Either way, he was only too pleased to be invited to travel with her. He agreed to her request.

And just to be on the safe side, once in England, they would be a Mr & Mrs Peter and Dorothea Fletcher, a Swiss cuckoo clock-maker and his wife.

Chapter 39

"It's like trying to run a wagon without oil. It begins to creak.
The German race begins to creak. As a whole, it is pale, thin
and sunken-eyed. Sooner or later a crisis is inevitable... They
are pale, weary and without life."

Madeleine Zabriskie Doty,
American Peace Activist, Germany 1918

As law and order had broken down towards the end of
the war, Ursula had been one of the thousands involved
in pitch battles on the streets of German cities. There had
been demonstrations, protests and riots demanding the
end of the war, the end of the monarchy, franchise reform
and better food distribution, amongst other things. There
were socialists, communists, anarchists, Pan-Germanists,
Spartacists, radical youth, police, army, and many more
groups fighting with or against one another.

A new government, a transition from monarchy to a
republic, and the armistice, had seen many of these protests
dissipate.

Ursula had won. She had been on the winning side
in all but one of her internal conflicts. Only the battle for
food remained.

The fight for the vote for women in particular, had dominated her entire adult life. But what do you do when such an all-encompassing battle is finally won? You go to vote of course. In her case for the Weimar Coalition. But what then? No more plotting protests. No more shouting the odds against counter mobs demanding the authorities 'send hysterical females to the trenches'. And no more serving on a soup kitchen for the Fatherland come to that. It was all over. Time to return to normal life. Whatever that was.

The decision as to what to do next, had been somewhat decided for her. Which she had to admit to herself was something of a relief. The demand for better food production and distribution was not over, and an opportunity to be heavily involved in this fight landed nicely in her lap.

The well-to-do woman with the car whom she had met during the fracas in the marketplace had been in touch to ask her to work on a farm as her representative. The idea was to produce free milk for the starving. It had been explained that Ursula did not need any farming expertise. Rather she just needed an auditor's eye. To keep watch over the farmer to ensure things were done correctly. He was a bit of a rough diamond apparently, who may no doubt try to pull the wool over her eyes, or to be more exact produce milk behind her back. And she was to deal with all the paperwork and distribution. There were some things about the logistics of the project that were still unresolved because the man who had been the initial contact between the farmer and Frau Ute had died of the flu during the negotiations, but without hesitation Ursula had agreed to take on the task.

******

The work had gone surprisingly well. The old farmer seemed to be a far more decent fellow than Ursula had been led to expect. Once they had developed some rapport, mutual respect and trust, he had confided to her that he had not behaved well during the war. And had told her some, though she suspected not all, of some of the shenanigans he had got up to. For her part, she had told him of the riots, some of them involving battles with the authorities, in which she had been involved.

The milk they were producing was making them and their employer feel better about themselves, but they were just one farm. It was too little, too late. The Allied blockade was still continuing, and the German poor were in a worse condition than ever.

During the war Ursula had become a good photographer, always keen to take the sort of interesting images, often of people suffering in some way, that the censors ensured did not appear in the newspapers. She had believed they would be a useful historical document after the war, when the defeated English would be held to account.

Recently, during her milk distribution rounds in the city, she had set up her camera apparatus on a street corner in the poverty stricken East End of Berlin, and taken photographs. She suspected the images would be good ones. There would be none of the usual problem of taking blurred or ghostly pictures of moving people. Her models had been stationery. Just lying there, with no energy or motivation to move. Her usual comment on seeing photographs that had come out well, was to state that she was 'pleased with them'. If she was right about the quality of these images, that was not a term that would be appropriate. There would be nothing pleasing about them.

On returning to the farm she had told Klaus what she had seen and hopefully captured on film. He assumed she must be exaggerating, though he noticed how quiet and withdrawn she had become since.

Now she had the photographs back from the printers. She invited Klaus to view her handy work. The two of them saw shocking images of starving children. While she had been on the streets, Ursula had concentrated so hard on getting good photographs that she had managed to distance herself somewhat from the horror in front of her. But now she had nowhere for her eyes to hide. There was not much that could shock an old farmer who had seen it all, but these images did the job. Human skeletons with bulging eyes and bloated bellies. On one occasion Ursula had captured a girl of about eight years of age looking directly down her lens. It was the most haunting image of them all. The child's face was expressionless, but to Klaus it wasn't. It was enquiring. Why have you done this to us farmer?

"I'd put animals down in that state," he said grimly.

"Remember I told you how I met Frau Burchardt originally?" asked Ursula. The farmer nodded so she continued. "There was another woman there, a friend of mine called Dorothea. She is travelling to England soon. They must learn what their blockade is doing to us. To our children."

******

Despite her years of nursing in the city, during which time she had seen many a terrible sight, Dorothea had been shocked and horrified by Ursula's photographs. It had not been that long since she had been in the Berlin East End herself, and conditions had been bad then, but at least the war effort had been helping people. Ursula's soup kitchen for example. But now it was clear that the economic, political and social collapse of the country had left its poorest in a terrible state, with no one save a few philanthropists such as Frau Burchardt to help them. Dorothea was therefore only too pleased to do her bit to help, promising to carry the images of the starving into England when she travelled there.

It transpired that Emmeline Pethick-Lawrence was away in Canada and would remain so for some time, so after swopping letters with Kitty, it was decided that the best course of action for Dorothea once in England was to get the images to an ex-Suffragette friend of Kitty's, Norah Smyth. It was explained that she was the photographer who had captured so many remarkable images of the British Suffragette campaign. She would have the press contacts and financial wherewithal to ensure the photographs would be circulated throughout England. She lived in Bow in the East End of London. It was also where another friend of Kitty's from the Suffragette days, Ruby Nash, lived. Norah and Ruby had both worked for Sylvia Pankhurst, initially as Suffragettes and then during the war doing social work. Kitty suggested Dorothea contact Ruby. Norah was not the most streetwise of people, whereas Ruby and her husband were. It would be best for Dorothea to deliver the photographs to them, and they could also give her advice on anything she needed while in England.

Dorothea remembered the name. Emmeline had mentioned the Nashes during a conversation years ago. Dorothea had thought at the time that they had sounded like just the sort of down-to-earth people she would enjoy meeting.

On contacting Norah, the advice was that while she would ordinarily have been honoured to take up the cudgels on behalf of Germany's starving children, she was alas already too busy helping Sylvia Pankhurst set up a new campaign to stop the British government starting a new war, against the Bolsheviks in Russia. Sylvia was galvanising East End dockers to get them to refuse to load armaments onto ships potentially bound for the new socialist republic. Norah did not think she could give the project the time it both deserved and needed. But she would be prepared to accept the photographs and get them passed on to a contact of hers, Sister Dorothy Buxton. Norah knew the nun was importing illicit copies of German and Austro-Hungarian newspapers into Britain, so was already aware of the deprivation of German children and was keen to do something about it. Norah had immediately swopped letters with the Sister about the photographs, and an agreement made to use the images in a campaign, using as a title the old war-time call to arms for Sylvia's Bow nursery, 'Save the Children'.

Chapter 40

"We do not like to be robbed of an enemy. We want someone to hate when we suffer… If so-and-so's wickedness is the sole cause of our misery, let us punish so-and-so and we shall be happy. The supreme example of this kind of political thought was the Treaty of Versailles."

Bertrand Russell, Sceptical Essays

The Lester Sisters were much loved East End philanthropists and social workers. They had supported Sylvia's East London Federation of Suffragettes before the war and, like its leader, were pacifists. This had led the three women to become good friends. And this had brought the sisters in to contact with Nash.

The straight-laced, salt-of-the-earth sisters found him quite shocking at times, and did not really appreciate having their Christian names, Muriel and Doris, shortened to Mu & Dot, but nonetheless they very much liked and respected him. And the feeling was mutual.

Nash had been one of the local volunteers who had helped redecorate and refurbish an old chapel that the sisters had bought at the start of the war in Eagling Road, Bow. Their brother, Kingsley, had died around the same time, and as a tribute to him the old chapel was renamed Kingsley Hall. It was set up as a 'peoples' house' for worship, study, fun and friendship, and included a school for adults and a nursery.

And after her rather ill-deserved fame as an ace footballer had spread, Ruby had been roped in to organise boys' and girls' football at the centre. The hall had also been a twenty-four hour soup kitchen during the war, and given he was a creature of the early hours, Nash had sometimes helped out in the middle of the night, keeping air raid wardens supplied with soup or his own warming beverage of choice, a cup of alcohol-infused tea.

Muriel and Doris had been born a year apart but they were so alike that people tended to assume they were twins. They dressed alike and had exactly the same hair-style. But all but one person in the East End could just about tell them apart. The exception to the rule was Nash, who had once made the mistake of confiding this to his wife, who had immediately informed the sisters. Like Ruby, they had been most amused by this, so to get some retribution for him always being so cheeky towards them, they resolved to play a little ongoing joke on him. Whenever they came in to contact with their friend Nashey, they passed themselves off as each other.

Muriel had sent Nash a note to ask him to pop round to see her at Kingsley Hall. It was at the far end of Bow from where he and Ruby lived, about a twenty minute walk away. He duly made his way over there and on entering the hall, was immediately met with an apology from his host.

"I'm so sorry Nashey, Muriel couldn't be here after all, you'll have to make do with me I'm afraid," said Muriel.

"Never mind Dot, always a pleasure to see you girl, you know that," he said with a saucy smile on his face. "Now, what can I do for you?"

Muriel explained that earlier in the war when Dr Alice and her local colleague Dr Barbara had discovered what the national infant mortality rate had been, they had gone to Sylvia with the information. It was decided to start a new campaign to appeal for funds. Sylvia had called it 'Save the Children'.

She went on to explain that the two doctors had written articles in the Woman's Dreadnought newspaper, laying out the appalling statistics and telling people of their work in East End nurseries and clinics. They explained that they were unable to get government grants for the heaviest costing items, namely food and milk. They called on people to send funds for milk, eggs, medicines, doctors and nursing. Or if they couldn't spare money perhaps they could send arrowroot, barley, Glaxo or Virol. The Save the Children campaign had helped keep the nursery going throughout the war.

Muriel appeared to have forgotten that Nash was married to someone who, through most of the war, had been Sylvia's administrator of the clinic and nursery. None of this was new to Nash. But his curiosity had certainly been aroused

"Yeah, Ruby's told me as such. So come on Dot, I'm a cat what's ready to cop it for the ninth time. Cut to the chase. What you up to girl?"

Muriel was well aware that she had been in danger of telling her grandmother to suck eggs somewhat. But the point was that she wished to ease into the conversation gradually. She eventually wished to speak on a most delicate matter. She was about to make it clear that she knew not just one but two things about Nash which were supposed to be highly confidential. Very few people knew this information and she should certainly not be one of them.

"Well, Nashey, will you promise me you won't be affronted by what I am about to say? I most sincerely do not wish to raise your hackles."

"Hackles is it?" said Nash mock seriously, amused at the term. "Well, seeing as it's you Dot, I'll promise not to raise 'em. No matter what you have to say for yourself. How's that?"

It was clear to Muriel that the big man was in a good mood. She considered it a good idea to come back with her own light hearted refrain. She knew how he liked such badinage. A few months earlier, just before the Germans had given up their aerial bombing campaign, an air-raid warden had popped into her all night soup kitchen and told her a joke that she thought she could now use. She didn't think it was terribly funny, but the warden was a similar sort of rough diamond to Nashey, so perhaps it appealed to that sort of chap. And Nashey's very own Christian name, Alexander, was mentioned in the joke.

"Jolly good," she said. "By the way, someone in Bow has just started a new business. He has put up a sign outside his establishment stating his name. A.Swindler. I said to him goodness me that looks mighty bad as it is. You must include your first name, Alexander or whatever it is. He said I know but I don't exactly like to do it. I said why not? What is your first name? He said, Adam."

The joke teller looked at the old East Ender with an air of expectancy.

Nash didn't realise it was a joke for a moment and looked back at Muriel nonplussed. Why on earth was she telling him this tale? Had she asked him over to talk about a feller called Swindler? And then it dawned on him, but his expression didn't change. Then, with a serious look on his face, he leant forward conspiratorially to whisper some advice.

"Word to the wise Dot. Don't work the music halls any time soon." He then burst out laughing, shaking his head with incredulity. "A dam swindler. Gawd help us!"

Joke over, it was time to find out why he had been summoned.

"So, come on, what you after Dot?" he asked.

She couldn't put it off any longer. Muriel took a deep breath and then let out the bombshell.

"Well, it has come to my attention Nashey, that you have been helping conscientious objectors evade justice, and also that you have squirrelled away somewhere a young soldier who has gone on the run."

She saw Nash's countenance change with scary speed. As his face darkened, she was afraid that he would not keep to his promise. She immediately felt intimidated.

"Who's been talking?" he asked solemnly.

"Now, you know I cannot possibly tell you that Nashey. If I did you would no doubt chastise the poor chap most severely."

In her naivety she had inadvertently told Nash that the informant was male. That reduced the number of suspects. And she would have referred to Freddie as a boy rather than a chap. Nash also doubted she would have referred to any of his mostly middle class conscientious objectors as poor men. He had a prime suspect. A man whom Nash knew frequented the Lester Sisters' hall. The poor old devil was known to go round there for a chinwag and some free coffee or soup. It was Kosher Bill.

Nash put his theory to the test.

"You wait till I get hold of that daft old sod. I'll give him kosher when I see him."

It got the response he was looking for.

"Now Nashey, you know poor Bill isn't all the ticket. You can't go…"

"Keep your hair on," cut in Nash to reassure her. "Bill's all right with me. I was just getting it out of you. But I wanna know how he found out about the soldier boy. It weren't nothing to do with him."

Relieved that Nash was keeping to his promise, Muriel felt emboldened to add something.

"He told me a policeman from the army had been to see him, asking about a fourteen year old soldier, who had disappeared in the area. And that the soldier was a friend of yours. Of course Bill honestly didn't know what he was talking about. He was just relieved the man did not ask him about conscientious objectors."

Nash just nodded and disappeared into deep thought for a few seconds. He would need to find out from her in due course the full details of what she knew of his business, but for now he was content to find out what she was up to.

"So, what's all this got to do with you Dot?"

Muriel didn't want to sound condescending so

considered for a moment before she spoke. She needed to choose her words carefully

"Do you know why the Allies finally won the war Nashey?"

"Tanks weren't it?" said Nash. "We had new ones what pushed the Hun back. They didn't have as good tanks as ours."

"Ah yes, but why did the Germans not build their own new tanks? They had tanks after all, every bit as good as the Allies' original ones. Surely they could have restored the status quo by improving theirs to the same degree as the Allies? Throughout this terrible war, whoever gained the ascendancy for a moment soon lost it when the other side countered. The sides were too well matched for over four years were they not?"

"Yeah but the Hun were knackered this time round weren't they? Their Spring Offensive nearly won 'em the war but they didn't pull it off."

Nash had not understood what 'status quo' meant, just as Muriel had never before heard the expression 'knackered', but they were both able to interpret successfully.

"Ah, ha, you're on the right track there," said Muriel. "Their last push had left the Germans in a most vulnerable position. They were no longer able to feed their war effort. They had exhausted themselves economically."

"Run out of money and munitions eh?" said Nash. "Well, it was either that or one side or another were gonna run out of men sooner or later."

"And food. The Germans could no longer feed themselves at home. I have seen a photograph of a horse which collapsed dead in a German city street. It was immediately set upon by the people and stripped to its bones in minutes. For the meat do you see? The German people are starving."

"Poor bleeders. Mind you, if we hadn't started protecting our merchant ships with convoys last year and started that allotment campaign and the rationing, we would have been in the same boat by now wouldn't we?"

"Indeed we would. But whilst we managed to largely stop the German u-boat successes, the Germans were unable to stop the Allies' blockade of their ports. The cordon of British warships stopping any imported food getting in has starved the Germans into defeat. But the terrible thing is that despite the war ending, British ships continue their blockade."

"Yeah, I've heard. It ain't right," agreed Nash. "The war's over for Gawd's sake."

"It is to force the Germans into signing a peace treaty of course. The armistice and the German fleet's surrender has not truly ended the war. One of our politicians has said he wants to squeeze the Germans until the pips squeak. We want our pound of flesh."

Nash was not aware that there had been an allusion to Shakespeare but he understood full well what Muriel meant.

"Sounds like it's the Hun who need a pound or two of flesh," he said, disgusted. "To eat, poor bastards."

"Quite so," agreed Muriel. "The people of Berlin and Vienna are starving to death. German children are suffering from malnutrition and rickets. Their bones are like rubber. TB is rife. They have no clothing. There are paper bandages in their hospitals."

Nash grimaced and then narrowed his eyes.

"How do you know all this Dot? It ain't something you read about in the papers is it?"

"A Sister of the church who is of my acquaintance has been importing newspapers from Germany and Austria-Hungary, then translating them into English and is about to start publishing extracts in a magazine. All very under the table as one might put it. A special licence has to be obtained from the government to import such things, and of course no such licence has been issued."

Nash just nodded and waited for her to continue. He assumed she was about to ask him to do something involving this illegal enterprise. If a woman of the cloth was involved, she wouldn't have the sort of street wisdom to keep herself out of gaol without help from the likes of him. But what it had to do with his objectors or Freddie, he couldn't imagine.

Muriel adjudged it was time to make her request.

"And you will of course not be surprised to find that I have asked you here to request a favour." Nash just nodded so she continued. "As you know there is a terrible shortage of wood, due to the need for so many coffins because of this accursed influenza. But I was wondering if you could use your contacts in the wood trade to secure enough wood to make a large cross."

Nash was disappointed. It turned out all she wanted was a bit of wood for some religious thing.

"Yeah, I daresay I can get me hands on some wood for you," he said with a rather bored sigh in his voice. "How big do you want this cross of yours to be?"

Muriel spotted the indifference, but she was confident his interest would increase shortly.

"As big as a cross being carried in a procession from Bow to the House of Commons by a conscientious objector and a fourteen year old soldier can be," she said matter-of-factly.

"Eh?" exclaimed a wide eyed Nash.

"I would like your fourteen year old soldier boy and a conscientious objector of your choosing to carry a cross at the front of a procession to Parliament, publicising the plight of children in war ravaged countries."

"Don't want much do you?!" The sarcasm failed to hide the startled horror in Nash's voice. "They'll be arrested for sure. And they'll be asked who's been helping 'em right enough. And that's Ruby as well as me in trouble."

"I know I am asking an awful lot Nashey," said Muriel softly. "But I ask it nonetheless."

"I'll have to speak to Ruby," said Nash, immediately realising that anything but a straight 'no' to a Lester sister was sure to be taken as a 'yes'. "She's got most to lose. She can be a conniving little vixen mind. Especially now she's a copper. If anyone can work out how to get round the law, she can. Talk about it takes one to know one."

Muriel knew not to show any signs of counting her chickens. She made all the right respectful noises. There was further discussion over a cup of tea of exactly how much Dot and Muriel knew of the conscientious objectors and the boy soldier, before Nash was on his way to see his wife.

******

Muriel Lester was to make a speech when the protest march reached the Houses of Parliament. It was hoped that there would be hundreds there to hear her speak about the need to feed the children in war ravaged countries.

Some horrendous photographs of the starving children of Germany had been blown up on to huge placards, but they were so disturbing that it was decided not to show them after all. The photographs had been papered over and a simple message added. 'We do not want any children anywhere to go hungry'.

People were to be asked to donate funds to buy milk to send to Europe. If one couldn't afford to make a donation, giving second-hand clothes would also be most welcome.

At the end of her speech, Muriel would introduce Sister Dorothy Buxton, who had imported a newspaper which featured appalling photographs of German starvation. The nun would describe some of the terrible images, not just those in the newspaper but also others passed on to her independently from a German woman living in Berlin, of children in the city's East End suffering from malnutrition and rickets.

The main organiser of the whole event, Miss Eglantyne Webb, would follow this by informing the crowd that it was the Allied blockade that was causing such suffering to millions of children. It was then Muriel's turn to introduce the two men, or to be more precise the man and the boy, who had carried the cross at the front of the march, all the way from Bow. A soldier and a conscientious objector. She would go on to provide the crowd with some of their back-story, before finishing the day's proceedings with a call for reconciliation and peace for all.

That was where things were to get complicated. Sister Buxton and Miss Webb were in breach of government restrictions laid down in the Defence of the Realm Act. They would surely be arrested by the police.

In a perverse way, it was rather hoped that some of the crowd would be there to attempt to disrupt the meeting; heckling, throwing rotten fruit and so on. This was because any publicity was good publicity. One of Sylvia's jobs had been to contact the press and tell them of the protest and what was to be said outside the House. She also confirmed that she would be there in person. The press knew that anything to do with Miss Pankhurst always made good copy, so they would surely be there in numbers to capture the proceedings in word and photograph.

There was also another reason why the organisers needed the meeting to end in a Suffragette-like melee. While Sister Buxton and Miss Webb were being arrested, and other police were hopefully having to deal with a scrum of protesters, hecklers, spectators and press, Nash would attempt to squirrel his two charges away, unnoticed.

The authorities would not have known the identity of the two males carrying the cross until Muriel Lester let the cat out of the bag at the end of the proceedings. And it was crucial from Muriel's, as well as Nash's, point of view that there was no mention in the speeches that the soldier and conscientious objector were army runaways. The whole point of the two cross-bearers was that a soldier, who had been so keen to go to war he had lied about his age to get into the army, and a conscientious objector, who had rejected fighting, were coming together in a show of reconciliation. The fact that the soldier was clearly young enough to be the objector's son, was a nice profound bonus as far as Muriel was concerned.

Ruby had managed to swop shifts around with colleagues to ensure the day of the march was her day off. It had cost her having to work the following two Sundays, but she wanted to be at the protest when off duty, in her civvies, to at least add moral support. But she was going to carry her largest shopping bag with her. In it would be her police uniform into which she could change quickly if need be. And in her pocket her police identification card. If there was any trouble involving her husband, she might be able to do something to help him. Pretend to arrest him or something and get him away. Plans had to be fluid to the point of having no plan at all.

Chapter 41

"It came and went, a hurricane across the green fields of life, sweeping away…in hundreds of thousands and leaving behind it a toll of sickness and infirmity which will not be reckoned in this generation."

The Times newspaper

The celebratory end of war crowds had spread the flu quicker than ever. Medical schools had been closed, their third and fourth year students now being used to help on hospital wards. Theatres, cinemas, dance halls, churches, women's football matches and any other public places that had the potential to crowd people close together, were shut down. Streets were being sprayed with chemicals.

And even the weather was not helping. Late autumn downpours had seen rivers spill over their banks. The harvest had been delayed and lowered the yields of vegetables.

Much of this created a lot of work for the police. And Ruby was not enjoying her job these days. She found herself having to be a pedant; picking on people, chivvying them along, stopping them from gathering together, telling people in queues for a doctor's surgery, pharmacy or greengrocer to keep a space between themselves and the person in front.

It was all very necessary but petty nonetheless. It was not why she had joined the police force. But she felt that she could not very well resign with the police still so short of officers. Someone had to do the job, and it might just as well be her.

And at least she was working on her own, and not having to put up with that rum character Pemberton. Since he had been given separate duties soon after the strange incident in Shoreditch station, Ruby had barely seen hide nor hair of him.

Nash still believed Pemberton may have simply taken a shine to her, and had followed her for that reason. But his wife disagreed. She had been a good looking woman her entire adult life, and had received plenty of stares and glances from men over the years. She knew lechery when she saw it. And she was convinced Pemberton had no such interest in her. He had never so much as glanced at her in that way. No, his interest was more professional. He had been trying to get something on her. Probably because he didn't approve of women in the police force. Perhaps he had heard that she had done well with the ambulances and so on, and decided that if he was to climb the greasy pole above her, he needed to put her down somehow? If Sergeant Granger thought him green as grass as he had put it, Pemberton needed to show that he wasn't. But he had not been able to get anything on her at work, so had taken to following her off duty. He had probably heard that she was married to a man with a certain reputation. Hanging around when she was with her husband, might be the best opportunity of getting something incriminating on his colleague.

But it hadn't worked. She concluded that he must have realised she and her husband had spotted him at the station and given him the slip. Whatever his plans had been, he appeared to have given them up.

It was thus with some disappointment that Ruby was told that she was being put back to work with PC Pemberton. She did not want to appear annoyed or frustrated at the news, so simply nodded and asked the obvious question.

"Some of the lads back from the flu are they sergeant? PC Pemberton joining me on crowd control again?"

"No," admitted Granger. "We are still low on numbers. But we are required to provide officers to accompany a march that's starting in Bow, then heading through the City and finishing in Westminster. The City police and our lads over in Westminster are particularly stretched at the moment, so officers from this station will accompany the march throughout. It's only a small affair, I doubt there will be many along, organised by some women asking for help for children in war-ravaged countries. We are very short staffed ourselves so just two officers will have to suffice. You and Pemberton have worked together in the past, you have experience of Westminster from your Trafalgar Square duties, and have both done well with your recent work, so I have chosen the two of you for this duty."

When Granger had reached the part about children in war-ravaged countries, blood had drained from Ruby's face. Her mind started to race.

Christ, it's the bloody march Nashey is involved with! I was going on it with him! Freddie and one of the conchies are carrying the cross at the front of the bloody thing! And now me, and Pemberton of all people are going to be accompanying it. This can't be a coincidence. What the hell...?

That's as far as her deliberations took her before Granger cut in.

"WPC Nash?" he asked. "Are you listening to me?"

"Sorry sarge," she answered, before quickly making up a little white lie. "It was just that it was supposed to be my day off. It's my husband's birthday see. I was supposed to be treating him to a day out. We were going over to..."

"Sergeant. It's sergeant. I've told you before WPC Nash," came the interruption in a tone making no attempt to hide the exasperation felt. "And no, you cannot expect to pick and choose your days off when half the force are down with the flu. It's all hands to the pump now."

Ruby just stood there, trying to think quickly on her feet.

"Have I made myself clear, WPC Nash? Do you have anything more you wish to say?" asked Granger.

Ruby was desperate to glean more information from her superior.

"Er, well, yes there is something sergeant," she said. "These children in war ravaged countries, do they include German children?"

Granger frowned at first, before a moment of realisation had him believing that he understood what was behind the question. His expression and tone of voice changed to a knowing, patronising one.

"Not that the subject of a march should concern a police officer, as you are expected to do your duty irrespective. But yes I daresay Hun children are included as being from a war ravaged land."

"It's…" Ruby hesitated. "Just that the idea of helping Germans in any way, may be provocative for some people. Might there be trouble? Should we not have more than two police officers in attendance? Are you sure a woman police officer would be up to it? Perhaps some officers on horseback would be better?"

Ruby hated playing the scared little woman but she needed to see how determined her sergeant was to have her on the march.

Granger waved away her concerns, stating that everyone had too much on their plates at the moment to worry about some little march that was probably going to be no more than a handful of women holding placards. If anyone did give it a moment of thought, they would probably assume the march was just about children in France and Belgium.

A moment of clarity hit Ruby unpleasantly in the face like a drunk's breath.

What a load of old codswallop! He *should* be concerned about it being for German children. And he's made it quite clear in the past he doesn't consider a mere slip of a WPC adequate at handling crowds if there's any trouble. He should have his biggest, burliest officers on it, and get more in from other divisions if he's that short of manpower. Granger wants to get something on me! Pemberton had turned up immediately after the spotlight incident at the football match. He's Granger's spy. Bastards!

She had believed at the time that she had gotten away with her little subterfuge at the football ground. Clearly not.

******

Nash was having a well-earned rest in his armchair, after a long day of running around cajoling, trading and making deals about, and if all else failed, pilfering timber.

His peace was interrupted by his wife walking through the door. She had opened said door to enter, but her expression reminded Nash of a joke that he had once seen in Punch. A man wearing a football scarf and carrying a rattle had returned home. He had obviously just been to watch his team play, and they must have lost. He was so distraught that he had walked straight through his front door without opening it. The door had a man's silhouette-sized hole in it. His wife asked him, '5-0, 6-0, 7?' Ruby now had a face on her that suggested her team had just lost 10-0, and they had been lucky to get nil.

Nash was fairly confident that he had not done anything wrong since using poor Maud's dead body to make a point to the landlord. His wife had read the riot act to him about that. But after he had taken a severe verbal beating she had eventually forgiven him. And even if she had somehow found out that he had just half-inched a coffin from outside a rival funeral directors, he was sure she wouldn't be too worried about it. Nevertheless, her expression suggested he tread very lightly.

"Rubes?" was all he said. It was enough.

His wife proceeded to tell him about the march, her sergeant and PC Pemberton.

"Fuck 'em," said Nash. "Just take the day off ill. What they gonna do, sack you? Not with half the Met down with the flu they ain't. And even if they do, so what? They got nothing on you. In fact, don't take the day off. Just tell 'em to stick their job where the sun don't shine."

"No," sighed Ruby, before continuing with a surprising air of contentment in her voice. "I am going on that march as a police officer. Remember I joined the police to help women. Miss Webb and the Lester sisters are arranging it, and Sylvia's also involved, and you know what she's like for getting people together. There's bound to be a lot more people on the march than the police think. And I suspect most of them will be women. I'm going to protect them the way us Suffragettes never got protected by the police."

"But it's obviously a snare," complained Nash. "Darling, they must have a plan to get you to do something that as a copper you shouldn't. They must finally have something on me and plan for Pemberton to try and arrest me, at which time you'll come to my rescue."

Ruby gave her husband an old fashioned look before answering.

"And since when did you need rescuing from the likes of Pemberton, you villainous old sod. If he's stupid enough to try to arrest you on his own, he'll be kissing the cobbles quick enough won't he?"

"And then, when you don't arrest me for thumping a copper, they'll have you darling," said Nash with the confidence of someone who has just won the argument. "Pemberton will tell his bosses he shouted out for help and you ignored him. They'll come mob-handed to arrest me later and you'll be for it an' all."

"So Pemberton's going to get himself thumped just to get me is he darling?" scolded Ruby. "They're not going to go to all that trouble just to throw me out the force. And besides, why would they think you would be at a women's protest about giving food to children abroad anyhow? No, whatever they have planned for me, I won't rise to the bait. I will do my duty as a police officer, straight down the line, and then there's nothing they can do about it. And afterwards I will very much enjoy walking up to Sergeant Granger and telling him exactly where to stick his job. I've had enough of being a copper."

Nash did not understand his wife's logic at all. Why go to the trouble of going on the march as a policewoman if you were going to tell them where to stick their job straight afterwards anyway? But experience had told him that any further argument with his wife on this matter would only lead to him being verbally outgunned. So he bit his tongue.

"All right darling, have it your way," said Nash with an air of resignation. "And don't worry, I'll be there but I'll keep well out of it."

Chapter 42

"I realise that patriotism is not enough. I must have no hatred towards any one."

Edith Cavell, British nurse
executed by Germany for spying

They wondered if they might be the only Germans travelling on the ship, so fearful of an adverse reaction to their accents, had made a pact to keep conversation between themselves to a minimum while on board. But they were surprised to find several of their compatriots, sounding as if they were businessmen, accompanying them. Apparently German toys, clocks, china, glassware, jewellery and haberdashery would be on sale in Britain soon enough if these men had their way. Peter muttered sarcastically to Dorothea that the war was, after all, merely a capitalist one so of course it was business as usual now. She nodded grimly in knowing agreement.

On disembarkation, Peter donned an anti-flu germ mask while he bought their rail tickets, hoping this would blur his voice to make the origin of his accent less detectable. It seemed to do the trick. The ticket clerk at Harwich Docks railway station, who was also wearing an anti-flu mask, was used to hearing foreign accents and didn't bat an eyelid.

Enjoying the anonymity that a port affords, the couple strolled up the platform alongside the waiting train, and hand-picked an empty six-seat carriage for themselves.

Their London hotel, a grand Victorian affair adjoining Liverpool Street station, was impersonal at check-in, which was just how they liked it. They freshened up in their room before returning to the reception area to ask the concierge to call them a taxi. The first hint of informality was when the man couldn't help but raise an eyebrow, not at their accents, but when their destination was given as Bow. After recovering his well-trained deadpan countenance, he recommended they ask their taxi driver to remain at their destination until they were ready to be brought back to the hotel, as he doubted they would be able to secure the services of a passing cab in such an area.

Wishing to keep his utterances to a minimum, Peter simply nodded, but he had no intention of doing as advised. He and Dorothea planned to visit Mr & Mrs Nash for a few hours. Showing them the photographs alone would take some time, and their hosts could no doubt give advice on how to return to the hotel by public transport.

Ruby would have liked to have met them off the train from Harwich, but she and Nash were both too busy. She had consequently sent them a map to help them find their address, which the taxi driver was only too pleased to have at his disposal.

On knocking at their destination a huge scary man answered the door with his usually abruptness. But once they had introduced themselves, the two Germans were told to come in, take the weight off their feet and make themselves at home. They were amazed by the warm welcome they received from their English hosts.

Before their guests had arrived, Ruby had told her husband that when the time came, to speak slowly and avoid as many cockneyisms as possible. So when the new arrivals mentioned the fear of their accents being unwelcome in London, Nash was quick to reassure them in his best slow, loud, condescending, speaking-to-foreigners voice.

"Don't worry about all that," he said. "We have so many Jews, Irish and God knows what round here, nobody knows where anyone's from. We had a German fellow working in a local toy factory for a while during the war, on the quiet like. He were called Niederhofer. We managed to pass him off as Swiss. The girls in the factory liked him. Nobody ever said nothing about where he was from. It got a bit difficult in the end mind you, so we got him away on a boat to Holland."

Dorothea got the gist but had missed a few meanings so asked Peter for a translation. Apart from the confusing double negative in one sentence, Peter had understood well enough and made a quick aside to her in German.

Peter was too wary of his surroundings at this point to tell them he was also a toy-maker. He preferred to let his hosts hold court.

Ruby told them an anecdote about how the English viewed foreigners. She and her husband had met on board the Titanic. She had worked in the a la carte restaurant, where the very few Italians on board were employed. But when she had attended the British inquiry into the disaster, some survivors gave evidence to the effect that the British had been stoic; it was all the Italians who had panicked. It would seem that anyone with a foreign accent on board the ship was an Italian as far as the British were concerned!

The punchline had been delivered with such scorn in her voice, it was clear to her audience what Ruby thought of such ignorant xenophobia. This had her guests relaxing a little.

When the conversation got around to employment, the Nashes were told they had a toy-maker and a nurse in their house. To which Nash was quick to tell them that his friend Sylvia would be very pleased to employ the both of them. The quality of the toys had gone downhill since Niederhofer had left her factory, and there was always a need for another good nurse at Sylvia's nursery. At this point Ruby piped in that better still, as she was worried about being a German in England, Dorothea could work in the Montessori section of the Mother's Arms. Working there with a Christian name that ended in an 'a', she was bound to be assumed to be Italian! This had her audience smiling politely.

And from this acorn of a conversation, which had been just small talk to make the new arrivals feel at ease, came a potential great oak. By the time the Nashes had walked their guests to Old Ford station, from where a train would drop them at Broad Street, a terminus a short walk from their hotel, Peter had agreed to do a little work at Sylvia's toy factory. And Dorothea had promised that when she returned from America she might indeed work at the nursery. Perhaps she and Peter could try their hand at living together in the East End, not of Berlin, but of London. She had come to realise that people of the eastern end of cities were pretty much the same the world over. It was the politicians of the West Ends who started wars.

Peter had taken this all with a large pinch of salt. It was a typically fanciful slice of Dorothea pie in the sky. He would certainly work at the toy factory, but only to pay his way in England while he waited for Dorothea to return. And only then if he was treated well. Otherwise he would return to Germany. If he was still in Bow when and if Dorothea returned, he would then see where the wind blew the two of them.

******

Ruby got a day off in lieu of her having to work the day of the march. It was her first day off for weeks. She would spend part of it at a travel agent's office.

She thought that she and her husband should, if possible, accompany Peter to see Dorothea off at Southampton. Ruby was originally from Southampton and her family still lived close to the docks. She needed to visit her much loved mother soon in any case, so perhaps she could combine such a trip with seeing off her new German friend. And with so many troops returning from the war via Southampton Docks, she wondered whether the train service from London to her home city might be better than usual. They would surely be running lots of trains there to pick up the soldiers. But she wondered whether they might be charters. And if they were, would the trains down to Southampton be available to the public? Or would they run there empty? Of course the trains back to London would be packed to capacity, but that was not a concern.

Ruby decided to ask Thomas Cook & Co for advice. They would know. And they would certainly be able to book her the tickets she needed. She would journey to Cook's head office at Ludgate Circus, in the City.

She could have got there by just one change of tram, but her husband suspected she might be under surveillance, so he had his wife join him on part of a trip he was taking round some of his old haunts. If she were being followed this would give Nash time to spot the spies and deal with them. Ruby thought he was being rather overly dramatic, but she wanted to make the most of her day off by accompanying him in any case.

They both particularly wanted to see the Lester sisters, so made them the first port of call. The sisters felt that it was time for a confession. After all, the war had ended, and it was clearly the end of an era. They told Nashey about the joke they had both been playing on him for years. Ever since Ruby had tipped them off. Muriel was Dorothy and Dorothy was Muriel. Nash's face was a picture. There wasn't a dry eye in the house thereafter, among the women at least.

They then popped along to see Freddie's mother to let her know the latest news of her boy. Nash was then going to oversee the departure from Shoreditch of his few remaining objectors. They were about to go home to face whatever music the authorities had in store for them. Each had a fictional cover story as to where they had been since disappearing off the government's radar. Ruby didn't know any of the objectors, so after leaving Freddie's place she made her way to Ludgate Circus, promising her husband she would keep her wits about her.

Ruby was in the Thomas Cook building quite some time. It became clear that there was much more to being a travel agent than she realised. Perhaps it would be a job she might be interested in doing in the future. She had travel experience of sorts after all.

On arrival back in Bow, she had some time to kill before she was to attend a meeting to discuss what was to become of Rose. So given that since becoming a police officer she hadn't had time to visit her old employment colleagues, she popped in to see them all at the nursery and toy factory. And she even sheepishly stuck her head inside the Cost Price restaurant and came away with some food. Vegetarian of course.

With Nashey still out seeing people, Ruby also had time to simply relax at home, but six years of firstly Suffragette and then war work had left her hyperactive. Nothing needed doing around the house, so she popped some things she no longer needed, including the vegetarian dish, round to the vicar's wife. Jenny would see to it everything found a good home.

She then spent the rest of the day with Sylvia, Norah, Alice and a few other friends and neighbours including Maud's closest relatives. It was decided that Rose would be put up for adoption. Sylvia promised she would keep a watchful eye on the process and make sure the little one was sent to a good home. She confided that she herself now had new, adopted siblings. Her mother, Mrs Pankhurst, at the ripe old age of sixty no less, had started a second family of adopted orphans. There were so many war orphans that people of all persuasions were doing their bit by taking them on.

Chapter 43

"The people...are depressed and horrified at the terms of the armistice especially that the blockade is not to be raised which means for so many a gradual death. One woman said to me the idea of continuing to exist and work on the minimum of food...was so dreadful, that she thought it would be the most sensible thing to go with her child and try to get shot in one of the numerous street fights."

Countess Evelyn Blucher:

English Wife in Berlin,

a private memoir...1918

Nash had spoken to Freddie and the conscientious objector John Jameson, whom he suspected would be keen, and both had agreed to stand together at the head of the Save the Children procession. Freddie would be wearing his full army uniform except he would not be donning any headgear, so people could see how young he looked. And fortunately he had not thought to clean said uniform, so he would be marching with the mud of France still on it, albeit with a bit of Bow gutter filth added to increase the dramatic effect.

And just to make his message clear to everyone, the

objector would also be wearing his army uniform. This, with a white shroud wrapped around it, to represent both purity and death, with the words 'I am a Conscience Objector' written all over the ensemble.

But Nash was still concerned about the problems inherent in getting his two soldiers away to safety at the end of the proceedings. No doubt they would be safe enough during the march, other than perhaps the odd piece of rotten fruit or a paper bag full of urine thrown at the 'bastard conchie'. But by the time the procession arrived at Westminster, the authorities would have been informed of their presence. And they may have calculated that the soldiers were probably deserters. Whether or not they knew the identities of the runaways, they would surely take them away. Whoever they were, such soldiers needed to be taken out of the public gaze and dealt with.

With this in mind, Nash went to see his old friend Sylvia. From her days leading the East London Federation of Suffragettes in Bow, much of which was spent avoiding arrest by a police force keen to return her to prison, she would know what to do for the best. She understood how the government's mind worked.

He laid out his concerns and awaited her advice.

"I am flattered that you charge me with this Nashey," she said. "Muriel tells me that Miss Eglantyne Webb, a wealthy woman far better situated than she to take the Save the Children cause further, has hired the Royal Albert Hall to acquire publicity and raise funds. When I first arrived in London as a little art student down from Manchester all those long years ago, I took the very same venue for my mother's new cause. Mother was much vexed and told me so, as only she could, by heated telegram. As you can imagine the great hall costs a goodly sum to take. Mother was fearful I had wasted the funds. She believed the place would echo! Instead of which the place was filled of course. And Mrs Pethick-Lawrence, our great fund-raiser, earned her nickname 'the greatest beggar in London' by gaining pledges from all there that day. Mother's fledgling women's suffrage society had become a great movement almost overnight."

No one was a bigger fan of Sylvia Pankhurst than Nash, and despite his years working for her, he had never heard this tale before. But he was not sure what point she was trying to make.

"The history lesson's all well and good Sylve but what's all that got to do with my boys?" he said bluntly.

Sylvia was used to Nash's ways so did not take offence. She simply held up a palm to tell him to have patience and indulge her.

"If you will forgive me Nashey," she said politely. "Once mother's Women's Social & Political Union had become established, the government got up to so many tricks to retard us in those early years, yet all it did was afford us publicity, which was of course what we craved almost above all else. Now, I suspect they have learnt their lesson. I believe they will refrain from arresting your chaps at the march because they will not wish to give Save the Children any additional publicity. They will want the procession to go off without incident and in so doing, not fuel the Albert Hall flame. They will be hoping that Miss Webb fails where I succeeded. They will be hoping for echoing walls in Kensington. So I am inclined to advise you to let the soldiers take their chance."

"Don't stop the coppers following my boys away from the House and then carting 'em off, quiet like, as soon as they're out of sight of the papers and their cameras do it?"

"I doubt that will be the case for the boy Freddie," advised Sylvia. "I suspect the army may have no interest in what would be the embarrassment of court-marshalling a child who should never have been accepted into their ranks in the first place. But I agree they may well arrest your conscientious objector in some Westminster back street."

"We'll see about that," said Nash, with grim determination.

The ex-Suffragette did not ask him to enlighten her. History told her that it was best not to know.

******

The march to the Houses of Parliament was going to be much larger than the police had expected. In fact, far better attended than even Ruby had thought likely. There were several hundred gathering, and almost as many spectators to see them set off. Most of the protesters were, as Ruby had assumed, women. Some had children along. It made sense given that the march was about children, but Ruby felt uneasy because there must be a chance the protest would meet with resistance along the route, and if it did, it would be no place for little ones.

Pemberton was in the crowd, as well as Freddie, and Nash's conscience objector. And Ruby knew her husband was somewhere in the vicinity too, though she'd be damned if she could spot him. He really was a master of lurking undetected. Perhaps he was looking out the window of one of the pubs. Or peering round the corner from one of the surrounding alleyways. Down the side of Anderson's India Rubber Company was favourite. Ruby looked around casually as if she was lost in thought, but her scan revealed no sign of her husband.

There were a few men dotted about, seemingly there with their wives and girlfriends. Ruby also spotted a couple of characters whom she knew to be nasty bits of work who were drinking friends of her husband's. Apparently they owed him a favour, so once the speeches outside the Houses of Parliament had brought the procession to a close, it had been agreed that they would grab and manhandle the conscientious objector as if they were carting him off to give him a good hiding down an alley. The reality was that they would be getting him away to safety before the police knew what was happening.

Ruby was thinking about how she was going to ensure that she was as far away from these characters as possible when the march got to Westminster, when she noticed a slightly incongruous little knot of four other men who had just arrived. They were gradually easing their way through the crowd towards the front of the procession. Had they been a larger group she may have been concerned they were there to infiltrate and disrupt the march. But just four of them were not too much to worry about.

She reviewed their efforts with mild contempt. Typical men; they get here late but won't take their rightful place at the back. She considered stopping and telling them to stay where they were, but the whole procession was lining up in such good natured fashion, with no abuse of the marchers issuing forth from any disapproving voices, she thought why show a police presence when it wasn't needed? She thus kept to the periphery of things.

Another glance round the throng and there was still no sign of her husband. But even if she had known where her husband lay in wait, she wouldn't have been able to see him.

Nash had been round to see Sylvia one last time. While there he had picked up a set of keys from her. They were to the shop she had rented as her first East London Federation of Suffragettes headquarters. The old double bay-fronted shop had closed down recently and Nash thought there was a good chance the locks had not been changed since Sylvia had rented the place. And even if they had, he could jemmy the back door easily enough.

Having earlier told the objector where to be and when, and also picked up Freddie from Bert & Elsie's and dropped him nearby, Nash had let himself into the shop without any problem. He had been right about the locks. The shop looked out on to Bow Road, with a panoramic view of where the protesters were now lining up ready to start their march.

He stood in the unlit gloom several feet back and off to the side from the window. Nobody could see him, but he had his eyes on everyone, especially the men.

The soldier and the conchie shook hands as if they had never met before, though Freddie had in fact dropped off a message with Jameson in the past. Nash had supplied each of them with a piece of wood. Jameson's was a six foot long plank; Freddie's was a bit of four by two. And now, for everyone in the procession and the onlookers to see, the two of them were making hard work of hammering a few nails in to their pieces of wood to make a rough cross. Freddie suddenly pulled up a thumb shaking it in pain. Much laughter ensued from the surrounding audience.

Nash looked on shaking his head ruefully. Silly little sod can't even bang a nail in, and that bleeding Quaker ain't much better.

It was then he saw the man he had last seen outside the hall in Holborn. He was part of a group of four men. Nash recognised the man he had knocked out on the ferry, and although he only saw them from afar, and for the briefest moment, he was pretty sure the other two were probably the men lying in wait for him at Silvertown.

He had been worried that Ruby being on the march was a ruse for the police to get her, when in fact the authorities were getting their net ready to throw over him. Ruby was bait.

They must have received information about two army deserters, one of whom was also a conscientious objector, being supplied by Nash to head the march. Once they had captured the men they could probably beat information out of them about the man who had helped them escape justice. But that could not be taken for granted. And how much did these deserters know about their protector in any case? Much better to catch him in the act, actually delivering the men to the march. But there was always the chance he wouldn't risk turning up at the march himself. That's where Ruby came in. They wanted her to be suspicious as to why she had been chosen for the march.

That way her loving husband would be there for sure, to protect her if nothing else.

The attempt to grab him at Silvertown was clearly by government men, but they may not have known at the time the identity of the man they only knew as Smith. But because of her connection with Sylvia, Holborn Man must have begun keeping a watching brief on Ruby around that same time, and in due course also became aware that her husband was the man his colleague had come into painful contact with on the Woolwich ferry. And when the information about Sergeant Granger's suspicions of Ruby and the intelligence concerning her husband's part in this march, crossed his desk, he must have got together with the police and come up with this little ruse.

Nash was furious with himself. As soon as they had tried to grab him at Silvertown he should have closed down his operation and gone to ground. He had gotten sloppy. He should never have used Kosher Bill. And God knows what Bert's old woman Elsie might have told anyone who would listen. She never stopped talking. And if do-gooders like the Lester sisters knew all his business, no wonder the bloody government and police did as well.

He wanted to punch something in his anger. The shop had been a general store selling anything and everything. The first object in Nash's immediate reach was a glass jar of sweets. The sugar shortage meant specialist sweet shops were a thing of the past. Punching it would make a nasty mess of his hand, and he suspected he was going to need both of his fists in full working order before the hour was out.

The moment of anger had passed. He took a deep

breath and cleared his head. The problem he faced was simple. The opposition were there to pick up him and his two charges. Pemberton would probably escort Ruby away too, but she was essentially a side show.

What to do? He looked around the shop for inspiration. The owners of the shop had covered most of the fixtures and fittings with sheets. There was not much to see. But an open tin box full of big thick paint brushes took his eye. Could he sneak to the corner and throw one to draw Ruby's attention. No, Ruby would have a policeman's hawk-eyes watching her.

He noticed that the paint brushes were not stock. Some of them had paint on them. There was also a tradesmen's set of steps; a large collapsible five-step A-frame affair. Its two legs had been pushed together and leaned against a wall. Next to it was a trestle table. There were tins of paint and rolls of wallpaper everywhere. When he had first opened the door to the shop, his nostrils had been assaulted by the smell of paint, turpentine and wallpaper paste, but such had been his concentration on the task at hand, he had barely registered it. He now realised that the owners were in fact still in business. They had been in the middle of decorating when they had probably gone down with the flu. Or perhaps they had called in decorators precisely because they were down with the flu. Having a shop closed for once, which was usually open all hours, was an ideal time to get the place spruced up. Inspiration duly arrived.

The procession was starting from the Gladstone statue, just a few yards along Bow Road from the shop. Six years earlier, Nash had been half way up a ladder, painting the hands of Gladstone red, when a stranger, one

Sylvia Pankhurst, had appeared on the street looking for a property to rent. Inquisitive about the lack of respect being shown a politician she herself had little regard for, she had asked him what he was up to. He had informed her that he was painting the hands red to comment that Bryant & May, the local factory owners who had commissioned the statue, and Gladstone himself, had blood on their hands. The former had run effectively the largest sweat shop in Victorian England, and such a horror had taken place on Prime Minister Gladstone's watch. Sylvia had been impressed and a conversation had ensued that included Nash pointing out that a suitable nearby shop was available for rent. It had been the start of Nash's indoctrination into the Suffragette fold.

Nash now looked around the shop on the off chance that the decorators had left a pair of overalls behind. No luck. He probably wouldn't have fitted into them anyway. He would have to do as he was. Having opened the back door of the shop, which led into an alley, he grabbed hold of a large white sheet and carefully draped it over his head and down his back. A mirror on the wall offered him a chance to peruse his handy work. He thought the man in front of him looked like something between a bride walking up the aisle and one of them Arab fellers. Perfect. You couldn't see who he was unless you stood right in front of him. A large paint brush and a can of paint were tossed into a metal bucket, which was then picked up with one hand, before he slid the other through the steps and hauled them up on to his shoulder. Ready.

He walked down a couple of alleys and into Bow Road. It seemed almost compulsory for workman to whistle, so

Nash played the role to the full. The crowd ignored the whistling workman as he set up for work, leaning his ladder against the statue. In the unlikely event of anyone giving him any mind, they would probably have assumed that the council were about to paint those red hands back to their original grey.

Ruby was doing her duty, walking around the periphery of the crowd, arms linked behind her back in the prescribed manner. She had not even noticed the workman nearby. She was too busy looking at Sergeant Granger, who had just hove into view.

Pemberton was patrolling the other side of the crowd, close to the sergeant. Granger must have seen his male constable but ignored him, and made a beeline for his copperette.

"WPC Nash," he said, nodding in greeting. "We received information that this protest was going to be rather larger than anticipated. More than a two officer job clearly. But we've got so many off with the flu at the moment, I thought I'd get out from behind my desk, stretch the old legs and do a bit of crowd control myself for a change."

"Thank you sergeant, it's all very good natured at the moment as you can see," said Ruby, looking around to add emphasis to her words. "But no doubt the sparks might fly a bit once we set off and people see what's written on the placards."

"Indeed," said Granger. "Well, I'd better get along and introduce myself to the leaders of the march. Carry on WPC Nash."

And with this, Granger disappeared into the throng, leaving Ruby suspicious. She had noticed that he did not look up to glance at the placards. He should have. It would have been natural enough for anyone to do so in response to what she had just conveyed, let alone a police sergeant charged with keeping order at a march full of placards that could incite trouble.

Nash kept an eye on this conversation while he went through the motions of a workman setting up. Thanks to the regular wallpapering work he had done at home, he had acquired the confident, efficient movements of the seasoned professional decorator. He draped the sheet between the top of the ladder and the statue, forming a thin white wall between himself and the crowd, while trying to keep one eye on the four government men. The numbers assembled for the march had become so large that it was becoming increasingly difficult to do this, but it also meant it was now very difficult for the opposition to keep an eye on his wife.

He was aware that when he walked into a crowded pub, the multi voices all drowned each other out. He couldn't hear a word of what was being said. But should someone mention his name, or something else that was very specific to him, somehow his ears latched on to it. No doubt it was the same for everybody. And with this in mind, Nash waited for his wife to come within earshot. She needed to be close enough so he could speak to her without overly raising his voice. And simply calling out 'Ruby' would not be a good idea with so many prying ears about.

Nash used lots of old Cockney phrases. One was 'Funny Cuts!' The term was the name of a comic newspaper. He used it in the same way others might use 'clever Dick!' When his wife made a witticism at his expense, it was his retort of choice.

A long minute later, said wife wandered, deep in

thought, close to the statue. Nash quickly flicked a glance around the crowd. None of the opposition appeared to be looking his or Ruby's way.

"Funny Cuts! Don't look round sharp!" said Nash, just loud enough to make sure his wife would hear it within the din of the crowd.

She might have stiffened a fraction. Or it could have been his imagination.

He need not have worried. Ruby had heard her husband and repelled the impulse to ignore his instruction. Instead, she looked casually across at Pemberton and caught him peering at her. He quickly turned and walked in the opposite direction, appearing for effect to busy himself doing a kindly policeman routine talking to a woman with a small child. Another casual tilt of the head had her focussing on Granger. His attention wasn't on her. Rather, he was looking at the group of men she had noticed earlier, and one of them was looking directly back at him. Something was wrong.

Ruby looked back at Pemberton to ensure he had not returned his gaze, but he was still on his haunches with his back to her talking to a four year old, so she slowly turned and looked around the crowd as far as the statue. Her husband was glaring at her. He nodded almost imperceptibly over his shoulder for her to follow him.

******

As the procession set off, five men were gathered together in heated argument. There was quite a blame game going on. The government men were furious with the police in general and Sergeant Granger in particular. As far as they were concerned, it must have been Granger's arrival that had spooked her. If he had not insisted on being there to arrest her himself, an act of pure indulgence, they would have got her and her conchie loving husband.

Now a decision had to be made. They had no interest in arresting the boy soldier in any case. His usefulness had only ever been in his potential for luring Nash to deliver him to the procession. But do they now cut their losses by going ahead and arresting the conchie? Or do they leave him as bait on the off chance that Nash will still attempt to help him escape?

Granger needed to check what to do with his superiors back at Leman Street. But he knew he was in trouble. He decided that he needed to pluck a rabbit out of a hat. He would act on his own initiative for once. It could not make matters any worse, and it just might save the day. And his bacon.

The sergeant had come to know that there was friction between his copperette and her landlord over the non-payment of rent. He now hoped to use this to his advantage.

The police were not allowed to enter someone's home to arrest them. And Granger knew he must abide by the law. Breaking it would have the hot water in which he was already in, have its temperature raised to scalding, and might even result in some clever lawyer getting Nash off on some technicality. But the war's Defence of the Realm Act, which was still in operation despite the end of hostilities, gave government men much more far-reaching powers.

Granger went to find Pemberton, who had sneaked

off to have a lie down in the Black Maria which had been brought from Leman Street to take away their prisoners. Pemberton was not feeling well but Granger was far too stressed to worry about his constable's well-being. He told Pemberton to hurry up and track down the Nashes' landlord and tell him that he was urgently required to immediately go round and knock on his tenants' door. Some government officials would be accompanying him.

The sergeant explained the plan to his government colleagues. The landlord would get the Nashes to open up, and then they would pile in. They would grab them and haul them outside, where he and his constable would be waiting to slap the handcuffs on them.

The government men were less than enthusiastic. The whole point of the exercise had been to catch Nash in the act of helping army runaways. Without achieving this, there was no hard evidence linking him to either soldier standing at the head of the procession.

Granger countered that with Nash under lock and key they would be in a much better position to cajole his guilt out of the conchie. And if that failed, they could always beat it out of him.

They might enjoy laying a fist or two on him, but the conchie implicating Nash would only be useful to the government men if they could catch the bastard in the first place, and from what they had heard about him, it would be easier said than done.

Standing on a street corner, with many hundreds of people marching past them chanting at the top of their voices, was not an ideal place to hold such a conversation. But with their main prey having disappeared into the ether, and with it only being an outside chance said ether was actually the inside of his own home, they were not in the best mental spot to come to a rational, lucid decision.

It also had to be conceded that if their quarry was not at home, the best chance they had of nabbing him later was if they did not arrest his conchie. The objector and the boy too for that matter, could still be useful bait. So somewhat reluctantly, they agreed to Granger's plan.

Pemberton was sent off on his mission. PC Betts, the constable who had driven the Black Maria there, was literally given his marching orders. He would have to leave the vehicle with his sergeant and go to accompany the procession.

While Pemberton was fetching the landlord, Granger just had time to face the unedifying embarrassment of having to run up the main road to Bow police station to ask for reinforcements because he had just allowed a sizeable, controversial procession to set off through the streets of the capital with nobody but a solitary wet behind the ears constable to patrol it.

******

A fraught half an hour later a posse of four government men and the owner of the property stood outside the front door of the Nash residence. Sergeant Granger stood in the yard at the rear of the property, truncheon in hand ready to intercept anyone making a break for it out the back. Pemberton was with him, but barely in body and not at all in spirit. He was having a much needed sit down on the Nash's outdoor toilet, and was feeling far too ill to do anything other than notice how his seat of choice and the floor of the little shed in which it was housed, had been scrubbed particularly clean. He concluded that the flu was certainly bringing a whole new level of cleanliness to the East End.

The landlord rapped on the front door of the house. When there was no answer, he received a nod to go ahead and use his key. In he piled with his supporting players right behind him.

They were met with a void. No people. No sign of life. There wasn't any food in the scullery. No cutlery or crockery in the kitchen. No clothes in the bedroom. Not a newspaper, tin of tobacco or anything else in the parlour.

Everything had been scrubbed and swept. The place was as a clean as a whistle. Spotless to the point where it was clear that it had been done with some pride. The men dashed upstairs. Maud's half of the house had been cleaned and cleared too. The beds, stove and furniture were the only things remaining in the house. This had clearly not been done in the past half hour. Whoever had done this had been buying their meals off the pie man for the past day or two.

Granger was called in by the others. The back door wasn't locked. And it was he who had the pleasure of finding the only thing that had been left in the house. Just inside the back door lay a pile of clothing, neatly folded, with a hat and a pair of shoes lying just to the side. Granger picked up a skirt, followed by stockings, a shirt, jacket, whistle & chain and truncheon. It was WPC Nash's police uniform and accoutrements.

Chapter 44

"A whole nation of children are starving worse than in the war. The fortunate ones die. Many more infants are dying in Berlin this year. The rest are starting their life with a physical and mental inefficiency that will make life a burden...A million children have died of TB and hunger."

Countess Blucher: English Wife

in Berlin, a private memoir...1918

Nash found the article for which he was looking.

SAVE THE CHILDREN PROCESSION ATTRACTS HUGE CROWD TO WESTMINSTER. ONE ARREST

A Save the Children procession from Bow, East London to The Houses of Parliament was led by its organiser Miss Eglantyne Webb and a young boy who was most joyous and gay in his little soldier's outfit. The march was to highlight the need for milk to be sent to war-torn countries to feed poor children. It was quite the occasion, with large, cheering crowds attracted along the route and at Westminster. The

organisers hoped that the success of the procession will help them attract a good audience to their fund-raising event next month at the Royal Albert Hall in Kensington. There was only one unsavoury incident, when some ruffians spirited away a man at the end of the march. Our reporter on the spot was able to ascertain that the man was believed to be a deserter from the army, who had been dragged away to have some rough justice dealt to him. The police were unable to apprehend the vigilantes and the man has not been found. Only one arrest was reported, that of Miss Webb for inciting the crowd during her speech outside the House.

"Little soldier's outfit indeed," scoffed Ruby. "Makes Freddie sound like Little Lord Fauntleroy. And I suppose Miss Webb might also have mentioned in her speech that it was the continuance of the Allied blockade, months after the war has finished that caused the need for such an event. And no mention of a conscientious objector and soldier sharing a cross. What a report! The newspapers down here are just as bad as those in London. They toe the line, even now the war is over."

"At least Sylvia was right about the police leaving Freddie alone," said Nash. "Didn't even arrest Sister Buxton did they? They were in a right old mess after they missed us I'll wager."

"And your mates got your conchie away into the bargain." said Ruby. "How did you manage to get those characters to help a conchie anyway?"

"Told 'em he weren't all the ticket. He'd copped a bit

of shellshock on the line earlier in the war," replied Nash with a matter-of-fact hunch of the shoulders.

"My husband's a clever bastard I'll say that for him," said Ruby as if said spouse was not standing beside her.

"I don't know so much. It don't take a lot to run rings round coppers," said Nash, with a cheeky grin on his face.

"This one it does," said his smiling ex-copperette wife, while she meted out some police brutality care of a truncheon made from a speedily rolled up Southampton newspaper.

Dorothea, leaning forward with her arms folded and resting on the ship's railing, glanced sideways at her new English friends, amused.

Author's Notes:

As with my previous novels, this book has been exhaustively researched and I have stuck closely to the facts. Almost everything in this novel is I'm afraid, most terribly, historically accurate. For example, after the war had ended, horrendous photographs showing the level of starvation in Germany, started to be smuggled into Britain, very much against the government's wishes. The Save the Children charity was founded in response to this, to provide milk for starving German children.

******

A novel set mostly during the war to end all wars, about the worst pandemic in history, had the potential to be an unremittingly dark read. But throughout my research, events presented themselves that appeared at the very least rather idiosyncratic to my twenty first century mind, and often downright eccentric. So I chose to use examples to bring some light in to the proceedings. One might say literally in the case of the women's football match. Britain's first ever floodlit football match, which was a woman's match in the war, really did end in chaos after a spotlight failed and a second one had its power boosted to the point where players and crowd alike were so dazzled that in the ensuing pandemonium an urchin ran off with the ball. And a dead zoo elephant really did end up on the menu of a Dresden bar restaurant.

******

My previous novel, Suffragette Autumn Women's Spring, set from 1912-1914 had originally been intended to also cover the war years up to women finally winning the vote in 1918. As background I did a huge amount of research into the Allied Home Front during the war, and became increasingly amazed at how little the 'Spanish' Flu Pandemic of 1918/19, was mentioned throughout the plethora of research resources available.

When dealing with how the war finally came to an end, books concentrating on the military side of the conflict, ignore the flu. There might be the odd sentence or two about how the armies were having to cope with losses incurred from the outbreak, but that's about all. Works specifically about the Home Front sometimes, though not always, give brief details of the flu. But like the military books, there is little analysis of the flu's role in bringing the war to an end. Perhaps something as seemingly mundane as influenza, is not considered interesting enough to consider when writing of war.

But yes, the war was finally ended by military means, the Germans being forced to the armistice negotiation table by military defeat. But this reversal came about because the

Germans could no longer feed their war effort. They could no longer feed themselves at home. Their Home Front had collapsed amidst starvation and the popular uprising that sprang from it, and this led to their military collapse.

The Allied blockade had successfully put huge pressures on German food resources for four years, but Germany had managed to keep going and they had themselves come close to starving Britain to defeat in 1917 with their successful u-boat campaign, which sank huge numbers of merchant shipping attempting to bring foodstuffs into Britain.

The final year of the war saw Britain introduce a better organised food system, firstly by introducing 423 National Kitchens across the country to feed those in need. Sylvia Pankhurst's Cost Price restaurant was something of a template for these, though the kitchens were different in that one took the food home to consume it there. An efficient and fair rationing system followed. Germany, in comparison, had a poorly organised piecemeal soup kitchen and specific food days set-up, as well as a less well organised, less fair rationing system.

Britain's superior food system was a huge boon to morale just when the worst ravages of the flu pandemic hit. It enabled The Home Front to keep going and to continue to feed the Military Front. Germany's Home Front morale, in comparison, collapsed under the weight put upon it by the flu. The German state started to collapse too and starvation followed, which continued until the Allied blockade was finally lifted, well into 1919.

As Sylvia suspects in the novel, the flu was not worse in Spain. It was simply that Spain was the only country telling the truth about its effects.

The mutated virus was unusual in that it tended to attack the strong rather more than the weak because it caused the immune system to attack itself. People essentially drowned in their own fluids produced by the immune system as its response to the virus. The stronger one's immune system, the more likely one was to die. It thus killed a disproportionate number of people who were at the peak of their powers, aged between 20 and 35. Fit young people like soldiers and those who otherwise would have been the strongest of those on the Home Front.

The flu pandemic killed approximately 50 million people worldwide. In terms of total deaths, it remains the worst outbreak of any disease in history.

The numbers directly killed by the Spanish Lady in Britain and Germany were very similar. 228,000 and 226,000 respectively. It is impossible to quantify exactly how many other Germans died as a result of malnutrition made worse by the flu, but 200,000 is a reasonable estimate.

It may have been the Spanish Flu that effectively ended the Great War.